THE PENGUIN POETS

The Penguin Book of Caribbean Verse in English

Paula Burnett was born in 1942 in Chelmsford, Essex, and was educated at the local high school and Oxford University. In 1968 she produced for the B.Litt. degree a critical edition of an Elizabethan prose romance. She went on to teach English in a London comprehensive school. Since 1973 she has been mainly at home with her three children. It was during a period when the family lived in Jamaica that she began work on an anthology of Caribbean poetry. Since returning to London in 1979, she has taught part-time at Kingston Polytechnic and the Roehampton Institute.

THE PENGUIN BOOK OF

CARIBBEAN VERSE

IN ENGLISH

Selected and edited by Paula Burnett

I have crossed an ocean
I have lost my tongue
from the root of the old one
a new one has sprung

– Grace Nichols

PENGUIN BOOKS

Penguin Books Ltd, Harmondsworth, Middlesex, England
Viking Penguin Inc., 40 West 23rd Street, New York, New York 10010, U.S.A.
Penguin Books Australia Ltd, Ringwood, Victoria, Australia
Penguin Books Canada Ltd, 2801 John Street, Markham, Ontario, Canada L3R 1B4
Penguin Books (N.Z.) Ltd, 182–190 Wairau Road, Auckland 10, New Zealand

First published 1986

The Acknowledgements on pages 443–8 constitute
an extension of this copyright page

Made and printed in Great Britain by
Cox & Wyman Ltd, Reading
Filmset in Trump Medieval (Linotron 202) by
Rowland Phototypesetting Ltd,
Bury St Edmunds, Suffolk

For Michael, who took me to the Caribbean

CONTENTS

PREFACE   xix

INTRODUCTION   xxiii
    The Language Continuum   xxv
The Oral Tradition   xxvii
    Before Emancipation   xxix
    From Emancipation to Black Liberation   xxxv
The Literary Tradition   xliii
    The Eighteenth and Nineteenth Centuries   xliii
    The Twentieth Century   li
Conclusion   lxiii

NOTE ON THE TEXT   lxv

THE ORAL TRADITION   I
Anonymous
    Work-songs, I and II   3
    Dancing Songs, I and II   3
    Guinea Corn   4
    Songs, I and II   4
    My Deery Honey   5
    Freedom a Come Oh!   6
    Song of the King of the Eboes   7
    Negro Song at Cornwall   7
    A Negro Song   7
    A Popular Negro Song   8
    Quaco Sam   8
    Sangaree Kill de Captain   9
    War Down a Monkland   9
    Two Man a Road   10
    Mas' Charley   10
    I Have a News   10
    There's a Black Boy in a Ring   11

Contents

Them Gar'n Town People 11
Itanami 12
Michael McTurk
Query 13
Deh 'Pon Um Again 13
Edward Cordle
Lizzie and Joe Catch a Thief 16
Lizzie and Joe in Court 17
Lizzie Discourses on the Small-pox 18
James Martinez
Dis Time No Stan' Like Befo' Time 19
My Little Lize 21
Marcus Garvey
Keep Cool 22
Centenary's Day 23
Slim and Sam
Sandy Gully 24
Johnny Tek Away Mi Wife 24
Anonymous
Sly Mongoose 25
Dis Long Time, Gal 26
Linstead Market 26
Dog Shark 27
Sammy Dead Oh 28
Glory Dead 28
Trouble Oh 29
Rastafarian chant
Zion Me Wan Go Home 30
Louise Bennett
Back to Africa 31
Colonization in Reverse 32
Dutty Tough 33
Excitement 34
Independance 35
Independence Twenty-One 37
Bruce St John
Bajan Litany 39
Subtlety 39
Wisdom 40
'Lord Kitchener'
Miss Tourist 41

Contents

'The Mighty Sparrow'
    The Yankees Back   43
    Get to Hell outa Here   44
'The Mighty Chalkdust'
    Brain Drain   46
Marc Matthews
    Guyana Not Ghana   48
Delano Abdul Malik De Coteau
    Oui Papa   49
    Motto Vision 1971   50
Paul Keens-Douglas
    Tell Me Again   56
    Wukhand   58
F. 'Toots' Hibbert
    Never Get Weary   61
Peter Tosh
    African   62
Jimmy Cliff
    The Harder They Come   63
Legon Cogil and Carlton Barrett
    Dem Belly Full   64
Bob Marley
    Trenchtown Rock   65
Christopher Laird
    The Sea at Evening   66
Frederick Williams
    De Eighties   68
Bongo Jerry
    Mabrak   69
Eddy Grant
    War Party   72
Lillian Allen
    Belly Woman's Lament   73
    I Fight Back   74
Linton Kwesi Johnson
    Bass Culture   75
    Reggae fi Dada   75
Mutabaruka
    Free Up de Lan, White Man   79
    Revolutionary Poets   80
    The Change   81

Contents

You Ask Me   82
Oku Onuora
Last Night   83
Pressure Drop   83
Reflection in Red   84
Brian Meeks
Las' Rights   87
The Coup-clock Clicks   88
Michael Smith
Black Bud   90
I an I Alone *or* Goliath   91
Valerie Bloom
Trench Town Shock (A Soh Dem Sey)   94
Wat a Rain   95

THE LITERARY TRADITION   97
Anonymous
From *A Pindarique Ode on the Arrival of His
    Excellency Sir Nicholas Lawes etc.*   99
Francis Williams
From *An Ode to George Haldane etc.*   101
Nathaniel Weekes
From *Barbados*, I and II   102
James Grainger
From *The Sugar-Cane*, Books II and IV   104
John Singleton
From *A General Description of the West Indian
    Islands*
Book II   106
Book III   107
Anonymous
From *A Poetical Epistle etc.*   110
From *Jamaica, a Poem in Three Parts etc.*   111
J. B. Moreton
Ballad   112
James Montgomery
From *The West Indies*   113
M. J. Chapman
From *Barbadoes*   115
African Dirge   116

William Hosack
   From *The Isle of Streams*, Stanzas x–xiv   117
   Stanzas xlv–li   118
Robert Dunbar
   From *The Cruise*   121
   From *The Caraguin*   121
Henry Dalton
   The Emigrant Ship   124
Horatio Nelson Huggins
   From *Hiroona*:
   The Introduction   126
   Canto xii, §§ 23–6   127
Egbert Martin
   Trade   130
   National Anthem   131
Thomas MacDermot
   From *San Gloria* (from Columbus's Soliloquy)   132
   Cuba   132
   A Market Basket in the Car   133
Donald McDonald
   A Song of Those Who Died   134
   Breakfast in Bed (Influenza in War-time)   135
   A Citizen of – the World   135
Alfred Cruickshank
   God or Mammon   137
   Let Us Be Frank   138
   The Convict Song   138
W. Adolphe Roberts
   On a Monument to Martí   140
   Peacocks   140
   The Maroon Girl   141
   A Valediction   141
Claude McKay
   Fetchin Water   142
   Subway Wind   143
   The White House   144
   If We Must Die   144
   Baptism   145
Jean Rhys
   Our Gardener   146
   Obeah Night   147

Contents

Frank Collymore
  Ballad of an Old Woman   151
  Monkeys   152
  Triptych   152
J. E. Clare McFarlane
  On National Vanity   153
Philip Sherlock
  Jamaican Fisherman   154
  Pocomania   154
  Dinner Party 1940   156
  A Beauty Too of Twisted Trees   156
Una Marson
  Kinky Hair Blues   158
  Brown Baby Blues   159
  Gettin de Spirit   160
  Politeness   160
  To Wed or Not to Wed   161
  Repose   162
Vivian Virtue
  Waifs   163
  The Hour   163
A. J. Seymour
  From *The Guiana Book*   165
  From *For Christopher Columbus*   168
  The Well   169
  I was a Boy   170
Phyllis Allfrey
  The Child's Return   171
  Love for an Island   171
Eric Roach
  Love Overgrows a Rock   173
  Piarco   174
  At Guaracara Park   175
George Campbell
  History Makers   177
  In the Slums   177
  Holy   178
Barbara Ferland
  Ave Maria   180
  Orange   180
  Expect No Turbulence   181

John Figueroa
Birth is . . .   182
Portrait of a Woman (and a Man)   182
At Home the Green Remains   184

Wilson Harris
Charcoal   185
Laocoön   185

A. L. Hendriks
Hot Summer Sunday   187
Boundary   187
The Migrant   188
Will the Real Me Please Stand Up?   189
From 'D'où venons nous? Que sommes nous?
   Où allons nous?', VI   190

Basil McFarlane
Arawak Prologue   193

Gloria Escoffery
Twins   195
No Man's Land   195
Farewell to a Jovial Friend   196
After the Fall   196

Louis Simpson
Jamaica   198
Arm in Arm   199
The Battle   200
The Inner Part   201
Back in the States   201
A Fine Day for Straw Hats   202
Working Late   204

James Berry
My Father   205
Ingrown   206
Back to Hometown Kingston   206
From Lucy: Holiday Reflections   207
Distance of a City   208
Fantasy of an African Boy   209

Jan Carew
Our Home   211
The Cliffs at Manzanilla   212
Faces and Skulls   212

Contents

Martin Carter

University of Hunger 214
From I Come from the Nigger Yard 215
Till I Collect 216
There is No Riot 216
For a Man Who Walked Sideways 217
The Great Dark 217
As New and as Old 218
Bent 219
Our Number 219

Evan Jones

Genesis 220
Walking with R.B. 221
November, 1956 221
The Song of the Banana Man 222
The Lament of the Banana Man 224

Shake Keane

Shaker Funeral 226
Coming Back 228
From *Volcano Suite*: Soufrière (79) 1 230

Daniel Williams

We are the Cenotaphs 232

Andrew Salkey

Remember Haiti, Cuba, Vietnam 235
Soufrière 235
Clearsightedness 236
Postcard from Mexico, 16.x.1973 237
A Song for England 238
Dry River Bed 238

Henry Beissel

Pans at Carnival 241

Derek Walcott

A Far Cry from Africa 243
From *Another Life*, Chapter 20 244
Forest of Europe 247
The Spoiler's Return 249

Edward Kamau Brathwaite

Horse Weebles 255
Starvation *and* Blues 257
Schooner 260
Harbour 261

Contents

Edward Lucie-Smith
   The Wise Child   264
   Your Own Place   264
   The Hymn Tunes   265
   Imperialists in Retirement   266
Abdur-Rahman Slade Hopkinson
   The Madwoman of Papine   268
   Tycoon, Poet, Saint   269
   December 1974: a Lament   271
Ivan Van Sertima
   Volcano   272
Edward Baugh
   Colour-scheme   273
   Truth and Consequences   273
   The Carpenter's Complaint   274
   Country Dance   274
Howard Fergus
   Forecast   276
   Ethnocide   276
   Lament for Maurice Bishop   277
Claire Harris
   Framed   278
   Policeman Cleared in Jaywalking Case   278
Mervyn Morris
   Brief   281
   The House-slave   281
   The Early Rebels   281
   To an Expatriate Friend   282
   For Consciousness   283
   Valley Prince   283
   Family Pictures   284
   One, Two   285
   Peace-time   286
LeRoy Clarke
   Where Hurricane   287
E. A. Markham
   Don't Talk to Me about Bread   290
   An Old Thought for a New Couple   291
   Rewrite   291
   Late Return   292
   Grandfather's Sermon and Michael Smith   296

Contents

Dennis Scott
Homecoming   299
Grampa   300
Uncle Time   301
Epitaph   301
For the Last Time, Fire   302
Mouth   303
Version   304
Weaponsong   305
More Poem   305
Anthony McNeill
Don   306
The Victors   306
Residue   307
Saint Ras   307
Dermis   308
A Wreath for the Suicide Heart   309
Judy Miles
Suicide?   310
Seasons Greetings, Love and Revolution   311
Kevyn Arthur
Gospel   312
I Saw Three Ships   313
Pamela Mordecai
Tell Me   314
For Eyes to Bless You   315
Shooting the Horses   315
Roger McTair
Guerillas   317
Politics Kaiso   318
Olive Senior
Ancestral Poem   320
Epitaph   321
Wayne Brown
Noah   322
Ballad of the Electric Eel   324
England, Autumn   325
The Bind   326
Faustin Charles
Fireflies   327
Sugar Cane   328

Contents

Cyril Dabydeen
   Rehearsal   330
   Words and Legacy   330
   The Fat Men   331
   Fruit, of the Earth   332
Marlene Philip
   Oliver Twist   333
   Salmon Courage   334
Lorna Goodison
   The Mulatta as Penelope   337
   For Don Drummond   337
John Robert Lee
   Return   340
   Kite   341
   third world snapshots   342
John Agard
   Waiting for Fidel   343
   Pan Recipe   343
Victor Questel
   Tom   345
   This Island Mopsy   346
Grace Nichols
   Waterpot   348
   Without Song   349
   Old Magic   349
Kendel Hippolyte
   good morning   350
   Jah-Son/ another way   351
Dionne Brand
   From *Epigrams to Ernesto Cardenal in Defense*
     of Claudia   356
   From *Military Occupations*   357
David Dabydeen
   Slave Song   363
   Men and Women   364
Fragano Ledgister
   On Parade   365
   The Cities Have Fallen   365
Frederick D'Aguiar
   Letter from Mama Dot   367
   On Duty   368

Contents

BIOGRAPHICAL AND EXPLANATORY
NOTES   369

GLOSSARY   431

INDEX OF POETS   441

ACKNOWLEDGEMENTS   443

PREFACE

The literature of the Caribbean has in recent years been attracting more attention from the literary establishment, and not before time, considering that the English literature of the region is more than two and a half centuries old. To those who belong to the English-speaking world this literature offers an important perspective without which our world picture loses some depth. Caribbean writers can share with us their unique identity of culture, place and history; they offer a vantage point on the South which speaks to us directly with no need for translation, and, through the diaspora, contribute a crucial focus to the image which the societies of the North have of themselves. They speak to their own people, but also to the English-speaking world at large.

There have been no substantial anthologies of Caribbean poetry for more than a decade – a decade of unprecedented literary activity. Earlier anthologies have not attempted to give, as this volume does, a comprehensive survey of the growth of a Caribbean literary tradition from its beginnings in the eighteenth century, nor have they given weight to the parallel tradition of oral poetry, born from song, which is here given thorough representation for the first time. The first poems in this book are examples of slave songs from the eighteenth century. The oral tradition is then traced through to the performance poets of today (only those poets known primarily as performers will be found in this section), while the remainder of the book covers the parallel literary tradition from the eighteenth century to the present. Hitherto, Caribbean poetry has usually been treated as a literary unit. This division of the book into two sections is intended to focus attention on the oral tradition as a distinct and important cultural phenomenon with its own excellences, and to facilitate study of the interplay between the oral and literary traditions, which is one of the most exciting aspects of

Caribbean poetry today. That very cross-fertilization may make it increasingly difficult in the future to divide the poetry in such a manner, but for now, in this historical survey, it seems a useful distinction.

An obvious difficulty arises in any attempt to survey an oral tradition in a written medium. The oral poems chosen here have been selected in part because they are also effective on the page. Readers should bear in mind that there are many other poems which are excellent in performance but flat on paper. The impact of lists and repetition, for instance, which tend to look contrived in print, is vastly different on the ear, while the musical sequence of tempo, rhythm, pitch, volume and tone which would be employed in performance can barely be hinted at on the page, by variations of typography and layout.

The English-speaking Caribbean is taken here to include all those territories in the Caribbean region where the official language is English, including the mainland countries of Guyana and Belize, which are referred to throughout by these names, not their former ones of British Guiana and British Honduras. The criterion used to assess whether a poet qualified for inclusion in this volume was the simple one of whether a significant contribution had been made to Caribbean culture. A narrow consideration of place of birth was found to contain difficulties, particularly at both ends of the time-scale: during slavery, when some of the most perceptive, extant portrayals of West Indian society came from European-born immigrants, and now, when there is a rising generation of the children of West Indian emigrants, born in Europe and North America, who still regard themselves as Caribbean.

I should like to record here my great debt to Mervyn Morris and Edward Kamau Brathwaite, who were the first to be kind. I am also very grateful for the generosity of Louis James, Knolly La Fortune, Ann Boys, Keith Waithe, Austin Clarke, Lloyd Brown, Darcus Howe and the staff of Race Today. My thanks for their willing help go to the library staffs of the University of the West Indies at Mona and St Augustine (particularly Dr Margaret Rouse-Jones), at the Institute of Jamaica, at the Commonwealth Institute, London (particularly Christiane Keane), at the Royal Commonwealth Society Library, London, and the British Library. Danielle Gianetti generously put her knowledge of Eric Roach's work at my disposal, as, most kindly, did Barbara Lalla and Ray Frammer with their research on 'Quaco Sam'; David Lockwood, Curator of Museums, Dumfries, and Lionel Burman, Keeper of Decorative Arts, Merseyside County Museum, Liverpool, also offered expert help.

In the end, my thanks go to all the Caribbean poets, whose book this is – including those whose work is not represented here. I have chosen what seemed to me the best and the most interesting, with an eye on representativeness, both within a poet's work and in the selection as a whole. Personal taste varies, of course, and no one else would have made quite this selection, but I hope my choice will satisfy those who are already on familiar terms with Caribbean poetry, and open a stimulating new window for those who are not.

Paula Burnett
Wimbledon,
July 1984

INTRODUCTION

Caribbean literature is, of course, first of all by and for Caribbean people. Like any culture, it gives expression to a particular people's experience. But Caribbean literature is also international in a special sense, both because it is a unique cultural hybrid, and because the Caribbean experience is being lived and explored artistically in Europe and North America as well as in the Caribbean region itself. The English-speaking Caribbean is uniquely placed, both geographically and historically, at the meeting-point between three continents – Europe, Africa and America – and between three poetic traditions – the British, the West African and the North American. Over the last fifty years, written Caribbean poetry has tended to shift from a more traditional European orientation, with the emphasis on form and a highly wrought surface, to a mode which is closer to the vernacular, influenced by the oral traditions of Africa and the dominance of modernism in the American tradition. The fragmentation of the Caribbean's people into island and scattered expatriate communities, while it broadens perspectives, also makes effective communication essential, but it is not only their own people that the poets of the Caribbean today are addressing. They are both philosophers of the modern world, and ambassadors for the South in the North. The Caribbean offers us a literature about the process of growth through, or in spite of, a history of exploitation and prejudice, about the turning of negatives into positives and the creative synthesis of ancient traditions, and is therefore relevant to all peoples engaged in the search for forms of creative cohabitation: the assertion of cultural self without the denial of that assertion to others, and the sharing of as much as can be shared. Its recurrent themes are universal: the gritty celebration of survival and the festive celebration of an inheritance of place, tongue and tradition; the lament for the lost and the quest for identity; the championing of faith and hope in the teeth of betrayal and disillusion. The poets of the English-speaking Caribbean have much to say to all those who care about the future, and who are prepared to look critically but constructively at the past.

This book begins at the beginning. The history of the region is a bitter story of slavery, cruelty and exploitation, as bitter as any other in the world's existence, but exceptionally well documented. As always, we are dependent on a scribal culture for our knowledge of a past oral culture, but enough can be gleaned from the accounts of the cultural life of the slaves by eighteenth- and early nineteenth-century poets and diarists to give us a picture of a rich and vigorous African tradition adapted to the New World. The early songs included here represent a good proportion of the surviving material, and should thus be regarded merely as indicators of the range that was current at the time. The early writers offer the best means we have of picturing a society based on slavery. Some degree of racial bias is evident in all white writers until well into the twentieth century, but it would be naïve to reject their works as 'un-Caribbean' because of this, when in fact the complexities of racial prejudice and interaction have been instrumental in shaping the Caribbean society of today. If the examples of the early literature given here seem on the whole moderate, it is because there seemed no point in giving a further airing to the more extreme and obnoxious views. The pieces from the early period have been chosen because they illustrate the creolization of a European literary tradition through the portrayal of a uniquely Caribbean landscape, society or experience, which is the first stage in the establishment of a distinct Caribbean literature.

The two and three-quarter centuries which have elapsed since the earliest surviving English literature of the region chart a growth which mirrors the political progress. In the period which has seen the transitions from slavery to abolition and emancipation, and from colonialism to independence, the poetry has developed from a dependence on English literary models to an increasing awareness of the black heritage, which in this final quarter of the twentieth century is at last getting the respect and admiration it has always deserved as both the culture of the majority and a rich and unique expression of the human condition.

The Language Continuum

A similar growth pattern can be observed in the language chosen for poetry or song. The oral tradition has always used the vernacular, but it is only in the twentieth century (with one or two exceptions) that poets in the literary, standard English tradition have begun to explore ways of working the rich ore of dialect in literary contexts. The majority of the poems here are in standard English, but many are either in one of the vernaculars of the Caribbean (which are accessible to non-speakers with the occasional help of a glossary), or make partial use of one. The creative juxtaposition of various tones of voice is a distinctively Caribbean literary device of great range and subtlety.

The first choice of a Caribbean writer is always which point of the language continuum to use. As George Lamming has said, English is a Caribbean language. Unlike most of his European counterparts, the West Indian who speaks 'BBC' English is probably also master of a local vernacular, and can draw on any point of the language range between market dialect and courtroom English. The complexity of the heritage results in a great verbal flair and ready wit. The art of the pun is employed here as a delicate poetic tool, while the Trinidadian tradition of 'picong' – from French *piquant*, satiric sparring with words – is typified by the superficially light verse which fledges a well-aimed dart.

The term 'dialect' is a problem in itself, in that it implies reference to a 'high culture' norm. Edward Brathwaite's alternative, 'nation language', is a worthy attempt to get round this, but doesn't seem to be taking over in popular usage. 'The vernacular' seems an accurate and useful term, relatively uncontaminated with pejorative connotations, and is therefore preferred here.

Just as the richness of the English language is derived from its history as a hybrid, the process is carried further with the English of the Caribbean. Not only have the main cultures of Europe impinged on one another there, but also the languages and traditions of West Africa have survived a process of attrition with remarkable tenacity. The hybrid tongues which result have an enormous range of nuance and vigour of expression, with the limitation that only the locals catch every resonance. The isolation of island communities, their varied histories, and the huge extent of the region (over a thousand miles of sea separate Jamaica and Trinidad, for example), have resulted in marked linguistic differences, although these are probably no greater than regional differences within the British Isles.

The vernaculars of the English-speaking Caribbean show strong African influence in their syntax and intonation although they are based on an English vocabulary, with some influence from the other European languages of the region, Portuguese, Spanish, French and Dutch. Words of African origin can be counted in hundreds, although these often have a cultural significance out of proportion to their numbers in that they are frequently either everyday words, to do with the preparation of food, for instance, or indispensable terms denoting personality or feeling, where the English equivalent is relatively prosaic. In several of the islands where the official language is English, the vernacular is a French-based patois, living witness to the long struggle for domination in the region between France and England. This is true of many of the Windward Islands (Derek Walcott's St Lucia, for instance), while in Trinidad, which attracted large numbers of French-speaking refugees from the Haitian revolution of 1791, a widespread French patois fell into disuse only during this century. Ruled by the Spanish until 1797 and only seven miles off the coast of Venezuela, Trinidad is also markedly affected by the Latin American culture, the distinctive orchestration of calypso music being one manifestation of this.

The language situation in countries such as Trinidad and Guyana is of relatively recent origin compared with that in Barbados and Jamaica, in that the majority of their territories have been settled only in the last century and a half, via large-scale immigration, chiefly from India but also from other countries in the Far East such as China and Indonesia, with the result that today about half the people of those countries are of Indian descent – or East Indian, as they say in the Caribbean, to distinguish them from the indigenous Indians, or Amerindians, misnamed by Columbus. The language and culture of the East Indians are surprisingly little evident in the poetry of the region – the two Dabydeens are beginning to redress that, while Derek Walcott has led those of non-Indian descent in taking up Indian subjects in his work. In the field of the novel, however, the East Indian heritage is well covered by the Naipaul brothers and Samuel Selvon, among others. The Amerindian languages are even more 'invisible', apart from place-names and a few words, some of which have become universal such as 'hurricane' and 'barbecue', but many, particularly Guyanese, writers have drawn on Amerindian myths in their work in a conscious attempt to stem the cultural erosion which those ancient traditions have suffered.

It remains the meeting of the West African languages with English (in all its regional variety) which has been the major determinant of the English-speaking Caribbean's own language. If it is easy to understand why a language which was the official medium of communication should become an indelible part of a culture, it is more remarkable that languages and cultures which were proscribed should survive their persecution; on arrival from Africa, new slaves were separated as far as possible from others of the same language group to speed up the process of adjustment and reduce the chance of rebellion. The British never made the mistake of underestimating the importance of language.

It is clear from the history of Greek and Latin that the languages of imperialism tend to outlast the empires. In a recent poem Derek Walcott comments on the British empire in the Caribbean: 'It's good that everything's gone, except their language, / which is everything.'*

THE ORAL TRADITION

Definitions of oral literature are inevitably open to argument, but agreement is generally given that it is not incompatible with a written literature. There are some societies (and were more) which do not make use of writing at all and in which all verbal culture is necessarily oral. In the Caribbean, the Amerindian and early Afro-Caribbean cultures came into this category. Other societies with perhaps universal literacy and a complex tradition of written literature

* 'North and South', *The Fortunate Traveller*, New York and London, 1982.

may, at the same time, have vigorous oral traditions and a highly sophisticated oral literature. Ruth Finnegan argues, for instance, that modern popular culture is essentially an oral literature.* The definition has to depend on the manner of transmission, and in the late-twentieth-century world of audio-visual technology there is a special sense in which the wheel has come full circle, with the live sound in the ascendancy once more. The majority people of the English-speaking Caribbean, those of African descent, have lived this cycle in a unique and impressive way, using the power of the word both for survival and renewal from the earliest days, and in recent years making creative use of the new technology.

Inevitably, where there is an oral tradition alongside a written tradition with literacy the norm, distinctions become blurred and a good deal of cross-fertilization from one tradition to the other occurs. Many of the poets in the oral section of this book make use of the printed word as well as live or recorded performance, while many of the poets in the remainder of the book have written 'oral' poems, or have been much influenced by the oral tradition, or are widely respected as performers of their work. This in no way invalidates the concept of an oral tradition with its own patterns of development and characteristic styles, distinct from those of the written tradition.

It is tempting to analyse the difference in simplistic terms: to say that the oral tradition is black, while the written tradition is white, or that the oral tradition is in the vernacular while the written tradition is in standard English, or that the one is popular while the other is elitist, or even revolutionary as against conservative. While each of these distinctions is partly valid, each also is, in some sense, downright untrue. There seems to be only one logical criterion: the division in this book is according to a rule of thumb as to the medium of transmission characteristically used by the poet, so that those who are known primarily as performers, either live or by recordings, are in the oral section.

The only exception is the inclusion in the oral section of the 'newspaper poets', the poets of the popular tradition who wrote vernacular verse mainly of a satiric or humorous charac-

* Ruth Finnegan, *Oral Poetry*, Cambridge University Press, 1977.

ter, which was published as a regular column in local newspapers, before the advent of the radio age. That writers such as McTurk, Cordle and Martinez are essentially in the oral tradition is shown by the way in which a later poet such as Louise Bennett has made parallel use of newspaper publication and performance – live, on radio, and later on television and by sound recording. It is also worth bearing in mind that in societies with, until recently, only partial adult literacy, the newspaper was often read out loud, so that poems such as these probably did reach their biggest audience in an oral form.*

The oral section here also includes examples of songs, from the eighteenth century to the present. The oral tradition was typified by the sung word long before it adapted itself to spoken poetry, and the musical tradition has continued alongside the spoken, most remarkably in its twin contemporary phenomena of calypso and reggae, art forms original to the Caribbean but in the African tradition, in that the roles of singer and song-writer are combined, the ability to improvise is highly esteemed, and a serious purpose is not seen as incompatible with popular appeal. Token representation has been given here to these musical traditions, and to the folk-song tradition, since they are crucial to the oral tradition as a whole; to survey them properly would take another book. The interplay between the musician-poets and the poets of the spoken word, who sometimes use music, is a rich cross-fertilization which should not be ignored by those who care about how poets reach audiences.

Before Emancipation

The common assumption that, in the words of a well-known critic, the Caribbean people 'for several centuries . . . lived destitute and inarticulate in a political, social and cultural void' is quite wrong.† From what little has survived of

---

* Edward Lucie-Smith in his autobiography, *The Burnt Child*, London, 1975, p. 26, relates, for instance, 'As dusk fell, all the servants but my nurse, and any casual callers who might be present, gathered on the back verandah to listen while one of their number read aloud, in a laborious singsong, from the day's newspaper.'

† Hena Maes-Jelinek, in *West Indian Literature* (ed. Bruce King), London, 1979, p. 182.

the oral literature of the slaves it is possible to build up a picture of a complex cultural phenomenon of great vigour and originality: a tradition of vocal self-expression in which all members of the community were involved and which played a part in all aspects of community life, not just the festive or ritualistic. The traditional African forms of this song were so strong that they have adapted to a new world location, the English language and the Christian religion without losing their characteristics, which are as much alive in the oral culture of the Caribbean today as they ever were.

It seems likely that African languages gradually gave way to English as the medium for song during the eighteenth century, as the Caribbean-born slaves began to assert a local identity. Sir Hans Sloane at the beginning of the century gives examples of songs in African languages,[*] but by the last decade of the century there seem to have been plenty of examples in English for commentators to choose from. Sloane heads his songs 'Angola' and 'Koromanti', but as late as 1807 Robert Renny noted the tribal distinctions in the music: 'Their tunes are generally characteristic of their national manners; those of the Eboes, for instance, being soft and soothing, of the Koromantyns, heroic and martial.'[†] In ritualistic contexts versions of songs in African languages still survive, the exact form and meaning of the words having been lost, but the authority of their sound persisting.

The call-and-response structure of the choral singing which came from Africa and is still found in Caribbean folk-songs differs from the European ballad-and-chorus, which tends to have much longer units. The antiphonal units of the 'jamma' or work-song seem to be determined by the work in hand, so that the chorus has a phrase on each exhalation. The leader, or 'bomma', takes the initiative and sets up the rhythm, into which his companions interject the short chorus phrases. Moreton relates, 'when working, though at the hardest labour, they are commonly singing',[‡] but the jamma seems to have

[*] Sir Hans Sloane, *A Voyage to the Islands Madera, Barbados, Nieves, S. Christophers and Jamaica, with the Natural History of the Herbs etc.*, 2 vols., London, 1707, vol. I, p. L.

[†] Robert Renny, *A History of Jamaica*, London, 1807, pp. 168–9.

[‡] J. B. Moreton, *West India Customs and Manners*, London, 1793, p. 152.

been particularly associated with the cultivation of the West African staple food, the yam, which the slaves grew on their own provision grounds: 'to tek out yam widout jamma' is a Jamaican proverb for an impossibility. 'Guinea Corn' is an example of a typical work-song which could be extended by improvisation, while Alfred Cruickshank's 'The Convict Song' offers a twentieth-century adaptation to the literary tradition.

A similar call-and-response pattern was also used to dance to: Lewis tells us, 'the principal part of the music to which they dance is vocal; one girl generally singing two lines by herself, and being answered by a chorus'.* Several commentators note how the singing and dancing was kept up all night: '... they will meet on Saturday nights, hundreds of them in gangs, and dance and sing till morning; nay, sometimes they continue their balls without intermission till Monday-morning.'† By the time Jekyll was collecting folk-songs in Jamaica at the beginning of this century he was able to detect a considerable European influence on the dance steps and tunes, and the effect of English children's ring-games on the Caribbean ring-games,‡ but there is no doubt that the tradition of singing and dancing in a ring was brought originally from Africa. Moreton tells us, 'When dancing, they form themselves into a circular position, adjoining some of their huts, and continue all in motion, singing so loud, that of a calm night they may be heard at about two miles distance.'§ These weekend festivities were intensified at Christmas, 'pickney Christmas' (Easter), and crop-time (harvest); after Emancipation, 1 August became a festival too, while in islands with a predominantly Catholic culture, and particularly Trinidad, the Mardi Gras pre-Lenten revelry became important.

The election of kings and queens and other dignitaries to preside over these festivities can be paralleled in European culture. The carnival tradition from Catholic Europe was a Christian adaptation of an older pagan festival, a spring

* M. G. Lewis, *Journal of a West India Proprietor*, London, 1834, p. 80.

† Moreton, op. cit., p. 155.

‡ See Walter Jekyll, *Jamaican Song and Story*, London, 1907, New York, 1966.

§ Moreton, op. cit., p. 156.

fertility rite and saturnalia, in which the established order was overturned, while variants of the festivity in which those normally under authority assume the dominant roles for the duration of the festival are widespread. The colonists perhaps realized that the occasional taking of liberties under licence was a useful psychological safety valve which tended to promote more willing submission for the rest of the year, but to their own people the kings and queens of the revels were symbolic and satiric roles, and the assumed persona tended to carry weight long after the performance.*

The tradition of satiric song, and particularly satire by impersonation, is derived from Africa but was readily transplanted to the Caribbean. On a slave plantation subjects for mimicry were not far to seek. Renny speaks of the slaves' 'talent for ridicule, of which they are possessed in an uncommon degree', and says their subject was often 'the follies or foibles of their masters and mistresses'.† Local gossip and scandal were also favourite topics, particularly with some sexual innuendo; according to Sloane 'their Songs are all bawdy, and leading that way',‡ and to judge by the examples which Moreton gives, this was particularly true of the dancing songs.

The topical nature of many of the songs meant that new ones were constantly being composed. The ability to compose extempore and wittily was highly valued in the West African cultures and its esteem continued in the Caribbean. Renny relates, 'The songs of the Negroes are commonly *impromptu*; and there are amongst them individuals, who resemble the *improvisatori*, or extempore bards of Italy.'§ Forms in which composer and performer are one, and in which improvisation plays a key role, are still central to the oral tradition today, with manifestations as diverse as calypso and the DJ's dub. There seems to have been a continual invention of topical songs on each estate, some of which caught on and were sung repeatedly until a new favourite ousted them. Lewis describes

---

* It is possible that the strong Caribbean tradition of using sobriquets derives from this.

† Renny, op. cit., p. 169.

‡ Sloane, op. cit., p. L.

§ Renny, op. cit., p. 168.

how the old favourite, 'We Varry Well Off' was 'still screamed about the estate by the children', while 'for several days past' a new song among the adults, 'Hey-ho-day! Me No Care a Dammee!' 'had been dinned into my ears incessantly'.* This constant innovation and trial by popularity, analogous to the modern pop-music situation, is confirmed by Hosack's description of Jamaican market women coming down from the mountains: '. . . together, all, the last new song they sing'.†

Occasionally a particular song would catch the popular fancy to such a degree that it crossed the divide from the transiently popular to the established and traditional. One such is the song, 'Take Him to the Gulley', which Lewis noted as popular in 1818 although it referred to an incident which took place in another part of Jamaica thirty years earlier.‡ This particular incident then passed into the story-telling folklore of the Anansi tradition (Anansi is the West African/Caribbean spider folk-hero whose exploits are part-told, part-sung), Jekyll recording in 1907 a story, 'Dry-Bone', in which it is incorporated,§ while as far away as Guyana there is a folk-song, 'Me Na Dead Yet', which, from the similarity of the phrase, may be descended from the same incident.¶ Likewise, Jekyll gives early versions of songs which are current today, such as 'Linstead Market' and 'There's a Black Boy in a Ring', which, as 'There's a Brown Girl in the Ring', has become part of the popular culture of the whole English-speaking world since it topped the hit parade in Boney-M's version and found its way into nursery songbooks.

The versatility to adapt and vary a particular song by the manner of performance, which is so typical of both oral poets and popular musicians today, has its roots in the early days. Louise Bennett tells how traditional songs could be given a completely different tone by being sung to a different beat or in a different key: 'Bitter Sarrassee', for instance, has both mento and waltz-time versions, while 'De Ribber Ben Come Dung'

* Lewis, op. cit., p. 232.

† William Hosack, *The Isle of Streams*, London, 1879, st. IV.

‡ Lewis, op. cit., pp. 322–4.

§ Jekyll, op. cit., pp. 48–51.

¶ A version of the song is recorded on *Bamboo Fire and Other Folk Songs of Guyana*, The Emmel Singers, National History and Arts Council of Guyana, HAS 1187 LP, n.d.

can be sung in the major key, in which case its excitement predominates, or in the minor, when the narrative takes on a more tragic aspect.* 'Linstead Market', for all the pathos of its words, is usually sung now to quite a cheerful tune.

Nearly two centuries ago, Moreton distinguished two basic types of song, the 'witty' and the 'pathetic': 'I have often laughed heartily, and have been as often struck with deep melancholly at their songs';† but it is from Robert Renny in 1807 that we have one of the fullest early descriptions of what we have come to call the blues. After describing the 'banja or merriwang . . . an imperfect kind of violoncello, which is played by the fingers, and produces only a simple monotony of four notes', he goes on:

> . . . it is impossible to hear this music, and remain un-affected with the dismal melody produced by the Negro, who, sitting in the door of his cabin, enjoying the coolness, and delighting in the stillness of evening, accompanies it with a melancholy song, expressive of his feelings. The melody, simple as it is, touches the heart, and cannot fail to draw tears from the affectionate, the melancholy, or the contemplative.‡

This clearly belies the common assumption that the blues is a North American form not found in the Caribbean.

Later writers have attempted to define the particular quality of the blues, that reconciliation of grief and joy without diminution of either, which has an effect analogous to the catharsis of tragedy. Eseoghene Lindsay Barrett, himself a poet, has captured its essence: 'The blues insists on naked-ness. Truth is the bone of strength. The flesh is purpose. The blues supports defiance in the face of pain. The blues is not pain.'§ To the enslaved, exiled and abused blacks it was an important tool for survival: to sing of suffering and sorrow was to commute their pain. And it is this voice from the New World, the blues, which has, more than any other, come to speak for the oppressed everywhere.

* Louise Bennett, interview with the editor, 14 March 1984.
† Moreton, op. cit., p. 152.
‡ Renny, op. cit., p. 168.
§ Eseoghene Lindsay Barrett, *The State of Black Desire*, Alençon, France, 1966, p. 48.

The attempt to catch its voice through words alone has preoccupied the poets of the Caribbean. Una Marson's blues poems, modelled on those of Langston Hughes in America, are the first to capture the true blues rhythm and tone, but it is to Edward Brathwaite that we have to look for a full realization of its poetic potential. His 'Blues' has all the right archetypal resonances: the sense of loss, the frame of reference which is simultaneously specific and universal, the heavy rhythm with its felt pauses at the end of each vocal phrase, and the solace which comes from making song of pain.

Although the oral culture of the Caribbean is unmistakably African in origin, even within the period of slavery it had a unique West Indian form, in that it reflected a new society in a new language. For economy of statement and depth in simplicity, songs such as 'One, Two, Tree' and 'Sangaree Kill de Captain' are hard to beat. The slave had learnt to address his master with the deft irony of song; with the wit, for instance, of an appeal to the overseer's Christian faith, in 'Tink dere is a God in a top'. By comparison, the political message of the 'Song of the King of the Eboes' is relatively crude and atypical, although no doubt effective as a rallying song. The dangers attendant on such a lack of subtlety are illustrated only too well by the story attached to the song, a copy of which became a significant item of evidence in the trial of the 'King' for sedition, which led to his execution. The tradition of oblique reference was a very African form; but where the ability to couch wisdom in riddles and proverbs had been esteemed as an accomplishment in African culture, in the Caribbean it acquired the added function of a tool for survival. It is 'Quaco Sam', however, which sums up better than any other song the realities of life on the plantations. It is a magical celebration of the independent spirit, which persists, against all odds, in its obstinate gaiety.

From Emancipation to Black Liberation

In the nineteenth century, on to this vigorous culture was grafted the language of the Bible and the Christian liturgy, and with it, gradually, literacy. The evangelization of the slaves had begun in the mid eighteenth century, with the Moravians first in the field, but missionary activity became widespread only after the abolition of the slave trade in 1807. At Emancipation in 1834 the British and Foreign Bible Society offered a combined volume of the New Testament and Psalms to 'every emancipated negro who had learnt to read', but were disappointed that so few passed their stringent test. When the unclaimed volumes were put up for sale shortly afterwards, the demand was huge. Mrs Campbell, recounting this in 1853, analyses the role of the non-conformist churches with their black congregations: 'The Baptists have obtained a very extensive influence over the minds of the black people in Jamaica, who have regarded them as much in the light of defenders from temporal oppression as in that of instructors of religion.'*

Instead of imposing an alien pattern of worship, the evangelists had the wisdom to adapt their services to the existing cultural patterns of their converts: eventually, except in a few cultic enclaves, possession by the Holy Spirit replaced African spirit-possession, while the call-and-response structure became a feature of black worship. Antiphonal responses were, of course, not new to the liturgy, but the particular manner in which preachers would, and do, evoke response from their congregations is very much a black, New World, phenomenon. The chiming of assent in such phrases as 'Yes, Lord' or 'True, true' is mirrored in everyday speech, and has been adapted to the oral poetry by James Martinez and Bruce St John, for instance. St John's most famous poem, 'Bajan Litany', is witty just because it cheats the expectation of that chiming assent; where a litany should be ritualistic, his suffers a rebellion in the ranks and makes its satiric point with delicious humour.

The Bible is part of the linguistic reservoir of Caribbean people in general, but the language of the Old Testament and Revelation in particular has been formative on the characteristic speech of Rastafarians, giving a sonorous authority to the songs of many reggae musicians and dub poets (see page xli below). Hymns too have an important place in the region's oral culture. Edward Lucie-Smith writes about their effect on him, but it is today's young oral poets who

---

* (Mrs Campbell), *Suggestions Relative to the Improvement of the British West India Colonies*, London, 1853, p. 15.

have learned to harness their linguistic power to a new use.

With the increase in literacy, at first through the efforts of the missionaries, a culture which had been entirely oral began to utilize the written word. The newspapers of the Caribbean were the first to capitalize on the new readership. In the late nineteenth and early twentieth centuries, daily papers often ran regular columns of vernacular verse, which rapidly gained huge popularity. Their writers were mostly educated men turning their hand to an effective piece of journalism, and were not in any sense poets from the world they portrayed, but they were important as founders of a new popular tradition, which has had a far-reaching influence. Perhaps marrying the contemporary British vogue for humorous dramatic monologue in the vernacular to the long-standing local tradition of humorous dramatic impersonation, writers such as Michael McTurk and Edward Cordle wrote for a new readership who, for the first time, saw their own lives reflected in literary form.

McTurk dealt with a wide range of subjects, not always in a humorous vein, and occasionally, although he was white, went right to the heart of the problem of being black in a white-dominated world, as in 'Query'. He wrote under a male persona, 'Quow', often addressing a fictional friend 'Jimmis', but it is the female persona as 'letter-writer' which has become typical of the verse monologue tradition.

Cordle's famous 'Lizzie and Joe' series, chronicling the daily ups and downs of the couple as recorded by Lizzie in letters to her friend Suzie, was spirited and funny, dealing with timeless themes such as marital relationships, quarrels with neighbours and the problem of opulent relatives returned from abroad, but it also touched on topical matters which verged on the political, and dared to be critical of the establishment. During the smallpox outbreak of 1902, the authorities imposed a trade embargo on Barbados to stop the disease spreading: Cordle pointed out the state of near-starvation to which this reduced the people. He also criticized local officials for pocketing funds sent from London. His satire on the authorities was counterbalanced by an element of caricature in his presentation of his main characters. The ordinary people were portrayed as quarrelsome and outspoken, the men unfaithful, the women domineering and jealous to the point of violence to their rivals (never to the fickle male). This powerful stereotype has dominated the tradition, cropping up in the work of Louise Bennett and the young poet, Valerie Bloom.

The vernacular tradition was, from McTurk onward, crossing the divide from the oral to the scribal, championing the language and way of life of a people who had hitherto seen print as the preserve of the ruling class. Implicit in this was the weaning of words from music, and the consequent need to find structural patterns via words alone. McTurk tried out a number of rather rambling metres for his verses, but Cordle stuck to a regular four-line rhymed stanza, whose humdrum rhythm became indelibly associated with the tradition. The tendency to jog along in rhythm and thought is not, however, a problem inherent in the metre, as other poets' use of a similar form illustrates: Louis Simpson, Phyllis Allfrey and Jean Rhys, for instance, all explore the potential for emotional tension between a simple metre and a tragic content, with powerful results. To a generation raised on the even rhythms and rhyme of hymns, however, the ballad quatrain had an enormous popular appeal, but in this adaptation to the regular prosody of traditional English verse the African tradition underwent its biggest metamorphosis. It is only in relatively recent years, and again through experimenting with music, that poets of the oral tradition have learned to use, rather than be used by, metre.

Another association which has proved hard to break is that of the vernacular and light verse. The prejudice against the everyday language of the ordinary people was entrenched and persistent, and it is only very recently that vernacular poetry has been taken at all seriously by the academic establishment. As late as 1962, in *The Independence Anthology of Jamaican Literature*, Louise Bennett's work was not put in the poetry section at all but under 'Miscellaneous', while earlier poetry anthologies ignored the vernacular altogether. The Jamaica Poetry League did once invite Louise Bennett, but to read someone else's work; she very properly declined to do so, until they had someone else read *her* work. The educational establishment had been labouring for years to teach those whose language was the vernacular to speak standard British English, which was the passport to social advancement, and it did not readily succumb to an acknowledgement that the vernacular could be the language of art: the worth of vernacular poetry could be denied, if not its popularity.

It was often also the poets themselves who resisted the idea of the vernacular as a potential medium. It was the Englishman, Walter Jekyll, compiler of the first (1907) collection of Jamaican folklore in words and music, who persuaded the young policeman, Claude McKay, to try his hand at vernacular poetry. There is an unmistakably literary quality to much of McKay's two volumes of vernacular verse published in 1912. He imitates the sentimental themes and interesting stanzas of Robert Burns, who had been such an inspiration to the growing Victorian interest in folklore (of which Jekyll was a product) and indeed earned himself the title of 'Jamaica's Bobbie Burns', but even in those early days a distinctively Caribbean consciousness was coming through, in local scenes and human drama drawn from his personal experience as a constable. McKay went on, however, to America, where he concentrated on his preferred medium, standard English. Jekyll's vision of a unique society celebrated in a unique language had to wait till later in the century for realization.

It is largely thanks to one woman's warmth that the prejudice against dialect has gradually melted away, and that a climate has been established in which a whole new generation of creative users of the vernacular could flourish. As a girl at school, in love with literature and trying her hand at poetry, Louise Bennett was given a copy of McKay's *Constab Ballads* by a teacher. Later, she became aware of Cordle's work, perhaps learning from him how to combine hilarious entertainment with serious satire, but these literary influences were minor compared with the effect on her of the vigorous rural folk culture, which was like a revelation to her when she went to her grandmother's funeral in St Mary at the age of ten. Realizing that the stuff of poetry was all around her in the drama of ordinary people's lives and in the language which they spoke, she began to write and to perform. A professional performer since her debut in 1938 at the age of nineteen, and a published writer since the *Gleaner* began to carry her verse on Sundays in 1943, 'Miss Lou' has become internationally known and loved as a poet, a performer and a champion of the folk. She is a serious folklorist who has done more to promote respect for ordinary people and their culture than any academic could have done, while as a poet she has placed a hallmark on the comic-satiric verse style which is proving hard to surpass, and has had a far-reaching effect on both the rising generation of vernacular poets and those poets who use mainly standard English.

Other persona poem sequences which owe something to this tradition are the two banana-man poems of Evan Jones (who was early in the field) and the Lucy poems of James Berry, while the Lambchops and Philpot poems of E. A. Markham and the Mama Dot poems of Frederick D'Aguiar are extending the tradition with a new sophistication. Paul Keens-Douglas's work, which also belongs in this tradition in that it consists mainly of humorous dramatic monologues with a cast of recurrent characters, is important because it offers a gallery of Caribbean icons, some of them rather rambling and facile, but a serious attempt none the less to portray the essence of a society through a series of symbolic vignettes. That they sometimes waver between prose and poetry matters only to a reader, not a listener; at his best he can develop a small incident to a rich comedy, while in 'Wukhand' there is an almost heroic pathos.

By the 1980s there is almost no major poet of the English-speaking Caribbean who does not have the vernacular as one of the languages of his poetry, but it is still to the oral tradition that we have to look for forms independent of the English literary tradition. In the last fifteen years a whole new cultural phenomenon has developed in response to modern technology, which has finally broken the old association of the vernacular with comedy, and is, in fact, a remarkable re-invention of an ancient tradition.

Here the word is still intimately bound up with the music. During the sixties, the popular music of the Caribbean had begun to attract world-wide notice, and in Kingston studios reggae was being created from the older Jamaican music of ska and mento. In those post-Independence years political optimism soon evaporated, and young people who felt betrayed by the establishment tended to turn to music for self-expression. Where most popular music was content to be entertainment, Caribbean popular music developed a significant political content, sometimes a simple protest against poverty (like the Marley song 'Dem Belly Full') and sometimes a complex satire (as in Sparrow's 'Get to Hell outa Here'). These are forms of poetry in the old vocal-music tradition. Calypso, for instance, is in direct descent from the African tradition of satiric song (its association with carnival dates only from the beginning of this century). The singer-songwriters are the court-jesters of modern society; they must first entertain, but of equal importance is the serious meaning of what they have to say, so that wit goes hand in hand with perceptive comment, whether on politics, society or the human condition. A musical accompaniment, by fulfilling the entertainment need, frees the lyricist to be as pointed as he wishes: the words of many of Trinidad's political calypsos, for instance, read more like newspaper leaders yet work as popular songs.

One of the offshoots of the new musical technology was the role of the disc jockey. Large numbers of people could be entertained cheaply by having one person play many artists' records, but in Jamaica, in particular, some of the DJs took this a stage further by themselves contributing to the art. Records were manufactured with a 'dub' side, that is, an instrumental version of the song with the vocal track removed ('dubbed out'), so that the DJ could improvise a half-spoken, half-sung, witty, often topical, and often satiric contribution over the music: the old Afro-Caribbean tradition was surfacing again in response to the new situation created by modern technology. Those who were interested particularly in the power of the word realized the artistic potential of this form and began to compose poems to be performed to music. It seems that around 1970 several young Jamaicans began to be popular with audiences for their poetry, notably Mutabaruka and Oku Onuora, and in England, Linton Kwesi Johnson, while Malik was doing a similar thing in Trinidad. Where the calypsonians and reggae musicians had dealt in music, with words, these 'dub poets', as they have come to be known, deal in words, with music, and are just as much at home speaking their poems to an audience as they are in dubbing them over a musical accompaniment. In several cases, poets have issued both voice-only and musical recordings of their work, but acknowledge the part played by music in helping them to reach a wide audience. Although recording tends to 'fix' both text and delivery, most poets insist on the concept of the uniqueness of each performance, and resist the notion of a script, although some have also published books of their work. Skilled performers with distinctive stage presences (several of them have studied at the Jamaica School of Drama), they will sometimes adapt to the voice the electronic techniques of the recording studio – reverberation, for example.

Their standpoint tends to be that of the urban poor, oppressed by a prosperous establishment, and their language, like many of the reggae musicians', is influenced by Rasta-farian speech. The Rastafarian celebration of Africa, regarding the black man outside Africa as exiled, in 'Babylon', is a recurring theme, although Linton Kwesi Johnson has firmly asserted a 'Black British' identity. They tend to employ the sonorous Rastafarian fusion of Biblical phraseology and 'I'-dominated terms* to lend weight to their message, and use proverbs and allusions to popular lore, such as folk-songs and children's rhymes, as a kind of folk wisdom in support of their case. Expert in the skilful manipulation of sound pattern, they often manage to translate the rhythms of reggae into speech patterns, while highly charged phrases from, say, the songs of Bob Marley are quoted for their talismanic value (the repetition of set phrases is one of the universal characteristics of oral literatures). They will use irony but are rarely funny; with them, laughter always has a serious edge. In the hands of a gifted poet and performer such as Michael Smith, whose murder is a reminder both of the violence of society which these poets reflect in their work and of the high price which can be paid for outspokenness, as much now as in the days of the 'King of the Eboes', the art of oral poetry has reached a genuine maturity.

In the end, it is through the oral poets that the Caribbean identity can be explored and celebrated in all its particularity. Although the long-hoped-for political federation failed, it may prove possible to weave a corporate cultural identity from the various national strands. The All Ah We performance group's tours of the Caribbean in the seventies with over 150 perform-ances, Marc Matthews's launching of He And She in London, Lillian Allen's adaptation of the dub style to a Canadian and feminist viewpoint – these are all indications of an international spirit which strengthens rather than weakens ties.

---

* See note on 'ITYOPIA', page 387 below.

The celebration of survival in Michael Smith's poems, or of love in Christopher Laird's, or Linton Kwesi Johnson's elegy for his father, are unmistakably Caribbean, but also universal.

THE LITERARY TRADITION

The Eighteenth and Nineteenth Centuries

There is a surprisingly large body of early verse either from or about the British West Indies. It reflects the prevalent European tastes, following well-established literary models and employing a poetic diction in which the slaves are referred to, if they are mentioned at all, by epithets such as 'sable' or 'sooty'. For virtually two centuries the written poetry of the region was, with one exception, the product of the white ruling classes, the only literates. It is of interest today, not because it is great literature, which it is not (although much of it is competent and pleasing verse), but because it offers an insight, however incomplete, into a unique society and into that society's growth towards moral and cultural integrity.

The process of creolization was under way from the beginning. The earliest surviving poems of the region (which may mask a body of lost literature) are anonymous occasional poems, of which the earliest one known to have been published in the West Indies is an ode welcoming a new governor to Jamaica in 1718. The charm of its classical fancies comes, for us, to a shuddering halt with the inclusion, in its portrayal of rejoicing crowds, of the 'branded, shackled Slave'. That the scene is Caribbean is painfully inescapable. The sensibility, or lack of it, here, is poles apart from the sensibility of Francis Williams, who also wrote an ode welcoming a subsequent new governor. Although it is in Latin it seemed right to include it here because it is of so much interest, and because none of Williams's poetry in English has survived.

Williams is the first black poet in the literary tradition, in fact the only one for another century and a half. A freeborn Jamaican, he was chosen by John, second Duke of Montagu, to become the subject of an experiment 'to discover, whether, by proper cultivation, and a regular course of tuition at school and the university, a Negroe might not be found as capable of literature as a white person'. He was dispatched to England for education, studying eventually at Cambridge, and when he returned to Jamaica the well-intentioned Duke tried to get him appointed to the Governor's Council. While the experiment to educate Williams was a success, no parallel experiment had been initiated to change the prejudice of colonial society, and having been refused entry to government service, Williams set up a school in Spanish Town – arguably a more valuable enterprise in any case. Despite what must have been a traumatic experience, he retained enough pride in his identity as a black man to claim a black muse for his art: a notion which, though couched in the terminology of European culture, was remarkable for its intellectual independence and far-sightedness. Williams's appellation of the new Governor as 'Caesar of the setting sun' and his choice of the Latin language indicate a fine awareness of the ironies of a colonial situation, and a subtle reminder of the fragility of empire.

The prevalent mode in the eighteenth century, however, was an exotic version of pastoral, modelled on the classics and Thomson's *Seasons*. The form chosen was usually blank verse, and the scale of these works was substantial. For all their mediocrity, the early poets were confident, fluent and productive, and it was in the descriptive genre that a truly Caribbean poetry began to emerge. A new landscape, a new climate and a new society were being claimed for art; and even at this early stage, a new manner of treatment was beginning to emerge.

Nathaniel Weekes's *Barbados*, the earliest poem in this category, published in London in 1754, presented the island landscape as a garden created for man's recreation: the appropriate setting for civilized activity. The 'daily destin'd Labours' of those who maintained the garden were unquestioned, and the detail of their lives irrelevant to the scene. The planter class was simply substituted for the British gentry, and barely visible slaves for barely visible peasants. The image was of a golden age, but the confidence of the period complacently placed it in the present, an idyll which was available in real life on a tropical island, tamed by ordered cultivation. Already, however, the Caribbean version of pastoral had other dimensions. Weekes stated his purpose in *Barbados* as 'to describe her various Fruit / Explore her Treasures, and her worth rehearse'; the last aim involved a topical plea to the British not to begrudge a good price for sugar, a warning against the threat posed by France, and a request for adequate defence. Weekes was making use of an artistic tradition to make a case, and an awareness of the power of art to persuade has been integral to Caribbean poetry ever since. Even in a genre such as pastoral, it has rarely been simply decorative.

James Grainger's *The Sugar-Cane*, published by Weekes's London publisher in 1764, was a functional poem of a different kind. Modelled on Virgil's *Georgics*, which had come into vogue at the end of the seventeenth century and had been imitated by poets such as Christopher Smart and John Dyer with their poems on the cultivation of hops and raising of sheep, it added the colonial dimension to these handbooks of rural husbandry by taking the cultivation of sugar-cane as its subject. Grainger, in his 'West India georgic', offers a serious guide to all aspects of the management of a sugar plantation, including such topics as soil and weather-lore, the purchase of slaves, and their medical care. He favoured the abolition of 'heart-debasing slavery' but imagined a future in which

> Servants, not slaves; of choice, and not compell'd;
> The Blacks should cultivate the Cane-land isles,

displaying an ambivalence typical of the more philanthropic planters. Although Grainger's poem is the only one from the early period to receive any notice from the English literary establishment and is still anthologized, whether much of it is poetry remains open to question. Weekes, when embarking on an account of the cultivation of the cane, had quailed, fearing his subject fitter 'for Prose than Song', but Grainger, acknowledging Dyer's example, pressed on. His poem contains some good passages, and is of considerable social interest, but as poetry it is in the main distinguished by its mediocrity.

His preface gives a good indication of the spirit in which several early poets embarked on specifically West Indian topics: '. . . as the face of this country was wholly different from that of Europe: so whatever hand copied its appearances, however rude, could not fail to enrich poetry with many new and picturesque images.' Here was an El Dorado of new poetic material, waiting, like the rich, volcanic soils, for exploitation. The aspiring poets saw themselves as participants in a new Arcadian scene, with nymphs and swains disporting themselves on the grass, in accordance with tradition, but in the shade of palm trees and with a banquet of barbecued meat, tropical fruits and rum. The main, descriptive set-piece of Weekes's poem is an elaborate account of an alfresco turtle feast, for example. At the same time, the vogue for the picturesque was gaining ground, and the search for the exotic within Europe, among the grandeur and terrible steeps of the Alps, was here outdone by a landscape and climate both dramatic in the extreme. The natural cataclysms of hurricane, earthquake and volcanic eruption became the standard subjects of this literature, with an increasingly romantic overlay as the style carried over into the nineteenth century. As early as 1767, John Singleton described with awe his descent into the sulphurous crater of Montserrat's volcano, in a spirit already far removed from the ordered garden imagery of Weekes's *Barbados*. Here again, the classics provided appropriate imagery; if the crater put him in mind of the ancients' Hades, a slave funeral recalled ceremonies to ancient gods: the imagery of the past was once more being rediscovered in a living present. The account of the authentically African-style funeral is impressive almost in spite of Singleton's presentation, with the dignity of the event rising above his label of 'primitive'.

Already by the mid eighteenth century, the question of the status of the negro could not be avoided. Where the author of the 1718 ode was able to mention casually the 'branded, shackled Slave', confident that no note extraneous to a scene of rejoicing had been struck, less than forty years later no writer could have approached the subject with any less delicacy than Weekes, who, like many of his age, circumvented the moral problem by admitting the theological argument of the equality of all mankind in the eyes of God, while defending the worldly institution of slavery. It is hardly surprising that those, like Weekes, and in the nineteenth century, Chapman, born and raised in the West Indies tended to accept the arrangement of society there, while in general, outsiders – new settlers and visitors – raised the first voices of protest. The movement for the abolition of slavery is of interest here for two reasons: first, because those of its supporters who described the West Indian scene tended to give the slave himself a central position in the frame, where before he had been, at best, peripheral to the main concern; and second, because it reveals that sense of the ethical power of the word which has given rise to some of the best Caribbean poetry.

The anonymous eighteen-year-old author of 'Jamaica' and the 'Poetical Epistle' raised a brave and early poetic voice against slavery. Five years after Lord Mansfield's historic ruling in the case of the negro, Somerset, which established that rights over slaves could not be asserted in England, but ten years before the setting up of the Commission for the Abolition of the Slave Trade, he was publishing moving appeals on behalf of the slaves, making skilful use of what had already become the region's literary tradition. He rejected the cultivation of sugar-cane as a potential subject:

> Th'ingrateful task a British Muse disdains,
> Lo! tortures, racks, whips, famine, gibbets, chains,
> Rise on my mind, appall my tear-stain'd eye.

Employing the by now familiar West Indian theme of the lusciousness of tropical fruits compared with those of England, he gives it an original twist by finally preferring slavery-free England to the exotica of the Caribbean, which include the monstrous 'fruit' of the planters' inventiveness in torturing their slaves. With similar subtlety he uses the classical names commonly given to slaves at that period so that, for the first time, they are portrayed as potential rulers, philosophers and patriots, who should be accorded the respect which Christian, eighteenth-century Europe accorded to the great pagans of Greece and Rome. This young poet was also one of the first to invert the terminology of civilization: to him, the 'Barbarians' are the European slave-traders – a theme later to be taken up by James Montgomery.

Moreton's ballad takes this process of empathy a major step further by not only entering into the experience of a slave woman, abused by master and overseer, but also speaking with her language, so that, although Moreton's intention may have been in part frivolous, the pathos of her predicament comes through. This is the earliest appearance of the vernacular in the literary tradition, antedating its first concerted use as a language for written poetry by more than a century.

Montgomery's poem *The West Indies* was commissioned

for Bowyer's handsome folio volume, *Poems on the Abolition of the Slave Trade*, published in 1809, two years after abolition became law. Montgomery was already well known as a hymn-writer, and although his rhetoric can be a cumbersome vehicle, his poem was effective in its time: the following year it was reissued in a cheaper format, and passed through several subsequent editions before emancipation was finally achieved in 1834. An excerpt from it is included here on the grounds that the pathos of its portrayal of the Caribs' extinction and the middle passage's horrors* makes a unique contribution to the literature dealing with Caribbean history. Although Montgomery did not visit the Caribbean himself, he did have West Indian connections (both his parents died as Moravian missionaries in the West Indies when he was a child), and in any case, his subject was in part a case for the historical imagination: the Caribs were, in most territories, long gone, and the British slave trade recently ended, but Montgomery warns that it should not therefore be consigned to oblivion, 'for were it ever forgotten, it might be revived in some future age of the world, as a new discovery in commerce and policy'.

As a last-ditch stand against the tide of Emancipation, M. J. Chapman offered his poem *Barbadoes* in defence of the old status quo. A competent poet, he painted a descriptive picture of his society on the old pastoral model, giving a landscape in which the happy negroes are picturesque additions to the sylvan scene, watched over by a paternalistic planter. It is subtly different from a work by the Scottish-born William Hosack which appeared in the same year, 1833, the year in which the Emancipation Bill was passed. His *Isle of Streams*, as it was subsequently titled, was a picturesque portrait of Jamaica, again on the old model, though using a new vehicle, the Spenserian stanza, but it is significant as the first Caribbean poem in the literary tradition in which the foreground is almost entirely occupied by black figures. Where earlier writers and Chapman would glance at the black community in passing from one aspect of the planter's life to another,

---

* The equatorial leg of the slave-ships' triangular voyage, Europe to Africa to the Americas and back to Europe, was known as the middle passage. See note to James Montgomery, page 396.

Hosack's Jamaica seems to be almost entirely peopled by blacks – as indeed it was. His descriptions of the midday recreation of the slaves, and of their Christmas festivities, show a warm interest and a keen eye for the details of a scene, but he writes still as an outsider, an observer looking on sympathetically from a distance.

Robert Dunbar, on the other hand, wove into his poem, *The Caraguin*, one of the earliest close-up portraits of a black person, the obeah-woman, Mimba, who is given an in-depth description, full of Gothic exaggeration admittedly, but interesting in that it offsets the old woman's hag-like appearance with an evocation of a noble ancestry, a young woman's love and pride, and a lifetime of suffering. This is a real step forward. It is clear from the poem itself (the mention of 'Orissa', for example), and from Dunbar's copious notes to his poems, that he took a scholarly interest in all aspects of West Indian life and other people's research on the subject. Others, such as John Singleton, had described the practice of obeah in mocking terms, but Dunbar was the first to treat it with respect, as an ancient and powerful tradition.

Dunbar was also one of the first to progress from the descriptive tradition, in which it was already difficult not to be hackneyed, to treat Caribbean subjects in narrative verse. Chapman had experimented with narrative episodes in his descriptive poem, but Dunbar was the first to write a full-length narrative poem, and to include the South American dimension. This set the scene for what became a tradition of Guyanese narrative poetry, of which Egbert Martin's 'Ruth', a sentimental story of the loss and hardship involved in migrant labour, told in a lilting metre reminiscent of Longfellow's *Hiawatha*, is one of the earliest and best-known examples.* Guyana was the first territory to develop a distinct national literature, although it is now becoming increasingly possible to distinguish a Trinidadian or Jamaican tradition, for instance. The chief agent of this was Guyana's difference from the islands in being a continental country; her writers turned naturally to the vast forests and rivers of the hinterland, and to the lives and myths of the indigenous peoples, for subjects.

* Martin is represented here by other work, as 'Ruth' does not lend itself to short excerpts.

As a country with many new people and much new settlement in the late nineteenth century, Guyana also developed a vigorous tradition of patriotic verse, designed to strengthen new bonds and allegiances. All of the territories shared this to a certain extent, just as they shared the Victorian tradition of loyalty to Britain which lasted well into the twentieth century. That poetic vein is represented here by Egbert Martin's prize-winning verses for the national anthem, composed for Queen Victoria's Jubilee in 1887.

Most of it was unremarkable, late-Victorian verse, spongy with sentiment and soft verbiage, but for all his similar weaknesses, it is to Horatio Nelson Huggins that the honours of the later nineteenth century must go. He turned to stories heard as a child in St Vincent to compose what may be tentatively called the Caribbean's first epic poem. It has as its subject the events leading up to the deportation of the Caribs (five thousand of them) from the island by the British in 1797, which Huggins presents with full tragic weight, as the guilty assertion of empire over a doomed race. His portrayal of the Caribs is coloured by a nineteenth-century romanticism – an elaboration of the 'noble savage' concept in which a Gothic excitement is derived from the account of blood rites – but their proud independence, and the courage with which it is defended, are presented with respect and admiration. His heroine, Ranèe, is a gentle Carib maiden (raised partly by Europeans and in love with a white man, Norman), whose tender Christian heart leads her to thwart her tribe's human sacrifice, but it is the hero, Warramou, a nobly born warrior's son, who holds the dominant role in the poem, which comes to a climax with his final prophecy in the Christian God's name that ultimately justice will be done: the great wrong done to the Caribs will be avenged in time by a corresponding expulsion, this time of the imperial power, the British themselves. The choice of an apocalyptic image of divine wrath, the eruption of St Vincent's volcano, shows Huggins at his most masterly: by making Warramou predict the 1812 eruption which was history by his own day, he lent weight to his real prophecy as to the future of the British in the island. He manages his long poem, in twelve cantos, with a confident sense of narrative and drama, using an easy, flowing style which, if not often inspired, is likewise rarely uncomfortable,

·and he should perhaps be forgiven the occasional remarks which grate on the modern ear, as to the primitiveness of the Caribs or the faithful devotion of the negro slaves to their masters, for the grandeur of his overall concept, and the courage with which, in nineteenth-century colonial society, he envisaged the ultimate collapse of the British empire. It is this, perhaps, which accounts for the non-publication of his poem until thirty-five years after his death.

The pathos of the virtual extinction of the Caribs had become a commonplace of the Caribbean literary tradition, but hitherto its moral implications had always been evaded by laying the guilt at the feet of Spain. Huggins, for all his imperfections, was the first to relate it to the British, and the first to question the whole role of empire. The exotic pastoral which began so tamely has grown muscles: Singleton's volcano which offered the romantic frisson of awe has turned into a terrible instrument of divine wrath, while Weekes's Eden has been corrupted by experience. Like Adam unparadised, the Caribs are expelled from their homeland, leaving the British as guilty usurpers. Huggins's lonely and original vision was a genuine precursor of the twentieth century.

The Twentieth Century

The first significant poet of this century symbolizes the way in which the old narrow literary tradition has been opened up. Where earlier poets (with the exception of Francis Williams) had been white, or virtually so, he was black; where they were middle- or upper-class, he was working-class, changing from wheelwright to police constable to poet and novelist. Claude McKay was also, as has been discussed above, the first poet (with the exception of Moreton) to bring the vernacular into the literary tradition, making the first move in that search for a poetic language which could bear the full weight of the Caribbean experience – a search which has dominated the century. In America, McKay changed over to standard English, to champion the wider cause of the black man. The compassion which had made him ill at ease as a policeman and which had informed moving vignettes of Jamaican life in the vernacular poems now lent a passionate depth to his American themes of white racism and the black man's heroic resistance to it. He was the first to weave into Caribbean poetry the strand of North American experience which has come to dominate the diaspora in more recent years. As an indication of the way in which the Caribbean's frame of reference was changing, his 1920 poetry collection was the first from the region to be published simultaneously in both London and New York.

Through contact with what has since come to be called the Harlem renaissance, he was enabled to come more fully into his heritage as a black man, and since his time, black solidarity has remained an essential dimension of the Caribbean consciousness. The interaction between Caribbean people and the major black liberation movements has been complex and fertile. Marcus Garvey, like McKay a Jamaican, and the founder of the United Negro Improvement Association in 1914, was another to catch the black American imagination, while later leaders of widespread black movements, Michael X and Stokely Carmichael (now Khame Ture), were of Trinidadian origin. The influence of the negritude movement of the French-speaking world in the thirties and forties was at first more literary than political in the English-speaking Caribbean, but the North American black movements of the sixties had an immediate impact, creating a climate in which the Jamaican cult of Rastafarianism, which had originally been of only minority and local appeal, could attract a huge, new, world-wide following, among young people in particular. It is against this background that the poetry of the twentieth century needs to be seen.

Hand in hand with black consciousness went the demands for independence. The nationalist, anti-colonial movements of the forties and fifties had their roots in the first decades of the century, but, despite this, the ethos of 'mother England' died hard. Many West Indians were, in fact, to pay the supreme price for their patriotism. Their contribution to the First World War is reflected in the poetry. Thomas MacDermot's poetry included patriotic war themes, while Donald McDonald published in London in 1918 a volume of verse from which the proceeds were to go to the West Indies Contingent Fund. W. A. Roberts, who had been a war correspondent in France, published a volume of poetry in New York in 1919, with several poems on France's war-time suffering. The

Second World War, too, was written in to the Caribbean experience, although fewer people were directly involved in the fighting. Louis Simpson, who fought with the Americans in Europe from 1943 onwards, wrote some of the finest poems to come out of that war. Others, at home in the West Indies, were learning to live with American bases (as in the Slim and Sam song and many calypsos of the period), while Philip Sherlock provides us with an updated version of McDonald's ironic 'Breakfast in Bed'.

In the early years of the century, loyalty to Britain was not felt to be incompatible with loyalty to one's native soil. Two poets of the twenties, Thomas MacDermot in Jamaica and James Martinez in Belize, illustrate the transitional phase which Caribbean poetry was passing through. Both wrote patriotic and nationalistic verse in a sentimental post-Victorian style, and both tried their hands at vernacular verse. MacDermot, who was posthumously elected Poet Laureate by the Jamaica Poetry League, was, despite his deliberately Jamaican subject-matter, in the old tradition of the patrician writer, a defender of empire, whose allegiance was as much to Britain (and her literary tradition) as to Jamaica. Martinez, who grew up on the Honduran lumber camps, had little formal education and wrote more often in a light vein, producing verses for popular consumption in the newspaper (hence his inclusion with other newspaper poets in the oral section), and giving his book a deprecatory title, *Caribbean Jingles*, although his serious sense of his role in establishing a national literature comes through in distinctively Belizean themes, such as life in the mahogany forests, the lumber-camp festivities, and so on. Significantly, MacDermot's best work is in standard English, while Martinez is better in the vernacular. Between them, they illustrate the tension between the literary and vernacular traditions in Caribbean poetry, a tension which has found a true creative resolution only in the last twenty years.

Una Marson, the Caribbean's first woman poet of note, was caught in the same dilemma. Like McKay, she was a Jamaican who became involved in black movements outside the Caribbean, this time in Europe, and like his, her poetic voice drew on a wide range of language and tone. Like him, she was most successful when working within a classical form,* but she is most interesting for being the first to attempt to capture in verse the distinctive qualities of black music, with her blues poems (following the example of the American, Langston Hughes), and to imitate the emotion and rhythm of black worship, but much of her experimental work is naïve without any real folk strength. One of her weaknesses is a tendency to vacillate uneasily between the vernacular and a faded poetic diction. She wrote very much as a woman, and was an early feminist, involved in women's-improvement organizations. Her personal verse has a tragic post-Victorian pathos, distinguished by a quiet sincerity.

The twenties and thirties were on the whole lean years, though. A number of people, particularly in Jamaica, were writing and publishing privately slim volumes of verse, but the cream of the Romantics and Victorians was pretty thin buttermilk by this late stage. The conservative spirit of the Jamaica Poetry League was to remain something of a strait-jacket to Jamaican poetry for several decades, although it performed the valuable service of stiffening the concept of a national literature. Its founder, J. E. C. McFarlane, published the first Caribbean anthology in 1929, *Voices from Summerland*, which was answered from Guyana by Norman Cameron's *Guianese Poetry, 1831–1931*; although much of their contents is verse rather than poetry, they had a symbolic importance which transcended their weaknesses.

Alfred Cruickshank's isolated voice was in a way typical of the period. Like Huggins, he illustrates the way in which it was possible, for someone who cared passionately enough, to invent a voice almost from nowhere to communicate his concerns. His fat volume of energetically committed poetry deploys satire in neat metric packages in what has since come to seem a very Trinidadian style. His verse is unpretentious, openly political, and effective. Again, it reads like an offshoot of journalism, but this quality of having its feet on the ground is one of the strengths of the Caribbean poetic tradition. Whether or not one agrees with Cruickshank's views, there is no doubt as to what he thinks, and the wit with which he puts it across is likely to win some converts.

* A surprisingly high proportion of the most successful early poems, by a wide range of writers, are sonnets.

It was in the forties that a real movement towards a Caribbean literature began to get off the ground, and this was largely due to the vision of a handful of people, who realized that local publishing was essential if the talents of local writers were to be given a climate in which they could develop. In 1942 Frank Collymore edited (from its third issue) the region's first lasting literary magazine, *Bim*, in Barbados. In 1943 the first edition of *Focus* appeared in Jamaica under Edna Manley's editorship, followed by A. J. Seymour's *Kyk-over-al* in Guyana in 1945. There had been a few earlier literary periodicals in the thirties (notably Albert Gomes's *The Beacon*, published in Trinidad in 1931–3 and 1939) but they had mostly been short-lived and there had been nothing to compare with the far-reaching importance of these three.

Focus, which, after a long gap since its early editions of 1943, 1948, 1956 and 1960, has in 1983 made a welcome reappearance, was in the forties associated with the new left-wing politics, an affiliation shared by Gomes's *Beacon* and Seymour's *Kyk-over-al*. From the beginning, *Bim* was more a simply literary magazine, and has been the longest-lasting and the most influential of all. Most major writers of the Caribbean and a host of minor ones have found their first readership through its pages and, apart from a recent pause following the death of its long-standing editor, it has continued in regular publication. The early nationalist intentions of these periodicals was from the start combined with a sense of a wider, federationist role. While it is true that George Lamming was associated with *Bim*, Wilson Harris with *Kyk-over-al* and George Campbell with *Focus* in the early years, non-local authors were never excluded, and anthology numbers of *Bim* and *Kyk-over-al* soon took on a distinctly federationist character. Discussion of concepts such as that of a West Indian literature rapidly gained the centre of the stage, while Seymour showed his vision in giving space, right at the beginning, for a series of articles on the vernacular. He also made an important contribution by setting up the Miniature Poets series, which gave pamphlet-sized first publication to a number of young writers who have since become major figures on the Caribbean literary scene. With the break-up of Federation imminent, *Kyk-over-al* lost its momentum, ceasing publication in 1961.

In the fifties, the Pioneer Press in Jamaica was issuing cheap titles of local interest, including, as well as the poems of MacDermot, volumes on folklore and dialect. But apart from these various local opportunities for publication, the single most important outlet for Caribbean writers was Henry Swanzy's BBC Caribbean Service programme, *Caribbean Voices*, which ran from 1945 to 1958, maintained high standards and, in Naipaul's phrase, 'spread a new idea of the value of writing'.*

The fruits of this literary infrastructure were already beginning to emerge by the end of the forties. The major new talent was the precocious nineteen-year-old St Lucian, Derek Walcott, whose *Epitaph for the Young* and *25 Poems* were privately published in Barbados in 1949. In his autobiographical poem, *Another Life*, he tells of the 'exhilaration' which George Campbell's *First Poems*, published in 1945, gave him. Here was something spare, plain, socially concerned, and unmistakably West Indian. A. J. Seymour's early works, culminating in *The Guiana Book* of 1948, were more consciously literary than Campbell's, but included some fine early attempts to capture characteristically Caribbean rhythms and scenes (and to use the indigenous myths of the Amerindians), as did Shake Keane's *L'Oubli* of 1950. These pioneers of rhythmic experiment were backed by a craft which gave their work substance even when it was not wholly successful. Wilson Harris, too, experimented with rhythmic repetition and a naïve manner before settling into his characteristically intricate and intellectually athletic style. The old derivative literariness typical of the Jamaica Poetry League had been rightly rejected by the new generation of writers in *Focus*, *Bim* and *Kyk-over-al*, but some of the new plainness was plain bad. Here at last, in Derek Walcott and Wilson Harris, was a new beginning: two enormous talents who could be literary in their own way, a quintessentially Caribbean way.

The fifties saw the beginning of the long emigrations, with many writers seeking both an income and a publisher abroad.

* See V. S. Naipaul's Introduction to his father's work, *The Adventures of Gurudeva and Other Stories* (by Seepersad Naipaul), London, 1976, p.10.

The novelists, many of whom had begun as poets,* were the first to be successful, with metropolitan publication for the best of the poets tending to come later, in the sixties. Louis Simpson was the exception to this, finding a publisher and academic recognition in America from 1949 on, and, with four poetry collections behind him, winning the Pulitzer Prize in 1964. In the eighties, with Walcott published by Faber in London and Farrar, Straus & Giroux in New York, with Edward Brathwaite and Louis Simpson published by Oxford University Press, and with the novels of Wilson Harris, Jean Rhys and the Naipaul brothers widely available in Faber or Penguin editions, it is easy to forget on what a fragile process the transition from local to world status can depend. The role of the specialist publishers, such as Heinemann and Longman, and, in particular, of the small presses and regional journals† is still crucial.

The politically committed writing of the forties took on a new urgency in the fifties, with the work of Martin Carter, who was an important forerunner of the protest poets of today. A political prisoner in the British Guiana of the fifties, he gave a lyric voice and a moral strength to the anti-colonial movement.

The sixties brought independence for the major territories of the British West Indies, and an increasing artistic concentration on the search for a characteristically Caribbean expression. The vernacular culture was drawing the attention of artist and academic as the manifestation of a unique identity, a source of powerful imagery and a positive answer to cultural derivativeness. It was only now, for instance, that Louise Bennett began to receive serious recognition; the first substantial collection of her poetry was published in 1966. Walcott

* For reasons of space, most of the early poets who went on to become well-known novelists, such as George Lamming, Roger Mais and Samuel Selvon, are omitted here. Wilson Harris and Jean Rhys are represented because of the particular light shed on their prose works by their poetry, while such writers as Andrew Salkey and Jan Carew are included because they have maintained a role as poet alongside their work as novelists.

† New Beacon and Bogle L'Ouverture in London, for instance, Williams-Wallace in Toronto, Savacou in Jamaica, or The New Voices in Trinidad.

Introduction

continued to publish impressive volumes of poetry exploring, among other things, potential Caribbean archetypes, such as Crusoe and Adam, while Brathwaite, who came to the fore in the mid-sixties, turned to the earlier folk-based sound-patterning experiments of Seymour and Keane, and realized that a unique poetic language could be created along similar lines as a vehicle for a Césaire-like heroic portrait of the society.

Like many Caribbean writers who had lived abroad, from McKay and Marson on, Brathwaite had had his racial consciousness sharpened by life at Cambridge and in Ghana. As a historian, the critical perspective of colonialism as expressed by Frantz Fanon, like Césaire from Martinique, came naturally to him; he was concerned to substitute for the white mask the face which was true to African roots, although, unlike some of his followers, he was never uncharitable to the generation of immediate ancestors with their 'white' ideals, the 'Toms'. He became the poet of the black experience in English as Césaire had become in French, giving in his trilogy, *The Arrivants*, 1967–9, an epic of journeys, of suffering and of discovery which is both an indictment of historical injustice and a celebration of a race. His poetic language is musical, a finely patterned skein of sound and rhythm, drawing on folk speech and culture to create a distinctively Caribbean sound, but never allowing the sound alone to dominate. There is always a tough intelligence at work and a rigorous sense of the overall design in his large-scale work (he has now published a second volume in his second trilogy, and plans a third trilogy to complete the opus), although the powerful lyrical and pictorial qualities of much of his work are so seductive that the reader or listener is unaware of the underlying craft. In a special way, Brathwaite's work spans the two traditions of the oral and the literary. His masterly manipulation of rhythm and sound-pattern cries out for an oral delivery (he has, in fact, issued recordings of his major poems, and draws large audiences as a performer), but the subtlety of his work is such that it repays study on the page and in relation to both the French and English literary traditions.* The younger generation owes him a great deal, both as critic-cum-publisher and as exem-

* He is included here in the literary section because his work reaches its widest public as words on the page rather than as sound.

plar: he was the first to extend the vernacular mode to its full range in non-dramatic poetry, and to give adequate expression to the sum of Caribbean experience.

The early seventies witnessed an unprecedented sequence of important publications, as well as the first pan-Caribbean arts festival, Carifesta, held in 1972 in Guyana. In the same year, Walcott's autobiographical poem, *Another Life*, an odyssey of the growth of the imagination – epic in the same sense as Wordsworth's *Prelude* – was published. This major work of contemporary English literature describes the growth of a uniquely Caribbean consciousness, through Walcott's own development from child to young man, ending with his departure from the St Lucia of his childhood to study in Jamaica. Here he had found the ultimate archetype of the Caribbean experience, the individual, whose growth to maturity is shaped by his unique environment, culture and history.

It is the archetype which emerges from that host of Caribbean writers who have drawn on childhood experiences, for whom the loss of childhood has a particular significance and poignancy, involving, through migration, divorce from a whole world of experience, and as such is closely bound up with the ancient and universal referends of pastoral: the alienation from a metropolitan society which fails to deliver what it promises, and the consequent yearning for the happiness and innocence of a rural childhood. The search for a lost golden age here becomes a quest for an elusive ideal society, attainable, in the end, neither in the far cities nor in the islands. McKay's contribution to the tradition had been mawkish with nostalgia; E. M. Roach, as one who stayed, could write honestly of the Caribbean dilemma, torn between the 'cage' of the islands and the cities' 'scorn'.

Walcott (another who stayed, although he now spends more of his time in America) acknowledges the pull of cities, as he imagined, devoted to art, and examines his own past without sentiment, although not without feeling. His poem, while intensely specific and personal, is also universal, achieving a fine balance between its positive, celebratory mode, recording the love for family, friends, partners and island, and its elegiac mode, recording a succession of deaths and failures. From this the symbolic figure of the artist emerges, uniting the imagery of endurance and sacrifice in his priest-like role as myth-maker, communicator of the revelation which alone can sustain his society.

This long poem of twenty-three chapters is handled with consummate skill, with an intricate web of linked imagery giving cohesion to the whole work. Having relinquished his first ambition, to be a painter, in favour of poetry, preferring to painting's two dimensions the multi-faceted resonance of the word, the 'crystal of ambiguities', Walcott here constructs a complete language of imagery, like a painter. If he had written nothing else, his reputation would be secure on this one work. As it is, he has continued to explore the Caribbean predicament and the dilemmas of the modern world in a succession of fine collections of poems, while his work in the theatre complements his poetry. Like Brathwaite, he bridges both traditions, the oral and the literary, with several magnificent poetic dramas which celebrate the folk culture and synthesize new myths from old traditions, while a vernacular *tour de force* such as 'The Spoiler's Return', in the Trinidadian tradition of 'picong', is as triumphant a transference of the vernacular music into print as Brathwaite's 'Horse Weebles', 'Starvation' or 'Blues'.

The Trinidadian, Wayne Brown, whose fine collection, *On the Coast*, was also published in 1972, has been criticized for being too much in Walcott's manner, but this is carping. Three Jamaicans – like Wayne Brown, about ten years younger than Walcott and Brathwaite – also came to the fore in the early seventies. They had studied abroad, Mervyn Morris at Oxford, Dennis Scott and Anthony McNeill in America, and were finding a new tough poetic language in surrealism. Like Walcott and Brathwaite, they returned to the Caribbean, and writing from within an ongoing Caribbean experience have been able both to use it and go beyond it as they wished. They are particularly good at laying bare the paradoxes and complexities of human feeling, and bring a keen intelligence to bear on private and public topics alike. While there are similarities between the three, each has a wholly distinctive voice, as should be clear from the selection of their work in these pages.

The confident poetic voice of Brown's *On the Coast*, Scott's *Uncle Time*, Morris's *The Pond* and McNeill's *Reel from 'The Life-Movie'* is mirrored in the work of the expatriates, E. A.

Markham, James Berry, A. L. Hendriks, Shake Keane and
Andrew Salkey, most of whom were publishing and reading in
the British poetry world as well as the British black com-
munity from at least the early seventies. Between them, they
illustrate the way in which the vernacular or oral spirit has
been growing within the literary tradition. All use the ver-
nacular as one of their poetic voices, although it is Berry who
is closest to the oral tradition, with his Lucy poems in
the humorous monologue style. Markham has made more
satiric use of this form with his Lambchops and Philpot
poems, which display a knife-sharp wit. Like Markham in his
sense of the absurd is Keane, another 'small-islander' who has
long shared the sardonic worldliness of northern capitals. A
jazz musician, his feeling for the rhythm of ordinary speech
and its rhetorical manipulation in poetry has produced some
fine work. In recent years both have turned increasingly to
their island roots, but both are now indelibly urban spirits.

Markham and Keane, who have lived in France and Ger-
many, are like A. L. Hendriks in that they bring an inter-
national perspective to the Caribbean focus which goes
beyond the English-speaking world. Hendriks's work does not
have the coruscating brilliance of Markham's, but it is always
well made and humane, often with a quiet humour. Andrew
Salkey, who like Keane has moved on to America, can also be
witty, although his poetry aligns itself more with the overtly
political tradition, particularly in its Latin American form. He
thus forms a bridge between the scribal, hieratic tradition of,
say, Neruda, and the essentially folk-based protest poetry of
the dub poets, for instance. His tone is vernacular and spare,
and at his best he achieves a startling directness of image and
idea. John Figueroa is perhaps the oldest champion of the
eclecticism which these poets display in their lives and work.
His assertion that nothing from any of the world's cultures 'is
alien to me' holds a breadth of vision which transcends racial
boundaries; by comparison, those who censure Walcott for
reading St John Perse while praising Brathwaite for reading
Césaire seem blinkered.

The internationalists do, however, face a real problem, that
the cultural Joseph's coat can end up as nothing more than
camouflage. Salkey's collection, *Away*, published in 1980, ex-
plores the recurrent Caribbean theme of isolation: the isolation

from the desired larger world felt by those raised on remote islands, and the isolation from 'home' which is substituted for this in attaining the metropolitan dream. Another kind of isolation is now emerging as a Caribbean theme, most strikingly in the recent work of Martin Carter. This is the defensive recoil into an inner solitude of a fine sensitivity trampled by the brutal outcome of events. Those who 'weep with a laughter beyond mirth', in Walcott's phrase, can take refuge in art. Carter, in describing 'our time's disgraceful space', does not attempt to separate himself from the judgement, yet the tragic despair of betrayed idealism is, in being expressed, transmuted, for the act of morally concerned creation is, in itself, a positive process: the tenderness with which Carter can say 'Shrimp is our number' gives cause for hope.

The best of the young generation of poets, several of them women, like Carter combine rigorous truthfulness with compassion. Sexual relationships and social roles are probed, and the new, grimmer aspects of the Caribbean experience portrayed with uncompromising directness. They are not all bleak visions, however; Kendel Hippolyte, in his fine poem, 'Jah-Son/ another way', for instance, conjures a defiantly optimistic conclusion.

It is significant that the voices of women should be increasingly firm in Caribbean poetry. From the earliest beginnings of the literature to the present, they have been the most exploited sector of the Caribbean's people: spanning the centuries an identical pathos informs both Moreton's ballad and Lillian Allen's modern lament. Una Marson took up the theme, and more recently the struggle for a specifically feminist liberation has motivated writers as various, and as widely spaced around the world, as Pamela Mordecai, Claire Harris, Marlene Philip, Lorna Goodison, Grace Nichols and Dionne Brand. The women of the Caribbean have come through a history of extreme hardship with great humanity and perseverance. That this strength should now be harnessed to poetry is a hopeful sign: we should not be surprised that their voices are authoritative.

CONCLUSION

Caribbean poetry has come a long way. From its beginnings in the portrayal through two cultures, derived from Africa and Britain, of a divided society, it has forged an identity which is unique and resilient. From the eighteenth century (which produced the earliest surviving poetry), both traditions, the African and the British, were being creolized simply by virtue of mirroring a unique society. The few slave songs to have survived are not African songs from the West Indies, but West Indian songs in the African tradition, while the early poems in the literary tradition, although modelled on English literature, were establishing from the start a distinct genre, because of their new subject-matter and the reasons why poets were taking up their pens.

In the search for an adequate poetic language, the poets of the twentieth century have experimented with the vernacular in relation to standard English, coming up with a number of different, personally successful solutions. Neither extreme viewpoint, that only poems in the vernacular can be truly Caribbean, or that only standard English can be used, does justice to the range of language use in the English-speaking Caribbean. The obvious dangers of self-isolation by too extreme a use of the vernacular, however authentic, when the whole of the English-speaking world awaits as a potential audience, have to be balanced against the loss of that unique cultural identity which can result from exclusive use of standard English. Some of the most interesting recent work experiments with the juxtaposition of standard English and the vernacular; Martin Carter, LeRoy Clarke and Kendel Hippolyte, for instance, have all made subtle use of the varied tones of voice thus available. It is the literary tradition's relatively recent 'discovery' of the oral tradition (in the same sense in which Columbus 'discovered' America), which is perhaps the single most important poetic event of this century. The poets of the Caribbean are leaders in the world-wide attempt to find a poetic language which can communicate with the majority of the people, not just an elite of initiates, a language which can be both simple and profound.

The Caribbean experience, which they offer to share with us, presents in an extreme form the dilemma of modern society, in that the tension between the old and the new may prove to be a test to destruction. It has to find roots in a community in which outside influences and scattered families are the rule. It has to establish an identity free of both the old colonial dependency and the subtler danger of becoming yet another US satellite. To find a role in a world dominated by East–West power blocs and their commercial stranglehold on primary producing countries, it has needed to express solidarity with black liberation movements and with the Third World, conscious that its own racial and socio-economic situation is unique, not to mention fragmented within itself.

The Caribbean crisis of identity is a malaise which Wayne Brown relates to the world-wide contemporary problem of a 'fundamentally religious dissatisfaction with a world that is no longer clearly organized, or with clear answers to offer'. In the long term there remains the ultimate truth that, as he says, 'the empires rise and fall . . . only the art stays'.* But in the here and now, what the poets are agreed on is that poetry matters, and has a crucial role to play in making an unjust world more just.

P.B.

---

* 'The century of exile', *Jamaica Journal*, vol. 7, no. 3, 1973.

NOTE ON THE TEXT

American spellings have not been anglicized since they often indicate a whole American experience. Within the Caribbean, usage varies, but seems to be undergoing a gradual shift from the British to the American convention.

To make the vernacular poems easier on the eye, the use of the apostrophe to indicate omission has been restricted to those words offering real difficulty without it.

For the reader's convenience, an attempt has been made to impose, with the poets' consent, some consistency on the presentation of the vernacular (with the exception of the orthography in some early texts). Where pronunciation is not significantly different from standard, the standard English spelling is retained, while where the vernacular pronunciation is distinct this is suggested by a phonetic spelling. If the non-Caribbean reader bears in mind some of the commonest characteristics of the vernacular, it should present few difficulties: voiced 'th' becomes 'd', unvoiced 'th' becomes 't' and 'v' becomes 'b'; 'o' tends to be broadened to 'a' or 'ah'; initial 'h' tends to be dropped, and added to words with an initial vowel; with pronouns (as in the West African languages) there is no distinction in case between subject and object, and pronouns (generally) double as possessives; difficulties can arise over the use of the singular noun for the plural, and over the lack of distinction between the tenses of verbs (again paralleled in the West African language group), but in context confusion is rare. The doubling of words for emphasis is also derived from Africa. The convention of representing the Caribbean broad 'a' by the spelling 'aw' in words such as 'Lawd' has been abandoned as confusing, in that it also, and more logically, represents the Cockney 'aw' sound which is closed with a 'w'; instead, the phonetic 'aa', 'ah' or 'ar' is used.

Paradoxically, it can be easier for a non-Caribbean person to make sense of the vernacular on the page (particularly in that many writers use a scribal compromise between the spoken and written languages), than to follow it aurally, since voice inflexion, which reflects the intonation of the tonal West African languages, can seem impenetrable, although in fact the words being used are familiar. There is, unfortunately, no simple answer to the problem of transcribing an oral language; phonetic symbols are logical but lost on the uninitiated, and everything else is compromise.

Above all, it is a language whose music lies in being spoken, and readers are requested to voice what the inner ear receives from the page.

On the principle that annotation is useful for those who need it, and that those who don't need it will ignore it, relevant information, sometimes with explanation for non-Caribbean readers, is included with biographical notes on the contributors after the texts. A full bibliography of poetry publications (including sound recordings where appropriate) follows each biographical note. A glossary of words unfamiliar to non-Caribbean readers is given at the end of the book. Terms requiring fuller explanation and those used in an idiosyncratic way are included in the notes.

THE ORAL TRADITION

Gal if yuh love me an yuh no write it
How me fe know?
Gal if yuh love me an yuh no write it
How me fe know?
Gal if yuh write it an me cyaan read it
How me fe know?

Talk it ah mout!
Talk it ah mout!
Talk it ah mout!

– Anonymous

ANONYMOUS

Work-songs

I
Tink dere is a God in a top,
No use me ill, Obissha!
Me no horse, me no mare, me no mule,
No use me ill, Obissha.

II
If me want for go in a Ebo,
Me can't go there!
Since dem tief me from a Guinea,
Me can't go there!

If me want for go in a Congo,
Me can't go there!
Since dem tief me from my tatta,
Me can't go there!

If me want for go in a Kingston,
Me can't go there!
Since massa go in a England,
Me can't go there!

Dancing Songs

I
Hipsaw! my deaa! you no do like a-me!
You no jig like a-me! you no twist like a-me!
Hipsaw! my deaa! you no shake like a-me!
You no wind like a-me! Go, yondaa!
Hipsaw! my deaa! you no jig like a-me!
You no work him like a-me! you no sweet him like a-me!

II
Tajo, tajo, tajo! tajo, my mackey massa!
O! laud, O! tajo, tajo, tajo!

You work him, mackey massa!
You sweet me, mackey massa!
A little more, my mackey massa!

Tajo, tajo, tajo! my mackey massa!
O! laud, O! tajo, tajo, tajo!
I'll please my mackey massa!
I'll jig to mackey massa!
I'll sweet my mackey massa!

Four songs recorded by J. B. Moreton in Jamaica, 1793

Guinea Corn

Guinea Corn, I long to see you
Guinea Corn, I long to plant you
Guinea Corn, I long to mould you
Guinea Corn, I long to weed you
Guinea Corn, I long to hoe you
Guinea Corn, I long to top you
Guinea Corn, I long to cut you
Guinea Corn, I long to dry you
Guinea Corn, I long to beat you
Guinea Corn, I long to trash you
Guinea Corn, I long to parch you
Guinea Corn, I long to grind you
Guinea Corn, I long to turn you
Guinea Corn, I long to eat you.

Recorded 1797

Songs

I
New-come buckra,
    He get sick,
He tak fever,

He be die;
He be die.
   New come, *etc.*

II
One, two, tree,
   All de same;
Black, white, brown,
   All de same;
   All de same.
     One, two, *etc.*

Recorded by Robert Renny in Jamaica in 1799

My Deery Honey

Shatterday nite aucung lau town,
   Chan fine my deery honey,
Run round de lebin street,
   Chan fine my deery honey,
Look behind de guaba bush,
   Chan fine my deery honey,
Vosh me pot, au vosh um clean,
   Chan fine my deery honey,
Au put in paze, au put in poke,
   Chan fine my deery honey,
Au bine me pot, au bine um sweet,
   Chan fine my deery honey,
Au sweep me ouse, au sweep um clean,
   Chan fine my deery honey,
Au clean me knife, au clean um shine,
   Chan fine my deery honey,
Au mek me bed, au mek um soff,
   Chan fine my deery honey,
Au mek um up, au shek um up,
   Chan fine my deery honey.

Recorded in 1805 by Samuel Augustus Matthews in
St Bartholomew

Freedom a Come Oh!

Talla ly li oh
Freedom a come oh!
Talla ly li oh
Here we dig, here we hoe.

Talla ly li oh
Slavery a gone oh!
Talla ly li oh
Here we dig, here we hoe.

Talla ly li oh
King George me a go.
Talla ly li oh
Here we dig, here we hoe.

Talla ly li oh
We nuh wuk no more!
Talla ly li oh
Here we dig, here we hoe.

Talla ly li oh
Massa he a go.
Talla ly li oh
Here we dig, here we hoe.

Talla ly li oh
Freedom a come oh!
Talla ly li oh
Here we dig, here we sow!

Folk-song, composed about 1807

Song of the King of the Eboes

Oh me good friend, Mr Wilberforce, make we free!
God Almighty thank ye! God Almighty thank ye!
  God Almighty, make we free!
Buckra in this country no make we free:
What Negro for to do? What Negro for to do?
  Take force by force! Take force by force!

CHORUS
To be sure! to be sure! to be sure!

Negro Song at Cornwall

  Hey-ho-day! me no care a dammee!
  Me acquire a house,
  Since massa come see we – oh!

  Hey-ho-day! neger now quite eerie,
  For once me see massa – hey-ho-day!
  When massa go, me no care a dammee,
  For how them usy we hey-ho-day!

A Negro Song

  Me take my cutacoo,
  And follow him to Lucea,
  And all for love of my bonny man-O:
    My bonny man, come home, come home!

  Doctor no do you good.
  When neger fall into neger hands,
  Buckra doctor no do him good more.
    Come home, my gold ring, come home!

A Popular Negro Song

(alluding to a local incident which took place thirty years earlier – see note, page 371)

'Take him to the Gulley! Take him to the Gulley!
 But bringee back the frock and board.' –
'Oh! massa, massa! me no deadee yet!' –
'Take him to the Gulley! Take him to the Gulley!
        Carry him along!'

> Four songs recorded by Matthew Gregory Lewis in Jamaica,
> 1816–18

Quaco Sam

Come, cousin Cuba, me yerry some news,
Me yerry say you buy one new pair a shoes,
Me yerry say you buy one dandy hat –
Come tell me, cousin Cuba, wha you pay fe dat?
        Wid me ring ding ding an me pam pam pam,
        Me nebber see a man like-a Quaco Sam.

Me yerry say one dance deh a Berry Hill:
Unco Jack fe play de fiddle, one hog deh fe kill;
Come tell me, cousin Cuba, how ebry ting 'tan,
Mek me ax sista Susan, mek me call sista Ann.
        Wid me ring ding ding *etc.*

Regen' gown me hab, me gingham coat;
Hankecha tie me head, tanky-massa be me troat –
An da warra mo me wanty? me hat, me junka fan,
Fe go da Berry Hill fe go see Quaco Sam.
        Wid me ring ding ding *etc.*

Oh Lard! how me wi dance when me yerry fiddle an drum!
Me no tink pon backra wuk, me no care fe fum-fum!
Me wi dance de shay-shay, me wi dance de 'cotch reel,
Me wi dance till ebry craps a me foot-battam peel.
        Wid me ring ding ding *etc.*

Monday marnin, Driber Harry, jus da cock da crow,
Tek him cudjo da him han, pop him whip da busha do'.
Wid me hoe da me shoulder, wid me bill da me back,
Me da mash putto-putto, me da tink pan Unco Jack.
    Wid me ring ding ding *etc*.

Me tek me road da cane-piece, weh de people-dem da run,
An all come behin' me, get de fum-fum.
Wid de centung da me back, chacolata da me pan,
Me da wuk, me da laugh, me da tink pan Quaco Sam.
    Wid me ring ding ding *etc*.

      Folk-song, composed between 1812 and *c*. 1825

Sangaree Kill de Captain

Sangaree kill de captain,
   O dear, he must die;
New rum kill de sailor,
   O dear, he must die;
Hard work kill de neger,
   O dear, he must die.
     La, la, La, la *etc*.

    Recorded by J. M. Phillippo in Jamaica, 1843

War Down a Monkland

War down a Monkland,
War down a Morant Bay,
War down a Chiggerfoot,
The Queen never know.
  War, war, war oh!
  War oh! heavy war oh!

Soldiers from Newcastle
Come down a Monkland
With gun an sword

Fe kill sinner oh!
  War, war, war oh!
  War oh! heavy war oh!

Folk-song, composed in 1865 and recorded by Walter
Jekyll in Jamaica, 1907

Two Man a Road

Two man a road, Cromanty boy,
Two man a road, fight for you lady!
Two man a road, down town picny,
Two man a road, fight for you lady!
Two man a road, Cromanty win oh!
Two man a road, Cromanty win.

Mas' Charley

Mas' Charley say want kiss Matty,
Kiss with a willing mind.
Me rarabum why!
Colon money done!
Me rarabum why!
Colon money done!

I Have a News

I have a news to tell you all about the Mowitahl men;
Time is harder ev'ry day an harder yet to come.
They made a dance on Friday night an failed to pay the
    drummer,
Say that they all was need of money to buy up their August
    pork.
Don't let them go free, drummer! Don't let them go free,
    drummer!

For your finger cost money to tickle the poor goat-'kin.
Not if the pork even purchase self, take it away for your
  labour,
For your finger cost money to tickle the poor goat-'kin.

There's a Black Boy in a Ring

There's a black boy in a ring, tra la la la la,
There's a black boy in a ring, tra la la la la,
There's a black boy in a ring, tra la la la la,
He like sugar an I like plum.

Wheel an take you pardner, jump shamador!
Wheel an take you pardner, jump shamador!
Wheel an take you pardner, jump shamador!
For he like sugar an I like plum.

Them Gar'n Town People

Them Gar'n Town people them call me follow-line,
Them Gar'n Town people them call me follow-line,
Them Gar'n Town people them call me follow-line,
Somebody dying here ev'ry day.

A ten pound order him kill me pardner,
A ten pound order him kill me pardner,
A ten pound order him kill me pardner,
For somebody dying here ev'ry day.

Den number nine tunnel I would not work deh,
Den number nine tunnel I would not work deh,
Den number nine tunnel I would not work deh,
For somebody dying here ev'ry day.

Five songs recorded by Walter Jekyll in Jamaica, 1907

Itanami

One morning de captain wake.
Captain wake, he wake de boatman,
Boatman wake, he wake de bowman,
Bowman wake wid de paddle in he han:
All ah wan is a lang an strang . . .
Lang an strang is too much for me,
Lang an strang is Itanami!
   Itanami, Itanami
   Itanami, Itanami oh!

Captain, captain, put me ashore!
Ah don wan to go any more!
Itanami gon frighken me,
Itanami gon drownded me,
Itanami gon wuk me belly,
Itanami gon too much for me!
   Itanami, Itanami
   Itanami, Itanami oh!

Folk-song

MICHAEL McTURK

Query

Da Backra one fo go a hebben?
Da Backra one fo raise like lebben?
Da wa' a-we po Negah do?
Make a-we no fo raise up too?
Da we a Lamb – no see we wool,
No make dem Backra make we fool,
Dem sef a Goat, no see dem hair,
Dem no wan' cut de 'tory fair.
Da wa, make a-we no a see
In all dem Pictah Histarie
A negah-hangel deh wid wing?
A puzzle somet'ing yeh dis t'ing.
Wa' fashin Jonah bin nyam w'ale,
Biout he no 'crape de 'cale?
Da man bin hungry true fo fiss,
A narrah puzzle 'tory dis.
Da wa' make duck an fowl no one,
Fo waak 'pon watah in de pon'?
Wa' makc fowl fingah no get 'kin?
Dem 'tory dis too puzzlin.

Deh 'Pon Um Again

Hi, Jimmis, nagah, matty man, you deh 'pon um again,
W'en man is no can 'peak wid mout', he blige fo cratch wid
  pen.
Da true you bin a Hinglan go pick dem Bacra brains,
A hope you no go go 'train up youse'f an so get sick fo you
  pains.
He 'tan' like you bin a do so, if a so, a wan 'tupid hact.
Cause you nagah lika buck-dag, an dah is a naked fact.
W'en you bin ware lang cote an beebah you bin put yiye-glass
  a you yiye;

But you yiye can' twis' fo hol' um, so a no t'ink you sa 'tupid
  fo try.
But bet you bin ware fingah-tacking, 'peak de wo'd, now tell
  me no true,
An you bin gat 'tick no so umbrella? Hi, Jim, you bin
  somet'ing fo true,
W'en you bin a 'tep so mannis', w'en you wan' 'kin you teet'
  fo laff,
You put you fingah 'crass you mout', so gi'e two fine-fine
  caff,
But ratta like dem ol' ol' hole, ol' fiah-'tick soon catch,
W'en fowl is meet weh wood-anch deh he blige fo loose two
  'cratch;
Like me too Jim, you no can bear um, you blige come back
  again,
Come pick you libbin' a Demeradah wid reglah 'crape a de
  pen.
But w'en you bin deh a Hinglan! – now put you 'pon you
  hoat',
You no bin crabin' fo piece a sal'-fis'? – a bet nagah you bin
  wan' um bad,
Da wa' de fus' t'ing you bin want a Demeradah soon as Mail
  bin pass de Fo't.
'Cause you no 'tan like dem Ba'jan nagah wa libbin' pon
  'cookoo an shad'.
Now Jim leh me gi'e you piece a 'vice, hear good, so 'membah
  an try,
No come wid no lang-lang 'tory, awe no wan' no Hinglis' lie.
Dem ol' Demeradah wan do fo awe, we know dem a'ready by
  haat,
An we no wan' fo l'arn new lesson – a haness no fit awe ca't.
Make you matty w'en dem hear you t'ink dem dreamin in
  dem sleep,
Leh we hab an de same as fus' time, an no come cut you
  Hinglis' too deep.
Da Ba'jan like hebby Hinglis', dem tongue lang like mason
  trowel,
W'en dem ha' fo call wan fowl-hen name, dem ha' fo call um
  fowel,
Wa'k good, no make brigah kill you, no you wan bin a
  Hinglan town.

Me a keep me wan yiye 'pon you, an me sa' reddy fo 'queeze
you down;
If you begin any mannis' 'tory, no so wo'k up youse'f in a row,
You sa' see somebody a come wid dem bo'-'tick, – an dem
call a nagah, Quow.

EDWARD CORDLE

Lizzie and Joe Catch a Thief

Wha ebah Joe an me duz lib we likes to hab um neat,
Ess um eben is uh two rooms um mus be nare de street,
An palisadin rung de frunt wid paint fuh mek um gran,
An in de back uh palin rung uh little piece uh lan.

An little way oukside de tung wha yuh kin raise uh pig,
An raise yuh ducks an fowls an got yuh piece uh lan fuh dig.
Ess yuh wan tea enny marnin yuh kin alwuz sell uh egg,
An wen uh man kin help heself he en got cause fuh beg.

De place dat we is libbin now we keeps uh little stock,
We got two pigs an sum yung squabs an sum hens an uh cock.
We fines it hahd to feed dem fuh stocks teks coppahs well,
But still we got fuh do um, and de pigs nare fit fuh sell.

Chile, two nights runnin we did hear sum body rung de place,
An doh Joe went oukside and luk he en see not uh face.
Nex nite we set up fuh he an um wuz gettin late
Wen Joe luk out, an, gal, he see uh man rite in de gate.

He run an Joe behin he up tuh Miss Cubbin wall,
An tryin fuh jump obah he get a puhty fall,
An Joe cud hahdly hole he – de brute bees wuz suh strong,
An fate he wud did get away ess deh did ressle long.

But me hole on an hollah an all de peetle run,
Gal, ess yuh had bin up deh yuh wud did see sum fun,
Fuh ebry body lick he till he wuz narely dead;
He had wan cut rite cross he nose an wan pun top he hed.

But, chile, de way tings stirrin de peetle bung fuh steal,
So ess yuh eben ketch dem yuh bung fuh hah sum feel;
He beg we not fuh lock he up an he did beg we so
Joe gie he wan lick fuh de las an den we leh he go.

Yuh trete we bad, fuh sense we move yuh en bin up we way,
We talks bouk you an Samyil an Rosie ebry day.
Yuh bettah come.to-morrah, yuh en got uh ting foh do.
So gubbye gal remembah uh gwine luk fuh yuh fuh true.

Lizzie and Joe in Court

Uh nebah cross dese courts agen ess uh live un hundred
    yares,
Yuh nebah gets no jestice, how dese false witnus swares,
An dem dat got fuh try you en eben wut deh pay.
Uh wud back me Josif gence dem in law-wuk enny day.

Joe carry up six peetle fuh artikles uh de peace,
An all he frens exvise he tuh hiah Mistah Reece,
But uh tell he keep yuh munny, yuh kin tauk as good as he,
Wah yuh gwine gie he pockit yuh bettah give tuh me.

De case cum off yestidah, an, gal, yuh shoud bin deh,
Aftah deh hare de witnusses Joe beg tuh have a say,
Yuh shoud bin deh tuh hare he! gal, he wuz sumting gran,
He plea he case moh bettah dan enny lawyah in de lan.

Yuh coud did hare uh pin drop, an Joe wuz gettin hot
Wen uh hare de Magistrit hollah ouk, 'Uh doan want all dah
    rot.
You foolish peetle fancy we got nuttn else tuh do
But listn tuh de rubbish uh ingrunt men like you.'

Susie, uh nebah bin suh rouse in all muh livelong days,
Uh try tuh keep muh tempah dung in ebry kind uh ways,
But uh coudn keep um longah an uh hollah ouk: 'Uh know
Dat ess he wuz uh whiteman yuh woudn tell he so.'

An den he tell de pleceman 'put dah ole umman ouk'
An de foolish bighed niggah tek an pull muh all abouk.
Uh didn mean tuh get up an uh hole on pun de seat,
But he pull muh all de way dung stares an chuck muh in de
    street.

Uh en gwine let um drop so, Joe got tuh use he pen,
An ess um coss muh munny uh kin alwuz fine uh fren.
De guvnah got fuh see muh an hare de unfair ting,
Ess he doan satisfy muh uh will write home tuh de King.

Lizzie Discourses on the Small-pox

Hi, mawning Susie, how yuh is? yuh get de small-pox yet?
Uh know who en gwine hah dem an dah is me, uh bet.
De doctahs kin say whah deh like, um en small-pox at all,
Um en no moh small-pox dan dah ole palin is uh wall.

Deh might leave de peetle in deh house deh only meks dem
    wuss;
And wen deh dead deh duz not eben put back duss to duss
But carries dem bout five mile ouk an drops dem in de sea,
An dah is why nuh fishermun cahn sell nuh fish tuh me.

Uh hare deh sennin all de peetle right down from Districk A:
Um cos de cuntry tummuch, fuh all dem gettin pay.
Whah deh carry dem at all fuh? dahs whah uh wahn fuh
    know;
Not Brustah, not de Gubnah heself cuhn mek me go.

'Deed ess dah Brustah wuz fuh cum to tek Joe out he bed
Uh woud did hah to try an drag de eyes ouk uh he head;
Ess Joe did eben hah dem I is uh ole time nuss,
An foh deh bring he outside deh woud hah fuh kill muh fuss.

Uh know dat deh had better gie de peetle food fuh eat;
Bumby you is gwine see dem like dead rats in de street.
Deh gwine drop dung wid hungry – de men cahn get nuh
    wuk,
Deh en not able not fuh buy uh lump uh salt fuh suck.

Wen we big peetle hungry we kin draw weself in tight
An we kin stan de hungry till wen we gets uh bite,
But little childrun diffrunt, um nuf fuh drive yuh wile
Wen yuh en got not uh biskit fuh gie yuh starvin chile.

Yuh come up nice las Sundy, we had de food fuh wase,
Fuh uh didn feelin too nice an uh did hahdly tase,
Pahaps wen yuh cum up fuh true we wun han not uh bite,
An fate uh woud be too glad, um woud only serve yuh right.

JAMES MARTINEZ

Dis Time No Stan' Like Befo' Time

Sometime I sit an wonder long;
True, true.
Dere's somet'ing sure is goin wrong;
True, true.
De time is sur'ly getting bad —
It's nough to mek a feller mad —
I r'ally now am feeling sad;
True, true.

We never know w'at's gwine to be;
True, true.
De time dat's comin we can't see;
True, true.
If we could see de distant day,
W'en we bin use to draw we pay,
We wouldn't squander it away;
True, true.

Dis time no stan' like befo' time.
True, truc.
We country now is not so fine;
True, true.
De days gone by dat we done spen',
Dere was nough money bout to len'
An dere was good an gen'rous frien'.
True, true.

Time change fo true wid everyt'ing;
True, true.
An dere's some awful change it bring;
True, true.
De motar cars an t'ings we meet,
W'en we go out upon de street,
Is nough to wreck yo narve complete;
True, true.

De children now is lef too free;
True, true.
Dey's nat like how we use to be;
True, true.
Dey walk de street at day an night,
An do such t'ings befo' yo sight,
Wid no regard fo wrong or right;
True, true.

De parants now is much to blame;
True, true.
Dey's nat like dose from w'ich we came;
True, true.
Dey do nat tek de proper care,
To teach de young respec' an fear,
Fo people who's advance in 'ear;
True, true.

Oh, everyt'ing is goin wrong;
True, true.
De debil sure is growin strong;
True, true.
For all aroun us we can see,
De many snares he's have fo we,
Dis wo'ld is wicked as can be;
True, true.

But dis here win' is gettin chill;
I bin a sittin here so still.
De kittle's b'ilin now I guess,
I better tek a sup an res' —
To r'ally keep de system up,
Dere's not'in like a hearty sup.

My Little Lize

Who is de prutties' gal you say?
Oh, hush up man an go away.
Yo don't know w'at yo talkin bout;
Yo ought to go an fin' dat out.
De prutties' gal dat one can meet
Dat ever walk along de street;
I guess yo never seen my Lize;
If yo had seen her – bless yo eyes,
Yo would be sure to 'gree wid me,
Dat she's de sweetes' gal dat be.
Why man! where was yo all dis time,
Dat yo don't see dis gal of mine?
Her skin is black an smoode as silk;
Her teet' is jus' as white as milk;
Her hair is of dem fluffy kin',
Wid curls a-hangin, black an shine.
Her shape is such dat can't be beat;
So graceful, slender an so neat.
W'ene'er she turn her eyes on you,
Dey seem to strike yo t'rough an t'rough,
Dere's not a sweeter lookin face;
An lips dat mek yo feel to tas'e.
Her hands is small an so's her feet,
Wid such a pair of enkles neat!
W'en she goes out to tek a walk
She sets de people all to talk.
De gals dey envy her wid fear,
Dey feel so cheap w'en she is near.
De boys dey lif' dere hats an try
To win a smile as she pass by.
But w'at's de use o talkin' so;
An try such beauty here to show!
Yo better see wid yo own eyes
Dis sweet an lovely little Lize;
For if I try de evening t'rough,
I couldn't quite explain to you.

MARCUS GARVEY

Keep Cool

Suns have set and suns will rise
Upon many gloomy lives;
Those who sit around and say:
'Nothing good comes down our way.'
Some say: 'What's the use to try,
Life is awful hard and dry.'
If they'd bring such news to you,
This is what you ought to do:
   Let no trouble worry you;
   Keep cool, keep cool!
   Don't get hot like some folk do,
   Keep cool, keep cool!
   What's the use of prancing high
   While the world goes smiling by.
   You can win if you would try,
   Keep cool, keep cool.

Throw your troubles far away,
Smile a little every day,
And the sun will start to shine,
Making life so true and fine.
Do not let a little care
Fill your life with grief and fear:
Just be calm, be brave and true,
Keep your head and you'll get through.
   Let no trouble worry you;
   Keep cool, keep cool!
   Just be brave and ever true;
   Keep cool, keep cool!
   If they'd put you in a flame,
   Though you should not bear the blame,
   Do not start to raising Cain,
   Keep cool, keep cool.

Centenary's Day

(from UNIA Convention Hymns, 1934)

A hundred years have passed and gone,
  And we are toiling still abroad;
But we are not dismayed, forlorn,
  Nor hopeless of redeeming God.

Our fathers bore the stinging lash
  Of centuries of slavery's crime;
But we are here without abash,
  For we shall win in God's good time.

We wish no evil, harm or hurt,
  To those who kept us down so long;
We join with them in ways alert,
  To guard good freedom's happy song.

To Afric's shore we're bound again,
  In freedom's glory won at large;
In thoughts we claim a just bargain,
  To sail in liberty's fair barge.

The world is conscious now of wrongs
  To us the sufferers had done;
But now to each, who claims, belongs
  The truth – the light of God's own Son.

We wish to live in peace alone,
  And bless all men for goodness' sake:
We praise the Lord on Glory's throne;
  To Him our Altars we do make.

SLIM AND SAM

Sandy Gully

A went to Sandy Gully fe go get a bite
Dem set dung mi name an a feel alright
De very day a start to work de man dem a strike
Waai!

Dem say de pay we a get is good
An if yu complain dem say wi rude
But look pon de price we a pay fi food
Waai!

If a had a gun a woulda heng myself
If a coulda swim a woulda shoot myself
If a had a rope a woulda drown myself
Waai!

Mus-Mus Mussolini yu know yu soft
Anyting befall yu, Hitler is de cause
Dat's de reason why we goin bus yu heart
Waai!

Hitler mek mi show yu a ting or two
Yu goin lose dis war, don't care what yu do
An when yu hear de end yu goin pupuputoo
Waai!

Johnny Tek Away Mi Wife

After Johnny wear mi clothes,
After Johnny eat mi food,
After Johnny sleep in mi bed,
Johnny tun roun an tek mi wife.
   Lard, what a misery!
   Wherever I see Johnny,
   People, people goin to sorry to see
   De grave fe Johnny an de gallows fe me.

ANONYMOUS

Sly Mongoose

I
Sly mongoose
Dog know you ways
Sly mongoose
Dog know you ways
Mongoose went to de master's kitchen
Pick up one of de fattest chicken
Put it in de wais'-coat pocket
Sly mongoose

II
Sly mongoose
Dog know you name
Sly mongoose
Ma ma, dog know you name
You dress like an old crusader
You talk like ah soap-box preacher
Don't tell me, you not me brother
Sly mongoose

Ah say sly mongoose
Ma ma, dog know you name
Ah say sly mongoose
Ma ma, dog know you name
You dress like a cunning lawyer
You talk like a Young Pretender
Don't tell me you know me mother
Sly mongoose

(Additional verses by Knolly La Fortune)

Dis Long Time, Gal

Dis long time, gal, me never see you,
Come mek me hol your han.
Dis long time, gal, me never see you,
Come mek me hol your han.
   Peel-head John Crow siddung pon tree-top
   Pick off de blossom;
   Mek me hol your han, gal,
   Mek me hol your han.

Dis long time, gal, me never see you,
Come mek we walk an talk.
Dis long time, gal, me never see you,
Come mek we walk an talk.
   Peel-head John Crow *etc.*

Dis long time, gal, me never see you,
Come mek we wheel an turn.
Dis long time, gal, me never see you,
Come mek we wheel an turn.
   Peel-head John Crow *etc.*

Mek we wheel an turn till we tumble dung,
Mek me hol your han, gal.
Mek we wheel an turn till we tumble dung,
Mek me hol your han, gal.
   Peel-head John Crow *etc.*

Linstead Market

Carry me ackee go a Linstead market:
Not a quatty wut sell.
Carry me ackee go a Linstead market:
Not a quatty wut sell.
   Lard, wat a night, not a bite,
   Wat a Satiday night.
   Lard, wat a night, not a bite,
   Wat a Satiday night.

Everybody come feel up, feel up:
Not a quatty wut sell.
Everybody come feel up, squeeze up:
Not a quatty wut sell.
   Lard, wat a night *etc.*

Mek me call i' louder: ackee! ackee!
Red an pretty dem 'tan!
Lady, buy yu Sunday marnin brukfas',
Rice an ackee nyam gran'.
   Lard, wat a night *etc.*

All de pickney dem a linga, linga,
Fe weh dem mumma no bring.
All de pickney dem a linga, linga,
Fe weh dem mumma no bring.
   Lard, wat a night *etc.*

Dog Shark

Daddy eat dog shark, malingay,
Daddy eat dog shark.
Tek dem one by one, malingay,
Tek dem one by one.

Pickney couldn't walk, malingay,
Pickney couldn't walk.
Tek dem two by two, malingay,
Tek dem two by two.

Rover couldn't bark, malingay,
Rover couldn't bark.
Tek dem t'ree by t'ree, malingay,
Tek dem t'ree by t'ree.

Sissy eye turn dark, malingay,
Sissy eye turn dark.
Tek dem four by four, malingay,
Tek dem four by four.

Mooma couldn't work, malingay,
Mooma couldn't work.
Tek dem five by five, malingay,
Tek dem five by five.

Daddy eat dog shark, malingay,
Daddy eat dog shark.
Tek dem one by one, malingay,
Tek dem one by one.

Sammy Dead Oh

Sammy plant piece a corn dung a gully, mm
An it bear till it kill poor Sammy, mm
Sammy dead, Sammy dead, Sammy dead oh, mm
Sammy dead, Sammy dead, Sammy dead oh, mm

A no tief Sammy tief mek dem kill him, mm
A no lie Sammy lie mek him dead oh, mm
But a grudgeful dem grudgeful kill Sammy, mm
But a grudgeful dem grudgeful kill Sammy, mm

Neighbour cyaan bear to see neighbour flourish, mm
Neighbour cyaan bear to see neighbour flourish, mm
Sammy dead, Sammy dead, Sammy dead oh, mm
Sammy dead, Sammy dead, Sammy dead oh, mm

Sammy gone dung a hell fe shoot blackbud, mm
A no lie Sammy lie mek him go deh, mm
But a grudgeful dem grudgeful kill Sammy, mm
Sammy dead, Sammy dead, Sammy dead oh, mm

Glory Dead

Glory dead when white man come,
    Glory dead, glory dead.
Glory dead when Buckra come,
    Glory dead, glory dead.

Trouble Oh

Climbin up de mountain,
Creepin on me knee,
Lookin for me Jesus
To tell me troubles to.
   For it is trouble oh, trouble oh,
   De whole world in trouble oh,
   Trouble oh, trouble oh,
   De whole world in trouble oh.

Wake up in de marnin,
Find it hard to go,
Wait upon me Jesus
To tell me troubles to.
   For it is *etc.*

Come home late de odder night,
Sick an tired o life,
Wait upon me Jesus
To tell me troubles to.
   For it is *etc.*

Now me corn ain flower,
All me yam ain grow,
Wait upon me Jesus
To tell me troubles to.
   For it is *etc.*

Seven folk-songs

RASTAFARIAN CHANT

Zion Me Wan Go Home

Zion, me wan go home,
Zion, me wan go home,
Oh, oh,
Zion, me wan go home.

Africa, me wan fe go,
Africa, me wan fe go,
Oh, oh,
Africa, me wan fe go.

Take me back to Et'iopia lan,
Take me back to Et'iopia lan,
Oh, oh,
Take me back to Et'iopia lan.

Et'iopia lan me fader's home,
Et'iopia lan me fader's home,
Oh, oh,
Et'iopia lan me fader's home.

Zion, me wan go home,
Zion, me wan go home,
Oh, oh,
Zion me wan go home.

LOUISE BENNETT

Back to Africa

Back to Africa, Miss Mattie?
You no know wha you dah seh?
You haf fe come from somewhe fus
Before you go back deh!

Me know say dat you great great great
Granma was African,
But Mattie, doan you great great great
Granpa was Englishman?

Den you great granmader fader
By you fader side was Jew?
An you granpa by you mader side
Was Frenchie parlez-vous?

But de balance a you family,
You whole generation,
Oonoo all barn dung a Bun Grung –
Oonoo all is Jamaican!

Den is weh you gwine, Miss Mattie?
Oh, you view de countenance,
An between you an de Africans
Is great resemblance!

Ascorden to dat, all dem blue-yeye
White American
Who-fa great granpa was Englishman
Mus go back a Englan!

What a debil of a bump-an-bore,
Rig-jig an palam-pam
Ef de whole worl start fe go back
Whe dem great granpa come from!

Ef a hard time you dah run from
Tek you chance! But Mattie, do
Sure a whe you come from so you got
Somewhe fe come back to!

Go a foreign, seek you fortune,
But no tell nobody say
You dah go fe seek you homelan,
For a right deh so you deh!

Colonization in Reverse

Wat a joyful news, Miss Mattie,
I feel like me heart gwine burs
Jamaica people colonizin
Englan in reverse.

By de hundred, by de tousan
From country and from town,
By de ship-load, by de plane-load
Jamaica is Englan boun.

Dem a pour out a Jamaica,
Everybody future plan
Is fe get a big-time job
An settle in de mother lan.

What a islan! What a people!
Man an woman, old an young
Jus a pack dem bag an baggage
An tun history upside dung!

Some people doan like travel,
But fe show dem loyalty
Dem all a open up cheap-fare-
To-Englan agency.

An week by week dem shippin off
Dem countryman like fire,
Fe immigrate an populate
De seat a de Empire.

Oonoo see how life is funny,
Oonoo see de tunabout?
Jamaica live fe box bread
Out a English people mout'.

For wen dem ketch a Englan,
An start play dem different role,
Some will settle down to work
An some will settle fe de dole.

Jane say de dole is not too bad
Because dey payin she
Two pounds a week fe seek a job
Dat suit her dignity.

Me say Jane will never fine work
At de rate how she dah look,
For all day she stay pon Aunt Fan couch
An read love-story book.

Wat a devilment a Englan!
Dem face war an brave de worse,
But me wonderin how dem gwine stan
Colonizin in reverse.

Dutty Tough

Sun a shine but tings noh bright;
Doah pot a bwile, bickle noh nuff;
River flood but wata scarce, yah;
Rain a fall but dutty tough!

Tings so bad, dat now-a-days wen
Yuh ask smaddy how dem do,
Dem fraid yuh tek it tell dem back
So dem noh answer yuh!

Noh care omuch we dah work fa
Hard-time still eena we shu't,
We dah fight, Hard-Time a beat we,
Dem might raise we wages, but

One poun gahn ahn pon we pay, an
We noh feel noh merriment,
For ten poun gahn ahn pon we food
An ten poun pon we rent!

Salfish gahn up! mackerel gahn up!
Pork an beef gahn up same way,
An wen rice an butter ready,
Dem jus go pon holiday!

Claat, boot, pin an needle gahn up,
Ice, bread, taxes, wata-rate!
Kersene ile, gasolene, gahn up
An de poun devaluate!

De price a bread gahn up so high
Dat we haf fe agree,
Fe cut we yiye pon bread an all
Tun dumplin refugee!

An all dem marga smaddy weh
Dah gwan like fat is sin,
All dem deh weh dah fahs wid me,
Ah lef dem to dumplin!

Sun a shine an pot a bwile, but
Tings noh bright, bickle noh nuff!
Rain a fall, river dah flood, but
Wata scarce an dutty tough!

Excitement

Fling weh de wash pan, drop de cloes!
Put ahn yuh blue-boot, Fan!
Bans a excitement outa street!
Come march wid soja man!

Pluck up yuh courage, ready up
Yuh weapon fe defen!
No fight nah bruck yet, but yuh cyaan
Tell how de day wi en!

For doah dem mout nah gwan bad,
Doah dem jussa march an sing,
Dem got a banner write up wid
Nuff dangerous sinting!

See it yah now! 'We unemploy',
'Away wid –!' Whai, me dead!
Koo pon de name dem write dung broad!
We boun fe have blood-shed!

Susie, yuh grab de fryin-pan!
Jane, tek dis junk-a-brick!
May, pahn de scrubbin-board! Me got
A coocoomacca stick!

Jane, see yuh lickle bwoy all outa
Breat a run come deh!
Pickney, wha happen? Talk plain mek
We hear wha yuh dah seh.

Lard, listen nuh, im seh dat big crowd
Gadder roun one man
What deh dung-tung dah gwan wid gun
Like real Wile-Wes cow-han!

Him seh de man bahl 'Keep back!'
Him han dem mek so, 'zoom!'
Dive fe him pocket, swips two gun
An shoot de asphalt 'boom!'

What a braveness, eeh Miss Mattie!
What a greatness, eeh Mas Joe!
Dem shoulda mek a big glass case
An put dat man pon show!

Is what Jamaica people wase time
Go a movies fa
When dem got nuff free excitement
Outa street side yah?

Independance

Independance wid a vengeance!
Independance raisin Cain!
Jamaica start grow beard, ah hope
We chin can stan de strain!

When daag marga him head big, an
When puss hungry him nose clean;
But every puss an daag no know
What Independance mean.

Mattie seh it mean we facety,
Stan up pon we dignity,
An we doan allow nobody
Fe tek liberty wid we.

Independance is we nature
Born an bred in all we do,
An she glad fe see dat Government
Tun independant too.

She hope dem caution worl-map
Fe stop draw Jamaica small,
For de lickle speck cyaan show
We independantness at all!

Moresomever we must tell map dat
We doan like we position –
Please kindly tek we out a sea
An draw we in de ocean.

What a crosses! Independance
Woulda never have a chance
Wid so much boogooyagga
Dah expose dem ignorance.

Daag wag im tail fe suit im size
An match im stamina –
Jamaica people need a
Independance formula!

No easy-come-by freeness tings,
Nuff labour, some privation,
Not much of dis an less of dat
An plenty studiration.

Independance wid a vengeance!
Wonder how we gwine to cope?
Jamaica start smoke pipe, ah hope
We got nuff jackass rope!

Independence Twenty-One

Independence tun Big-Smady!
Independence proud cyaan done!
Him a halla tell de worl seh
'Me ketch up a Twenty-one!

'Is twenty-one 'ears since me barn
Tun Caribbean nation!'
Independence feel so boasify
Him order Celebration!

From January to December!
From Negril to Morant Bay!
Fe de whole 'ear Independence
Got a birtday every day!

Frien an fambily an stranger,
So dem ketch de Birtday fever,
Join de party, show dem motion,
Even skip across de ocean!

For dis yah Independence,
A no pyah-pyah Independence,
Is de one-time-in-a-lifetime
Independence Twenty-one!

Barn and grow outa Jamaica-people
Struggle pon de lan,
Outa kin-teet and yiye-water,
Barn an grow tun twenty-one.

But dat a jus de cotta;
De load lef fe come me frien!
When drum done beat, yanga done dance.
Every sweet-dream haf fe en'.

So cow a grow him yeye dah open,
Look an learn from wat yuh se'.
If yuh call Tiger Massa, him nyam yuh.
Wat sweet a mout can hot belly.

Mek sure say look-so, tan-so,
Chat an laugh can tun cuss-cuss.

Man spit white but blood deh a him t'roat,
So careful who yuh trus'.

No mek no duppy fool yuh.
One finger cyaan ketch flea.
If yuh no go a man fire-side, yuh no know
Omuch fire-stick bwile him tea.

Tek wat yuh can get so get wat yuh want,
No play buggy-widouten-top!
Bignadoa, an cocohead no deh a barrel.
De higher de horse de hotta de drop.

Sometime moonshine, sometime dark.
When yuh tink yuh right, sometime yuh wrong,
But, no pain, no Balm, no macca, no Crown;
Heaby hamper-load mek jackass back strong.

Dark-night got peeny-wally!
Doah de dumplin tun fla-fla,
Bright sun shine tru lickle key-hole!
Marga cow is bull muma!

Independence tun Big-smady!
Independence proud fe true!
Walk good yah Independence,
An good-duppy walk wid yuh.

BRUCE ST JOHN

Bajan Litany

(*Fast*)	
Follow pattern kill Cadogan	Yes, Lord
America got black power?	O Lord
We got black power	Yes, Lord
Wuh sweeten goat mout bun 'e tail	O Lord
Bermuda got tourism?	Yes, Lord
We got too	O Lord
De higher monkey go, de more 'e show 'e tail	Yes, Lord
Jamaica got industry?	O Lord
We got industry	Yes, Lord
Jamaica got bauxite?	(*Silence*)
(*Louder*) Jamaica got bauxite?	Yes, Lord
Choke 'e collar, hang 'e tie, trip 'e up	
trousers, t'row 'e down boots	O Lord
Trinidad got army?	(*Silence*)
(*Louder*) Trinidad got army?	O Lord
We got too	Yes, Lord
Stop friggin' spiders fuh twice de increase	O Lord
England got family planning?	Yes, Lord
We got too	O Lord
Wuh in ketch yuh en pass yuh	Yes, Lord
Follow pattern kill Cadogan	O Lord
Lord, Lord	Yes, Lord
Lookah we tho' nuh	O Lord
We heading fuh trouble!	Yes, Lord!
O Lord	O Lord!

Subtlety

'Cordin to de present perdicament,
You policy li'l too plain.
Too much nail, too straight, too much
Hammerin – need to be
Quiet an greasy like a screw!

Twis'in an turnin like a
Forward, cuttin in an
Scorin like a winger, swerve
In de air an break pun de
Turf! Jook yuh tap-root
Down to de knuck
Suck in whuhever drop so dat
When dem stem yuh fuh
Dislodge yuh, yuh turn de key
In de lock an yuh
Shove home de bolt an is
Trouble yuh kin
Gi' dem, yuh get muh?

Wisdom

Yuh t'ink we foolish?
We gine ban South Africa an invite the U.S.A.,
We gine kill apartheid an lick up black power;
Ashe cyaan play nor Sobers needuh.
You t'ink we foolish?

Springbok keep yuh wine we gine tek Yankee aid
Pay fuh get um
Buy dem tings
Keep Sam producin
Keep 'e people wukkin
An le' 'e help 'eself
Yuh t'ink we foolish, t'ink we foolish?

Lef out Rhodesian an bring in Canadian
Sell dem de beaches we kin tek to de hills
T'ink we foolish?

Industry fuh so
Hotel like peas
Doan min' de squeeze when dey tek to de breeze
We kin cut an contrive,
T'ink we is fools nuh.
Evah fool got 'e sense,
T'ink we foolish?

'LORD KITCHENER'

Miss Tourist

A tourist dame,
I met her the night she came,
She curiously
Asking about my country,
She said, 'I heard about bacchanal
And the Trinidad carnival,
So I come to jump in the fun
And I want you tell me how it is done.'
 I say, 'Do, do come in town Jou'vert morning,
 Find youself in a band,
 Watch the way how the natives moving,
 Hug up tight with ah man,
 Sing along with the tunes they playing,
 And now and again you shouting
 "Play mas! Carnival!"
 Miss tourist, that is bacchanal.'

The following day
We went to Maracas bay.
Every step we walk
She start with this Jou'vert talk.
She said, 'Kitch, from what I've been told,
Carnival is out of this world.
Just the thought is worrying my brain:
Well, let me hear that lesson again!'
 I say, 'Do, do, *etc.*

Jou'vert morn
You'll swear that is here she born!
We holding hand,
Jumping in a Jou'vert band.
When the rhythm hot up the pace,
She say, 'Play mas!' shaking she waist,
'Kitch, will you phone Hotel Normandie
And tell them don't leave no breakfast for me.'
 I say, 'Do, do, *etc.*

She turn and say,
'Kitch, I now feel to break away!'
She say, 'Come on, man!'
And drag me in front the band!
Mama, when we reach Independence Square,
She kick and she raise she dress in the air,
Bawling, 'Becchenel! Becchenel!
I am the Queen of the Kenevel!'

'THE MIGHTY SPARROW'

The Yankees Back

Well, the day of slavery back again!
Ah hope it ain't reach in Port of Spain.
Since the Yankees come back over here
They buy out the whole of Pointe-a-Pierre.
Money start to pass, people start to bawl,
Pointe-a-Pierre sell, the workmen and all.
   Fifty cents a head for Grenadians,
   A dollar a head for Trinidadians;
   Tobagonians free, whether big or small;
   But they say, they ain't want Barbadians at all.

Well, it look as if they going mad
To sell the Refinery in Trinidad.
Ah hear they tackling the Pitch Lake,
But ah keeping cool for Heaven's sake.
Next time they will buy Ste Madeleine Cane –
Then it's easy to capture Port of Spain.
But when they buy Trinidad and you think they stop,
They taking Tobago for lagniappe.
   Fifty cents a head *etc.*

Ah watching me girl friend, Lillian;
They have a funny intention
Bunching with Olga and Doris
Who intend to start their foolishness.
But if they think the Yankees making joke,
This time, ain't no fun: it's strictly work!
Not because they come back in barrage,
Remember, the Sparrow still in charge.
   Fifty cents a head *etc.*

Whenever this place have Yankees
Women does make we suffer like peas,
But now, it's entirely different,
The Yankees don't want entertainment.

The way they pack up in Pointe-a-Pierre,
They entertaining one another down there.
To any woman who want Yankee money,
Turn Grenadian and work like a donkey!
   Fifty cents a head *etc.*

Get to Hell outa Here

I am going to bring back Solomon
Who don't like it, complain to the Commission
None of them going to tell me how to run my country
I defy any one of you to dictate for me
I am no dictator, but when I pass an order
Mr Speaker, this matter must go no further
I have nothing more to say
And it must be done my way
Come on, come on, come on, meeting done for the day
This land is mine, I am the boss
What I say goes and who vex loss
   I say that Solomon will be Minister of External Affair
   If you ain't like it, get to hell outa here

I am going to do what I feel to do
And I couldn't care less who vex or who get blue
And if you want to test how ah strong in an election
Leh we bet some money, ah giving odds ten to one
I control all the money that pass through this country
And they envy me for my African Safari
I am politically strong, I am the weight of town
Don't argue with me, you can't beat me in John John
Who's not with me is my enemy
And dust will be their destiny
   If I say that Solomon will be Minister of External Affair
   And you ain't like it, get to hell outa here.

Who the hell is you to jump and quarrel?
Look, P.N.M. is mine, lock, stock and barrel
Who give you the privilege to object?
Pay you' taxes, shut up and have respect
I'm a tower of strength, yes

I'm powerful but modest . . . unless
I'm forced to be blunt and ruthless
So shut up and don't squawk
This ain't no skylark
When I talk, no damn dog bark
My word is law so watch you' case
If you slip you slide, this is my place
    And I say that Solomon will be Minister of External Affair
    And if you ain't like it, get to hell outa here.

Brain Drain

Just because some teachers go away
To improve their status and their pay,
Many people calling this thing Brain Drain,
But I say they should be shame.
They ain't see Horace James and Errol John
Teaching drums to foreign sons,
They would never see our best footballer
In the States as professionals.
   Police and soldiers went to Expo
   And only one true calypsonian go;
   And when foreign artistes come
   They does get lump sum,
   While calypsonians must sing for rum;
   And when steelbandsmen teach outsiders
   To tune a pan for kisses and favours –
   All that is what I call Brain Drain.

So many good technicians away,
So many doctors and engineers don't stay,
But on teachers and nurses they put a stain,
And when *they* leave, people bawl 'Brain Drain!'
Look, C. L. R. James, that great writer,
He should be at U.W.I. teaching literature.
Cricketers like Legall and Ramdeen
Still teaching the English to bat and spin.
   Foreign artistes coming here and getting jobs,
   And Andrew Beddoe can't make some bobs!
   Why not put in every school a steelbandsman
   To train children to beat pan?
   Our children don't know what's B-flat on pan,
   While the U.S. Army and all have steelband!
   That is what I call Brain Drain.

Men like Peter Farquhar and Sukie
Should be given jobs in the Ministry.

We wasting brain in this our nation –
Forget party affiliation! –
And we does use we Drain to make we mas:
Tourist come click-click in photograph –
All we mas pictures in America
And Saldenah getting cah-cah-dah!
   Our culture fruits are draining away,
    And we ain't doing nothing to make them stay!
    Tobago goat race, crab race, bongo, limbo,
    And stickfighting draining out slow.
    O yes, we are living on yankee sad songs like bugs,
    While we parang and folk song going to dogs.
    That is what I call Brain Drain!

MARC MATTHEWS

Guyana Not Ghana

Buxton, Fyrish, Cove-an-John, Bush Lot, Mahaica,
no, ah said, Guyana, not Ghana.

Pompeii, Tanta doux, Bhagwandeen car for hire
Sai John, Saturdee night, sweet shop, gas light,
shinin on shame-face in de trench water.
No, ah said, Guyana, not Ghana.

Black puddin, corn pone, swank, cuss-cuss an sugar
jinghi seeds, back-dam mettagee,

buxton spice, no mango sweeter
when you eat passion fruit don' drink wine nor water
is in Buxton, ah say, de first girl ah love,
five years old; she was from Africa

Pass Plaisance? ah ask, no, she say, further
Georgetown was far

she say pass dat
days an nights she spen' on de water
Africa to de Brazilian border
ah believe her

Pardon, said de English school teacher
I was dreaming of las' lick, jamoon, rum and coconut water

to John Bull potagee daughter
ah said: Guyana could a' been Africa
but for Brazil and a heap o' water.
No, ah said, Guyana, not Ghana.

DELANO ABDUL MALIK DE COTEAU

Oui Papa

He could Trimble
ah mountain
pouning drum
rap like Moses
rap like John
ah say
Mih Daddy was strong
  so strong
  Lord all mighty.

He coulda level
de ground
wid ah sweeping gaze
sa-cri-fice
ah wuk fuh days
  an days
  L-O-O-R-D
Mih Daddy was good
  real good
  ah tell yuh

He coulda dodge
dem Poleece
tunning beast
  blow dong
  trample
  slay an shout
in de Butler riots
ah talking bout
M-A-N
Mih Daddy get mad
  real mad
  Yuh hear mih

Den he open dese eyes
an make mih wise yes

he say SON
is lil people sweat
make up big pappy gain
is poor people always
in de rain
U'hmmmm
Mih Daddy was poor
    still poor
        poor fella.

Motto Vision 1971

I born
from
a force
ripe
small
Island
an ah bitter
now
like a paw-paw
seed
SPIT ME OUT
buh Grenada soil
plant dey
on mih mind too
an miles ah sea
rough up time
in me
When mih mind
was green and fresh
as sea weed,
come an go
to an fro
make mih
like ah loose buoy
in St George's land
-lock harbour
now all dem boys

drift far too
from Grand'anse
sexy – smell
an dah dazzling strip
of sun on sea
blazing
on black backs
rowing till sunset,
salt crystals fine now
like specks of diamonds
in mih mind.
— WHO SAY DE FLYING FISH —
woman voice singing out
an de lambie shell
TOOTING from de wharf
big steamers blowing
doing de Town,
an Marryshow
was de stern
face voice
rich in mih ears
de day in school
he say
an we voices echo
THE WEST INDIES
MUST BE
WEST INDIAN!
an ah take in
Marryshow voice
like de first time
ah hear de sound
of de waves
breaking on land,
THE WEST INDIES
MUST BE WEST INDIAN!
An Marryshow
Motto-Vision
row boat
did run aground
in ah Federal
Funeral,

An de buoy
just drift bout
sick to hear
— SEND DEM BACK —
black like me,
vomit sounds an bad
'LICKS in de POLICE VAN'
for bad english
— SEND DEM BACK —
— SEND DEM BACK —
BLACK
like me
to land
BLACK LIKE ME
IN THAT LAND
OF HOPE AND
G-L-O-O-O-R-Y
an de flying fish
woman cry out loud
and de lambie shell
Toot out loud
and sad
for all dem people going
on dem big steamers
blowing
dong
St George's Town

An ah drink
rum
like sea water
ah nearly drown
in dey Independence
Blood c-l-a-a-t
flags
up politics
up prices
leh we see fuh weself
up to de
up side
dong
shit house

Parliament
plan
left over
HOLDS
fuh rotten fish smell
in ah Carifta
Basket
– poor effort
fuh de poor –
marketing off fuh
deyself an de UP CLASS
cutting dong an
bleeding WE
eversince molasses
was black blood
an sugar was
bitter
bitter vomit
an sweet sailing
fuh dem tourist
Havens
spreading out
more an more
by West Indian
Islands now.

An I know
Toussaint dead
in France
an Garvey dead
in England
an Fanon dead
in America
an I cry
BLACK POWER
fuh we
an all dem
restless souls
to rest in peace
in dey home
    lands
an wid force

dey take me
handcuff
cross de sea
to Nelson Island
an from dah
small
force ripe
Island
I taste
de sourness
of despair
an I hear de waves
an echoes of voices
saying
THE WEST INDIES
MUST BE WEST INDIAN!
an I spit
at de feet
of dem West Indian heads
who band deyself
in Sodomy
to ban
an defeat
dis vision
of seeing ALL
as Black an
one force
United
for — LIFE —
an I feel
de power
of de sea
in de hour
we bathe
an sun weself
on EXILE Island,
wid machine guns
covering we
black backs
hunched wid tension
locked back in

before sunset,
salt crystals fine now
like gelignite
in mih mind.
An I hear Powell
talking
SEND DEM BACK
in de land
of HOPE AND
G-L-O-O-O-R-Y!
an I know
Time rough
Time ripe
so come back home then
Come back home
THE WEST INDIES
WILL BE WEST INDIAN
NOW
Fuh dis MOTTO VISION
speed boat
load up wid
— ALL POWER TO THE
PEOPLE —
an it ruffling up
ideas,
Hope dazzling
mih eyes
like a new day
by de sea
an hearing waves
an echoes
of West Indian
Voices
returning.

PAUL KEENS-DOUGLAS

Tell Me Again

Tell me again
bout de big island
an de small island,
bout de rich island
an de poor island,
how all ah we is one,
an how Cari – com
an Cari – gone,
tell me again.

Tell me again
how I love you
an you love me,
an how blood ticker dan water,
an how we is brudder
an we is sister,
an yu won't cut me t'roat
cause we come on de same boat,
tell me again.

Tell me again
how oil don't spoil,
how we have plenty dollars
but no sense,
an how money is no problem
but de problem is no money,
tell me again.

Tell me again
bout psychology an biology,
bout modern technology,
how he goin by plane
an she goin by boat
an we goin by guess,
tell me again.

Tell me again
how weed don't kill
so yu could smoke it still,
an how it good for yu eye-sight,
an is ah religious ting,
an yu is ah real rahtid rasta,
tell me again.

Tell me again
how she tell you
dat he tell she
dat dey tell dem
dat you tell me,
tell me again.

Tell me again
bout de sweet Caribbean,
bout palm tree an easy life,
bout Greenidge meantime
an Trinidad time,
an how is ah waste ah time,
tell me again.

Tell me again
bout your poetry
an my poetry,
an how I stupid
an you smart,
an how we is Douen,
an we 'fraid de light,
an how dialect cool
but not for school,
tell me again.

Tell me again
how we have plenty pitch,
an we fix Walter Raleigh boat,
but we can't fix de road,
how we invent steelband
an we love carnival,
an how ah should do like Starsky
an hush,
tell me again.

Tell me again
yu don't understan
when ah say,
'God gave me toots
an He tooks dem backs
dat's why
when I speaks
my spats flews',
tell me again.

Tell me again
how de Redhouse red
an de 'Doc' well read
an we goin red
an better red dan dead,
tell me again.

Tell me again
how everybody
mus come home;
tell me again
loud an clear;
tell me again
let me cuff yu in yu damn mout'!

Wukhand

Sah gimme ah wuk nah.
Ah lookin ole but ah strong.
Never mind ah skinny sah,
Ah could wuk like ah beas.
Ask anybody, ask dem sah:
Clean yard, shine car, cut grass,
Ah tekkin anyting sah.
Yu see dis hand sah, it like stone
Never mind it lookin marga.
Dis hand could pelt cutlass
Like Sampson pelt de ass jaw,
Dis hand clear bush from Toco to Town,
When tree see me dey does bawl;

If dey could ah run, is ah straight case,
Cause I is de man with de Lightnin in me hand.
Me blade does flash in de sun
Like fish gainst river stone,
An when ah finish, is me one standin
An all bush lay down, quiet quiet.
Yes sah, dis hand is a wukkin hand.
Yu lookin at me sah,
With me pants foot roll up,
An me mareno lookin holy, holy,
Never mind dat sah; look sah, look me hand
Tough like mangrove root,
Hard like iron cable.
Dis is ah hand sah, ah real hand, ah wukkin hand,
Ah hand with ah past, ah present an ah future.
Dis hand chuck banana, sah,
Cut dem, draw dem, an stack dem,
Under sun, under moon, an in de dark,
An when de back cry out, an foot say stop,
Dis hand still goin like ah champ,
Ah stroke to de left, an ah stroke to de right.

Dat was me, de man with de iron hand.
Dont judge me by me size sah,
Ah lookin' small, ah know dat,
But me hand sah, watch it.
Dis hand have character,
Dis hand throw net like was feather,
An when dis hand pull back sah,
Was fish in any weather.
Ah catch dem, cut dem, clean dem
Ah couldn't afford to eat dem.
Yes sah, dis is ah hand sah.
When dis hand was ah boy sah,
It throw stone, pelt rock,
Wash in river, an cook on fire.
It get cut, bruise, bounce, burn, an break.
Dis hand sah, grow up strong.
It help police pull hose
When man house start burnin down,
It tired pullin car out ah ditch,

It break fight under plenty strain,
But is ah wukkin hand sah.
An dis hand sah, have touch,
Crack ah egg, pick ah flower,
Caress ah woman, ahhhh, sah
As gentle as de mornin sun
Growin fierce, but not destroyin
Beautiful sah, beautiful.
An dis hand have speed sah,
Yes speed.
See dis hand sah, pull ace sah,
From any part ah de pack,
An so it pullin ace, is so it wukkin hard.
But dis hand is ah honest hand sah.
Dis hand pick up two hundred dolla
Lying dey in open street,
An dis hand send it straight to de station.
Yes sah, dis hand make headline,
De paper call me de 'honest hand'.
Wha yu say sah?
Yu eh have no wuk?
Yu makin joke sah.
How yu mean yu eh have wuk?
Ah rich lookin fella like yu,
Stand up in front yu big house,
An dress up as if is weddin yu goin to.
Ah know is joke yu jokin sah,
But dis hand could take ah joke.
What sah? dis is not yu house?
Yu just stan up here waitin on taxi?
But look me crosses with dis niggerman,
Ah stan up here only wastin me time with he,
Ah poor man like me, with arthritis,
Me dam hand near fallin off,
An he can't even sponsor ah cup ah coffee.
Only posing up in front de people place.
Ah have a good mind to arrest yu.
Look man, move out ah me sight yu hear?
Before ah leggo de hand on yu.
Well, yes.

F. 'TOOTS' HIBBERT

Never Get Weary

I was down in the valley for a very long time
But I never get weary yet
I was down in the valley for a very long time
But I never get weary yet
I was born and raised in a little old shack
With my poor family
With my poor family
   I was born before
   Christopher Columbus
   And I was born before
   The Arawak Indians
   Trod in creation
   Before this nation
   I'll always remember
   I can't forget

I was walking on the shore and they took me in the ship
And they throw me overboard
And I swam right out of the belly of the whale
And I never get weary yet
They put me in jail and I did not do no wrong
And I never get weary yet
Say they put me in jail and I didn't get no bail
And I never get weary yet
Never get weary yet
   I know I was from before
   Christopher Columbus
   And I was born before
   The Arawak Indians
   Trod in creation
   Before this nation
   I'll always remember
   I can't forget
   Never get weary yet

PETER TOSH

African

Don't care where you come from
As long as you're a black man, you're an African
No min' your nationality
You have got the identity of an African

Cos if you come from Clarendon, you are an African
And if you come from Portland, you are an African
And if you come from Westmoreland, you are an African
    Don't care *etc.*

Cos if you come from Trinidad, you are an African
And if you come from Nassau, you are an African
And if you come from Cuba, you are an African
    So don't care *etc.*

No min' your complexion
There is no rejection, you are an African
Cos if your 'plexion high, high, high
If your 'plexion low, low, low
And if your 'plexion in between
You are an African
    So don't care *etc.*

No min' denomination
That is only segregation, you are an African
Cos if you go to the Catholic, you are an African
Or if you go to the Methodist, you are an African
And if you go to the Church of God, you are an African
    So don't care *etc.*

Cos if you come from Brixton, you are an African
And if you come from Neasden, you are an African
And if *etc.* (*with* Willesden, Bronx, Brooklyn, Queens,
Manhattan, Canada, Miami, Switzerland, Germany, Russia,
    Taiwan – *Fade*)

JIMMY CLIFF

The Harder They Come

O they tell me of a pie up in the sky
Waiting for me when I die
But between the day you're born and when you die
They never seem to hear you when you cry
   So as sure as the sun will shine
   I'm gonna get my share now, what's mine
   And then the harder they come, the harder they fall
   One and all
   Ooh the harder they come, the harder they fall
   One and all

Well the oppressors are trying to keep me down
Trying to drive me underground
And they think that they have got the battle won
I say forgive them, Lord, they know not what they've done
   Because as sure as the sun will shine *etc.*

And I keep on fighting for the things I want
Though I know that when you're dead you can't
But I'd rather be a free man in my grave
Than living as a puppet or a slave
   So as sure as the sun will shine *etc.*

LEGON COGIL AND CARLTON BARRETT

Performed by Bob Marley

Dem Belly Full

Dem belly full but we 'ungry
A 'ungry mob is a hangry mob
De rain a fall but de dutty tough
A pot a cook but de food nuh 'nough
   We're gonna dance to Jah music, yeh
   We're gonna dance to Jah music, yeh
   Forget your sorrows and dance
   Forget your troubles and dance
   Forget your sickness and dance
   Forget your weariness and dance
Ah say: cost of living get so 'igh
De rich and poor dey start to cry
And now de weak must get strong by singing
Ah what a tribulation
Sing: muh belly full but me 'ungry
A 'ungry man is a hangry man
A rain a fall but de dutty tough
A pot a cook but de food nuh 'nough
   We're gonna chuck to Jah music, we're chuckin, yeh
   You hear we're chuckin to Jah music, we're chuckin

BOB MARLEY

Trenchtown Rock

One good thing about music
when it hits, you feel no pain
One good thing about music
when it hits, you feel no pain
So hit me with music
Hit me with music now
So hit me with music
Hit me with music now
Ah say Trenchtown Rock: don't watch that
Trenchtown Rock: big fish or sprat
Trenchtown Rock: you reap what you sow
Trenchtown Rock: and everyone know
Trenchtown Rock: don't turn your back
Trenchtown Rock: give them so much rock
Trenchtown Rock: never let the children cry
Trenchtown Rock: cause you got to tell Jah Jah why
you're grooving in Kingston 12
grooving in Kingston 12
One good thing about music
when it hits, you feel no pain
So hit me with music
Hit me with music now
Hit me with music
Brutalize me with music now

CHRISTOPHER LAIRD

The Sea at Evening

I love the sea
when it's like this.
When you see is like this?
I love the sea.
Yeah.

Man,
that sea, man,
is full of my tears eh!
Yeah.
·Full of my tears man.
I mean,
you know what
memories
that does bring back man?
You know how much
memories that does bring back?

Man,
as the sun
sink into she
is like all my life there
you know man.
Yeah.

Boy, like them swells eh,
only moving slowly cross
she belly
like is she own hand caressing
she own self.
Yeah.
And all of that
eh man;
all them tears, them memories
and them;
all of them come
in one petulant

splash
on the beach.
Yeah.

Is like a woman you always had
you know,
who hold all you present and private
thoughts
and wishes
and dreams in she,
and all she do is throw them on the beach
and pull them back
and throw them out again
like some sort of insult man,
or some sort of bait eh.

Is like . . . man, like . . .
like she ain't care
bout you.
She ain't care bout you man.
But you know she care eh man.
Yeah.
You know she care like you care.
You know she want you love she eh.
You know she want you in she.
Yeah man.
In she.
But right now,
right now eh man,
she playing it cool man.
Yeah.

As the sun goes
she taking on all the night's
lights
and she glows and she glitters
and she sulks and she seduces
while she threatens.

Right now man,
I love the sea eh.
Yeah.
I love that sea man.
I love she bad.

FREDERICK WILLIAMS

De Eighties

Call me bad when me start walk de streets
Shouting, repatriation – repatriation
Give us what is ours an mek we go home

Me-say call me bad when me act out what me tinkin
An dem say, dis is a black
Sir Francis Drake
An for Jah-Jah sake – why not

Call me bad when, me wud start bun dem
Like acid, dem start panic
Dem say a who im a talk
Me trow me corn, me no call no fowl
Me is me, an we is we
An all who com after we is weeble
So me nah sow me seed pon stony ground

Call me bad, when me
Chant dung Judas, smile an Backwud style

Call me bad, den I will join de
Clan of rich – powerful – famous

Yes! call me bad, 'cause bad men
Dont sit on dem ass frustrated
Dem cus rass,
An free up dem selves

BONGO JERRY

Mabrak

Lightning
is the future brightening,
for last year man learn
how to use black eyes.
(wise!)

Mabrak:
        NEWSFLASH!
'Babylon plans crash'
Thunder interrupt their program to
announce:

BLACK ELECTRIC STORM
                        IS HERE
How long you feel 'fair to fine
(WHITE)' would last?

How long calm in darkness
        when out of BLACK
        come forth LIGHT?

How long dis slave caste
        when out of
        the BLACK FUTURE
comes
        I
        RIGHTS
        ?

Every knee
        must bow
Every tongue
        confess
Every language
        express

W
O
R
D
W
O
R
K
S

YOU

    MUST

        COME

to RAS
MABRAK,
Enlightening is BLACK
hands writing the words of
black message
for black hearts to feel.

MABRAK is righting the wrongs and brain-whitening –
    HOW?
Not just by washing out the straightening and wearing
    dashiki t'ing:
MOSTOFTHESTRAIGHTENINGISINTHETONGUE
  – SO HOW?

Save the YOUNG
from the language that MEN teach,
the doctrine Pope preach
skin bleach.

HOW ELSE? . . . MAN must use MEN language to carry dis
  message:

SILENCE BABEL TONGUES; recall and
recollect BLACK SPEECH.

Cramp all double meaning
        an' all that hiding behind language bar,

for that crossword speaking
        when expressing feeling

is just English language contribution to increase confusion in
        Babel-land tower –

delusion, name changing, word rearranging
        ringing rings of roses, pocket full of poses:

'SAR' instead of 'RAS'
left us in a situation
        where education
mek plenty African afraid, ashamed, unable to choose
        (and use)

BLACK POWA. (Strange Tongue)

NOT AGAIN!
Never be the same!
Never again shame!

Ever now communicate – for now I-and-I come to recreate:
sight sounds and meaning to measure the feeling
of BLACK HEARTS – alone –

MABRAK: frightening
MABRAK: black lightning

The coming of light to the black world: Come show I the
    way,
come make it plain as day – now – come once, and come for
    all
        and every one better come to RAS
for I come far, have far to go from here:

for the white world must come to blood bath
and blood bath is as far as the white world can reach; so
        when MABRAK
start skywriting,
LET BABYLON BURN
JEZEBEL MOURN
LET WEAK HEART CHURN
BLACK HOUSE STAND FIRM: for somewhere under
        ITYOPIA rainbow,
AFRICA WAITING FOR I.

EDDY GRANT

War Party

You invite me to a war party
Me no wanna go
Everybody seem to be inviting me to
A war party
Me no wanna go
Heard about the last one
So thanks but no thank you

You killed off all the Indians
And you killed off all the slaves
But not quite
So you killed off the remains
You look for me, and I'm looking for you
I can't believe what they say 'bout you is true
That you're a bad star, just like Pharaoh
You killed the children, just like Pharaoh
Now you sent a ticket for me
It don't have R.S.V.P.
  Oh Lord it's a war party *etc.*

You invited all our wise men
Many times before
To dance around your fires
And even out your scores
And when toll's taken of the valiant and the brave
The only decoration is the one upon the graves
Oh no you're a bad star, just like Pharaoh
You killed the children just like Pharaoh
Now you sent a ticket for me
And it don't have R.S.V.P.
  Oh Lord it's a war party *etc.*

Please don't send no ticket for me
If it don't have R.S.V.P.
Do you wanna go? Say no
Oh, do you wanna gonna go? Say no
Oh me no wanna go right now
Me no wanna go right now

LILLIAN ALLEN

Belly Woman's Lament

A likkle seed
Of her love fe a man
Germinates in her gut
She dah breed
Cool breeze
It did nice
Im nuh waan no wife
Just life
Wey fe do!

The likkle seed
Jus a grow
Bloat her belly
It noh know
How it change
Mek life rearrange

Ooman bruk
Nuh likkle wuk
Man gaan
Nuh waan noh ties
Just life
Wey fe do!

Anada heart
Start fe beat
Anada mouth
Deh fe feed
Plant corn
Reap weed

Wey fe do!

I Fight Back

ITT ALCAN KAISER
Canadian Imperial Bank of Commerce
these are privileged names in my country
but I am illegal here

My children scream
My grandmother is dying

I came to Canada
and found the doors
of opportunities well guarded

I scrub floors
serve backra's meals on time
spend two days' working in one
and twelve days in a week

Here I am in Canada
bringing up someone else's child
while someone else and me in absentee
bring up my own

And I fight back

And constantly they ask
'Oh beautiful tropical beach
with coconut tree and rum
why did you leave there
why on earth did you come?'

And I say:
    For the same reasons
    your mothers came

    I fight back

    They label me
    Immigrant, Law-breaker, Illegal
    Ah no, not Mother, not Worker, not Fighter

I fight back
like my sisters before me
I FIGHT BACK
I FIGHT BACK

LINTON KWESI JOHNSON

Bass Culture

For Big Yout

muzik of blood
black reared
pain rooted
heart geared;

all tensed up
in the bubble and the bounce
an the leap an the weight-drop.

it is the beat of the heart,
this pulsing of blood
that is a bubblin bass,
a bad bad beat
pushin gainst the wall
whey bar black blood.

an is a whole heappa
passion a gather
like a frightful form
like a righteous harm
giving off wild like is madness.

Reggae fi Dada

galang dada
galang gwaan yaw sah
yu nevah ad noh life fi live
jus di wan life fi give
yu did yu time pan ert
yu nevah get yu just dizert
galang goh smile inna di sun
galang goh satta inna di palace af peace

o di waatah
it soh deep
di waatah
it soh daak
an it full a hawbah shaak

di lan is like a rack
slowly shattahrin to san
sinkin in a sea af calimity
where fear breed shadows
dat lurks in di daak
where people fraid fi waak
fraid fi tink fraid fi taak
where di present is haunted by di paas

a deh soh mi bawn
get fi know bout staam
learn fi cling to di dawn
an wen mi hear mi daddy sick
mi quickly pack mi grip an tek a trip

mi nevah have noh time
wen mi reach
fi si noh sunny beach
wen mi reach
jus people a live in shack
people livin back-to-back
mongst cackroach an rat
mongst dirt an dizeez
subjek to terrorist attack
political intrigue
kanstant grief
an noh sign af relief

o di grass
turn brown
soh many trees
cut doun
an di lan is ovahgrown

fram country to town
is jus thistle an tawn
inna di woun a di poor
is a miracle ow dem endure

di pain nite an day
di stench af decay
di glarin sights
di guarded affluence
di arrogant vices
cole eyes af kantemp
di mackin symbals af independence

a deh soh mi bawn
get fi know bout staam
learn fi cling to di dawn
an wen di news reach mi
seh mi wan daddy ded
mi ketch a plane quick

an wen mi reach mi sunny isle
it woz di same ole style
di money well dry
di bullits dem a fly
plenty innocent a die
many rivahs run dry
ganja plane flyin high
di poor man im a try
yu tink a lickle try im try
holdin awn bye an bye
wen a dallah cant buy
a lickle dinnah fi a fly

galang dada
galang gwaan yaw sah
yu nevah ad noh life fi live
just di wan life fi give
yu did yu time pan ert
yu nevah get yu jus dizert
galang goh smile inna di sun
galang goh satta inna di palace af peace

mi know yu couldn tek it dada
di anguish an di pain
di suffahrin di prablems di strain
di strugglin in vain
fi mek two ens meet
soh dat dem pickney coulda get

77

a lickle someting fi eat
fi put cloaz pan dem back
fi put shoes pan dem feet
wen a dallah cant buy
a lickle dinnah fi a fly

mi know yu try dada
yu fite a good fite
but di dice dem did loaded
an di card pack fix
yet still yu reach fifty-six
before yu lose yu leg wicket
'a noh yu bawn grung here'
soh wi bury yu a Stranger's Burying Groun
near to mhum an cousin Daris
nat far fram di quarry
doun a August Town

MUTABARUKA

Free Up de Lan, White Man

Free up de lan, white man
free de Namibian
Free up de lan, white man
free all African

Mi nah gah compromise
wid nuh more lies
You lef your lan
run de Indian
call yourself American
now you inna fe me lan
a call yourself Sout African

Free up de lan, white man *etc.*

Now you call yourself wise
because you industrialize
but de matcrials you usc
is from de people you abuse
but we still call you frien
but now it seem like de frienship a guh en

Free up de lan, white man *etc.*

Now de proverb goes
only who know knows
Betta de fowl com see de daag dead
dan de daag com see de fowl head
an if de wata nuh run, it a guh stink like hell

Free up de lan, white man *etc.*

Som com wid Bible inna dem han
but on deir ships were big cannon
Wid Bible an cannon
dem set up a plan
Ship us beyon
control wi lan

Free up de lan, white man
free de Namibian
Free up de lan, white man
free all African
Free de black in Englan
free de Caribbean
Free all nations!

Revolutionary Poets

revolutionary poets
'ave become entertainers
babblin out angry words
about
          ghetto yout'
bein shot down
guns an bombs
          yes
revolutionary words bein
digested with
          bubble gums
          popcorn an
          ice cream
in tall(inter conti nental)
                    buildins

revolutionary poets
'ave become entertainers
oppressors recitin about oppressors
oppressin the oppressors
               where are the oppressed?

revolutionary poets
'ave become entertainers
sippin coffee an tea
explainin what it's like
to be down town
aroun town
up town dancin to
          bee gees

gettin night fever
while the
salvation army is still leadin the
        revolution

revolutionary poets
'ave become entertainers
revoltin against change
that's takin place
in their heads
while old ladies an others
are shot down dead
        can't write about that

yes
revolutionary poets
'ave all gone to the
creative art centre
to watch
the sufferin
of the people bein dram at ized by the
oppressors
        in their
            revolutionary
                poems.

*create problems
where th dont exist*

The Change

Yesterday
God was
white.
Good was white,
so
white was right.

Yesterday
evil was black
so
I took stock.
Today,
I changed.

Changed to evil?

You Ask Me

You ask me if I have ever been to prison.
Been to prison?
Your world of murderers and thieves
of hatred and jealousy
and . . . you ask me if I have ever been to prison?

I answer
Yes
I am still there
trying to escape . . .

OKU ONUORA

Last Night

got a peek
at the moon
last night
an didn't think of lovers

got a peek
at the moon
last night
an saw
a man with a load on his back

got a peek
at the moon
last night
an cried

Pressure Drop

hunga a twis man tripe
jus say 'eh'   man fight
man nerves raw
man tek a draw   c o o l
man jook up a tek in de scene
garbage dead-daag fly
'cho! but dis nu right'
man ready fe explode
man cyaan bear de load
                  pressure drop

dahta sigh
'lard! hear de pickney dem a cry'
man a pass say dahta fat
dahta smile   but dahta cyaan check dat
dahta haffi a check fe food fe put ina pat

dahta say all man want a fe get im han under skirt
bam!   she say she a breed
im vanish like when you bun weed
dahta wan wuk   dahta willin fe wuk
but is like say dahta nu have nu luck
or dem nu have enough wuk?
dahta say she nah ketch nu men
she say she nah falla nu fren
dahta confuse
too often dahta get use
dahta bahl
'lard! weh me a go do?'
            pressure drop

man flare
ina de slum man haffi live mongs rat, roach, fly, chink
'cho! de place stink'
man willin fe wuk
man nu wan fe bun gun ina man gut
man nu jus wan fe jook up an chat
man nu wan fe pap lack
but when hunger twis tripe an pickney bahl
time dread
eart tun red
curfew
man screw
gun blaze
knife flash
man run hot   when pressure drop

Reflection in Red

  an de beat well red
  an de scene well dread
  an de man dem a loot
  an shoot
        Laaard!
an de fia bun
an de blod a run

an some people jus doan
know weh fe tun
an de politicians a preach
an de preachas a pray
but tings a get worse
day after day
an den den den den den . . .
fram de eas' an de wes'
an de nart' an de sout'
a shout
peace . . .
an de man dem fram Rema
an Jungle a bungle
a dance an a prance
to some heavy reggae riddim
   an de beat well red
   an de scene well dread
   an de man dem a loot
   an shoot
an fe a lang lang time
de man Peta, Waila,
in de wilderness wailin:
   dere cannot be any peace, no peace
   until dere's equal rights, equal rights, equal rights
   an justice -tice -tice -tice -tice -tice -tice . . .
an de likkle dutty bagabone
a bubble to some heavy hyp-
notic survival
riddim an im madda
wid har han pon har jaw
a sing a sad, sad
song
a redemshan
an im bredda fram de crack
a dawn a dance a dance
wid death tru de bloody black
asphalt streets of de city
without any pity
an de people dem a wail:
free Michael Bernard
down with isms and schisms

it's written on de wall
babylon kingdom
mus
fall
natty dread bahl:
    dere cannot be any peace, no peace
    until dere's equal rights, equal rights, equal rights
    an justice -tice -tice -tice -tice . . .

BRIAN MEEKS

Las' Rights

Gunclick/
hopesfears
lovehate
the move
to make
this friday
comin on
strong a need
to see the John
or tell the baas
jus how the cash
real low
or where the
present alms
presented every
month should go:
bittahsulphah
acrid lifesmell
(or how the taste
of fresh white
bread upset
the bammi Negrah
yam an even
though the
price is high
the saltfish
low real low)
a new
suit a tery
lene for the
weddin next
week an Christ
masiscominthe
gooseisgettinfat
so please baas,

please put a
somethin
in you poor
bredda hat
/Gunflash/
done

The Coup-clock Clicks

1
today
the west
burns down.
Jones town
cries out
for water.
the rat a tat
staccato
automatic death
carves out its
place
in history.
children fall
at barricades,
crumpled faces
age
before their
time.

2
roun' one
i-told-you-so's
run sour
workers' blood
flows freely

roun' one.
confusion reigns
reaction smiles
and files
its blade

roun' one.
the blind man
hides the facts
in Rema.
Gleaner paints
a twisted picture

roun' one.
wall street
john crows
take a closer
perch, prepare
to pick the
pieces out.

3
can ill-timed
speeches
reassuring
words
prevent the
rising beast
from
feasting?

4
in Miami
the coup-clock clicks
toward the
time . . .

MICHAEL SMITH

Black Bud

Dem say
Who say?
Dem who always a say
   Sing a song a cent
   from way back then but
   black bud a cunny bud
   hard fi dead
a beg tropence
still behind
too far behind
doctor cyaan doctor she
nurse cyaan nurse she
knife a cut wi
blood a wash wi
claat' a wrap wi
police a lock wi
dem
     a
       knock
          pon
            one
little room
two panel bed
Junky Junky
like a smell
baton a mash wi
shot a tear wi
who fi dead?
stay
    behind
         fence
            wi a scale i
but knife, knife a cut wi
blood, blood a wash wi
claat', claat' a wrap wi

Cry-cry pickney still a cry
black bud a cunny bud
hard fi dead

I an I Alone
or *Goliath*

I an I alone
ah trod tru creation
Babylon on I right
Babylon on I left
Babylon in front of I
an Babylon behine I
an I an I alone inna de middle
like a Goliath wid a sling shot

'Ten cent a bundle fi me calaloo!
Yuh a buy calaloo, dread? Ten cent.'

Everybody a try fi sell someting
Everybody a try fi grab someting
Everybody a try fi hussle someting
Everybody a try fi kill someting

but ting an ting mus ring
an only a few cyaan sing
cause dem nah face de same sinting

'It's a hard road to travel
an a mighty long way to go;
Jesus, me blessed Saviour
will meet us on the journey home.' (*Sung*)

'Shoppin bag! Shoppin bag! Five cent fi one!'
'Green pepper! Thyme! Skellion! Pimento!'
'Remember de Sabbath day to keep it holy!
Six days shalt thou labour,
but on the seventh day shalt thou rest.'
'Hey, Mam! How much fi dah piece a yam deh?
No, no dat; dat! Yes, dat!'
'Three dollars a poun, nice genkleman.'

'Clear out! Oonoo country people
too damn tief!' 'Like yuh muma!'
'Fi-me muma? Wha yuh know bout me muma?'
'Look-ya, a might push dis inna yuh!'
'Yuh lie! A woulda collar yuh!'
'Bruck it up! But dread, cool down!'
'Alright, cool down, Rastafari.'

De people-dem tek everyting mek a muckle –
dem a try fi hussle down de price
fi mek two ends meet,
de odder a try fi push up de price
fi mek dem pickney backbone
get someting fi eat.
But two teet meet an dem a bark,
dem cyaan stan de pressure,
dem tired fi compete wid hog an daag
but dem mus aspire fi someting better
although dem dungle heap ketch a fire.

Cyaan mek blood out a stone
an cow never know de use a im tail
till fly tek it, but from dem barn
dem a fan de fly of poverty from dem ass
because dem never have a tail fi cover it.
'Watch me! Watch me!' 'Hey, handcart bwoy,
mine yuh lick dung me pickney-dem, yuh know!'
'Tief! Tief!' 'Weh im deh?'
'Look out, mek a bruck im friggin neck!'
'Im a one a de P dem!'
'Yuh see it? Zacky was me fren
but look how im life a go en?
Party politics play de trick
an it lick im down wit de big coocoomacca stick!'

Pickney dem a bawl,
rent to pay,
wife to obey,
but only Jesus know de way,
de meek shall inherit de eart
an de fullness thereof –
but look what she inherit?
six month pregnant an five mout fi feed!

'Cho, Roy, man, let me go no man?
Me no want no man inna '81!'
'So wha appen? It was only '80
yuh did a tek man? Cho, Doris, man,
consider dis late application.'

Dem waan mek love pon hungry belly
jus to figet dis moment of poverty
but she mus get breed
an dem haffi go face dem calamity.

'Joshua seh oonoo fi draw oonoo belt tight.'
'Which belt? when me tripe a come tru me mout'!'
'Wha appen, sah – yuh get deliver?
Yuh nah answer?' 'Hey, lady, yuh believe
in Socialism?' 'No, sah, me believe
in social living.'

'Calaloo!' 'Shoppin bag!' 'Green pepper!'
'Skellion!' 'Pimento!' 'Yellow yam!'
'Dutty Albert!' 'Hey, Tony!'
'Beg yuh a ten cent, no sah!'
'Mek yuh woan lef me alone!'
'Hey, sexy!' 'Sugar plum!' 'Honey-bunch!'
'Daag shit!' 'Cow shit!'

I an I alone
a trod tru creation
Babylon on I right
Babylon on I lef
Babylon behine I
an Babylon in front of I
an I an I alone inna de middle
like a Goliath wid a sling shot.

VALERIE BLOOM

Trench Town Shock (A Soh Dem Sey)

Waia, Miss May, trouble dey yah,
Ban yuh belly, Missis, do.
Mi ha one terrible piece a news,
An mi sarry fe sey it consarn yuh.

Yuh know yuh secon or t'ird cousin?
Yuh great-aunt Edit' Fred?
Im pick up imse'f gahn a pickcha show,
An police shoot im dead.

But a di bwoy own fault yah mah,
For im go out a im way
Fi gwan fahs wid police-man,
At leas' a soh dem sey.

Dem sey im a creep oba di teata fence,
Dem halla 'Who go deh?'
De bwoy dis chap one bad wud mah,
At leas' a soh dem sey.

De police sey 'tap or we opin fiah'.
But yuh know ow di bwoy stay,
Im gallop back come attack dem,
At leas' a soh dem say.

Still, nutten woulda come from i',
But wha yuh tink, Miss May?
De bwoy no pull out lang knife mah!
At leas' a soh dem sey.

Dem try fi aim afta im foot
But im head get een di way,
Di bullit go 'traight through im brain,
At leas' a soh dem sey.

Dry yuh yeye, mah, mi know i' hat,
But i happen ebery day,
Knife-man always attack armed police
At leas' a soh dem sey.

Wat a Rain

Wat a piece a rain, Miss Kate!
Mi nebba see it soh yet.
Whole week mi shet up eena house
Yuh wouldn' know how mi fret.

Mi dear mam! Yuh can sey it agen
For when it start de day,
Mi coulda tell anybody sey
Wi mus gwine hab hell fi pay.

As mi see di black cloud dem set up
Oba Big Mountain tap,
Mi tun to Joe-Joe an mi sey
'Jocy massa, rain gwine drap'.

Mi dear mam, as mi sey de wud,
A piece a lightning flash!
An before yuh sey 'who dat', Miss Kate,
De whole a yahd a wash.

One time de tunda clap so loud,
It nea'ly plit mi head,
Mi tun fe calla pon Joe-Joe
An fine im quinge up unda bed.

Five night an day it rain missis,
De house tun Noah Ark,
Puss, fowl, an goat an daag een deh
Mi could hardly fine place fe walk.

But wus of all mi dear Miss Kate,
De house tap start fe leak,
Tap, yuh noh hear nutten yet mah;
Mi cyaan feget de week.

Mi sey Miss Kate, fe de solid week,
Wi sleep pon one annoda,
For de whole a de bed wus wringing wet
'Cep' fe one likkle carna.

But good tings did come outa it,
For when mi tep a kitchen,
Mi see tup dung a fiahside,
Two big fat peely chicken.

Mi ketch dem put eena fowl kub,
Dem nebba hab no owna,
For mi look pon ebery fedda,
An mi noh see name nor numba.

Fish was lyin pon de step,
An swims de pon verandah,
Is a good ting mi lib a ribberside,
Oh yes – mi fine one ganda.

Mi tink it belong to Jacob Brown,
But mi fine i' unda cella,
Mi tek i' put wid mi chicken dem,
An no badda ask a foofah.

For Jacob tief mi one goat kid
An tief from tief God laugh;
An mi tell yuh sey de whole a Sta Fay
Long neck pear limb tear off?

It drap oba fe wi side o' fence
Soh now wi hab pear fe eat,
An Mary whofah fat sow drown
Gi' mi one shet pan o' meat.

Soh doah mi house did full o' san
An mi yahd tun sea, waan drain;
Mi still mek likkle profit mam,
Outa de likkle rain.

THE LITERARY TRADITION

there's no such thing as 'only literature'

– Edward Baugh

ANONYMOUS

From *A Pindarique Ode on the Arrival of His
Excellency Sir Nicholas Lawes, Governor of
Jamaica*

Sing first the Heroe in his Goodly Ship
With waving Pendants and her gilded Beak
    Breasting the surgy deep,
    Proud of th' important weight she bears,
    Her Head aloft she stately rears,
And her Old Foe beneath Disdains, not Fears:
    About Her ornamented Side
    The painted Dolphins sport and glide,
And court his gracious Hand in all their Pride;
The fierce devouring Tyrants of the Main
Forget their Nature, for a while are tame;
The Shark himself neglects his easy Prey,
Swims to the Vessel and doth Homage pay,
    Th' exulting harmless little Fry
    Wanton before their Enemy
Secure in Innocence whilst LAWES is by.

Our Prayers are heard, Our Fears dispers'd and fled,
No longer now the false destructive Seas,
Their Rocks, their Monsters, or their Rage we dread,
The labour'd Bark fast anchoring rides at ease,
Our Guardian safely Lands; (All Praise to Heaven,
For its best Gift to us in Him now giv'n.)
    The wide-mouth'd Cannons Roar,
    Bears the News from Shore to Shore;
Farther th' acclaiming Peoples mightier Voice,
And bless Great Brittain's Monarch in his Choice.

    Behold upon the winding Strand
    Crowds like its Pebbles numerous stand.
And press upon the Ruler of the Land
    With too obsequious Love
    Cluster'd in Throngs they move:

Herself neglecting see the pregnant Wife
Too fondly curious risques a double Life,
Old Age on Crutches limps to bless it's Eyes
As loath to lose so wish'd a sight before it dyes,
All Work and Labour's at a stand, as though
Of more Importance were the graceful Show
Than Gold, to all Things else prefer'd but You;
The branded shackled Slave makes Holy-Day,
    And is allow'd to Play,
     This once he expatiates free,
And tasts the unknown sweets of Liberty;
Life's Choicest Blessings all shall flow Great Chief from
   Thee.

FRANCIS WILLIAMS

From *An Ode to George Haldane, Governor of the Island of Jamaica*

Hoc demum accipias, multa fuligine fusum
  Ore sonaturo; non cute, corde valet.
Pollenti stabilita manu, (Deus almus, eandem
  Omnigenis animam, nil prohibente dedit)
Ipsa coloris egens virtus, prudentia; honesto
  Nullus inest animo, nullus in arte color.
Cur timeas, quamvis, dubitesve, nigerrima celsam
  Caesaris occidui, scandere Musa domum?
Vade salutatum, nec sit tibi causa pudoris,
  Candida quod nigra corpora pelle geris!
Integritas morum Maurum magis ornat, et ardor
  Ingenii, et docto dulcis in ore decor;
Hunc, mage cor sapiens, patriae virtutis amorque,
  Eximit e sociis, conspicuumque facit.
Insula me genuit, celebres aluere Britanni,
  Insula, te salvo non dolitura patre!
Hoc precor; o nullo videant te fine, regentem
  Florentes populos, terra, Deique locus!

(Accept this, uttered with much soot from a mouth that wishes to sing; not from the skin but from the heart comes its strength. Established by a mighty hand (God the creator gave the same soul to all his creatures, without exception), virtue itself, like wisdom, is devoid of colour. There is no colour in an honourable mind, none in art. Why do you fear so much, and hesitate, my Muse so black, to mount to the lofty abode of the Caesar of the setting sun? Go and greet him, nor let it be a source of shame to you that a black skin covers your fair body! All the more does moral integrity adorn an African, as does ardour of intellect, and attractive eloquence in a learned mouth. Rather, a wise heart, and love both of country and of virtue, distinguish such a man from his fellows, and make him outstanding. An island gave me birth, the renowned Britons nurtured me, this island which will have no cause to grieve while you, its father, thrive! This I pray; O may this land and place of God see you ruling without end over a flourishing people.)

NATHANIEL WEEKES

From *Barbados*

[I]

When frequent Rains, and gentle Show'rs descend,
To chear the Earth, and Nature's self revive,
A second Paradise appears! the *Isle*
Thro'-out, one beauteous Garden seems; now Plants
Spring forth in all their Bloom; now Orange Groves
Diffuse their Sweets, and load each passing Gale
With heav'nly Fragrance; the Citron too, now
Breathes its Hoard of rich Perfumes; while All,
Their various Odours join, and to the Mind
Inspire a Likeness of what *Eden* was.

Thro' Walks thick-set with Orange Trees in Bloom,
And Citron intermix'd, who does not like
To sport and range, when the cool Evening tempts
The social Mind to sober Exercise,
And sweet Discourse? still sweeter made by Mirth!
Beneath each pleasant Shade, Discreetly Gay,
Or innocently Fond, the Sexes meet,
By Love or Friendship Pair'd; while Others range
The various Walks, and chat of Scandal, Toys,
And Fashions now in Vogue; still reigning Themes
In all Assemblies of the Fair and Gay!

[II]

The Virtues of the *Cane* must now be sung;
The noblest Plant of all the western Isles!
What greater Subject can employ my Muse?
Not India's aromatic Groves, nor all
The Treasures of her Hundred Mines, can boast
A more important Trade, or yield to Man
A nobler Use. Here, Muse! your Pow'r exert,
The Subject now your utmost Pow'r demands.
To trace the *Cane* thro' all its various Toils,
Till full Perfection crowns its Use compleat,
Be now your Task to celebrate at large.

   To urge the Glory of your *Cane*'s success,
Rich be your Soil, and well manur'd with Dung,
Or, *Planters*! what will all your Labours yield?
A faithless Profit, and a barren Crop.
When heavy Rains in pleasing Floods descend,
And all your Land with finish'd *Holing* smiles,
Swift to the Task of Planting call your Slaves,
While yet the Weather favours your Designs.
Close watch, ye *Drivers*! your work-hating Gang,
And mark their Labours with a careful Eye;
But spare your cruel, and ungen'rous Stripes!
They sure are Men, tho' Slaves, and colour'd Black;
And what is Colour in the Eye of Heav'n?
'Tis impious to suppose a Diff'rence made;
Like you they boast sound Reason, Feeling, Sense,
And Virtues equally as great, and good,
If Lesson'd rightly, and instructed well.
Spare then your Tyranny, inhuman Men!
And deal that Mercy you expect from Heav'n.

JAMES GRAINGER

From *The Sugar-Cane*

From Book II

Then earthquakes, nature's agonizing pangs,
Oft shake the astonied isles: the solfaterre
Or sends forth thick, blue, suffocating steams;
Or shoots to temporary flame. A din,
Wild, thro' the mountain's quivering rocky caves,
Like the dread Crash of tumbling planets, roars.
When tremble thus the pillars of the globe,
Like the tall coco by the fierce North blown;
Can the poor, brittle tenements of man
Withstand the dread convulsion? Their dear homes,
(Which shaking, tottering, crashing, bursting, fall)
The boldest fly; and, on the open plain
Appal'd, in agony the moment wait,
When, with disrupture vast, the waving earth
Shall whelm them in her sea-disgorging womb.

Nor less affrighted are the bestial kind.
The bold steed quivers in each panting vein,
And staggers, bath'd in deluges of sweat:
The lowing herds forsake their grassy food,
And send forth frighted, woful, hollow sounds:
The dog, thy trusty centinel of night,
Deserts his post assign'd; and, piteous, howls —
Wide ocean feels: —
The mountain-waves, passing their custom'd bounds,
Make direful, loud incursions on the land,
All-overwhelming: Sudden they retreat,
With their whole troubled waters; but, anon,
Sudden return, with louder, mightier force;
(The black rocks whiten, the vext shores resound;)
And yet, more rapid, distant they retire.
Vast coruscations lighten all the sky,
With volum'd flames; while thunder's awful voice,
From forth his shrine, by night and horror girt,
Astounds the guilty, and appals the good.

From Book IV

On festal days; or when their work is done;
Permit thy slaves to lead the choral dance,
To the wild banshaw's melancholy sound.
Responsive to the sound, head, feet and frame
Move aukwardly harmonious; hand in hand
Now lock'd, the gay troop circularly wheels,
And frisks and capers with intemperate joy.
Halts the vast circle, all clap hands and sing;
While those distinguish'd for their heels and air,
Bound in the center, and fantastic twine.
Meanwhile some stripling, from the choral ring,
Trips forth; and, not ungallantly, bestows
On her who nimblest hath the greensward beat,
And whose flush'd beauties have inthrall'd his soul,
A silver token of his fond applause.
Anon they form in ranks; nor inexpert
A thousand tuneful intricacies weave,
Shaking their sable limbs; and oft a kiss
Steal from their partners; who, with neck reclin'd,
And semblant scorn, resent the ravish'd bliss.
But let not thou the drum their mirth inspire;
Nor vinous spirits: else, to madness fir'd,
(What will not bacchanalian frenzy dare?)
Fell acts of blood, and vengeance they pursue.

JOHN SINGLETON

From *A General Description of the West Indian Islands*

From Book II

But lo! the reaking surface of the vale
Presents its wond'rous horrors to the sight;
What tongue can speak, or pencil paint, the scene?
What words can brightest thought of fancy find,
Or fruitfullest imagination form,
To give the manifold idea birth?
Not all description's liveliest, varied tints,
Can the dread landscape to conception draw.
A steep it is, where tygers might repose,
And lions breed, free from the hunter's toils.
Like that abyss, where fabling poets place
The rugged portal of th'infernal bounds.

Within all terror and confusion seems:
There hollow noises, murmuring thro' the vault,
Surprize the list'ning ear; whilst from the deeps
The hoarse Cerberean yell dreadful ascends,
Three times full-echo'd from the distant hills.

A place it is, environ'd round with rocks,
And by immeasurable clifts immur'd.
The glorious planet of all-cheering day
There sheds a faint, dim light, which only serves
To spread a gloom more horrible around;
Whilst swift (like flitting ghosts) strange dismal shades,
In wild, delusive forms, incessant glide.

Sometimes, dank dews in hasty drops descend,
Or raw, unwholesome mists, wide-hovering hang,
And, darksome, roll around, fetid, and thick,
Gath'ring beneath th'encircling mountain tops.

Sometimes the rains, in sheets descending fall;
And, dashing on the fiery soil amain,
Rebounding foam. Sometimes enormous rocks
Rush headlong, tumbling from the ragged brow
Of some inferior hill, and sink below,

Half buried in the sulphurous unsound.
Here pensive melancholy might compose
Her solemn features, and, with horror chill'd,
As in a tomb, brood o'er her fancy'd ills.
  Beneath the surface of the doleful way
That ever burns, with wild infernal noise
Two cauldrons, huge, enormous, fiercely boil.
Not fiercer those for criminals prepar'd
By cruel law in fell barbarian realms,
Or in Batavian land; where oft they plunge
The base delinquent, foul with monstrous crimes,
In brazen cauldrons charg'd with molten lead.
The pitchy smoak in circling clouds ascends,
And flashing sudden gleams of stifled flame,
O'er the dun vale its sooty mantle waves,
Height'ning the dismal horror of the scene.
Oft do these cauldrons deep their brims o'erflow,
And with amazing ebullition rise;
What time, with dire combustibles o'ercharg'd,
The rumbling earth from its foundation shakes,
And, heaving, bursts; whilst the convulsive pit
With hideous ruin reaks, and spreads in air
Its flaky entrails flaming to the sky.
This wond'rous scene had fabling poets view'd,
They ne'er in Tartarus had plac'd their Hell.

From Book III

  Ah me! how differently th'untutor'd slave,
To no philosophy indebted, views
The obsequies of his departed friend,
And with his calm deportment puts to shame
The boasted reason of the polish'd world:
A moment dries his manly eye, untaught
To melt at death, the necessary end
Of all terrestrial things. His creed (the voice
Of nature) keeps him firm, nay, gives him joy,
When he considers (so the sages teach
Of Afric's sun-burnt realms) that the freed soul,

Soon as it leaves its mortal coil behind,
Transported to some distant world, is wrapt
In bliss eternal. There the man begins,
With organs more refin'd, to live again,
And taste such sweets as were deny'd him here,
The sweets of liberty. Oh glorious name!
Oh pow'rful soother of the suff'ring heart!
That with thy spark divine can'st animate
Unletter'd slaves to stretch their simple thoughts
In search of thee, beyond this gloomy vale
Of painful life, where all their piteous hours
Drag heavily along in constant toil,
In stripes, in tears, in hunger, or in chains:
These are the ills which they rejoice to fly,
Unless, by partial chance, their lot is cast
Beneath some kind indulgent master's sway,
Whose hands like their good genius, feeds their wants,
And with protection shields their helpless state.

   But see what strange procession hither winds,
With long continued stream, through yonder wood!
Like gentle waves hundreds of sable heads
Float onwards; still they move, and still they seem
With unexhausted flow to keep their course.

   In calm succession thus th'unruffled main
Rolls on its peaceful waters to the shore,
With easy swell, wave gliding over wave,
Till the spectator can no longer count
Their breaks incessant, but the numbers past
Are in succeeding numbers quickly lost.
Behold the white-rob'd train in form advance
To yonder new-made grave: Six ugly hags,
Their visage seam'd with honorary scars,
In wild contortive postures lead the van;
High o'er their palsied heads, rattling, they wave
Their noisy instruments; whilst to the sound
In dance progressive their shrunk shanks keep time.
With more composure the succeeding ranks,
Chanting their fun'ral song in chorus full,
Precede the mournful bier, by friendly hands
Supported: Sudden stops the flowing line;
The puzzled bearers of the restive corps

Stand for a while, fast rooted to the ground,
Depriv'd of motion, or, perhaps, impell'd
This way, or that, unable to proceed
In course direct, until the troubled dead
Has to some friend imparted his request;
That gratify'd, again the fun'ral moves:
When at the grave arriv'd the solemn rites
Begin; the slave's cold reliques gently laid
Within their earthy bed, some veteran
Among the sable Archimages, pours
Her mercenary panegyric forth,
In all the jargon of mysterious speech,
And, to compose the spirit of the dead,
Sprinkles his fav'rite liquor on the grave.
This done, the mourners form a spacious ring,
When sudden clangours, blended with shrill notes,
Pour'd forth from many a piercing pipe, surprise
The deafen'd ear. Nor Corybantian brass,
Nor rattling sistrum, ever rung a peal
So frantic, when th' Idaean dactyli
At their intoxicated feasts ran wild,
Dizzily weaving the fantastic dance,
And with extended throats proclaiming high
Their goddess Rhea, thro' the giddy croud.
Thus do these sooty children of the sun,
'Unused to the melting mood', perform
Their fun'ral obsequies, and joyous chaunt,
In concert full, the requiem of the dead;
Wheeling in many a mazy round, they fill
The jocund dance, and take a last farewell
Of their departed friend, without a tear.

ANONYMOUS

From *A Poetical Epistle, from the Island of Jamaica, to a Gentleman of the Middle-Temple*

Our tropic fruits, nurs'd 'neath a torrid sky,
With Britain's orchards, mild and fertile, vie.
Can England boast th'Anana's nectar'd taste?
The marrowy pear, a vegetable feast?
The flavour'd melon, or the juicy lime?
Or sugar-cane, the pride of India's clime?
Or milky apple, Venus to inspire?
Or cooling tamarind, that fans the fire?
Can ye, midst winter, pluck the summer's pride,
When all your gardens glow one snowy void?
Or can ye sit by yonder fairy stream,
Where orang'd boughs preclude the scalding beam?

But happy ye, who dwell midst Britain's isle,
Thrice happy men! if fortune deigns to smile.
No sighing slave there makes his heedless moan,
No injur'd Afric echoes forth his groan;
No tort'ring lord ransacks his fruitful mind,
Some unthought woe, some unknown rack to find.

At each new crime this labours in my breast,
And this each night denies a quiet rest:
Some Afric chief will rise, who, scorning chains,
Racks, tortures, flames – excruciating pains,
Will lead his injur'd friends to bloody fight,
And in the flooded carnage take delight;
Then dear repay us in some vengeful war,
And give us blood for blood, and scar for scar.

Kingston, Jamaica, 20 May 1776

From *Jamaica, a Poem in Three Parts, Written in That Island in the Year 1776*

And can the Muse reflect her tear-stain'd eye,
When blood attests ev'n slaves for freedom die?
On cruel gibbets high disclos'd they rest,
And scarce one groan escapes one bloated breast.
Here sable Caesars feel the christian rod;
There Afric Platos, tortur'd, hope a God:
While jetty Brutus for his country sighs,
And sooty Cato with his freedom dies!

Britons, forbear! be Mercy still your aim,
And as your faith, unspotted be your fame;
Tremendous pains tremendous deeds inspire,
And, hydra-like, new martyrs rise from fire.

J. B. MORETON

Ballad

(Air 'What care I for Mam or Dad')

Altho' a slave me is born and bred,
    My skin is black, not yellow:
I often sold my maidenhead
    To many a handsome fellow.

My massa keep me once, for true,
    And gave me clothes, wid busses:
Fine muslin coats, wid bitty, too,
    To gain my sweet embraces.

When pickinniny him come black,
    My massa starve and fum me;
He tear the coat from off my back,
    And naked him did strip me.

Him turn me out into the field,
    Wid hoe, the ground to clear-o;
Me take pickinniny on my back,
    And work him te-me weary.

Him, Obissha, him de come one night,
    And give me gown and busses;
Him get one pickinniny, white!
    Almost as white as missess.

Then missess fum me wid long switch,
    And say him da for massa;
My massa curse her, 'lying bitch!'
    And tell her, 'buss my rassa!'

Me fum'd when me no condescend;
    Me fum'd too if me do it;
Me no have no one for 'tand my friend,
    So me am forc'd to do it.

Me know no law, me know no sin,
    Me is just what ebba dem make me;
This is the way dem bring me in;
    So God nor devil take me!

JAMES MONTGOMERY

From *The West Indies*

Dreadful as hurricanes, athwart the main
Rush'd the fell legions of invading Spain;
With fraud and force, with false and fatal breath,
(Submission bondage, and resistance death,)
They swept the isles. In vain the simple race
Kneel'd to the iron sceptre of their grace,
Or with weak arms their fiery vengeance braved;
They came, they saw, they conquer'd, they enslaved,
And they destroy'd; – the generous heart they broke,
They crush'd the timid neck beneath the yoke;
Where'er to battle march'd their grim array,
The sword of conquest plough'd resistless way;
Where'er from cruel toil they sought repose,
Around, the fires of devastation rose.
The Indian, as he turn'd his head in flight,
Beheld his cottage flaming through the night,
And, midst the shrieks of murder on the wind,
Heard the mute blood-hound's death-step close behind.

The conflict o'er, the valiant in their graves,
The wretched remnant dwindled into slaves;
Condemn'd in pestilential cells to pine,
Delving for gold amidst the gloomy mine,
The sufferer, sick of life-protracting breath,
Inhaled with joy the fire-damp blast of death:
– Condemn'd to fell the mountain-palm on high,
That cast its shadow from the evening sky,
Ere the tree trembled to his feeble stroke,
The woodman languish'd, and his heart-strings broke:
– Condemn'd in torrid noon, with palsy'd hand,
To urge the slow plough o'er the obdurate land,
The labourer, smitten by the sun's fierce ray,
A corpse along the unfinish'd furrow lay.
O'erwhelm'd at length with ignominious toil,
Mingling their barren ashes with the soil,

Down to the dust the Charib people pass'd,
Like autumn foliage withering in the blast:
The whole race sunk beneath the oppressor's rod,
And left a blank among the works of God . . .

Thus, childless as the Charibbeans died,
Afric's strong sons the ravening waste supplied;
Of hardier fibre to endure the yoke,
And self-renew'd beneath the severing stroke;
As grim oppression crush'd them to the tomb,
Their fruitful parent's miserable womb
Teem'd with fresh myriads, crowded o'er the waves,
Heirs to their toil, their sufferings, and their graves.

Freighted with curses was the bark that bore
The spoilers of the west to Guinea's shore;
Heavy with groans of anguish blew the gales
That swell'd that fatal bark's returning sails;
Old Ocean shrunk as o'er his surface flew
The human-cargo and the demon crew.
– Thenceforth, unnumber'd as the waves that roll
From sun to sun, or pass from pole to pole,
Outcasts and exiles, from their country torn,
In floating dungeons o'er the gulph were borne . . .

Captives of tyrant power and dastard wiles,
Dispeopled Africa, and gorged the isles.
Loud and perpetual o'er th' Atlantic waves,
For guilty ages, roll'd the tide of slaves;
A tide that knew no fall, no turn, no rest,
Constant as day and night from east to west;
Still widening, deepening, swelling in its course,
With boundless ruin, and resistless force.

M. J. CHAPMAN

From *Barbadoes*

[I]

Still sparkles here the glory of the west,
Shews his crowned head, and bares his jewelled breast,
In whose bright plumes the richest colours live,
Whose dazzling hues no mimic art can give –
The purple amethyst, the emerald's green,
Contrasted, mingle with the ruby's sheen;
While over all a tissue is put on
Of golden gauze, by fairy fingers spun –
Small as a beetle, as an eagle brave,
In purest ether he delights to lave;
The sweetest flowers alone descends to woo,
Rifles their sweets, and lives on honey-dew –
So light his kisses, not a leaf is stirred
By the bold, happy, amorous humming-bird;
No disarray, no petal rudely moved,
Betrays the flower the collobree has loved.

[II]

While the noon-lustre o'er the land is spread,
The listening lizard hides his star-lit head:
The four-o'clocks their shrinking petals close,
And wearied man seeks shelter and repose.
The negroes now desert the master's field,
And seek the joys that dearest home can yield;
Their little children claim the mother's care –
Some cull the pepper, and their meals prepare;
Some dress their gardens; some a fish-net spin;
While childhood's merry laugh is heard within.
How calm and tranquil look those negro-huts,
Their fruit-trees round, and scattered cocoa-nuts!
Their dear security the negro loves,
While through his shrubs and vines he lordly moves.

African Dirge

O, why should we the dead deplore,
  Who bids us now 'farewell';
Since he has gone to Guinea's shore,
  For ever there to dwell?

Now, underneath the village-tree,
  That dear familiar place,
He breathes the air of liberty,
  Mid his departed race.

Why should we mourn for him who lives
  Amid the blessed blest?
It is alone the living grieves –
  The dead enjoys his rest.

Brother! remember us, as we
  Thus hail thy happy flight;
Brother! we soon shall follow thee –
  Till then a brief good night!

WILLIAM HOSACK

From *The Isle of Streams, or, The Jamaica Hermit*

Stanzas X–XIV

'Tis blazing noon, fierce, unrelenting noon!
Pale Phoebus from the pinnacle of heaven,
O'er panting labor beats – the dark Maroon
To the cool woods, or fishing stream is driven; –
Fair damsels to Siesta now are given –
Noon's twanging signal hark! the welcome shell
Delights all those who in the sun have striven,
And frees them quickly by its magic spell,
   To bathe in crystal pool, or doze in shady dell.

The naked children in the sun, excel
In snaring silver shrimps in shallows clear,
Their dainty pepper-pot to season well! –
Half nude Maroons, with casting-net and spear,
Dive deftly into pools, or disappear
Among the rapids, Otter-like, to drive
Fish into traps of stone, by dint of fear;
Whence, netted o'er, they cleverly contrive,
   To spear them in their nooks, or bring them forth alive.

But washerwomen, busy – black, and brown, –
Flog the round stones; as in the stream they stand:
Their dainty daughters, scorning to stoop down!
Spread out their clothes upon the smoothest sand, –
Singing, they dance upon them, hand to hand;
Marking the time, with gestures singular –
All unadorned, and gay like naiad band! –
Watched by white Gaulins, silent from afar;
   While the green Bittern screams, that they so noisy are!

The boys ascend the dark, round mango trees,
Retreat of owls, from glare of noon secured;
Deep from the sun, yet open to the breeze,
By rosy fruit and leafy walls obscured –

Where hunger need not be, nor thirst endured; —
Or climb the cocoa-nuts, with monkey skill,
By their great bread-and-water nuts allured;
Others to drink the cane-juice, seek the mill,
   Whereof, both young and old, are free to take their fill.

Again, o'er hill and dale, resounds the shell! —
Sharp summons to return afield again;
Groups follow groups, and mark the signal well: —
Wainmen now crack their sounding whips amain,
To start for fresh supplies of sugar-cane;
Boilers, impatient, roar, and coax, and scream,
To the 'good-stokers,' all their arts to strain! —
Who envy much the bath each cattle-team
   Takes every time it crosses the adjacent stream.

Stanzas XLV–LI

But hark! the sharp beat of the Afric drum,
Sounds through the trees, and fills him with delight.
He sees a band of noisy Mummers come
With faces masked, to mock him, coloured bright; —
Before his door they dance with all their might, —
Or frantically drag him, one and all,
Headlong — into the pleasures of the night! —
Untroubled by one thought that could enthral,
   Or mar the moment's madness for their Carnaval!

Each dancing maid intent he scans in turn;
Till one herself unmasks, to draw his eyes!
Knowing right well, for whom his heart doth burn —
Across the room to her at once he flies:
While she — coquettishly — feigns to disguise
Her own delight, but fails to do it well! —
Which quickly he observes, and also spies
Her agitated bosom's breathing swell!
   And deems her faultless form nought earthly can excel!

Even the little children dance apart,
In the safe corners, looking at their feet,

In mute attention, to acquire the art —
Until, anon, with merriment replete,
They stretch their weary limbs in slumber sweet,
Snugly, without the eddy of the throng; —
And though the Gumby's unabating beat
Continues — and the universal song,
   Serenely they repose these stirring sounds among!

Brightly o'er the delighted throng below
In holdings primative, and brackets rude,
All round the dancing booths the tapers glow,
'Gainst wall of woven palm-leaves, sheen-endued
With glossy verdure — little understood
By those who in the halls of fashion flit —
And ne'er can be, till personally viewed —
Where music never stops, nor dancers sit,
   Nor glee from morn till night, doth ever intermit!

More rapidly now drummers strive to beat —
With ear turned to the instrument, and eye,
Fixed stedfastly upon the busy feet
They regulate: — and of their harmony
Approve, or disapprove, by shout, or sigh —
A group of gazing mummers by them stand, —
Dreaming, — whom they regard not, 'midst their high,
And heated aspirations, to command
   A simultaneous movement, with unerring hand!

Meanwhile the sherbert passes gaily round,
Coffee and Christmas fruits, in ample store;
Each coat is off, and handkerchief unbound;
The Booths all round are filled from door to door.
Lips, that were closed an hour or two before,
Their teeth, all white as ivory display!
In laughter, rising to a joyous roar!
Songs are composed impromptu, such as they
   Deem not inferior to the poets' loftiest lay!

Thus they continue, till the morning star
Shines o'er the mountain summit, lone and bright —
And every village cock proclaims afar,
From out his leafy roost, the waning night —

And the fair moon hath quenched her modest light,
Deep, in the bosom of the western surge –
And all the stars begin to mock the sight –
And objects from the gloom of night emerge –
   Then scatter, soberly, the ways their lovers urge.

ROBERT DUNBAR

From *The Cruise*

The summit gain'd, how glorious the reward! –
Bursts on the eye, and thrills upon the heart,
Reality more bright than dream of bard,
Or triumphs of Lorraine's creative art:
The land lies stretch'd like an illumined chart,
The sea one glistering sheet of silver shines;
And the sun's fires such dazzling radiance dart,
That each far isle, that in the glare reclines,
Quivers, like leafy gold, in undulating lines.

White peasant-villages embower'd in trees,
And garden'd mansions, dot the wide-spread map;
While o'er them, to the east's undying breeze,
The princely palm unfolds his feather'd cap:
Plenty lies cradled in the isle's soft lap;
Canes clothe with waving wealth the smiling land;
The rural powers their hands exulting clap;
Havens, with dark hulls speck'd, indent the strand,
And towns, and bristling forts, emboss the silver sand.

From *The Caraguin*

Angelica has gain'd the dell; –
The Sybil quits her cane-thatch'd cell.
A coarse grey blanket-coat is braced
With hempen cord around her waist:
Around her shaking head is roll'd
A dingy turban's tatter'd fold;
'Neath which, contrasting with her hue,
Lumps of white wool show scant and few;
And on her turban's topmost round
A broad low hat of straw is bound.
Each wrist, and ankle, wears its ring
Of white and talismanic string,

Powerful to shelter by its charm
Each member from disease or harm.
Carved birds, and flowers, deep-scarr'd, bedeck
Her temples sunk, and wrinkled neck; –
O'er shrunken lip, and sharpen'd chin,
Straggled long bristles, white and thin;
And her gaunt form, with age low-bent,
Upon a snake-mark'd Staff she leant: –
Tradition dim of those old rods
To serpents turn'd by Pharaoh's gods,
When his false priests would madly try
In miracles with heaven to vie.

The sable dame was far renown'd;
The terror of the hamlets round;
Their oracle to learn Fate's will,
Their refuge in impending ill.
For her dark sorceries had force
To stay disease's cankering course,
Or cause foul pestilence and blight –
Where'er her hatred fell – to light.

[*Before answering Angelica's request for help in her
mistress's love affair, Mimba relates her own history:*]

Her answer, couch'd in barbarous phrase,
This sense, interpreted, conveys.
'Mistress,' she said, 'the Black Man's God
Conferr'd on me the snake-mark'd Rod.
Where Benin laves the fruitful plain,
King Toko held his ample reign.
Of all that throng'd the regal gate,
Seers, warriors, and men of state,
My Father, high above the rest,
With kingly preference was blest.
Priest of the Serpent, – his the power
To utter the propitious hour
When the conjunction of the stars
Favour'd premeditated wars,
Or when they sign'd those wars to cease,
And great Orissa will'd – Be peace!
The Harvest's wealth, too, he foretold,

And what ships from the white man's King
Would come, that year, for slaves and gold,
And what rich presents they would bring.
And nought did Toko undertake
Ere counsell'd by the mighty Snake.
That Father did to me impart
Some myst'ries of his sacred art;
And gave me an affianced bride
To him for whom alone I sigh'd,
A noble youth, the King's third son,
Who all my youthful heart had won.
My Mistress, — yes! — devouring years
Have long drank dry the spring of tears,
Yet never does the name of love,
Like whisper'd music from above,
Strike these dull ears, but o'er me gush
Old memories with impetuous rush; —
Dear shadows of the blissful past!
Of rapture too divine to last! —
I loved with the intense desire
Which thrills the Ethiop's breast of fire;
But, as I chanced, one day, to swim
On the wide river's dimpled brim,
Where the broad lotus screen'd the stream
From noon's intolerable beam,
And fig-trees spread their bowery shade,
A hostile tribe in ambuscade
Seized me, far distant from relief,
And bore me fetter'd to their Chief.
On amorous design intent,
The Royal Veil he quickly sent.
His passion I indignant spurn'd;
And love was soon to vengeance turn'd.
Death would have been my instant fate,
But Avarice prevail'd o'er hate:
Sold for a Slave, full threescore years
I've steep'd my bitter bread in tears;
The arts, my awful father taught,
Sole solace of my aching thought.'

HENRY DALTON

The Emigrant Ship

Her sails are spread, and colours flying,
   Music's strains are in the air;
But heavy hearts on board are sighing,
   As they hide their misery there.

The breeze is fair, the sun is shining,
   Nature smiling with delight;
The human heart alone repining,
   Forc'd from home to take its flight.

The birds around are singing sweetly,
   Flow'rs their perfumed fragrance shed;
The parting hour is passing fleetly,
   'Tis like parting with the dead.

The crowded decks are harshly creaking,
   With the numbers gathered there;
Friends in confusion friends are seeking,
   Each the woes of each to share.

And there is manly honest parting,
   Such as brave hearts only show;
And feelings bitter and disheart'ning,
   Such as lorn hearts only know.

The hour arrives, – 'Tis time for sailing, –
   See the rushing to and fro!
Here female voices loudly wailing,
   There the deeply hidden woe.

'Goodbye!' a thousand times is utter'd,
   'Heav'n bless you!' breath'd forth in tears,
The mournful benediction mutter'd
   By some patriarch in years.

Again, again, the hands are shaking,
   Friends are clasp'd in last embrace,
And the old parents' hearts are breaking,
   Turning from their children's face.

Relations now must part for ever,
   Torn from hearts they loved so well;
Alas! life's dearest ties they sever,
   When they breathe that word farewell.

The ship is on the ocean bounding,
   Friends their hands wave o'er and o'er;
And sorrow's accents loud are sounding,
   As that ship sails from the shore.

HORATIO NELSON HUGGINS

From *Hiroona*

From The Introduction

The clear transparent sea with light,
Which poured from sun in noon-day height,
Was full. In gradient depths below,
In sun-illumined brilliance, glow,
(Ablaze in every gorgeous hue
From molten gold to azure blue),
A thousand scaly forms of life
In peaceful rest, or playful strife.
And as the astonished eye passed through
One group, another came in view
In lower depths; and lower yet
The sheen and glow of others met
Th' unwearied eye, to view displayed
In living strata, grade o'er grade;
And ever where, beyond the view
The peerless light but just pierced through,
Some finny one would catch the beam,
And flash in momentary gleam.

On scenes of life and peace like these
In sky, in air, in teeming seas,
Yon glorious orb would daily rise:
And ah! 'twas surely Paradise
As yet in those primeval seas!
Not yet the keel of Genoese –
Grown now through new-born science bold,
In greed of fame and fabled gold,
Adrift from old exhausted world,
With sail to untried winds unfurled –
Had thrust profane intruding prow
O'er those fair seas, so sacred now
To plenty and to solitude,
To waken with awakening rude!

But now the fatal keels draw near
With freight of misery and despair,
To fray these islands of the sun
With darkest deeds that e'er were done,
Colon! thyself a righteous man,
Ah! could thine eye prophetic scan
The vista dark of coming years –
The wrongs, and agonies, and tears,
The black man's chains, the red man's ban,
That follow fast thy leading van –
Thyself, appalled, would surely shrink
As from some dreadful crime's dark brink;
Or, on thy knees, at least thy tears
Would mingle freely with thy prayers!

Canto XII, §§ 23–6

'But mark you well the words I say,
There comes, and quickly comes a day
When England's heel shall spurn these isles;
Although she lavish now her smiles
And spend her treasure and her blood
Shall deem them worthless, past all good;
Shall deem their keep not worth the cost;
Her millions spent shall reckon lost;
Regard West Indian tutelage
Not worth a single soldier's wage.
Abandoned all in sheer disgust,
Her stores and guns shall rot and rust,
Her battlements in slow decay
Uncared shall crumble day by day.
Your heartless Mother shall recall
Her best and wealthiest sons, and all
Shall quit the fated land who may –
Except the wretch who needs must stay:
All quit this god-forsaken shore
Where faith and hope are known no more.

Scared hence, as from some deadly sink
Affrighted capital shall shrink.

And enterprise starved out shall die;
What gold remains find wings and fly;
And princely commerce frayed away,
Poor drivelling trade alone shall stay.
Your bravest efforts shall be checked
By cold contempt or stern neglect,
Or crushed by unjust, cruel laws –
For England's lion has its claws!
Ah! wronged Hiroon, my country, then
Shall Heaven be known as just – white men
Flung forth from thee, O ocean gem,
As we are now flung forth by them!
Your very negro-slaves shall gain
Their freedom, fling away the chain
And claim to shake you by the hand,
And strut your equals in the land:
Ay! revolution strange and new,
Become its lord and master too.

Ha! ha! great *Bondieu* gives me eyes
To see what in the future lies;
And on them visions vast have broke.
See! See! yon mountain burst in smoke
And flame, which fiercely leaps and flays,
And all the mountain's sides ablaze:
No earthly flames! for see they spurn
The forest trees – 'tis rocks that burn!
And fire rolls down the mountain's side
And streams of flame like rivers glide.
And while the fiery torrents pour
Tremendous peals of thunder roar;
And up leaps lightning everywhere:
Vile smells of sulphur choke the air
Deep down its sides the mountain moans,
In pain and loud unearthly groans.
And all the hills round quake with fear
At th'agony of dread Souffrière.
And while the fierce, terrific glow
Fills all with hellish glare below
Above no sky is seen o'erhead;
But heavy mass of darkness spread,

'Gainst which the demon flames in hate
Spring up but cannot penetrate;
Through which no opening cleft is riven
To let descend one smile from Heaven.
The very sun sends through no light;
But for th'unearthly glare, 'twere night!
Such night above such glare below,
'Twould seem the gods had meant it so –
'Twixt heaven and earth such barrier thrown
As left the earth to hell alone!
Yet deathlier shudderings through me thrill
And horrors crowd on horrors still!
See! Can it be? God! can we trust
Our startled senses? yet we must!
See! Heaven no longer pours its rain
To bless the thirsty waiting plain;
But from that lurid darkness pour
Such showers as none e'er knew before
Of stones and rocks, and dust and mud
Which strike the earth with heavy thud:
Trees, houses perish, and not least
Your harvests – perish man and beast.

Confusion, terror and dismay!
Hiroona never saw such day.
And yet that day yourselves shall see;
And when it comes remember me:
Accept it as a pledge that all
That I foretell you shall befall
Hiroon – but now Hiroon no more
Since all her sons have left her shore –
All come to pass and nothing fail.'

EGBERT MARTIN

Trade

Some talk of trade as low and mean,
    Believing worth the patent right
Of him who guides the pen, or e'en
    Of him who glasses nature's light.
While art and written language tell
    The spirit portion of God's earth,
The tradesman hath its task as well,
    As noble and as full of worth.

The flaccid coxcomb we behold
    Like some abortive work of fate,
In unctuous folds of fashion rolled:
    Can he with truth be titled *great*?
Can he whose heart hath never thrilled
    One moment at another's pain;
One kindly action never willed
    Can *he* deserve the poet's strain?

And yet, with empty gaze and mien,
    A blushless cheek and voidless head,
Such will despise the tradesman seen
    Hard toiling for his daily bread.
Look! if you would behold the man,
    Whom God and nature crown a king,
A wide-earth noble would you scan?
    Behold him in some better thing.

Bold front whose eyes give way to none,
    Clean, honest hands tho' hard and black; –
Kind voice and free, tho' harsh of tone,
    Of ill, a share; of joy, no lack.
If such be found, to him all praise,
    Be he the lowest, vilest clown;
All honour, homage, reverence raise
    With words of light his manhood crown.

National Anthem

And, like a bird at rest
In her own ample nest,
    Let Britain close
Far-reaching wings and strong
O'er her colonial throng,
Guard, keep and shield them long
    From all their foes.

While o'er the Empire's bound
The Sun shall skirt his round,
    Shining serene
On one broad amity
Holding from sea to sea
Free rule and subjects free:
    God save the Queen.

THOMAS MacDERMOT

From *San Gloria*

From Columbus's soliloquy

A dark foreboding haunts me lest I die
Amid the careless beauty of this isle,
And these great heights, blue – forest-garmented,
That wave slow signals to the mighty deep,
Callous to smaller things, across my grave
Stare; while the green things tangle on the plain;
While the soft waters lip the sandy shore;
While dawns, arriving, spread their crimson flags;
And passing day gives all her tents to fire,
Seeking a new encampment; doves will coo
When, into deep oblivion sunk, my grave
Lies in the flood of life that blots out all,
While the great hills stare on, o'er shrub and vine,
Heeding my resting-place and me no more
Than slow grey lichens heed the rock they stain,
Or this huge trunk they moisten to decay.

Cuba

(What the heart of the Jamaican said to Cuba in 1895)

Sister! the sundering Sea
   Divides us not from thee,
The Ocean's homeless roar
   May sever shore from shore;
Beneath the bitter brine,
   Our hand is locked in thine.
Cold custom chides us down
   And stills us with a frown;
But we like lovers twain
   Are one in joy and pain,

Whose mutual love is known
  But may not yet be shown.
With clasped hands we convey
  The love we may not say.

A Market Basket in the Car

Why? doan't I pay me car-fare?
  Tuppence – same fe we two?
What you da mek you face for?
  You tink I is frighten fe you?

Because you Mudda see duppy
  So put whitey wash in you 'kin,
Seems as you tink you is Buckra;
  You nigga man – ugly no sin.

Doan dare you to come yah so push me,
  As in a dis car I is sit;
I pay me fare an I tell you
  De Gubbena self wouden fit

To come yah and f'erancing wid me,
  When I doan brek none o him rule;
Doan liard, nor tief, nor obeah;
  An keep all me pickney a school.

What you is saying? – O! 'nuttin'
  Dat is jus' what suiting you – Hi!
Keep grumblin an saying you 'Nuttin',
  While I drop you out a me eye.

DONALD McDONALD

A Song of Those Who Died

Think not of these as dead, the brave young souls,
Flashed into Life, not Death, when at the touch
Of England's need, they, putting all aside,
Counted their very lives as not too much
          To give for England.

Think not of these as dead, brave lives live on
In loving hearts, until those hearts are still,
And these who gave themselves at England's call,
Live on and share in England's life, and will
          Be part of England.

As tiny fibres bound and bound around
Each other, forming cables strong that hold
The greatest ships, so each who gave his all,
And brought to England's need a courage bold,
          Is part of England.

And so, while only to the hearts that loved,
Their names and worth are known, they have their part
With those, the great, who carried England on,
Guarding all down the years with strength of heart
          The name of England.

And ever through the years that are to come,
Our little Isle may speak of these with pride,
As those of us who took their place and died,
In England's hour of stress, and stand beside
          The great of England.

Breakfast in Bed (Influenza in War-time)

Breakfast in bed – how it conjures up visions
Of comfort, and leisure, and freedom from care,
There we can settle the Nation's dilemmas,
Plan all the wonderful things we would dare.

How we can feel for the chaps in the trenches,
Or talk of the horrors at sea – which we've read
Out of the papers, that lie all around us –
While we are having our breakfast in bed.

There with our bacon we settle the submarine,
Then with our toast we can toast to our Fleet;
Drinking our tea, we will drink to our Army,
How we would like these brave fellows to meet.

Next for War-work we commend the war-workers,
Glorious work they have done – so we've read,
So many things still we'd bring to their notice –
If we were not having breakfast in bed.

Shorter food rations we'd mention to Rhondda,
'Save or starve' maxims we have by the score,
Let us be up and encourage the people
(Kidneys and marmalade, please for some more).

'Greater activity, Army and Navy,
Statesmen, Munitioners,' that's what we've said;
(How we can preach of the beauty of energy
While we are having our breakfast in bed).

A Citizen of – the World

A reply to 'Le sans Patrie' of Madame Edith Dunaew, the
Russian authoress and traveller

Why vex thy soul that never Nations claim thee?
No homeland stirs thy pulses, cheers thy heart?
Throughout the world there's many who will need thee,
On every land a chance to play thy part.

To brighten lives that need the human brightness
Of thy young life, of thy strong will and power,
No land without its chances, love and pity
Will find a place to work in every hour.

A world-wide citizen thy claim may then be,
A prouder title than a nation gives,
One that makes life a very happy living
And leaves behind a memory dear that lives.

ALFRED CRUICKSHANK

God or Mammon

The fees! The fees! The mighty fees!
Is there anything else we crave as these?
At the gates of heaven, on the brink of hell,
There's a kick in the fees that pleases us well!
How they shake our knees! How they bend our necks,
And laugh at the buckler of Creeds and Sects!
Say, masters, say, for you must know,
Which way does the wind of Virtue blow?
See, Mammon smiles with a gracious nod,
And the second-fiddle is played by God!

In Church and State, in home and school,
Go get the fees! is the only rule;
Go get the fees! Get all you can,
To the measure and worth of every man!
Go make them fly! Go keep them high!
For the under dogs must pay or buy!
Say, masters, say, for you must know,
Which way does the wind of Virtue blow?
See, Mammon smiles with a gracious nod,
And the second-fiddle is played by God!

The under dogs with nought to sell
But brawn and sinews! It is well –
This scheme of things, so beautiful!
These trodden things, so dutiful!
They make your heaven, you make their hell,
The under dogs! – Oh, it is well!
Say, masters, say, for you must know,
Which way does the wind of Justice blow?
See, Mammon smiles with a gracious nod,
And the second-fiddle is played by God!

The under dogs! Oh, the under dogs!
The stepping stones of the demagogues,
Who, as they climb to a state of grace,
Leave the under dogs in the same old place,

In a scheme of things like a grinding mill
That crunches and crushes and grinds them still!
Say, masters, say, for you must know,
Which way does the wind of Justice blow?
See, Mammon smiles with a gracious nod,
And the second-fiddle is played by God!

Let Us Be Frank

Let us be frank and tell ourselves the truth.
To talk of Brotherhood in prose or rhyme
Is to deceive ourselves, to waste our time.
Love, justice, virtue, sacrifice – forsooth!
Are we not all still red in claw and tooth? –
A million years up from the ooze and slime
Climbing to God on stepping-stones of crime!
Let us be frank! Why palter with the truth?
Ah me! I shrink into myself with fear
When, in the silent hours of night,
Dreaming on life, again I seem to hear
The shrieks of babes and virgins in affright
Rising amidst the roar of bomb and shell
Wherewith we serve the God we love so well!

The Convict Song

Hard stones! Hard stones!
My manhood draining!
The light in me is waning
        Hard stones!
To lead me from the path of sin,
You make a hell and shut me in,
        Hard stones!

Hard stones! Hard stones!
My heart is breaking!
My flesh the sun is baking,
        Hard stones!

You drag my spirit in the dust;
You rob me of my human trust,
    Hard stones!

Hard stones! Hard stones!
My limbs are aching!
The beast in me is waking!
    Hard stones!
You make of me a shameless thing;
You make of me a tameless thing,
    Hard stones!

Hard stones! Hard stones!
My soul is moaning!
You hear my spirit groaning,
    Hard stones!
But from this hell when I come through,
I shall be harder far than you,
    Hard stones!

W. ADOLPHE ROBERTS

On a Monument to Martí

Cuba, dishevelled, naked to the waist,
Springs up erect from the dark earth and screams
Her joy in liberty. The metal gleams
Where her chains broke. Magnificent her haste
To charge into battle and to taste
Revenge on the oppressor. Thus she seems.
But, she were powerless without the dreams
Of him who stands above, unsmiling, chaste;
Yes, over Cuba on her jubilant way
Broods the Apostle, José Julian Martí.
He shaped her course of glory, and the day
The guns first spoke he died to make her free.
That night a meteor flamed in splendid loss
Between the North Star and the Southern Cross.

Peacocks

They came from Persia to the sacred way
    And rode in Pompey's triumph, side by side
    With odalisques and idols, plumes flung wide,
A flame of gems in the chill Roman day.
They that were brought as captives came to stay,
    To flaunt in beauty, mystery and pride,
    To preen before the emperors deified,
Symbols of their magnificent decay.
Then there was madness and a scourge of swords;
    Imperial purple mouldered into dust.
But the immortal peacocks stung new lords
    To furies of insatiable lust.
Contemptuous, they loitered on parade –
Live opals, rubies, sardonyx and jade.

The Maroon Girl

I see her on a lonely forest track,
Her level brows made salient by the sheen
Of flesh the hue of cinnamon. The clean
Blood of the hunted, vanished Arawak
Flows in her veins with blood of white and black.
Maternal, noble-breasted in her mien;
She is a peasant, yet she is a queen.
She is Jamaica poised against attack.
Her woods are hung with orchids; the still flame
Of red hibiscus lights her path, and starred
With orange and coffee blossoms is her yard.
Fabulous, pitted mountains close the frame.
She stands on ground for which her fathers died;
Figure of savage beauty, figure of pride.

A Valediction

Before the seas again divide
    And another page be turned,
Let these three things be written down,
    Reborn from days gone by:
The peak that rose through the morning mist;
    The firefly flames that burned;
And the Southern Cross in the hills of home,
    Hung low in a velvet sky.

CLAUDE McKAY

Fetchin Water

Watch how dem touris' like fe look
  Out pon me little daughter,
Wheneber fe her tu'n to cook
  Or fetch a pan of water:
    De sight look gay;
    Dat is one way,
    But I can tell you say,
Nuff rock'tone in de sea, yet none
But those pon lan' know 'bouten sun.

De pickny comin up de hill,
  Fightin wid heavy gou'd,
Won't say it sweet him, but he will
  Complain about de load:
    Him feel de weight,
    Dem watch him gait;
    It's so some of de great
High people fabour t'ink it sweet
Fe batter in de boilin heat.

Dat boy wid de karasene pan,
  Sulky down to him toe,
His back was rollin in a san',
  For him pa mek him crow:
    Him feel it bad,
    Near mek him mad,
    But teach him he's a lad;
Go disobey him fader wud,
When he knows dat his back would sud!

But Sarah Jane she wus 'an all,
  For she t'row way de pan,
An jam her back agains de wall
  Fe fight her mumma Fan:
    Feelin de pinch,
    She mek a wrinch

An get way; but de wench
Try fe put shame upon her ma,
Say dat she cook de bittle raw.

Dis water-fetchin sweet dem though
   When dey mek up dem min',
An nuff o dem 'tart out fe go,
    An de weader is fine:
      De pan might leak,
      Dem don't a 'peak,
      Nor eben try fe seek
Some clay or so to mek it soun';
Dem don't care ef dem wet all roun'.

Den all 'bout de road dem 'catter
   Marchin along quite at ease;
Dat time listen to deir chatter,
   Talkin anyt'ing dem please:
      Dem don't a fear,
      Neider a care,
      For who can interfere?
T'ree mile – five, six tu'n, – an neber
W'ary, but could do it for eber.

Subway Wind

Far down, down through the city's great gaunt gut
   The gray train rushing bears the weary wind;
In the packed cars the fans the crowd's breath cut,
   Leaving the sick and heavy air behind.
And pale-cheeked children seek the upper door
   To give their summer jackets to the breeze;
Their laugh is swallowed in the deafening roar
   Of captive wind that moans for fields and seas;
Seas cooling warm where native schooners drift
   Through sleepy waters, while gulls wheel and sweep,
Waiting for windy waves the keels to lift
   Lightly among the islands of the deep;
Islands of lofty palm trees blooming white
   That lend their perfume to the tropic sea,

Where fields lie idle in the dew-drenched night,
   And the Trades float above them fresh and free.

The White House

Your door is shut against my tightened face,
And I am sharp as steel with discontent;
But I possess the courage and the grace
To bear my anger proudly and unbent.
The pavement slabs burn loose beneath my feet,
A chafing savage, down the decent street;
And passion rends my vitals as I pass,
Where boldly shines your shuttered door of glass.
Oh, I must search for wisdom every hour,
Deep in my wrathful bosom sore and raw,
And find in it the superhuman power
To hold me to the letter of your law!
Oh, I must keep my heart inviolate
Against the potent poison of your hate.

If We Must Die

If we must die, let it not be like hogs
Hunted and penned in an inglorious spot,
While round us bark the mad and hungry dogs,
Making their mock at our accursed lot.
If we must die, O let us nobly die,
So that our precious blood may not be shed
In vain; then even the monsters we defy
Shall be constrained to honour us though dead!
O kinsmen! we must meet the common foe!
Though far outnumbered let us show us brave,
And for their thousand blows deal one deathblow!
What though before us lies the open grave?
Like men we'll face the murderous, cowardly pack,
Pressed to the wall, dying, but fighting back!

Baptism

Into the furnace let me go alone;
Stay you without in terror of the heat.
I will go naked in – for thus 'tis sweet –
Into the weird depths of the hottest zone.
I will not quiver in the frailest bone,
You will not note a flicker of defeat;
My heart shall tremble not its fate to meet,
My mouth give utterance to any moan.
The yawning oven spits forth fiery spears;
Red aspish tongues shout wordlessly my name.
Desire destroys, consumes my mortal fears,
Transforming me into a shape of flame.
I will come out, back to your world of tears,
A stronger soul within a finer frame.

JEAN RHYS

Our Gardener

I thought Ken a nice man
Ken was a pal
His other name's Taylor
My name's Sal

This happened yesterday
We were all there
I was sitting
In a grown-up chair

Dad had his camera
Back to the light
Ken was pottering
Out of sight

Dad called to Mummy
Picking flowers in the sun
Dad said 'ready?'
She said 'wait until I've done'

Ken came softly smiling
Cutlass in his hand
I thought a new game
Isn't he grand

Then he swung his cutlass
Struck Daddy's head
Blood came pouring out
Red, red, red

Ken struck a second time
Dad groaned and fell
He raised his head and looked at me
Then fell back and lay still

Mum didn't scream at all
Nor did I
Couldn't if I'd wanted to
Throat too dry

But she let the flowers fall
'Oh no' I heard her say
I saw the roses
Blowing away

She screamed when he hit her
Loud and shrill
Went on screaming .
I can hear her still

People came running
Ken didn't look round
He laughed as he was striking
Mum on the ground

Went on laughing
And this is what he said
'White flesh, white flesh'
Talking to my Mother, dead

This happened yesterday
It was still light
First comes sunset
Then comes night.

Obeah Night

A night I seldom remember
   (If it can be helped)
The night I saw Love's dark face
   Was Love's dark face
'And cruel as he is'? I've never known that
   I tried my best you may be certain (whoever asks)
   My human best

If the next morning as I looked at what I'd done
(He was watching us mockingly, used to these games)
If I'd stared back at him
If I'd said
'I was a god myself last night
I've tamed and changed a wild girl'

Or taken my hurt darling in my arms
(Conquered at last. And silent. Mine)

Perhaps Love would have smiled then
   Shown us the way
Across that sea. They say it's strewn with wrecks
   And weed-infested
Few dare it, fewer still escape
But *we*, led by smiling Love
We could have sailed
   Reached a safe harbour
Found a sweet, brief heaven
   Lived our short lives

But I was both sick and sad
   (Night always ends)
She was a stranger
Wearing the mask of pain
Bearing the marks of pain –
I turned away – Traitor
Too sane to face my madness (or despair)
   Far, far too cold and sane

Then Love, relenting
Sent clouds and soft rain
Sent sun, light and shadow
   To show me again
Her young face waiting
Waiting for comfort and a gentler lover?
   (You'll not find him)
A kinder loving? *Love is not kind*
I would not look at her
(Once is enough)
Over my dead love
Over a sleeping girl
I drew a sheet
Cover the stains of tears
Cover the marks of blood
(You can say nothing
That I have not said a thousand times and one
Excepting this – That night was Something Else
I was Angry Love Himself
Blind fierce avenging Love – no other that night)

'It's too strong for Béké'
   The black woman said
Love, hate or jealousy
   Which had she seen?
She knew well – the *Devil*!
– What it could mean

How can I forget you Antoinette
   When the spring is here?
Where did you hide yourself

After that shameless, shameful night?
And why come back? Hating and hated?
Was it Love, Fear, Hoping?
Or (as always) Pain?
(*Did* you come back I wonder
Did I ever see you again?)

No. I'll lock that door
Forget it. –
The motto was 'Locked Hearts I open
   I have the heavy key'
Written in black letters
Under a Royal Palm Tree
On a slave owner's gravestone
'Look! And look again, hypocrite' he says
   'Before *you* judge *me*'

I'm no damn slave owner
I have no slave
Didn't she (forgiven) betray me
Once more – and then again
Unrepentant – laughing?
I can soon show her
   Who hates the best
Always she answers me
   I will hate last

Lost, lovely Antoinette
How can I forget you
When the spring comes?
(Spring is cold and furtive here
There's a different rain)
Where did you hide yourself

After the obeah nights?
(*What* did you send instead?
   Hating and hated?)
Where did you go?
I'll never see you now
I'll never know
For you left me – my truest Love
Long ago

Edward Rochester or Raworth
Written in Spring 1842

FRANK COLLYMORE

Ballad of an Old Woman

There was an old woman who never was wed;
Of twenty-one children was she brought to bed,
      Singing Glory to God.

She gave them all her poor means could afford
And brought them all up in the Fear of the Lord,
      Singing Glory to God.

As soon as they grew up, each sailed away,
One after the other to the great U.S.A.,
      Singing Glory to God.

Sometimes they thought of her, sometimes they wrote,
Sometimes they sent her a five dollar note:
      Singing Glory to God.

And when in the course of the long waiting years
The letters ceased coming, she dried her tears,
      Singing Glory to God.

And when the old shed-roof collapsed from decay
She went to the Almshouse and walked all the way,
      Singing Glory to God.

And there she mothered many motherless brats
Who slept on her shoulder and pulled at her plaits,
      Singing Glory to God.

Then one day she sickened and next day she died;
They brought out the hearse and put her inside
      Singing Glory to God.

Only weeds and nettles spring up from her clay
Who is one with the Night and the Light of the Day.
      Singing Glory to God.

Monkeys

I think it quite a charming myth
That monkeys are our kin and kith;
But I've never yet met a Monkey who
Was pleased to entertain this view.

Triptych

I see these ancestors of ours:
The merchants, the adventurers, the youngest sons of
    squires,
Leaving the city and the shires and the seaports,
Eager to establish a temporary home and make a fortune
In the new lands beyond the West, pawning perhaps
The old familiar acres or the assured competence;
Sturdy, realist, eager to wring wealth from these Barbadoes
And to build, trade, colonize, pay homage to their King,
And worship according to the doctrines of the Church of
    England.

I see these ancestors of ours
Torn from the hills and dales of their motherland,
Weeping, hoping in the mercy of time to return
To farm and holding, shuttle and loom, to return
In snow or rain or shine to humble homes, their own;
Cursing the day they were cheated by rebel standards,
Or betrayed for their country's honour; fearing
The unknown land, the fever and the hurricane,
The swamp and jungle – all the travellers' tales.

I see them, these ancestors of ours;
Children of the tribe, ignorant of their doom, innocent
As cattle, bartered for, captured, beaten, penned,
Cattle of the slave-ship, less than cattle;
Sold in the market-place, yoked to servitude;
Cattle, bruised and broken, but strong enough to plough and
    breed,
And promised white man's heaven where they sing,
Fill lamps with oil nor wait the Bridegroom's coming;
Raise chorused voices in the hymn of praise.

J. E. CLARE McFARLANE

On National Vanity

Slowly we learn; the oft repeated line
Lingers a little moment and is gone;
Nation on nation follows, sun on sun.
With empire's dust fate builds her great design,
But we are blind and see not; in our pride
We strain toward the petrifying mound
To sit above our fellows, and we ride
The slow and luckless toiler to the ground.
Fools are we for our pains; whom we despise,
Last come, shall mount our withered vanities,
Topmost to sit upon the vast decay
Of time and temporal things – for, last or first,
The proud array of pictured bubbles burst,
Mirages of their glory pass away.

PHILIP SHERLOCK

Jamaican Fisherman

Across the sand I saw a black man stride
To fetch his fishing gear and broken things,
And silently that splendid body cried
Its proud descent from ancient chiefs and kings,
Across the sand I saw him naked stride;
Sang his black body in the sun's white light
The velvet coolness of dark forests wide,
The blackness of the jungle's starless night.
He stood beside the old canoe which lay
Upon the beach; swept up within his arms
The broken nets and careless lounged away
Towards his wretched hut . . .   •
Nor knew how fiercely spoke his body then
Of ancient wealth and savage regal men.

Pocomania

Long Mountain, rise,
Lift you' shoulder, blot the moon.
Black the stars, hide the skies,
Long Mountain, rise, lift you' shoulder high.

Black of skin and white of gown
Black of night and candle light
White against the black of trees
And altar white against the gloom,
Black of mountain high up there
Long Mountain, rise,
Lift you' shoulder, blot the moon,
Black the stars, black the sky.

Africa among the trees
Asia with her mysteries

Weaving white in flowing gown
Black Long Mountain looking down
Sees the shepherd and his flock
Dance and sing and wisdom mock,
Dance and sing and falls away
All the civilized today
Dance and sing and fears let loose;
Here the ancient gods that choose
Man for victim, man for hate
Man for sacrifice to fate
Hate and fear and madness black
Dance before the altar white
Comes the circle closer still
Shepherd weave your pattern old
Africa among the trees
Asia with her mysteries.

Black of night and white of gown
White of altar, black of trees
'Swing de circle wide again
Fall and cry me sister now
Let de spirit come again
Fling away de flesh an' bone
Let de spirit have a home.'

Grunting low and in the dark
White of gown and circling dance
Gone today and all control
Now the dead are in control
Power of the past returns
Africa among the trees
Asia with her mysteries.

Black the stars, hide the sky
Lift you' shoulder, blot the moon.
Long Mountain, rise.

Dinner Party 1940

'Do you mind the news while we eat?'
    So guests assenting
The well-bred voice from Daventry
Mingled with sounds from the pantry
And slowly through the ether spilled
Its syllables . . . not silencing
      augmenting
The show of wit which never fails
Thanks to 7.30 cock-tails . . . 'and at Narvik
  Where for five days a storm has raged
  a few were killed . . .'
'More mutton, Alice?' 'Yes, it's delicious, dear,
Yesterday at bridge I held three aces, three . . .'
     'in the Baltic
  it is reported from Stockholm that the
      soldiers fled
  leaving a number of dead' . . .
'But don't you like it cold with guava-jelly?'

The well-bred voice from Daventry
Did not grow less well-bred
And did not speak of more than three or four hundred dead,
And did not really silence the sounds from the pantry
  Or the show of wit which never fails
  Thanks to 7.30 cock-tails.

Cold mutton is delicious with guava-jelly
And does not seriously incommode
Like cold lead in the belly.

A Beauty Too of Twisted Trees

  A beauty too of twisted trees
  The harsh insistence of the wind
  Writes lines of loveliness within
  The being of this tortured trunk.
  I know that some there are that spring
  In effortless perfection still,

No beauty there of twisted trees
Of broken branch and tortured trunk
And knotted root that thrusts its way
Impatient of the clinging clay.

John who leapt in the womb has fled
Into the desert to waken the dead,
His naked body broken and torn
Knows nothing now of Bethlehem's peace,
And wild of mood and fierce of face
He strives alone in that lonely place.
Ezekiel too saw the dry bones live
The flames and smoke and conflicts give
A lightning flash to the dead man's sight
And Moses smote the rock, no rock
In a weary cactus-land to mock
Hollow men stuffed with straw, but a rock
That freely pours from its riven side
Water for those who else had died . . .

And hangs on a twisted tree
A broken body for those who see,
All the world, for those who see
Hangs its hope on a twisted tree.
And the broken branch and the tortured trunk
Are the stubborn evidence of growth
And record proud of strife, of life.

A beauty too of twisted trees.

UNA MARSON

Kinky Hair Blues

Gwine find a beauty shop
Cause I ain't a belle.
Gwine find a beauty shop
Cause I ain't a lovely belle.
The boys pass me by,
They say I's not so swell.

See oder young gals
So slick and smart.
See dose oder young gals
So slick and smart.
I jes gwine die on de shelf
If I don't mek a start.

I hate dat ironed hair
And dat bleaching skin.
Hate dat ironed hair
And dat bleaching skin.
But I'll be all alone
If I don't fall in.

Lord 'tis you did gie me
All dis kinky hair.
'Tis you did gie me
All dis kinky hair,
And I don't envy gals
What got dose locks so fair.

I like me black face
And me kinky hair.
I like me black face
And me kinky hair.
But nobody loves dem,
I jes don't tink it's fair.

Now I's gwine press me hair
And bleach me skin.

I's gwine press me hair
And bleach me skin.
What won't a gal do
Some kind of man to win.

Brown Baby Blues

I got a brown baby
Sweet as she can be.
I got a brown baby
Sweet as she can be.
But she ain't got no papa,
Cause he's gone to sea.

I love me baby
But she don't got no name.
I love me baby
She don't got no name.
Well wha' fe do,
Dat is not her shame.

Maybe she'll ask me
Why I is so black,
Maybe she'll ask me
Why I is so black,
An' she's so brown;
Lord, send her papa back.

My sweet brown baby
Don't you cry.
My sweet brown baby
Don't you cry.
Your mamma does love you
And you colour is high.

Gettin de Spirit

Lord gie you chile de spirit
Let her shout
Lord gie you chile de power
An let her pray –
Hallelujah – Amen –
Shout sister – shout –
God is sen you His spirit
Shout – sister – shout.

Shout sister – shout –
Hallelujah – Amen.
Can't you feel de spirit
Shout sister – shout
Hallelujah – Amen.

Join de chorus,
We feel it flowing o'er us –
You is no chile of satan
So get de spirit
And shout – sister – shout –
Hallelujah – Amen –
Shout – Sister – Shout!

Politeness

They tell us
That our skin is black
But our hearts are white.

We tell them
That their skin is white
But their hearts are black.

To Wed or Not to Wed

To wed, or not to wed: that is the question:
Whether 'tis nobler in the mind to suffer
The fret and loneliness of spinsterhood
Or to take arms against the single state
And by marrying, end it? To wed; to match,
No more; yet by this match to say we end
The heartache and the thousand natural shocks
That flesh is heir to; 'tis a consummation
Devoutly to be wish'd. To wed, to match;
To match, perchance mismatch: aye, there's the rub;
For in that match what dread mishaps may come,
When we have shuffled off this single state
For wedded bliss: there's the respect
That makes singleness of so long life,
For who'd forgo the joys of wife and mother,
The pleasures of devotion, of sacrifice and love
The blessings of a home and all home means,
The restful sympathy of soul to soul,
The loved ones circling round at eventide
When she herself might gain all these
With a marriage vow? Who would fardels bear
To pine and sigh under a single life
But that the dread of something after marriage,
That undiscovered nature, from whose ways
One scarce can sever, puzzles the will,
And makes us rather cling to single bliss
Than barter that we know for things unsure?
Thus dreadful doubt makes cowards of us all
And thus the native hue of resolution
Is sicklied o'er with the pale cast of thought,
And matrimonial rites, and wedded life
With this regard their currents turn awry
And lose the name of action.

(With apologies to Shakespeare)

Repose

Return, my heart, from wandering afar
Where tempests toss thy unpretentious bark,
Rest thee content to muse upon a star,
At dawn to hear the music of the lark.
Stay home and half forget the prisoned pain
That will not have thee rest in settled peace,
The simple joys of life thou canst retain,
From storms of ocean thou wilt find release;
Rest, then, my heart, thou knowest but too well
How strong and fierce relentless winds can blow;
How frail thy bark when tempests round thee swell,
How thou dost need the peace thou wouldst forgo:
For hearts do not upon the wild rocks break;
They only know deep hurt and ache on ache.

VIVIAN VIRTUE

Waifs

They shout no stranger, troublous news
Along the heedless street
Than wrongs their own loud page abuse,
The starveling waifs who cannot choose
But barter soul for bread:
Ragged, unkempt, uncouth,
Orphaned of joy and youth.

And yet their Nazarene Brother said,
Who had not where to lay His head,
Their angels in the highest place
Always behold the Father's face.

Nomads without a tribe or name,
Wild Ishmaels of the street,
They wander, whom Crime waits to claim . . .
Upon the highways of our shame
How urgently they spread
The warnings of our doom
Who still deny them room!

For better on our necks, said He,
A mill-stone and the swallowing sea,
Than to be cause of least offence
To one young spirit's innocence.

The Hour

This crowded night my People's kindling pride
Is one with all the thronging stars that dart
Their crystal lightnings down the uttermost part
Of brave Jamaican skies. Here in the wide
Embrace of Freedom met to stem a tide
Of tyranny, the rapture and the smart,

All the large patience of your suffering heart
I feel, my Country! and love stands justified.

Your nonage now is over. You must up,
Gird in the calling morning, set your face
With granite purpose to the mountain way.
Prepare your bosom for the bitter cup:
Steel for endurance in the wearing race:
Yours is the triumphing, if yours the stay.

A. J. SEYMOUR

From *The Guiana Book*

9

Slaves
Humming in the twilight by the shanty door
Oh Lord Jesus.
Slaves
Pouring out heart-music till it run no more
Oh Lord Jesus.

Slaves born in hot wet forestlands
Tend the young cane-shoots and they give
Brute power to the signal of the lash
It curls and hisses through the air
And lifts upon the black, broad backs
Roped weals in hideous sculpture
Oh Lord Jesus.

Some slaves are whipped
For looking at the Master's grown-up daughters
Picking their way across the compound,
And other slaves for trying to run away.
Oh Lord Jesus.

Some few found kindly-hearted owners
And they were used like human beings
But those were rare, Lord Jesus.

Before, it was the shining yellow metal
And now, the dark sweet crystal owned the land
And if the chattel and the cattle died
There always would be more to take their place.
Till, in its deep sleep
Europe's conscience turned
And strenuous voices
Broke chains and set the people free.
Oh Lord Jesus.

But there were other chains and earth was not yet heaven
And other races came to share the work
And halve the pay.

10
FIRST OF AUGUST

Gather into the mind
Over a hundred years of a people
Wearing a natural livery in the sun
And budding up in generations and dying
Upon a strip of South American coastland.

See a prostrate people
Straighten its knees and stand erect
And stare dark eyes against the sun.

Watch hidden power dome the brow
And lend a depth of vision to the eyes.

Gather into the mind
Over a hundred years of a people
Toiling against climate
Working against prejudice

Growing within an alien framework
Cramped, but stretching its limbs
And staring against the sun.

Sometimes the blood forgets the flowering trees,
Red with flamboyants in the hard clear sun
And traces memories from hotter suns,
Other green-brilliant trees beneath a sky
That burns a deeper and more vital blue.

The blood goes back —

Coming across to land from Africa
The winds would close their mouths, the sea would smooth
And leave the little ships gasping, then the Sun
Would stand above and gaze right down the masts.

Children dying in dozens below the decks
The women drooping in clumps of flowers, the men
Standing about, with anger carved upon their foreheads.

A ferry of infamy from the heart of Africa
Roots torn and bleeding from their native soil,
A stain of race spreading across the ocean.

Then the new life of chains and stinging swamps
Whips flickering in the air in curling arabesques.

Gather into the mind
Over a hundred years of a people
Wearing a natural livery in the sun
And budding up in generations and dying
Upon a strip of South American coastland.

II

Drums
Then again drums
African drums
Drums, then a pause, the drums, African drums
Drums.

The white hair like a snow cap on his head
That thin old negro had beat the rhythm for years
The Ibu rhythm, learnt in African forests
From hands as proud and serpent-veined as his.

The negro shuffles, stamping the hard earth
Drums, African drums
His eyes blind-shut or half-slit with the passion
Shuffling and stamping feet beating the earth.

That rhythm will search out the Ibu blood
And pull a laughing stranger in its dance
Drums, African drums.

The old man beats the troubled rhythm faster
And music jerks the dancer's head and arms
In puppet-action. The tension grows
Movements come Bacchic and then half obscene
Drums, African drums.

Then like a leaven, see the madness spread,
Drums, African drums.
Caught in the mounting wind of passion
Others come stamping in the hard-earth circle

With eyes now half-slit and now shut and blind
Drums, drums, African drums.

The old drummer tightens the frenzy again
The drum notes pursue each other fiercely
Climbing the curious archways of the blood
Snuffing out the brain – dancers topple balance
And running down the scale of evolution
Writhe like the snakes from sea or ovum seekers
Dancing upon their bellies on the ground.
Others are music-drunk – drums, drums, the drums.

Then the old man unwinds the dancers, lays
That wind of passion to rest within his drums
Right to the last note of the octave.

Drums, African drums.

From *For Christopher Columbus*

4

He dreamed not that the ocean would bear ships
Heavy with slaves in the holds, to spill their seed
And fertilize new islands under whips

Of many nail-knotted thongs – dreamt not indeed
Massive steel eagles would keep an anxious watch
For strange and glittering fish where now was weed.

He knew not that a world beneath his touch
Springing to life would flower in cities and towns
Over two continents, nor guessed that such

A ferment of civilization was set down
Would overshadow Europe whence he came.
He could not dream how on the nations' tongue

Discovery would marry with his name.
That to these simple Indians his ships brought doom
For cargo; that the world was not the same

Because his vision had driven him from home
And that as architect of a new age
The solid world would build upon his poem.

5
And so the day beginning.
                    In the vast Atlantic
The sun's eye blazes over the edge of ocean
And watches the islands in a great bow curving
From Florida down to the South American coast.

Behind these towers in a hollow of ocean
Quiet from the Trade Winds lies the Caribbean
With the long shadows on her breathing bosom
Thrown from the islands in the morning sun.

And as the wind comes up, millions of palm trees
Weave leaves in rhythm as the shaft of sunlight
Numbers the islands till it reaches Cuba
Leaps the last neck of water in its course.

The Well

Time spirals upright this unflowing river
This waterrise through the earth safely miracled
This phallus from the deeps unbound and liquid,

Reversal of the dying in the desert
No sea, no river but water tamed and rooted.

Drums are struck wells, see how the sound drops fathoming,
Deeper than touch, than sense, dark in the rhythms
Where consciousness turns in the layers of darkness,
Drowned past the memory, frozen and dantean,
Through the human into animalean layers.

Mirrors are secret wells, huge coins of light where
The spirit plumbing opens the dark portals,
As lovers find themselves in their beloveds,
Or artist vision, or the mystic, God
(O grace of dark flame in the iron silence)
Identity all worn and frontiers gone
Below where image quickens to its power
Below

I Was a Boy

I was a boy
And my kite was a rigid gun on my shoulder
As I marched in the dark of an Easter morning
To the sea and the sun.

And my mounting loop
Caught a glimpse of the sun.

And the sun skipped over the muddy sea
And the Risen Lord climbed the breezy heavens
On my brilliant weaving kite
That soared like a bird, was a swan, was an eagle
On my resurrection morning.

PHYLLIS ALLFREY

The Child's Return

For Jean Rhys

I remember a far tall island
floating in cobalt paint
The thought of it is a childhood dream
torn by a midnight plaint

There are painted ships and rusty ships
that pass the island by,
and one dark day I'll board a boat
when I am ready to die

The timbers will creak and my heart will break
and the sailors will lay my bones
on the stiff rich grass, as sharp as spikes,
by the volcanic stones.

Love for an Island

Love for an island is the sternest passion:
pulsing beyond the blood through roots and loam
it overflows the boundary of bedrooms
and courses past the fragile walls of home.

Those nourished on the sap and milk of beauty
(born in its landsight) tremble like a tree
at the first footfall of the dread usurper —
a carpet-bagging mediocrity.

Theirs is no mild attachment, but rapacious
craving for a possession rude and whole;
lovers of islands drive their stake, prospecting
to run the flag of ego up the pole,

sink on the tented ground, hot under azure,
plunge in the heat of earth, and smell the stars

of the incredible vales. At night, triumphant,
they lift their eyes to Venus and to Mars.

Their passion drives them to perpetuation:
they dig, they plant, they build and they aspire
to the eternal landmark; when they die
the forest covers up their set desire.

Salesmen and termites occupy their dwellings,
their legendary politics decay.
Yet they achieve an ultimate memorial:
they blend their flesh with the beloved clay.

ERIC ROACH

Love Overgrows a Rock

Only the foreground's green;
Waves break the middle distance,
And to horizon the Atlantic's spread
Bright, blue and empty as the sky;
My eyot jails the heart,
And every dream is drowned in the shore water.

Too narrow room pressed down
My years to stunted scrub,
Blunted my sister's beauty
And my friend's grave force,
Our tribe's renewing faith and pride:
Love overgrows a rock as blood outbreeds it.

We take banana boats
Tourist, stowaway,
Our luck in hand, calypsoes in the heart:
We turn Columbus's blunder back
From sun to snow, to bitter cities;
We explore the hostile and exploding zones.

The drunken hawk's blood of
The poet streams through climates of the mind
Seeking a word's integrity
A human truth. So, from my private hillock
In Atlantic I join cry:
Come, seine the archipelago;
Disdain the sea; gather the islands' hills
Into the blue horizons of our love.

Piarco

Whole villages come
cliqued, cawing like poggoes
round one they're posting
into alien seasons,
civilizations that broke
and twined us round their will.
Each brings him gifts –
a handclasp or a kiss,
jewels even, of tears,
to ease the boy's umbilical
severing from the clan,
yet moor him by love's hope
in the green pool of home.

They suffered centuries
of time's distilling
of the peasant blood,
of sighs from penury and pain
in their Homeric grappling
with the earth to gain this day,
this font through which the son
who rode the bison to the pond,
split cacao pods, cut canes,
threshed rice, reaped peas in season
shall name them to the world.
Their eyes are gleaming
with new years of dreams.

She waddles, wheels,
exhales a dragon breath
blasting the waving gallery,
children laugh and women scamper off.

She's come from Bogota;
and those there – read their names –
from Buenos Aires, Rio, Santiago:
they flew up the long Antarctica – touching
America del Sud
to rest like migrant birds
on our sea rock

at the equatorial hinge
of the American mass.

One lifts and noses
north for New York,
Toronto, Montreal;
then she'll bear east
across Atlantic on to London;
there, all Europe's cities
are a choice of journeys
Paris, Berlin, Rome –
and what is beyond is dreams.

Islands cage us
and we long to leave them;
the cities scorn us
and we long to love them.
Bite the earth's orange
and her pips are bitter.

At Guaracara Park

the bronze god running;
beauty hurtling through the web of air,
motion fusing time and space
exploding our applauses . . .

speed was survival there in the green heat
where the lithe hero dashed
from the leopard's leap,
fled to cover from the feral fang
or ran the antelope across the plains.

and speed and stamina were the warrior's pride
where impis of assegais and swords and shields
tore tigerish through the brush and raided
and bounced back upon the kraals
panting from wounds and weariness,
brandishing the trophies of their cradling war.

the slave ships could not break our bones
nor strip our tendons, nor the long slaving
years narrow our arteries nor disease
our lungs nor shrivel up our hearts,
but left love thundering to this running man.

not fame's wreath crowns him
but Ogun's aura now; that blaze of flame
that savaged history back beyond our memories
our dreams and searchings.
the blood of the fierce gods we lost,
the pantheon of the kraals made him immortal
or he would have been a scarecrow in the canes.

GEORGE CAMPBELL

History Makers

I
Women stone breakers
Hammers and rocks
Tired child makers
Haphazard frocks.
Strong thigh
Rigid head
Bent nigh
Hard white piles
Of stone
Under hot sky
In the gully bed.

II
No smiles
No sigh
No moan.

III
Women child bearers
Pregnant frocks
Wilful toil sharers
Destiny shapers
History makers
Hammers and rocks.

In the Slums

In the slums
Jewel staring eyes
Of human flies
Crowd the rims
Of our social order.
We avoid

The stench of slums
Everything uncomfortable
Insistence
Of staring eyes
Evidence
Of substanceless limbs.

Here are –
Bilious houses
At the womb-head
Of comfort
Riches
Pleasure.

Here are –
Magnificent skeletons
With shrinking skins
Shrinking
With our approval.
Here
Here is
The world we accept
From our glass houses.

Holy

Holy be the white head of a Negro.
Sacred be the black flax of a black child.
Holy be
The golden down
That will stream in the waves of the winds
And will thin like dispersing cloud.
Holy be
Heads of Chinese hair
Sea calm sea impersonal
Deep flowering of the mellow and traditional.
Heads of peoples fair
Bright shimmering from the riches of their species;
Heads of Indians
With feeling of distance and space and dusk:

Heads of wheaten gold,
Heads of peoples dark
So strong so original:
All of the earth and the sun!

BARBARA FERLAND

Ave Maria

From a church across the street
  Children repeat
Hail Mary, full of Grace.
  Skipping the syllables; Follow-the-leader pace.

A little girl, (the Lord is with thee,)
  White in organdy,
Lifts her starched, black face
  Towards the barricaded altar
Meadowed in lace.

(Blessed art Thou among women.)
  Her child's fingers rove the coloured beads
One after one.
  (Blessed is the fruit of Thy womb, –)
Yea; and blessed, too,
  Ripe fruit on trees, window-close,
Under a tropical sun.

Bend low the laden bough
  Child-high; sweeten her incense-laden breath
With food, good Mary. (Holy Mary, Mother of God,
  Pray for us sinners.) And for the blameless,
Now, before the hour of their death.

Orange

You must learn how to peel, man.
The fruit in your hand is ripe.
  Cut, so! Reel, as you ring it round,
          like a ball.
Hold the rind to your nose, man.
Smell, 'til your eyes burn. Then
Bite. And when the juice sweets your tongue,
Man,
  Let the seed fall.

Expect No Turbulence

Expect no turbulence, although you hold me fast,
For this, where late my love lay, beats no more.
Confute, perplex not; only shield me from the past.
What might have been is lost, not gone before.

Though in the night your surgent need impels
Your body to seek comfort, bruising me awake,
I will not shrink, though all your flesh repels;
Nor sanctuary deny, while we communion take.

For we, two lost, two hungry souls, will meet
At common board, with common need for bread.
You, in the wood, will gather berries sweet;
I, in the dark, taste the salt flesh of the dead.

JOHN FIGUEROA

Birth is . . .

Birth is too bloody; we resist the end
The throes, the after-birth and after-care
Of child and mother. Darkly unaware
We start the perfumed path whose sudden bend
At dawn to us reveals the unknown friend.
The agony of mother and child we fear,
We are solicitous, nor God nor air
We trust: without security we will not lend
Our precious selves to poor posterity.
Suppose our seed to Faith should swell
And make demands on our temerity!
Or throes like waves should dash the spell
That dreams ourselves the final verity
Against infinite shores to splintered shell.

Portrait of a Woman (and a Man)

Firmly, sweetly
refusing . . .
Tall for seventeen fit
for a tumble

        'A guess hard time
        tek her' she said
        referring to
        her mother's misfortune
        (her strict mother whose
        three men had left
        her holding five
        pledges to fortune.)

She came easily into
my arms
refusing only to kiss

'Any familiarity an
we stop right now'

Dixerat – as lachrymae rerum used to say.
She's in the public domain
she's lost her patent rights
but would not kiss

'A guess hard time tek her'

Love, yes
Tenderness, no.
Mating's fine
Involvement, woe.
Familiarity would spoil
The moment's glow.

'A guess hard time tek her'

She is in the public domain
she's copied, copied, copied.

'You have bad min
Doan tell nobody
Doan tell nobody
Doan mck mi do it
        mek mi
Doan mek mi do it
        mek mi
        laard:

You see I intend to be
A nurse
No need to apologize
(Laard it sweet!)

But if you try to kiss
Me I will scream.'

At Home the Green Remains

In England now I hear the window shake
And see beyond its astigmatic pane
Against black limbs Autumn's yellow stain
Splashed about tree-tops and wet beneath the rake.

New England's hills are flattened as crimson-lake
And purple columns, all that now remain
Of trees, stand forward as hillocks do in rain,
And up the hillside ruined temples make.

At home the green remains: the palm throws back
Its head and breathes above the still blue sea,
The separate hills are lost in common blue
Only the splendid poinsettias, true
And crimson like the northern ivy, tack,
But late, the yearly notice to a tree.

(England, 1948)

WILSON HARRIS

Charcoal

Bold outlines are drawn to encompass
the history of the world: crude but naked emphasis
rests on each figure of the past
wherein the golden sunlight burns raw and unsophisticated.
Fires of brightness are sheltered
to burn the fallen limbs of men: the green
spirit of leaves like smoke
rises to mark the barrow of earth
and dwindles to perfection. The stars
are sparks
emblems of fire
to blacken the limbs of each god who falls:
spendthrift creation. The stable dew-drop is flame.
The dew burnishes each star in preparation for every deserted
    lane.
Time lies uneasy between the paintless houses
weather-beaten and dark.
The Negro once leaned on his spade
breathing the smoke of his labour

the arch of his body banked to shelter or tame
fury and diamond

or else like charcoal to grain
the world.

Laocoön

The dry earth near this salt sea
is baked and parched
under the sun.

Ridges of shadow
mark the distant bush
at the far end of the fields.

The land is bounded
by ineffectual palings.
The sounding sea cannonades half-a-mile off the coast.

Versions of economic blockade in weather-charts of grain
come near however far into a scale that measures
what is great, commands what is small.
Humped back of rain is no plainer than nails
or crevices that scar the dumb blood, the bombed sea.
Seedtime
is no less clamant than stone-age cloud
men and women of science seek to employ in an orchestra of
    greed.
And the continuity of savage drum
is sun's loud shadow on the television tree of the sky,
    continuity
of savage spoil
the closeness of a blossom reflected in a bloated corpse,
    roadside drain's
snapshot in a glossy magazine.
Documentation of famine
consumes the eye
as if no masked flower or bark can startle into lucid battalion

save forgotten fate that comes
in the womb of converted horse in the Christmas supplement
of the colour magazine
in each photographed bone, statistic of blood
and the silence that encompasses it is virgin wood's
technology of the foetus of god.

Birth is never treason
(the printer's devil reads)
It is the encroachment of savage conscience within the
    full-fed reader's
body of death, hope of resurrection
in partial nature's, partial myth's,
pregnant miracle.

A. L. HENDRIKS

Hot Summer Sunday

Especially on hot summer Sundays
my Grandpa liked to rest
supine in the narrow bathtub
soaking in curved cool water
sometimes flipping his toes
or, quite child-like,
toying with a pale green soapcake,
but mostly
staying motionless, eyes closed,
lips half-smiling,
limbs outstretched.

That hot summer Sunday
when I looked at him
straightly lying, lips parted,
silent in the shallow trough,
a foam of white, frothed and lacy,
set as new suds
about his shaven jawbones,
it seemed he might stir,
whistle a relaxed sigh,
unclose those eyelids,
ask me to scrub his back.

Boundary

It was planted early,
Best we said confirm the line
Between the joining properties,
A border never to be trampled;

Relationships are better built
Through doors with doorbells
And sometimes a wicket-gate
Letting in to private gardens.

Besides it would blossom
Putting on crimson flowers
Over emerald leaves
To ornament our views.

It was tended deftly
Watered and clipped both sides,
At times better cared
Than even the dwellings,
Nurturing it our proud delight.

Were we to know that it would spread
Gnarled with rough limbs
Stiff with thorns,
Grow too quick for us,
High, impenetrable,
Bind the hinge of the wicket-gate,
Lash creepers across the doors?

The Migrant

She could not remember anything about the voyage,
Her country of origin, or if someone had paid for the passage:
Of such she had no recollection.

She was sure only that she had travelled,
Without doubt had been made welcome.

For a while she believed she was home,
Rooted and securely settled,
Until it was broken to her
That in fact she was merely in transit
Bound for some other destination,
Committed to continue elsewhere.

This slow realization sharpened,
She formed plans to postpone her departure
Not observing her movement en route to the exit.

When she did, it was piteous how, saddened,
She went appreciably closer towards it.

Eventually facing the inescapable
She began reading travel brochures,
(Gaudy, competitive, plentiful)
Spent time considering the onward journey,
Studied a new language,
Stuffed her bosom with strange currency,
Nevertheless dreading the boarding announcements.

We watch her go through
The gate for *Embarking Passengers Only*,
Fearful and unutterably lonely,
Finger our own documents,
Shuffle forward in the queue.

Will the Real Me Please Stand Up?

As soon as i saw i was naked
i put on mother's dress
but it smelled of pain
and had holes where vanity had poked through

so i tried on father's coat
but it was too small for me
his ego being dwarfish

my brother's jacket
almost fit
but he had need of it

the circus was in town
a clown! that's it i thought, a clown!
but i didn't like the laughter, it got me down,

tin-hat, wig of judge, robe of priest,
i tried them all, for a while at least.

Animals seemed simply suited
so i concocted a beast to clothe in:
the elegant tights of a black panther
jerkin of a chameleon
and the hood of a Capuchin monkey

but the one i loved
said i was so beautiful
no one would undress me to go to bed with

something kinetic being needed
i appeared like a flock of white birds
circling over a green field

but the other i loved
said birds and fields were reminiscent of scarecrows
or Leda's bestialism
and was i sure i wasn't unsympathetic to homosexuals.

Therefore i decided to undress completely,
i unrolled my skin,
it came off neat as a banana,
carefully unstrapped my backbone and my guts,
stripped the pink flesh from the creamy bones
and threw them along with the bag of organs into the north
    wind
however secreting the sex-parts in my pocket,
not for utility
but because of their sculptured aesthetic,
the tactile and visual values, you understand.

Now i am carefully scanning
that relentless closed-circuit
which cameras and screens
every   thing
and when i pick me out
i will write again.

From 'D'où venons nous? Que sommes nous? Où allons nous?'

VI
Je vis un rêve permanent qui ne s'arrête ni nuit ni jour
    – *Georges Enesco*

(a)
Looking out toward the stars
I see two, close, appear as sisters

like those who speak meaningly in whispers
when I pass near to them at corners
as though saying, He will find out,
One day he will know It,
whose secret has to do with blood . . .

The Church, frigid,
mothering a mystery
locked up in its body,
breeding formal echoes,
words with helpless usage,
the stabbed God of virgins
in Paradise peopled by the dead . . .

always in the kitchen
the scarlet smell of death,
entrails of fish and chickens . . .

my brother picks a key, hidden, from the long grass,
(near the pomegranate I know it is,
burst fruit makes stains across his trousers)
it unlocks nothing,
he pretends it is a dagger
the girls that they bleed . . .

the neighbour's
where that stitch of river,
private in forbidden grass,
receives me, naked, a trespasser,
yet keeps murmuring, You are my owner!
so my shame is very great
I cannot tell my brother . . .

>   (b)
A woman in the garden gathers lilacs,
Stalks flow like arrows from her hand,
Bluish blossoms attempt cool lanterns of warning

>   'The impression of time,
>   Its small imprinting,
>   Publishes the end;
>   the moment
>   Dives compulsively,
>   Flighted as the arrow of the dream!'

Her fingers
Her fingers
Her fingers

Bright agonizing secateurs
Deliberately massacring lilacs
Compelling them from earth
Holding them
To flared hungering nostrils
Putting these blossoms
Finally
Alive, yet gravid with the seed of death
Into trapped waveless waters.

(c)

I touch jig-saw fragments:
A splintered torso.

Where I handle edges
the sensation of being burned.

I must have loved
Once
For often in the music
A shadow rises,

At the centre of the night
One dream is real:
What I dream
Is the pond opened by a fish
The water's belly healing
Patently unscarred,
The sky pierced through by birds
Remaining as a virgin,
The woman's face
Not disguised to conceal blemishes;

I am frightened
By that Once
It is live-bait
Tugging a straight line
Down dark astonished waters.

BASIL McFARLANE

Arawak Prologue

We cross many rivers, but here is no anguish; our
dugouts have straddled the salt sea. The land
we have found is a mountain, magical with birds'
throats, and in the sea are fish. In the forests are many
fleet canoes. And here is no anguish, though storms
still the birds and frighten the fish from inshore shallows,
                                                          And
once it seemed the mountain moved, groaning
a little.

   In the sunless wet, after
rains, leaves in the tangled underbrush (like cool hands
of children on face and arms) glisten. I
am not one for society, and think how the houses throb with
                                                    the noise
of women up to their elbows
in cassava milk, when the dove-grey sea's breast is
soft in the lowering light – and the land we found
fairest of women.

           That bright day, the light
like clusters of gold fruit, alone, unknown
of any, the dugout and I fled the shore's
burning beauty; the first wave's shock
an ecstasy like singing, oh, and the sea's strength
entered these arms. All day
we climbed the hill
of the sea.

           It seemed I died
and found that bleak
Coyaba of the wise. The dugout
faltered in a long smooth swell. There were houses on the
water, aglow with light and music and strange
laughter. Like great birds, with
ominous mutterings and preenings, they

hovered on every side. Flat on the dugout's
bottom, I prayed deliverance. Where was the land, the
houses throbbing with the noise of women
up to their elbows in cassava milk?
                                    The towering birds
floated majestically on, dragging me a little in their
fabulous wake.
                        I tell this story in the evening, after
the smoke of pipes has addled the elders'
brains, and I am assured at least of the children's respectful
silence. I am no longer certain it happened to me.

GLORIA ESCOFFERY

Twins

This one arrived on time
with a stitch in his side,
will reach his finishing line
a plain man, as God made him, without a single stitch on.

That one arrived clutching his brother's heel;
his emblem a ladder for he scorns the flat race.
Backed against a wall he will find
the tendril of a flowering vine and swing
upwards though his angelic challenger
awaits him smiling among the branches;
some say his mother gave him that extra push.

He protests, waving liberty's torch
that singes his spirit a little.
Outwardly he wears shirts of pure silk, flame proof and
    shining smooth:
he washes and irons them himself.

No Man's Land

The body of a fourteen year old caught playing politics
Makes a hummock on the ground beside his ratchet knife
Which drew blood but cannot bleed for him.
The muzzle of a sawn-off shotgun masks the eye of one
Who, being a man (?), thinks himself a great gun.
The gully scrub cannot hide him for ever;
Silenced, he drops the gun and becomes a dead man.

Now the killer's 'baby mother' is caught by the press
    photographer;
For the morning paper and forever she throws up her arms
In the traditional gesture of prayer.
Wai oh! Aie! Eheu! mourns the camera shot matron

Whose stringy son, like a sucked mango seed,
Lies there no more use to anyone;
Soon to be inseparable from the rest of the levelled ground.
Why this pietà needs to be enacted in our land
No one can explain:
It clearly belongs within the pieties of a museum frame.
Is there no way but through this scene?

Farewell to a Jovial Friend

The shouldered box has nested deep,
The pallid bearers turned to weep
Their friend's cold sleep.
Who mourns his laugh
Curtails by half
The drabness of November.

The caged, carmine bud of lust
Mounded in splendour bows to dust;
Here rest, not rust.
This kiln bright clay
May rise to play
A song that's far from sombre.

Eternity begins to hone
The marrow in each seamy bone –
We die alone.
Dearth in the grain
Attunes our strain
For use as seasoned timber.

After the Fall

Swordscape, tombscape, flame ploughed
Where the old man gilt fingered reads, born; died;
Needs must in between have suffered, lied
Sighing at the milk spill hushing.
Now herself fallen

Silent as thin piped water
As linen on blanched stones pure
To her own epitaph a whisper
To the young sign painter, coon capped,
A shadow, to ginger farmers
A fragrance of nutmeg.

Let the young shout,
My dog, my house, my wife,
Pale water carriers in the land's dawn
Before the fall.

LOUIS SIMPSON

Jamaica

Far from your crumpled mountains, plains that vultures
    ponder,
White gulches, wounded to pythons from gunshot of
    thunder:
  What should I sing in a city of stone,
  Drawing the bow across skull, across bone?

On phosphorescent furrows drifting from the dark sand,
We felt the fish pluck, keel grate, were laughed at by the land,
  Saw searchlights comb corpses' hair in mangroves
  Malarial, birds beat to quiet coves.

The gull shuddered plashing from sharks; and under green
    glass
Delicate needles to death twitched in terror's compass;
  Crimson on blue blade, gaping like hooked gills
  The sun was drawn bleeding across the hills.

By the sunk schooner, the nets, canoes with broken backs,
Was a cathedral, now choral to currents: now shacks
  Show a negress, children swollen with gas,
  A man cuts coconuts with a cutlass.

This island seemed emerald in the steel furnace flame
To the pirate . . . Port Royal . . . his ship shed clothes as she
    came
  To lie in the bay's blue arms, lazy, lean,
  And gold glowed through the hull with a death sheen.

He lay on shore with a black and a gold-hearted girl
Whose laugh unhinged like a box of red velvet and pearl.
  She gave his enemies the Judas word
  Who came at cock-crow, each one with a sword.

Still she cherished in womb the chromosomes for whiteness.
Fish flittered about the father's bones, but she could press
  Her hands to the high jumper there, the warm
  Mulatto, ambitious in lizard form.

This got the start of my bestial, indolent race
With coarse skin, crazy laugh, nostrils like swords through
    the face:
  Athletes at sixteen, they dive deep and lie
  In women like waves: in such dark caves die.

Bitter pale beauty, the small salty jewels of sun
Fade by the ocean. But the fruit of the valleys run
  From plump bourgeois banana's yellow skin
  To the cruel cane, cutlass-bladed, thin.

Life is a winter liner, here history passes
Like tourists on top-decks, seeing the shore through
    sun-glasses:
  And death, a delightful life-long disease,
  Sighs in sideways languor of twisted trees.

     January 1942

Arm in Arm

    Arm in arm in the Dutch dyke
    Were piled both friend and foe
    With rifle, helmet, motor-bike:
    Step over as you go.

    They laid the Captain on a bed
    Of gravel and green grass.
    The little Dutch girl held his head
    And motioned us to pass.

    Her busy hands seemed smooth as silk
    To a soldier in the sun,
    When she gave him a jug of milk
    In which his blood did run.

    O, had the Captain been around
    When trenching was begun,
    His bright binoculars had found
    The enemy's masked gun!

Beside a Church we dug our holes,
By tombstone and by cross.
They were too shallow for our souls
When the ground began to toss.

Which were the new, which the old dead
It was a sight to ask.
One private found a polished head
And took the skull to task

For spying on us . . . Till along
Driving the clouds like sheep,
Our bombers came in a great throng:
And so we fell asleep.

The Battle

Helmet and rifle, pack and overcoat
Marched through a forest. Somewhere up ahead
Guns thudded. Like the circle of a throat
The night on every side was turning red.

They halted and they dug. They sank like moles
Into the clammy earth between the trees.
And soon the sentries, standing in their holes,
Felt the first snow. Their feet began to freeze.

At dawn the first shell landed with a crack.
Then shells and bullets swept the icy woods.
This lasted many days. The snow was black.
The corpses stiffened in their scarlet hoods.

Most clearly of that battle I remember
The tiredness in eyes, how hands looked thin
Around a cigarette, and the bright ember
Would pulse with all the life there was within.

The Inner Part

When they had won the war
And for the first time in history
Americans were the most important people –

When the leading citizens no longer lived in their shirt
   sleeves,
And their wives did not scratch in public;
Just when they'd stopped saying 'Gosh!' –

When their daughters seemed as sensitive
As the tip of a fly rod,
And their sons were as smooth as a V-8 engine –

Priests, examining the entrails of birds,
Found the heart misplaced, and seeds
As black as death, emitting a strange odour.

Back in the States

It was cold, and all they gave him to wear
was a shirt. And he had malaria.

There was continual singing of hymns –
'Nearer My God to Thee' was a favorite.
And a sound like running water . . .
it took him a while to figure it.

Weeping, coming from the cells
of the men who had been condemned.

Now here he was, back in the States,
idly picking up a magazine,
glancing through the table of contents.

Already becoming like the rest of us.

A Fine Day for Straw Hats

He bought an old ship's lifeboat,
gave it an engine,
and built on a roof extending
from the stern to the bow.
It looked like a house, but it ran.

He christened it *Seahawk*,
and we travelled across the harbor
to Port Royal . . . sand and coconuts,
a few houses and huts,
and a low wall with embrasures
for cannon. This was Fort Charles
where Nelson used to stand
gazing at the sun and the pelicans.

And there were streets and ruins
in the weedy ooze below . . .
the pirate town that vanished
in an earthquake long ago.

*

The trip back was monotonous . . .
the fan of the wake subsiding
in foam, the thrumming of the engine.

When a ship was anchored in the harbor
we would go slowly around it
and read the name on the stern.

There used to be white steamers,
the Grace Line, sailing the Caribbean.
We saw the *Empress of Britain*,

and once, the battle cruiser *Rodney*.
I imagined the big guns firing,
the flame and smoke of battle,
ships sliding beneath the waves.

*

One Christmas we were in the *Seahawk*
off Kingston. An excursion launch

was setting out, crowded with passengers,
straw hats and gaily colored frocks.

I gazed away, to the Palisades . . .
behind them a sleeve of smoke
unravelling . . . a ship at sea.

When I looked again the excursion launch
had vanished. There were only seagulls,
and a confused murmur
coming from the people on shore.

We steered where the launch had been
and circled. The garden boy
who also served as an able seaman,
fished up something with the boathook . . .
a man's straw hat.
He placed it on the seat and we stared at it.

Next day's *Gleaner* carried the story:
the launch had capsized,
more than forty were feared drowned.

I don't think I was frightened
so much as appalled. That this could happen
at Christmas, on a calm sea . . .

Nothing, the sea whispers, is certain.

*

Reflections of the harbor
flit on walls. On the veranda
leaves are rustling. In the afternoon
a breeze springs up, driving whitecaps
into shore. The tops of the palms
thrash and swerve.

Sea clouds are drifting over.
Years, and a house seems to drift
and hills appear to have moved.

But memory is secure,
it is anchored with a chain.
Nothing short of a hurricane
could ever tear it loose.

Working Late

A light is on in my father's study
'Still up?' he says, and we are silent,
looking at the harbor lights,
listening to the surf
and the creak of coconut boughs.

He is working late on cases.
No impassioned speech! He argues from evidence,
actually pacing out and measuring,
while the fans revolving on the ceiling
winnow the true from the false.

Once he passed a brass curtain rod
through a head made out of plaster
and showed the jury the angle of fire –
where the murderer must have stood.
For years, all through my childhood,
if I opened a closet . . . bang!
There would be the dead man's head
with a black hole in the forehead.

All the arguing in the world
will not stay the moon.
She has come all the way from Russia
to gaze for a while in a mango tree
and light the wall of a veranda,
before resuming her interrupted journey
beyond the harbor and the lighthouse
at Port Royal, turning away
from land to the open sea.

Yet, nothing in nature changes, from that day to this,
she is still the mother of us all.
I can see the drifting offshore lights,
black posts where the pelicans brood.

And the light that used to shine
at night in my father's study
now shines as late in mine.

JAMES BERRY

My Father

For being so black
so muscular so well curved
like a groomed show man
too fit everyday for barefoot
he made us boys feel
we could kill him

For laughing so deep
down notes from soprano
like a tied stallion sighting
a pan of water
he got all laughter stopped
to listen to him

For treating ticks
like berries gathering
and the halfdead cow
in a bath of herbs and oil
he sat all day in tall grass
sweet-talking weak jaws

For tipping out warm pockets
of sticky sugar plums
or sat-on bananas
or squashed up naseberries
he made children descend
on him for things past ripe

For expecting my mother
to make money like food
and clothes and be the sum
of every question
he made us go deadfaced
when he stayed in

For drawing his name 'X'
and carrying a locked head

to explain stars
like a treetop pointing
he made us acknowledge him
keenly in rage

Ingrown

See a man with sound eyes
wearing his glasses dark

all through keenest midnight
his silence gone severe

his seeing grown inward
allowing no more in

you see a man who dreads
the streets the rooms the gardens

deep deeper in himself
till his roots are his blooms

Back to Hometown Kingston

These faces are true,
all dark with the sun.
No one is snow bled
into enmity. This place
exhibits a welcome.

This wind brushes a laughing
sun. It shatters me how
my muscles let go:
I startle no one
with my black face.

From Lucy: Holiday Reflections

I'm here an not here. Me head's
too full of mornin sun
an sea soun' an voices
echoin words this long long
time I never have.

Seeing home again, Leela chile,
I bring back a mind to Englan
tha's not enough to share. For how
I eat a mango under tree,
a soursop ripened for me,
a pawpaw kept, brings back
the whole taste of sunshine
an how our own love ripen.

O I glad to see hard times
ease off some faces a little.
I glad to see the stream still
goin in the gully, though
where it gives up to sea
is a different face now.

Big fig tree gone as ghost.
Whole breed of nana midwives
gone. Givin-for-not'n gone
mixed with cash. I had to ask
a-where walled bank of fire an
wood ashes gone from kitchen
for paraffin smell? Then I see
me head lost the account
of everything and everybody.

I meet a young face I get
the pain we don't know each other.
An I see Cousin John fine-shin boy
stretch up to sixfoot man. I see
Puppa is bones in the groun',
Mumma can't see to climb mount'n
lan'. An smellin of pee, Aunty
Meg's in bed all through sunhot.

Then old Granny Lyn an kids have
no regular man voice about.

Leela, sweetheart, I glad glad
I came home. I glad you still
have wasp waist an, funny,
that you hair still short.
You see how food fill me out:
I promise to slim.

I glad you don't grow bitter.
I glad how the sun still ripen
evenin, so strong in colour.
An there, where I did go
to school with one piece of book,
I came, I walked in darkness,
an it was a soothin blot.

Too many sea waves passed between
us, chile. Let us remind the other,
'Length of time gets rope buried'.

Distance of a City

The travel was homespun.
By night
a lantern carrier beckoned us.

We covered the sea
like scattered wreckage. Villagers,
hidden workmen, came upon
stores, new tools, books.

This now is my town of regal presence.
Old stones hold up the flag, along
the river. Sounds here came

and modelled my echoes.
Steadily, wheels vibrate
dream-wheels. And a lot
of weariness faded here with sleep.

Well placed women saunter
in tiaras, in pearls, in finest fur.
Cleopatra's Needle stands.

Ethnic spirits in relics,
from South, from East,
from North and West, settle shapes
in the grandeur of rooms.

My belly is full of holes
like a tattered and flat hunting bag.
Bells ring: my belly is bottomless.
An alien sweat settles connections.

Ammunition I didn't make
explodes in my face
in a deathless no-return,
in a strange introduction bequeathed.

And a loser must practise
teaching now, must learn to excite
new emotions through eyes meeting.

Fantasy of an African Boy

Such a peculiar lot
we are, we people
without money, in daylong
yearlong sunlight, knowing
money is somewhere, somewhere.

Everybody says it's a big
bigger brain bother now,
money. Such millions and millions
of us don't manage at all
without it, like war going on.

And we can't eat it. Yet
without it our heads alone
stay big, as lots and lots do,
coming from nowhere joyful,
going nowhere happy.

We can't drink it up. Yet
without it we shrivel when small
and stop forever
where we stopped,
as lots and lots do.

We can't read money for books.
Yet without it we don't
read, don't write numbers,
don't open gates in other countries,
as lots and lots never do.

We can't use money to bandage
sores, can't pound it
to powder for sick eyes
and sick bellies. Yet without
it, flesh melts from our bones.

Such walled-round gentlemen
overseas minding money! Such
bigtime gentlemen, body guarded
because of too much respect
and too many wishes on them:

too many wishes, everywhere,
wanting them to let go
magic of money, and let it fly
away, everywhere, day and night,
just like dropped leaves in wind!

JAN CAREW

Our Home

Our Caribbean
a bandolier
of emerald isles
circling
the waist
of twin continents,
suspended
miraculously
between Atlantic deeps
and the sun;
archipelago of famished hearts
manacled
with silver sands
caged
inside
moon burnished seas,
behind the flash
of cotton eyes
and tiger-orchid teeth
secret Fanonesque dreams
linger.
Our Caribbean
where sufferers laugh
to keep from weeping
and limpets
laze
on golden beaches,
half a millennium
of pain
vanished
when Cuba
reclaimed
a stolen heritage.

The Cliffs at Manzanilla

I'll not forget
I swear
dawn's dreams that you had spawned
in a green time
Tawny breakers leaping high
like agile tongues to lick the salted spume
and wild palms spinning like green wheels
in the wind
Green rocks and amarillic shale
were altars where you died
at Manzanilla
Your prayers to Savacou and Hurricane
Immortal gods of Spirit and Flesh
were lost like echoes of the thrashing surf
in green indifferent hinterlands of silence
A cannonade of Lombards
overcame the magic
of the Lightning-Eel, the Thunder-Axe
and wreaths of foam were strewn
like flowers of the boiling seas
across the amber sand
To be or not to be a slave
left you no choice save suicide
My Carib ancestors I swear
I'll not forget
the green years of your saga
in an ocean sea
that bears your name
eternally.

Faces and Skulls

Time pleats dark flesh
around white bones.
My dreams need black flesh
to clothe them.
Time scrapes away my black face

then chiselling
a white skull appears
empty as ivory goblets
in tombs of Benin.

MARTIN CARTER

University of Hunger

is the university of hunger the wide waste
is the pilgrimage of man the long march
The print of hunger wanders in the land
The green tree bends above the long forgotten
The plains of life rise up and fall in spasms
The roofs of men are fused in misery.

They come treading in the hoof marks of the mule
passing the ancient bridge
the grave of pride
the sudden flight
the terror and the time.

They come from the distant village of the flood
passing from middle air to middle earth
in the common hours of nakedness.

Twin bars of hunger mark their metal brows
twin seasons mock them
parching drought and flood.

is the dark ones
the half sunken in the land
is they who had no voice in the emptiness
in the unbelievable
in the shadowless.

They come treading on the mud floor of the year
mingling with dark heavy water
And the sea sound of the eyeless flitting bat,
O long is the march of men and long is the life
And wide is the span.

is air dust and the long distance of memory
is the hour of rain when sleepless toads are silent
is broken chimneys smokeless in the wind
is brown trash huts and jagged mounds of iron.

They come in long lines
toward the broad city.
is the golden moon like a big coin in the sky
is the floor of bone beneath the floor of flesh
is the beak of sickness breaking on the stone
O long is the march of men and long is the life
And wide is the span.
O cold is the cruel wind blowing
O cold is the hoe in the ground.

They come like sea birds
flapping in the wake of a boat.
is the torture of sunset in purple bandages
is the powder of fire spread like dust in the twilight
is the water melodies of white foam on wrinkled sand.

The long streets of night move up and down
baring the thighs of a woman
and the cavern of generation.
The beating drum returns and dies away
the bearded men fall down and go to sleep
the cocks of dawn stand up and crow like bugles.

is they who rose early in the morning
watching the moon die in the dawn
is they who heard the shell blow and the iron clang
is they who had no voice in the emptiness
in the unbelievable
in the shadowless
O long is the march of men and long is the life
And wide is the span.

From *I Come from the Nigger Yard*

I come from the nigger yard of yesterday
leaping from the oppressor's hate
and the scorn of myself.
I come to the world with scars upon my soul
wounds on my body, fury in my hands
I turn to the histories of men and the lives of the peoples

I examine the shower of sparks the wealth of the dreams
I am pleased with the glories and sad with the sorrows
rich with the riches, poor with the loss
From the nigger yard of yesterday I come with my burden.
To the world of to-morrow I turn with my strength.

Till I Collect

Over the shining mud the moon is blood
falling on ocean at the fence of lights.
My mast of love will sail and come to port
leaving a trail beneath the world, a track
cut by my rudder tempered out of anguish.

The fisherman will set his tray of hooks
and ease them one by one into the flood.
His net of twine will strain the liquid billow
and take the silver fishes from the deep.
But my own hand I dare not plunge too far
lest only sand and shells I bring to air
lest only bones I resurrect to light.

Over the shining mud the moon is blood
falling on ocean at the fence of lights –
My course I set, I give my sail the wind
to navigate the islands of the stars
till I collect my scattered skeleton
till I collect. . . .

There is No Riot

Even that desperate gaiety is gone.
Empty bottles, no longer trophies
are weapons now. Even the cunning
grumble. 'If is talk you want,' she said,
'you wasting time with me. Try the church.'
One time, it was because rain fell
there was no riot. Another time,

it was because the terrorist forgot
to bring the bomb. Now, in these days
though no rain falls, and bombs are well remembered
there is no riot. But everywhere
empty and broken bottles gleam like ruin.

For a Man Who Walked Sideways

Proudful and barefoot I stride the street
who wants my shirt can have it.
Only the giver gets. The unwanted
unwants the world. The bruised heel of his foot
kicks like a meteor. And the dim dark behind
the blue illusion stands like an altar in a temple
in a forsaken land. Having failed to learn
how to die, they all perish ungracefully.
Laocoön, for all the snakes, struggled well.

The Great Dark

Orbiting, the sun itself has a sun
as the moon an earth, a man a mind.
And life is not a matter of a mother only.
It is also a question of the probability of the spirit,
strength of the web of the ever weaving weaver
I know not how to speak of, caught as I am
in the great dark of the bright connection of words.

And the linked power of love holds the restless wind
even though the sky shudders, and life orbits
around time, around death, it holds the restless wind
as each might hold each other, as each might hold each other.

As New and as Old

I
Every day is as old
as a new day is. Time
represents itself. Night fakes
the rule of stars; as we fake
light's good pencil. A child's
chalk ridden black board. Alphabet
of hope in a season of insects. Crawl
of the beast in a season of days. I
unapologetic, remember why every
day was once a new day. As new
and as old as my childhood roaming
among grass. The world is a cold
wind. It is a glass of sweet water
in a grim place of thirst.
Farewell rain. When again shall I
taste your high cloud? Having betrayed
old gods in an old day, we seek
now to betray new ones
in a new day.

II
This morning is new, but the sun
that made it is old. New and old
is the face of the world's great grief,
a kind of music we listen to and hear
when the toil of silence builds
our house of language in this wind's
throat, the grim larynx. A green leaf
on the branch of a tree fingers
our time's disgraceful space. We
are its measure.

Bent

On the street, the sun
rages. The bent back of
an old woman resurrects
the brimmed bucket of this world's
light and insupportable
agony. A damage of years.

Her bent back, time's bad
step, and the creeping out
is ash; is the crushed cloud
of an incredible want.

The last time I saw her
she was far more truthful
than the damage of the years
carried on her back. The
sky, blue and ever,
imitates her. Bent.

Our Number

The pins of the slack pin seine
irregular the horizon; the tide
has gone them bare. A most disturbed
seagull proportions a catch. The fisherman's
wife, another seagull, leans on the sky
counting shrimp.

Surrendering ourselves
we denizen an epoch of abuse
trying to defy with the seagull's
or seawife's similar desperation
the tide that naked skins us.
Shrimp is our number. Is so
we stay. Is a way
of counting born we.

EVAN JONES

Genesis

He was a young god
So he worked with furious abandon
Strewing his precious suns around
In largely useless galaxies

Grandiose in his use of mountains, water, sky,
But not merely bombastic
For the detail of the microscopic was ingenious
Beyond the imagination of his predecessors
And the uses, particularly, of form and colour . . .

But he wasn't sure
Not quite sure, even when he had finished,
Especially then,

That he had solved such questions as
The relation of stability to change . . .

Cycles of birth and death were a masterpiece
But they weren't, not quite . . .

Yet, oh, the thing was beautiful
Turning and glittering and many-coloured
Infinite in all directions in space and time
And yet completely self-complete . . .

But he wasn't sure

So, as a sort of flourish to his signature
An underline for curtain
He made an animal in his own image
Except of course, for the dimensions lost
Transferring from eternity to time
Gave it the last perception of his mind
The sense of incompleteness
The gap between the intended and the done
The utter sadness of magnificence not quite

He gave it that
And asked of it perfection.

Walking with R.B.

What my friend? Love this! I who have known
Dark mountains heaving to burn-blue sky,
Slept within sea-sound's continual sigh
Seen coral gardens with pearl seed sown . . .

I, love this infinite dullness, mossed stones
Too long piled up to be now pulled down,
Mouldering in mist's grey, fog's brown,
This plaster-patched ruin covering dog bones
Of dead minds and dust knowledge? I'll not
Love. Endure yet, study yet, receive
Proof of persistence, meanwhile grieve
Wastage of sense, youth vigour forgot.

My last year's speech.

                    In new autumn eve
Slow footed strolling Oxford's streets,
Sentiment surged, by dim retreats,
Grand sweep of the gothic, make believe,
By decadence, dreams, the fall of leaves,
And swallows darting from rotting caves,
Loving sadly this old grey city,
Gasworks, martyrs, mere antiquity,
And knowing the change that slow time brings
Admitting joy in customary things.

November, 1956

It were best to sleep
Elections will proceed without our aid.

Jakov has lost the old encounter
Of naked flesh with steel
He hangs, feet in the air
Cold from a Danube lamp post

Where are the cigarettes? I inhale
The taste of railway stations

All night waits, remembering
The greasy faces at the hot-dog stands.

Mahmoud should know you cannot breathe
Face downward in the sand
We are policemen for his pyramids
Illiterates have no traffic on canals.

Somewhere in neverland, the telepeople
Broadcast and count and cheer
The general who will keep them out of war
Protect their interest and provide them beer.

Best to sleep, allowing these
Events their passage, while the dawn
Creeps in on London like a white disease.

The Song of the Banana Man

Touris, white man, wipin his face,
Met me in Golden Grove market place.
He looked at m'ol' clothes brown wid stain,
An soaked right through wid de Portlan rain,
He cas his eye, turn up his nose,
He says, 'You're a beggar man, I suppose?'
He says, 'Boy, get some occupation,
Be of some value to your nation.'
   I said, 'By God and dis big right han
   You mus recognize a banana man.

'Up in de hills, where de streams are cool,
An mullet an janga swim in de pool,
I have ten acres of mountain side,
An a dainty-foot donkey dat I ride,
Four Gros Michel, an four Lacatan,
Some coconut trees, and some hills of yam,
An I pasture on dat very same lan
Five she-goats an a big black ram,
   Dat, by God an dis big right han
   Is de property of a banana man.

'I leave m'yard early-mornin time
An set m'foot to de mountain climb,
I ben m'back to de hot-sun toil,
An m'cutlass rings on de stony soil,
Ploughin an weedin, diggin an plantin
Till Massa Sun drop back o John Crow mountain,
Den home again in cool evenin time,
Perhaps whistling dis likkle rhyme,
   (Sung) Praise God an m'big right han
   I will live an die a banana man.

'Banana day is my special day,
I cut my stems an I'm on m'way,
Load up de donkey, leave de lan
Head down de hill to banana stan,
When de truck comes roun I take a ride
All de way down to de harbour side –
Dat is de night, when you, touris man,
Would change your place wid a banana man.
   Yes, by God, an m'big right han
   I will live an die a banana man.

'De bay is calm, an de moon is bright
De hills look black for de sky is light,
Down at de dock is an English ship,
Restin after her ocean trip,
While on de pier is a monstrous hustle,
Tallymen, carriers, all in a bustle,
Wid stems on deir heads in a long black snake
Some singin de songs dat banana men make,
   Like, *(Sung)* Praise God an m'big right han
   I will live an die a banana man.

'Den de payment comes, an we have some fun,
Me, Zekiel, Breda and Duppy Son.
Down at de bar near United Wharf
We knock back a white rum, bus a laugh,
Fill de empty bag for further toil
Wid saltfish, breadfruit, coconut oil.
Den head back home to m'yard to sleep,
A proper sleep dat is long an deep.
   Yes, by God, an m'big right han
   I will live an die a banana man.

'So when you see dese ol' clothes brown wid stain,
An soaked right through wid de Portlan rain,
Don't cas your eye nor turn your nose,
Don't judge a man by his patchy clothes,
I'm a strong man, a proud man, an I'm free,
Free as dese mountains, free as dis sea,
I know myself, an I know my ways,
An will sing wid pride to de end o my days
  (*Sung*) Praise God an m'big right han
  I will live an die a banana man.'

The Lament of the Banana Man

Gal, I'm tellin you, I'm tired fo true,
Tired of Englan, tired o you.
But I can't go back to Jamaica now . . .

I'm here in Englan, I'm drawin pay,
I go to de underground every day –
Eight hours is all, half-hour fo lunch,
M' uniform's free, an m'ticket punch –
Punchin tickets not hard to do,
When I'm tired o punchin, I let dem through.

I get a paid holiday once a year.
Ol age an sickness can't touch me here.
I have a room of m'own, an a iron bed,
Dunlopillo under m'head,
A Morphy-Richards to warm de air,
A formica table, an easy chair.
I have summer clothes, an winter clothes,
An paper kerchiefs to blow m'nose.

My yoke is easy, my burden is light,
I know a place I can go to, any night.
Dis place Englan! I'm not complainin,
If it col', it col', if it rainin, it rainin.
I don't mind if it's mostly night,
Dere's always inside, or de sodium light.
I don't mind white people starin at me,

Dey don' want me here? Don't is deir country?
You won' catch me bawlin any homesick tears,
If I don' see Jamaica for a t'ousan years!

. . . Gal, I'm tellin you, I'm tired fo true,
Tired of Englan, tired o you,
I can't go back to Jamaica now —
But I'd want to die there, anyhow.

SHAKE KEANE

Shaker Funeral

Sorrow sin-
bound, pelting din
big chorusclash
o' the mourners;
eyes red
with a shout for the dead,
yelling crash-
ing sadness in
the dusty tread
o' the mourners.

    Sweet Mother gone
    to the by and by,
    follow her to the brink o' Zion.

Wave wave
as they roared to grave
a drench song –
soulthunder –
was *aymens* through
the wind, shrieks flew,
and eyes were strong;
for 'twas madness gave
them dirge, that grew
made thunder.

Drums, flags,
pious rags o'
robes stenching
sweat;
mitre o' tattered
straw, bamboo crozier
wagged by wind's clenching –
deathwind that bragged
sorrow, smattered
o' sweat.

Saints in blue
bathrobes flew
about the ranks
o' the sinners,
and froth-lipped virgins
with powdered skins
and frocks that stank
with the slime and the stew
from the purged away sins
o' the sinners;

And heads were white
in starched cloth . . . Bright
was the blood from the eyes
o' the candles;
and the 'horn of the Ram
of the great I Am'
spoke hoarse in cries . . .
and crowned with the light
o' the Judah Lamb
were the candles.

    Lord delivered Daniel
    from shame's mouth,
    (o strong, o strong roll Jordan).
    Lord deliver our Mother
    gone to the Glory Home,
    gone to the Glory Home, gone to Zion.

All God's brothers
were loud, and the ten
holy lampers were
reeking in smoke;
and the 'valley of sod-
and-shadow,' Staff-Rod,
was blenched as the canker-
ing sweat o' men
and the reeking o' God
in the smoke.

    His willing be,
    Mother gone,
    Jordan deep,

but her soul is strong.
Follow her to the brink o' Zion.

And now the grave
was washed in a wave
o' wails and a
city o' stars

that dribbled and burned
in the tears that turned
hot sins, on the smoke-white pillars . . .
But their sorrow was yells,
and their faith was brave
as the blood-blemished lambs
piled big on the grave
their city o' wax and stars.

Sweet Mother gone,
King o' Mansions-over-Jordan.
O strong . . .
Leave her safe on the brink o' Zion.

Coming Back

Beaches are full of dirty nails after rain
a shivering heat in my belly
like love
like disaster like old words
I found once on a rusty tin in January
as a child speeding past my first temptation
don't go out go out either in the hot sun nor
in the pouring rain
pride like the sea secretes little by little
odd kinds of music
you might get old nails in your little foot
Don't come in come in
the house of the lord without a good hat
the whole congregation sitting up like little children

That time was the magic before he
hadn't exactly risen like glory over the place
where she would die

Then all the cornets and the small drums
would yell in my belly something like power
Would he really come one day
to make a sentence containing any or all of the following
all old nails on the beach
think of all the music you might lose just constructing
    sentences

people said so she said
everything seems easier when you learn the words
as I sped like disaster past my first temptation
the teacher and the preacher
careful or not needing to go out
in the dirty rain said
you would later have big trouble with a mustard seed

Old words and new coins in my rusty tin
dancing on one good foot looking
over the other shoulder
I felt I couldn't hold her but she
took me up from out of all of that wet wet tide
and loved me like I was a man

but really where drums and cornets and church choirs
replaced all my music
how could she take me out to pasture
though it was moonlight the rain purred
like beasts all through the August nights

that year much later
clusters of shining in wet sand
she secretly waited should I come surging back old nails
and pride shivering in my belly it really feels
a little like power something like love

From *Volcano Suite*

Soufrière (79) 1

The thing split Good Friday in two
and that good new morning groaned
and snapped
like breaking an old habit

Within minutes
people
who had always been leaving nowhere
began arriving nowhere
entire lives stuffed in pillow-cases
and used plastic bags
naked children suddenly transformed
into citizens

'Ologists with their guilty little instruments
were already oozing about the mountainsides
bravely
and by radio

(As a prelude to resurrection and brotherly love
you can't beat ructions and eruptions)

Flies ran away from the scene of the crime
and crouched like Pilate
in the secret places of my house
washing their hands

Thirty grains of sulphur
panicked off the phone
when it rang

Mysterious people ordered
other mysterious people
to go to mysterious places
'immediately'

I wondered about the old woman
who had walked back to hell
to wash her Sunday clothes

All the grey-long day
music

credible and incredibly beautiful
came over the radio
while the mountain refreshed itself

Someone who lives
inside a microphone
kept things in order

Three children in unspectacular rags
a single bowl of grey dust between them
tried to manure the future
round a young plum tree

The island put a white mask
over its face
coughed cool as history
and fell in love with itself

A bus travelling heavy
cramped as Calvary
thrust its panic into the side of a hovel
and then the evening's blanket
sent like some strange gift from abroad
was rent by lightning

After a dream
of rancid hope and Guyana rice
I awoke to hear
that the nation had given itself
two hundred thousand dollars

The leaves did not glisten when wet

An old friend
phoned from Ireland
to ask about the future
my Empire cigarettes
have lately been tasting of sulphur
I told her that.

DANIEL WILLIAMS

We are the Cenotaphs

I

We are the cenotaphs
Of the dozing dead,
Wherever they snooze
Under the low weather
Of the sullen soil.
We are hour-glass
Trickling through aeons of grained desires,
And centuries of pain wrapped in tall longitudes
Of hope.

I am my father.

We are the past;
We too have slain the younger brother,
And smitten the rock for water.

Not new the broken sun,
Piercing the silken sky
With splintered shafts
Of light and the day's death;
Always we clock
The sick rust of the salt years and our oxidized
Will; always the brown stain of our failure disfigures
The white linen of our hope.

II

Brackish we drink
The liquid years
From the cups of our fathers.
Feverish we sink
In the dam of despair
Where they were;
Where they clutched to each thread after every
Cutting twine, that hung lean from the tentacles
Of time.

I am my child.

We are the future;
We too mislaid their building brick,
We pulled down their stone.

Not then any new tragedy
Or travesty of love;
Always since genesis,
Love was anachronism.
Always the wolf
Chased the sober sheep and the hare ran hunted
Over acres of bush; always the Philistine quenched
From the cup of the wound.

III

We are the epitaphs
Stamped on this
Spinning tomb; star-
Less our sky, and the kiss
Of our season is cold.
We relate ghost tales
Of our fallen slain, and lugubrious is the luggage
Of memories bundled in the archives of the brain.

We are the past;
We too have slain the younger brother,
And smitten the rock for water.

Not new the broken sun,
Piercing the silken sky
With splintered shafts
Of light and the day's death;
Always we clock
The sick rust of the salt years and our oxidized
Will; always the brown stain of our failure disfigures
The white linen of our hope.

I am I.

We are the present;
We too erect and dig our graves
We have killed our dead.

Grey is the light
Lazing limp on
The page of our period
And the shadows fold.
But the blackbird on
The tamarind still strikes a gay allegro note,
And the winsome wind grimaces on the pond.

Only, in the street of the heart
Our hate has not succumbed;
Only, in the soul's nakedest part
Our love is benumbed.

We are all time;
Yet only the future is ours
To desecrate.
The present is the past,
And the past
Our fathers' mischief.

ANDREW SALKEY

Remember Haiti, Cuba, Vietnam

Here's something folk tales tell
us about, at night, but which
we lose sight of during the day:

Giants can be surprised.

That's something three slingshots
in our third of the world gauged
and defiantly stretched to success.

What's the light like now in the dark?

Look at the untouched stones
lying on our beaches
and the idle rubber bands
in our upturned hands!

Soufrière

Far and wide
outside St Vincent,
the man, who holds
the Soufrière postcard,
regrets the energy
used so prettily,
stilled by a stamp,
approved with a postmark,
tamed by firm fingers.

At this time, in America,
they'd tell you, Soufrière,
'Keep on keepin' on!'

For you've been a long time
on the boil, bulked
and gorged with layers

of hot rock and soup thick
earth, rolled in folds,
pleated and tucked
into molten waves
of mounting resentment
and anger, banging inside
the field-slave's head
for luck: see how he squints
like clinking marbles;
listen to him gritting his ancient teeth!
Bite, Soufrière, bite through
that top lip of ours,
through our bauxite gardens,
bordered by sugar cane and bananas!

How many of us know
how to wait for the gush
to blow, for the ashes
to cool, for the rocks
to dry, for the stone
to be handed on, deep
inside St Vincent and far
and wide outside?

Clearsightedness

(In memory of Claudia Jones)

In spite of what the quarrymen said,
she was sure she knew only too well
that she was born to see through stone,
to slash that broad back with her eyes
and tell her daughter about it, one day.

I remember we'd often catch her smiling,
brushing rock-dust out of her hair,
clapping her granite-veined hands,
slapping her long skirt with carpet-clatter,
and looking like a moving hive of hillside.

'I'm every bit as hard as they hit me,'
she liked saying, winking confidently.
'Remember, we live on a rock in water,
nothing surprises me, only my eyes.
I can see us striking back. I can see it.'

Postcard from Mexico, 16.x.1973

From Villahermosa,
in Tabasco,
out of the lowlands
of Veracruz
(Chiapas
only spitting distance away),
an upright, giant
Olmec head,
without benefit of clergy,
brings moonfaced greetings
on its African lips,
three thousand years old;

and the liana-twined palimpsest
of myth and mysterious history,
flat on the table before me,
says its message is clear,
says it swallowed whole
the Mexican Revolution,
says its head grew larger and larger
with headache after headache
at watching the progress
of Mexico's bouncing economy
leaping north over the border
like jumping beans nobody sees.

Look,
no Mexicans!

A Song for England

An a so de rain a-fall
An a so de snow a-rain

An a so de fog a-fall
An a so de sun a-fail

An a so de seasons mix
An a so de bag-o-tricks

But a so me understan
De misery o de Englishman.

Dry River Bed

he came back
by plane,
train,
bus
and cart

his expectations
were plain:
family,
eyecorner familiarity,
back-home self,
or so he thought

1
during the last stretch,
on foot,
over the hard dirt road,
a beggar smiled at him,
and held out his left hand,
like a reaping hook

he gave him
nearly all his small change

2
further along the way,
a tatter of children
offered him pebbly mangoes,
at a price

he handed over
the rest of his change,
without taking the mangoes

3
on the narrative veranda,
where all the village tales
had perched
and taken off again,
his mother stood,
as light as the money
he'd just given away

in his embrace,
her body, wrapped wire,
felt smaller
than he remembered,
her face drawn tight
and frightened

4
everything was diminished,
whittled by long urban knives:
the road outside,
the front garden,
the lean-to house,
the back yard,
the lives

5
all his family
and neighbours
were knocking softly
at death's door,
waiting patiently,

spit fringing their cracked lips,
wizened frowns

sliding
into their collapsed cheeks

6
the villagers clawed at him
and what little he'd brought back;

they picked him clean
as a eucalyptus

7
he quickly saw
that home was a dry river bed;
he knew he'd have to run away, again,

or stay and be clawed to death
by the eagle
hovering over the village;
nothing had changed

8
he walked alone,
for a while;
not even his footprints
sank behind him,
in the dust;

no niche,
no bounce-back,
no mirror, anywhere,
in which to see himself,
merely the sunlight
mocking everybody, everywhere,
and the circling eagle

HENRY BEISSEL

Pans at Carnival

Steel voice of a steel god
commands the groined shuffle and shake
man beat man beat she hard
holy rum and roti host
up and down the profane aisles
of this tin pan city
clinking clanking
pilgrimage in disguise
to cleanse the past from terror
and from fury what is to come
ringing in

the tympanum of a tin god
the blood hammering by heart
forges wrought shapes of music
hot from gaudy steel
on the anvil of ancient passion
to roadmarch this tin pan city
clinking into the savannah
of its clanking nightmares
in honour of the black sun
bottled in one million groins
shaking out

the crumpled world of another year
wasted – oh man hold she tight!
The world for forty-two hours caught
in the sphere of a steel pan
with its continents embossed in tune
with its people one and divided
in the shuffle and jump-up
on the tin belly of some god
blessing with cane and cocoa
cursing with cutlass and pride
beating time

creation from oil drums
of a world of sweat and laboured
masks obeying the ten metallic
commandments revealed in burning
rhythms on a mountain of flesh
from which leave is to be taken
by a grand public ascent
clanging up Henry Street
down rum and roti
the steel god the groin the black
sun beat man beat man!

DEREK WALCOTT

A Far Cry from Africa

A wind is ruffling the tawny pelt
Of Africa. Kikuyu, quick as flies
Batten upon the bloodstreams of the veldt.
Corpses are scattered through a paradise.
But still the worm, colonel of carrion, cries:
'Waste no compassion on these separate dead'
Statistics justify and scholars seize
The salients of colonial policy.
What is that to the white child hacked in bed?
To savages, expendable as Jews?

Threshed out by beaters, the long rushes break
In a white dust of ibises whose cries
Have wheeled since civilization's dawn
From the parched river or beast-teeming plain;
The violence of beast on beast is read
As natural law, but upright man
Seeks his divinity with inflicting pain.
Delirious as these worried beasts, his wars
Dance to the tightened carcass of a drum,
While he calls courage still, that native dread
Of the white peace contracted by the dead.

Again brutish necessity wipes its hands
Upon the napkin of a dirty cause, again
A waste of our compassion, as with Spain.
The gorilla wrestles with the superman.

I who am poisoned with the blood of both,
Where shall I turn, divided to the vein?
I who have cursed
The drunken officer of British rule, how choose
Between this Africa and the English tongue I love?
Betray them both, or give back what they give?
How can I face such slaughter and be cool?
How can I turn from Africa and live?

From *Another Life*, Chapter 20

II

The rain falls like knives
on the kitchen floor.
The sky's heavy drawer
was pulled out too suddenly.
The raw season is on us.

For days it has huddled on the kitchen sill,
tense, a smoke and orange kitten
flexing its haunches,
coiling its yellow scream
and now, it springs.
Nimble fingers of lightning
have picked the watershed,
the wires fling their beads.
Tears, like slow crystal beetles, crawl the pane.

On such days, when the postman's bicycle
whirrs drily like the locust
that brings rain, I dread my premonitions.
A grey spot, a waterdrop
blisters my hand.
A sodden letter thunders in my hand.
The insect gnaws steadily at its leaf,
an eaten letter crumbles in my hand,
as he once held my drawing to his face,
as though dusk were myopic, not his gaze.

'Harry has killed himself. He was found dead
in a house in the country. He was dead for two days.'

III

The fishermen, like thieves, shake out their silver,
the lithe knives wriggle on the drying sand.
They go about their work,
their chronicler has gone about his work.

At Garand, at Piaille, at L'Anse la Verdure,
the sky is grey as pewter, without meaning.
It thunders and the kitten scuttles back
into the kitchen bin

of coal, its tines sheathing, unsheathing,
its yellow eyes the colour of fool's gold.

He had left this note.
No meaning, and no meaning.

All day, on the tin roofs
the rain berates the poverty of life,
all day the sunset bleeds like a cut wrist.

IV

Well, there you have your seasons, prodigy!
For instance, the autumnal fall of bodies,
deaths, like a comic, brutal repetition,
and in the Book of Hours, that seemed so far,
the light and amber of another life,
there is a Reaper busy about his wheat,
one who stalks nearer, and will not look up
from the scythe's swish in the orange evening grass,
and the fly at the font of your ear
sings, Hurry, hurry!
Never to set eyes on this page,
ah Harry, never to read our names,
like a stone blurred with tears I could not read
among the pilgrims, and the mooning child
staring from the window of the high studio.

Brown, balding, with a lacertilian
jut to his underlip,
with spectacles thick as a glass paperweight
and squat, blunt fingers,
waspish, austere, swift with asperities,
with a dimpled pot for a belly from the red clay of Piaille.
Eyes like the glint of sea-smoothed bottle glass,
his knee-high khaki stockings,
brown shoes lacquered even in desolation.

People entered his understanding
like a wayside country church,
they had built him themselves.
It was they who had smoothed the wall
of his clay-coloured forehead,
who made of his rotundity an earthy

useful object
holding the clear water of their simple troubles,
he who returned their tribal names
to the adze, mattock, midden and cookingpot.

A tang of white rum on the tongue of the mandolin,
a young bay, parting its mouth,
a heron silently named or a night-moth,
or the names of villages plaited into one map,
in the evocation of scrubbed back-yard smoke,
and he is a man no more
but the fervour and intelligence
of a whole country.

Leonce, Placide, Alcindor,
Dominic, from whose plane vowels were shorn
odorous as forest,
ask the charcoal-burner to look up
with his singed eyes,
ask the lip-cracked fisherman three miles at sea
with nothing between him and Dahomey's coast
to dip rain-water over his parched boards
for Monsieur Simmons, *pour* Msieu Harry Simmons,
let the husker on his pyramid of coconuts
rest on his tree.

Blow out the eyes in the unfinished portraits.

And the old woman who danced
with a spine like the 'glory cedar',
so lissome that her veins bulged evenly
upon the tightened drumskin of the earth,
her feet nimbler than the drummer's fingers,
let her sit in her corner and become evening
for a man the colour of her earth,
for a cracked claypot full of idle brushes,
and the tubes curl and harden,
except the red,
except the virulent red!

His island forest, open and enclose him
like a rare butterfly between its leaves.

Forest of Europe

For Joseph Brodsky

The last leaves fell like notes from a piano
and left their ovals echoing in the ear;
with gawky music stands, the winter forest
looks like an empty orchestra, its lines
ruled on these scattered manuscripts of snow.

The inlaid copper laurel of an oak
shines through the brown-bricked glass above your head
as bright as whiskey, while the wintry breath
of lines from Mandelstam, which you recite,
uncoils as visibly as cigarette smoke.

'The rustling of ruble notes by the lemon Neva.'
Under your exile's tongue, crisp under heel,
the gutturals crackle like decaying leaves,
the phrase from Mandelstam circles with light
in a brown room, in barren Oklahoma.

There is a Gulag Archipelago
under this ice, where the salt, mineral spring
of the long Trail of Tears runnels these plains
as hard and open as a herdsman's face
sun-cracked and stubbled with unshaven snow.

Growing in whispers from the Writers' Congress,
the snow circles like cossacks round the corpse
of a tired Choctaw till it is a blizzard
of treaties and white papers as we lose
sight of the single human through the cause.

So every spring these branches load their shelves,
like libraries with newly published leaves,
till waste recycles them – paper to snow –
but, at zero of suffering, one mind
lasts like this oak with a few brazen leaves.

As the train passes the forest's tortured icons,
the floes clanging like freight yards, then the spires
of frozen tears, the stations screeching steam,
he drew them in a single winter's breath
whose freezing consonants turned into stones.

He saw the poetry in forlorn stations
under clouds vast as Asia, through districts
that could gulp Oklahoma like a grape,
not these tree-shaded prairie halts but space
so desolate it mocked destinations.

Who is that dark child on the parapets
of Europe, watching the evening river mint
its sovereigns stamped with power, not with poets,
the Thames and the Neva rustling like banknotes,
then, black on gold, the Hudson's silhouettes?

From frozen Neva to the Hudson pours,
under the airport domes, the echoing stations,
the tributary of emigrants whom exile
has made as classless as the common cold,
citizens of a language that is now yours,

and every February, every 'last autumn',
you write far from the threshing harvesters
folding wheat like a girl plaiting her hair,
far from Russia's canals quivering with sunstroke,
a man living with English in one room.

The tourist archipelagos of my South
are prisons too, corruptible, and though
there is no harder prison than writing verse,
what's poetry, if it is worth its salt,
but a phrase men can pass from hand to mouth?

From hand to mouth, across the centuries,
the bread that lasts when systems have decayed,
when, in his forest of barbed-wire branches,
a prisoner circles, chewing the one phrase
whose music will last longer than the leaves,

whose condensation is the marble sweat
of angels' foreheads, which will never dry
till Borealis shuts the peacock lights
of its slow fan from L.A. to Archangel,
and memory needs nothing to repeat.

Frightened and starved, with divine fever
Osip Mandelstam shook, and every

metaphor shuddered him with ague,
each vowel heavier than a boundary stone,
'to the rustling of ruble notes by the lemon Neva,'

but now that fever is a fire whose glow
warms our hands, Joseph, as we grunt like primates
exchanging gutturals in this winter cave
of a brown cottage, while in drifts outside
mastodons force their systems through the snow.

The Spoiler's Return

I sit high on this bridge in Laventille,
watching that city where I left no will
but my own conscience and rum-eaten wit,
and limers passing see me where I sit,
ghost in brown gabardine, bones in a sack,
and bawl: 'Ay, Spoiler, boy! When you come back?'
And those who bold don't feel they out of place
to peel my limeskin back, and see a face
with eyes as cold as a dead macajuel,
and if they still can talk, I answer: 'Hell.'
I have a room there where I keep a crown,
and Satan send me to check out this town.
Down there, that Hot Boy have a stereo
where, whole day, he does blast my caiso;
I beg him two weeks' leave and he send me
back up, not as no bedbug or no flea,
but in this limeskin hat and floccy suit,
to sing what I did always sing: the truth.
Tell Desperadoes when you reach the hill,
I decompose, but I composing still:

I going to bite them young ladies, partner,
like a hotdog or a hamburger
and if you thin, don't be in a fright
is only big fat women I going to bite.

The shark, racing the shadow of the shark
across clear coral rocks, does make them dark –

that is my premonition of the scene
of what passing over this Caribbean.
Is crab climbing crab-back, in a crab-quarrel,
and going round and round in the same barrel,
is sharks with shirt-jacs, sharks with well-pressed fins,
ripping we small fry off with razor grins;
nothing ain't change but color and attire,
so back me up, Old Brigade of Satire,
back me up, Martial, Juvenal, and Pope
(to hang theirself I giving plenty rope),
join Spoiler' chorus, sing the song with me,
Lord Rochester, who praised the nimble flea:

Were I, who to my cost already am
One of those strange, prodigious creatures, Man,
A spirit free, to choose for my own share,
What case of flesh and blood I pleased to wear,
I hope when I die, after burial,
To come back as an insect or animal.

I see these islands and I feel to bawl,
'area of darkness' with V. S. Nightfall.

Lock off your tears, you casting pearls of grief
on a duck's back, a waxen dasheen leaf,
the slime crab's carapace is waterproof
and those with hearing aids turn off the truth,
and their dark glasses let you criticize
your own presumptuous image in their eyes.
Behind dark glasses is just hollow skull,
and black still poor, though black is beautiful.
So, crown and mitre me Bedbug the First —
the gift of mockery with which I'm cursed
is just a insect biting Fame behind,
a vermin swimming in a glass of wine,
that, dipped out with a finger, bound to bite
its saving host, ungrateful parasite,
whose sting, between the cleft arse and its seat,
reminds Authority man is just meat,
a moralist as mordant as the louse
that the good husband brings from the whorehouse,
the flea whose itch to make all Power wince,

will crash a fete, even at his life's expense,
and these pile up in lime pits by the heap,
daily, that our deliverers may sleep.
All those who promise free and just debate,
then blow up radicals to save the state,
who allow, in democracy's defense,
a parliament of spiked heads on a fence,
all you go bawl out, 'Spoils, things ain't so bad.'
This ain't the Dark Age, is just Trinidad,
is human nature, Spoiler, after all,
it ain't big genocide, is just bohbohl;
safe and conservative, 'fraid to take side,
they say that Rodney commit suicide,
is the same voices that, in the slave ship,
smile at their brothers, 'Boy, is just the whip,'
I free and easy, you see me have chain?
A little censorship can't cause no pain,
a little graft can't rot the human mind,
what sweet in goat-mouth sour in his behind.
So I sing with Attila, I sing with Commander,
what right in Guyana, right in Uganda.
The time could come, it can't be very long,
when they will jail calypso for picong,
for first comes television, then the press,
all in the name of Civic Righteousness;
it has been done before, all Power has
made the sky shit and maggots of the stars,
over these Romans lying on their backs,
the hookers swaying their enormous sacks,
until all language stinks, and the truth lies,
a mass for maggots and a fete for flies;
and, for a spineless thing, rumor can twist
into a style the local journalist –
as bland as a green coconut, his manner
routinely tart, his sources the Savannah
and all pretensions to a native art
reduced to giggles at the coconut cart,
where heads with reputations, in one slice,
are brought to earth, when they ain't eating nice;
and as for local Art, so it does go,
the audience have more talent than the show.

Is Carnival, straight Carnival that's all,
the beat is base, the melody bohbohl,
all Port of Spain is a twelve-thirty show,
some playing Kojak, some Fidel Castro,
some Rastamen, but, with or without locks,
to Spoiler is the same old khaki socks,
all Frederick Street stinking like a closed drain,
Hell is a city much like Port of Spain,
what the rain rots, the sun ripens some more,
all in due process and within the law,
as, like a sailor on a spending spree,
we blow our oil-bloated economy
on projects from here to eternity,
and Lord, the sunlit streets break Spoiler's heart,
to have natural gas and not to give a fart,
to see them line up, pitch-oil tin in hand:
each independent, oil-forsaken island,
like jeering at some scrunter with the blues,
while you lend him some need-a-half-sole shoes,
some begging bold as brass, some coming meeker,
but from Jamaica to poor Dominica
we make them know they begging, every loan
we send them is like blood squeezed out of stone,
and giving gives us back the right to laugh
that we couldn't see we own black people starve,
and, more we give, more we congratulate
we-self on our own self-sufficient state.
In all them project, all them Five-Year-Plan,
what happen to the Brotherhood of Man?
Around the time I dead it wasn't so,
we sang the Commonwealth of caiso,
we was in chains, but chains made us unite,
now who have, good for them, and who blight, blight;
my bread is bitterness, my wine is gall,
my chorus is the same: 'I want to fall.'
Oh, wheel of industry, check out your cogs!
Between the knee-high trash and khaki dogs
Arnold's Phoenician trader reach this far,
selling you half-dead batteries for your car;
the children of Tagore, in funeral shroud,
curry favor and chicken from the crowd;

as for the Creoles, check their house, and look,
you bust your brain before you find a book,
when Spoiler see all this, ain't he must bawl,
'area of darkness,' with V. S. Nightfall?
Corbeaux like cardinals line the La Basse
in ecumenical patience while you pass
the Beetham Highway – Guard corruption's stench,
you bald, black justices of the High Bench –
and beyond them the firelit mangrove swamps,
ibises practicing for postage stamps,
Lord, let me take a taxi South again
and hear, drumming across the Caroni Plain,
the tabla in the Indian half hour
when twilight fills the mud huts of the poor,
to hear the tattered flags of drying corn
rattle a sky from which all the gods gone,
their bleached flags of distress waving to me
from shacks, adrift like rafts on a green sea,
'Things ain't go change, they ain't go change at all,'
to my old chorus: 'Lord, I want to bawl.'
The poor still poor, whatever arse they catch.
Look south from Laventille, and you can watch
the torn brown patches of the Central Plain
slowly restitched by needles of the rain,
and the frayed earth, crisscrossed like old bagasse,
spring to a cushiony quilt of emerald grass,
and who does sew and sow and patch the land?
The Indian. And whose villages turn sand?
The fishermen doomed to stitching the huge net
of the torn foam from Point to La Fillette.

One thing with Hell, at least it organize
in soaring circles, when any man dies
he must pass through them first, that is the style,
Jesus was down here for a little while,
cadaverous Dante, big-guts Rabelais,
all of them wave to Spoiler on their way.
Catch us in Satan tent, next carnival:
Lord Rochester, Quevedo, Juvenal,
Maestro, Martial, Pope, Dryden, Swift, Lord Byron,
the lords of irony, the Duke of Iron,

hotly contending for the monarchy
in couplets or the old re-minor key,
all those who gave earth's pompous carnival
fatigue, and groaned 'O God, I feel to fall!'
all those whose anger for the poor on earth
made them weep with a laughter beyond mirth,
names wide as oceans when compared with mine
salted my songs, and gave me their high sign.
All you excuse me, Spoiler was in town;
you pass him straight, so now he gone back down.

EDWARD KAMAU BRATHWAITE

Horse Weebles

Sellin biscuit an salfish in de plantation shop at pie
corner, was another good way of keepin she body an
   soul-seam together

she got she plot of cane, she cow, she fifteen pigeons in a
   coop,
razzle-neck fool-hens, a rhode islan cocklin,
yam, pumpkin, okro, sweet
potato, green pea bush

there is lard ile in de larder
an shark ile for de children's colds
there is easin ile for crusty locks
and castor oil with lime or salt or sugar for extreme
distress, and candle grease for sea-egg pricks an chiggoes

but she sells in de plantation shop at pie corner, hoping to
   make enns meet.

from she left school, taking up sewing since she was
   fourteen,
bringin forth myrtle, den eggbert, den
sammy an redsin de twin wuns

not a sarradee come you cahn fine she in there after leven
   o'clock
heat risin: smokin hisin outside: blackbirds hidin from sun
white: weighin out flour, choppin up salt beef, countin out
   biscuit

shovellin
oat flake out o de tin while she
frettin

evenin miss
evvy, miss
maisie, miss
maud, olive

how you! how
you, eveie, chile!
you tek dat miraculous bush
fuh de trouble you tell me about!

de cornmeal flour is flow thru she fingers like time
self, me chile

the saltfish barrel is dark like a well an is broaden out to a
    lake at de bottom
where de swink is splash into slippery conger-eels

the crystal sugar is shine like stars that does twinkle into de
    dark
o de ackee tree

but you tek
it!

ev'ry night fore uh gets
into bed.

uh bet-
'cha feelin less
poorly a'ready!

i int know, pearlie,
man, any-
way, de body int dead.

no man, you even lookin
more hearty!

a'ready!
then all uh kin say
an uh say it agen:
we got to thank god
fuh small mercies

an she is dream of tears of stone
of dark meroë water lapping at the centre of the world

but then is cries an hungry faces: children
who can hardly shit: t'in bones of ancient skeletones

the planter's robber's waggon wheels and whips
and she trapped in within her rusting canepiece plot.

so sar'dee nights when you hearin de shout
mister greedyman boltin he bars cross de gate
de pump-up glass lamp soon outin out

she is dust off she hanns
put back de rounn biscuit lid pun de barrel
help lock stock and socket de shop

collect what little they give she in small
change, handin back what she owe pun de frock

goin slowly down in de winks o de dark
to de half lot o' lann dat she callin a home

an not sayin a word to a soul what she see what she dream
   what she own

Starvation and *Blues*

Starvation

This is no white man lan'
an yet we have ghetto here
we have place where man cyaan live good
we have place where man have to sweat shit
we have place where man die wid im eye-water dry up
where he cyaan even cry tribulation
where de dry river rocks clog im in

i did swim into dis worl' from a was a small bwoy
an i never see harbour yet
ship cyaan spot no pilot light
i burnin through dis wall o silence
wid me dread

look how i look pan likkle fun:
herb, soun' system,
runnin a groun' wid de don drummon blues
summon de nyah bingeh
but non-a dem come

de eart' cole, you see me hyah,
de goodyear tyre dem tek flight

o dust, o nasty water
from de pat'ole, from de hasphalt,
an lan' pan tap de sufferer dem,
standin by pan de sidewalk,
inside de wayside cabin dem a-kall
a bus stap, hadvertisin'
SHERATON HOTEL

you see dis root o bottle
springblade risin
from de shacks; you see dis tall
vexation pan me face dat never favar talk
dat wan' to strangle
priest an politician; dat wan' to halt
de brothers in black space, de daughters
in dem dream a abyssinia, de white
black trenton in im cage

a barbican, a red hills,
a skyline drive, a babylon . . .
dis rage o crow dem
walkin pan de coffin wid it wheels,
stoppin at de station, police
station, haxin for sargeant brown
when de likkle pickney dem drown
ina drei gully

an de hungry belly
mekkin one wid me skull
wid me white cock o deat'
wid me fuse bok o healt'
wid me leakin drum . . .

leka dem pass
wha' de rass:
bus, taxi cab, limousine

i waitin here:
one day de grass goin green,
de tyre dem goin shred thru to de rim

de sheraton hotel goin flash
out all it light,
it money-makin room goin resurrect dem

self back down to gravel
an babylon gwine hear an
crash down to de groun'

wid i an i still here
wid i an i still standin here
wid dese blues
wid dese bogle blues
wid dese broken bokkle blues . . .

Blues

i woke up this mornin
sunshine int showin through my door
i woke up this mornin
sunshine int showin through my door
cause the blues is got me
and i int got strength to go no more

i woke up this mornin
clothes still scattered cross the floor
i woke up this mornin
clothes still scattered cross the floor
las night the ride was lovely
but she int comin back for more

sea island sunshine
where are you hidin now
sea island sunshine
where are you hidin now
could a sware i left you in the cupboard
but is only empties mockin at me in there now

empty bottles knockin
laugh like a woman satisfied
empty bottles knockin
laugh like a woman satisfied
she full an left me empty
laughin when i should a cried

this place is empty bottles
this place is a woman satisfied
this place is empty bottles
this place is a woman satisfied

she drink muh sugar water
till muh sunshine died

i woke up this mornin
sunshine int showin underneath my door
i woke up this mornin
sunshine int showin underneath my door
she gone an left me empty
and i should a died . . .

Schooner

A tossed night between us
high seas
and then in the morning
sails slack
rope flapping the rigging
your schooner came in

on the deck, buttressed
with mango boxes, chicken-
coops, rice: I saw you:
older than I would wish you
more tattered than my pride
could stand

you saw me
moving reluctant to the quay-
side, stiff as you knew me
too full of pride.
but you had travelled
braved the big wave
and the bilge-swishing stomach,
climbed the tall seas
to come to me

*ship was too early
or was I too late?*

walking still slowly
(too late or too early?)
saw you suddenly turn

ropes quickly cast off from the capstan
frilled sails were unfurled
water already between your hull and the harbour

too late too late
or too early?

running now
one last rope stretched
to the dockside
tripping over a chain –
chink in my armour –

but the white bows were turning
stern coming round squat in the water

and I
older now
more torn and tattered than my pride
could stand
stretch out my love to you across the water
but cannot reach your hand

Harbour

But love curdles to milk in this climate
love of companion to distrust
love of good woman to lust
love of the good soil
to rust

the white man will not take
the black man's eye to his brother
the brown man keeps his own corridor
lies become politics of getting on
rum explodes in the blood stream
the humming bird dreams of the thickening horn of the
    hornet

sing dance drum limbo
the chains have not been shucked
the shackles are not off

their links tinkle with money
the tight collar of history chokes on blue dollars
the eyes blaze back into their history
to discover damp, squid, black-fire; shame makes me laugh
shame brings its cracked twigs of terror

so the sick skin must be peeled
the canefields of pain must be cut-
lashed away: their juice like a soft
error; their trapped crystal traitors
the trash of their dry river beds
is chained to my feet
why is the sun of this colour

and the islands float, unmoored and moisture laden
lidded with dream and dew
and find no anchor of love, no hover
of hope in their back-
yard: they can find no safe hollow
the sun rises and sets, rages
bleeding bleeding the pages of history's horror

yet here in the cup of my word
on the lip of my eyelid of light
like a star in its syllable socket
there is a cripple crack and hobble
whorl of colour, eye

it is a cool harbour
death of the trapped fish is not its meaning
death of the bird's wing is not within its memory
safe for ships, the fisherman's labour
soft for ships, cloud, high, in shadow

prows cut their white teeth towards it
sails, halyard, the salt harp's sting

there is the smell of tar, of mango tang
locked sun of oranges, nailed boxes

charcoal stains, the stretched decks creaking
with wave heave, scrubbed skin of the whitewood

the sea's drummers

softly softly on sound: fire of starlight
blazed by white bellows; the black bulk heaving to starboard

it is a beginning

forests, canefields, move over the waters
seeds of the dead fruit: cashew, grape, guinep,

with their blind tendrils of freedom:
a long way the one eyed stare of the coconut will travel
steered by its roots, what its milk teaches,
till its stalk, with its flag and its cross-

sword, its mailed head and chained feet
walks over the arawaks beaches

EDWARD LUCIE-SMITH

The Wise Child

I couldn't wait. My childhood angered me.
It was a sickness time would cure in time,
But clocks were doctors slow to make me well.
I sulked and raged. My parents told me 'play' –
I stood in the garden shouting my own name.
The noise enlarged me. I can hear it still.

At last I've come where then I longed to go.
And what's the change? – I find that I can choose
To wish for where I started. Childhood puts
Its prettiest manners on. I see the dew
Filming the lawn I stamped.
                              The wise child knows
Not here, not there, the perfect somewhere waits.

Your Own Place

Invent it now. Your own place,
Your own soil. All inferior
Localities are done with.
Yet how is it to be made
Without things remembered? Sun
Thrown in fistfuls, and the sand
Of that ripe apricot; wind
Spiced with thyme and lavender
Blowing from one hill, at one
Season. But these bring with them
Disasters – the imperfect
Friendship broken, and the perfect
Love unconsummated. Sand
Which burns the foot, hill blocking
The view. So invent it now,
And arrive after the long

Voyage, alone, having left
A companion at each
Port, a lover in all the
Hot bedrooms, all the stifling
Cabins.

It is before dawn.
There is a cove with a few
Bare rocks. Your feet cling to them,
Naked, as the rest of you
Is naked. Women come laughing
Down to the shore. You call out,
Expecting to be embraced.
They strip and bathe, brush by you
Without a glance or a cry
As the light swells and brightens.

The Hymn Tunes

They often haunt me, these substantial ghosts,
Four-four, four-square, thumping in the brain;
Not always with the words their puritan
Plainness was made to, and yet always plain,
Bawdily forthright, loud for Lord of Hosts.
One must begin somewhere.
                            Where I began

I sang off-key on Low Church, tropical
Sunday mornings; organ-swept, never doubted
That the sure tunes had reason to be sure,
That some great good would come of what I shouted.
Later, across the sea, I sang in a tall
Gothic cathedral, where all sounds endure

Long seconds in the vault, but felt no change
In what the tunes were. And when, later still,
I learned new smut to sing to the old notes,
They stayed the same. Nothing changed until
I woke one day to find the rules were strange
I'd thought to obey.
                      Now a hymn-tune floats

Teasingly into the mind, patterns a day
To its rhythm, and nags like sudden speech
In a tongue one used to know – quietly said
Words which move forward, always out of reach;
Still, though I cannot grasp what it is they say,
God's tunes go marching through my echoing head.

Imperialists in Retirement

'I have done the state some service'
– *Othello*

Tender each to the other, gentle
   But not to the world which has just now
Snatched back its gifts. Oh fallen, fallen
   From your proconsular state! I watch
Perhaps too closely, with too much
   Easy pity, the old man's loving
Protective gesture – the old woman
   Accepting the arm of a blind man,
Leaning upon it. I look around
   At the faded chintz, at china chipped
By so many packings, unpackings.

I listen, too. This part is not so
   Easy. He is not resigned. He cries
Aloud for the state he kept. He wants
   Privilege still and power, the long
Moonlit nights of the steamship voyage
   Out to a new appointment. Whisky
And bridge and talk of what's to be done –
   The phrase again: 'They're children, really.'
And he beats with feeble hands against
   The immovable door of blindness,
The shut door of the years. 'Live in the
   Past,' he says. 'That's the thing. Live in the
Past.' And his wife soothes him, as one would
   A child when it's nearly his bedtime.
'One mustn't grumble,' she says. 'Times change.'

Her hands are reddened and swollen I
   Notice, saying goodnight. Her head shakes.
She stumbles a little in rising.
   Tonight she washes up. Tomorrow
She will scrub their kitchen on her knees.
   I see, as we go, the look of love
From her to him blind. Then the door shuts.

ABDUR-RAHMAN SLADE HOPKINSON

The Madwoman of Papine

Two Cartoons with Captions

I

Four years ago,
in this knot of a village north of the university,
she was in residence
where a triangle of grass gathered the mountain road,
looped it once, and tossed it to Kingston,
where grampus buses, cycling students,
duppies of dust and ululations in light
vortexed around her.
Ritualist, she tried to reduce the world,
sketching her violent diagrams
against a wall of mountains which her stare made totter.
Her rhythmic ideas detonated into gestures.
She would jab her knee into the groin of the air,
fling her sharp instep at the fluttering sky,
revise perspectives with the hooks of her fingers,
and butt blood from the teeth of God.

She cooked and ate anything. But, being so often busy,
she hardly ever cooked or ate.

What of her history?
These are the latitudes of the ex-colonized,
Of degradation still unmollified,
imported managers, styles in art,
second-hand subsistence of the spirit,
the habit of waste,
mayhem committed on the personality,
and everywhere the wrecked or scuttled mind.
Scholars, more brilliant than I could hope to be,
advised that if I valued poetry,
I should eschew all sociology.
Who could make anything of a pauper lunatic
modelling one mildewed dress from year to year?

Scarecrow, just sane enough occasionally
to pick-up filth and toast it on a brick.
She would then renew
the comic mime of her despair.

Clearly something was very wrong with her
as subject. Pedestrian. Too limited
for lyric literature.
I went away for four years. Then returned.

2

One loaf now costs what two loaves used to.
The madwoman has crossed the road
and gone behind the shops
nearer the university,
oriens et occidente lux,
the light of scholars rising in the west.
She wears the same perennial dress,
now black as any graduate's gown,
but stands in placid anguish now,
perfects her introverted trance,
with hanging arms, still feet,
chin on breast, forehead parallel
to the eroded, indifferent earth,
merely an invisible old woman,
extremist votary at an interior altar,
repeatedly rinsing along her tongue
a kind of invocation, whispered, verbless:

'O
Rass Rass Rass
in the highest.'

Tycoon, Poet, Saint

An island off the main.
Easy to cross to the metropolis
By plane or boat. Nevertheless, an island,
With deep if narrow channel in between.
Radio and television sets relay
News from the mainland marketplace.

An island off the main, which is to say:
Cut off, or not cut off, just as you please.

Thank God for sunshine, rich soil, regular
Abundant rain. From the small farms and orchards
Come grain and butter, vegetables and fruit.
A self-sufficient place. Sufficient too
As home for saint or poet.
But saint and poet have been irrelevant
Since God knows when. Time is progressive.

The prosperous boutiques around the coast
Buzz with the flower-shirted and knock-kneed
Pursuers of swift holiday distraction,
The tycoons from the mainland marketplace.
The beaches shriek with sunlight as it grills
Pallid flesh offerings.

                    Past the ring of farmland
That feeds, these days, the hotel coast,
The island rises in a stair of crags
To a skull-bald mountain, soundboard for the thunder.
All roads stop short. No one comes here.
(Too few have feet for crags, heads for heights;
Besides, the fun-shops lie the other way).

But scholars talk
Of two that share that igneous, cracked skull.
Their caves on opposite slopes: a saint; a poet.
Both sold their farms when the tycoons started touring;
Both pulled back to the lightning-pelted mountain.
Neither speaks to the other, not from testiness,
But too entranced by the shafts of golden lightning.

Once every month, though never on the same day,
Each scrambles down that runnelled face
And catches boat or plane
For the metropolitan main
To satisfy himself of lightning truth
(Lightning and gold
Are very old)
By proving it against
The expediencies of the marketplace.
And each,

On his way back to the mountain,
Surreptitious among the flowery tycoons,
Stops for a day at the beach.

December 1974: a Lament

And the euphorbia,
Snow on its branches, Lord.
Though our sun melts flesh,
The euphorbia whitens.
The year is dying.
My time is dying.
What have I planted, Lord?

And the poinsettia,
Blood stars the hedges, Lord;
Daytime and startime
The red spears cluster.
My year is dying.
My cry dies.
What have I planted, Lord?

And gungu also,
Pods weighting the branches, Lord,
Though Your children are poor.
(Cry thanks for fit food).
My year is dying, dying,
And blood runs thin.
What have I planted, Lord?

I cannot afford
Time's waste, fruit-
less sweat, point-
less talk. For time points.
And spears of poinsettia threaten.
Wasting I cannot afford.
Drive me to plant, Lord!

Grand trees I cannot afford.
The quick crops, Lord!
Ambition I cannot afford.
The cash crops, Lord!

IVAN VAN SERTIMA

Volcano

When I speak now
there are no urgent rumblings in my voice
no scarlet vapour issues from my lips
I spit no lava:
but I am a volcano
an incandescent cone of angry flesh
black brimstone broils within
the craters of my being.
When I speak now
no one can hear me
the thunder lies too deep too deep
for violent cataclysm:
My heat
is nothing but a memory now:
My cry
a terror of the long forgotten:
Time heaps high snow upon my passive flanks
and I stand muted with my furnace caged
too chilled for agitation.
But mark me well
for I am still volcano
I may disown my nature, my vesuvian blood,
so did my cousin Krakatoa
for centuries locked his fist within the earth
and only shook it when his wrath was full
and died to rock the world.
So, mark me well
pray that my silence shall outlive my wrath
for if this vomit ventures to my lips again
old orthodoxies villaged on my flanks
shall face the molten magma of my wrath
submerge and perish.

EDWARD BAUGH

Colour-scheme

The rainbow is the shape of God's desire:
all colours bend together, blend,
arching from end to end of earth,
curve of love and loveliness.

That's only a deception for the eye.
Skin-deep excuses are enough
to make a Memphis of the world.

The rainbow fades and aspirations die,
one red encroaches on the sky.
The rainbow, sign of God's desire,
is earnest of the final fire.

Truth and Consequences

When the mob swerved
at him
he screamed
'I'm not the man you're after.
I'm Cinna the poet.
I never meddled in politics!'

The mob knew better. 'Then tear him,'
it screamed back, 'tear him
for his bad verses!'

It was then he learned
too late
there's no such thing as 'only literature'.
Every line commits you.
Those you thought dead will rise,
accusing. And if you plead
you never meant them,
then feel responsibility

break on you in a sudden sweat
as the beast bears down.

The Carpenter's Complaint

Now you think that is right, sah? Talk the truth.
The man was mi friend. *I* build it, *I*
Build the house that him live in; but now
That him dead, that marga-foot bwoy, him son,
Come say, him want a nice job for the coffin,
So him give it to *Mister* Belnavis to make –
That big-belly crook who don't know him arse
From a chisel, but because him is big-shot, because
Him make big-shot coffin, fi-him coffin must better
Than mine! Bwoy, it hot me, it hot me
For true. Fix we a nex' one, Miss Fergie –
That man coulda knock back him waters, you know sah!
I remember the day in this said-same bar
When him drink Old Brown and Coxs'n into
The ground, then stand up straight as a plumb-line
And keel him felt hat on him head and walk
Home cool, cool, cool. Dem was water-bird, brother!
Funeral? *Me*, sah? That bwoy have to learn
That a man have him pride. But bless mi days!
Good enough to make the house that him live in,
But not good enough to make him coffin!
I woulda do it for nutt'n, for nutt'n! The man
Was mi friend. Damn marga-foot bwoy.
Is university turn him fool. I tell you,
It burn me, it burn me for true!

Country Dance

Those country folk dancing a *schottische*
to shac-shac and fiddle in the one-room
schoolhouse-cum-village hall
are not concerned with origins.

Miss Bibsy leads, rakish
in Sam's battered fedora.
Unstaid her sweep and bounce
of buttock. Read Africa.

We had come seeking the true folk
the immaculate idea untouched by irony,
and what could be truer than Bibsy's
callused heel stamping its assurance
on this hard ground?
Night, rolling in from the Atlantic
washes over the island
re-enacting migrations.
The sea's complaint is the sigh of the tribes.
And in the pause between two breakers
was that a skirl of bagpipes?
Doan worry bout dat, Sammy boy,
Scotlan is a districk in Barbados
from where, on a clear day, if you eye clean
you can make believe you seein the golden shores.
Night, rolling in from the Atlantic
washes over the island.
Later, picking my way
down the hill
in the dark
the music bounces in my head
like light.

HOWARD FERGUS

Forecast

There is a rumour
Mongst the clouds that it will rain
Trust none black or white

I know my humour
My cosmic rheumatism pains
Look for rain tonight

Ethnocide

The willing Arawak
Kissed by the lily lips of Spain
Demonstrated his belief
In Christianity
And self-extermination
Columbus in communion
Ate their bread
Drank their blood
And dyed their bed
He washed his hands
And thanked St Christopher
For the slaughter.

The hostile Carib
Dodged the holy hand of Spain
Affirming his belief
In ethnocide
And self-determination
Caonabo fed
His godly guests
The poisoned juice of cassareep
In a calabash of gold
The gods of Anacona drank
Their blood and thundered
Righteous laughter.

Lament for Maurice Bishop

BISHOP
high priest of Grenada
land of spice
and putrid sacrifice
why so sudden flight
in undressed wounds
standby for paradise

Blood clots on the sceptre
sully the bright sword
forged in revolution fires
your blood
your father's blood twice dead
the people's blood heavy
like a guillotine on your head

What evensong you sang
at Mount Moritz or Moriah
did you chant
Das Kapital or King James
did you breathe the names
of Marx and angels
was Fidel faithful to your call
helpless hero
before the lamentable fall

They say ghosts march past in silence
at Fort Rupert
sire's sepulchre
son's doomed altar
revolution's wasted rampart
Grenada's fell Golgotha

Will you come back to medicine your land
do armies muster where you are
do men still aspire
do sudden storm clouds tumble down
shipwrecking high desire

Bishop of Grenada
land of spice
were you embalmed
checked out so soon for paradise

CLAIRE HARRIS

Framed

She is in your painting   the one you bought when the taxi
snarled in market lines   you jumped out and grabbed a
picture of stilted wooden houses against the vivid island
even then there was recognition

She is the woman in a broken pair of men's shoes   her
flesh slipped down like old socks around her ankles   a tray
of laundry on her head   I am there too   but I would not
be like her   at supper she set the one plate and the whole
cup at my place   for herself a mug a bowl my leavings. . . .
they said I resembled her   I spent hours before the mirror
training my mouth to different lines

At night while I read   she folded the blanket on her
narrow board   coalfire smooth on her face   she boiled
scrubbed   ironed   the musk of soap and others soil like
a mist around her head   often she dreamed   I would have
a maid   like her   she laughed   I studied harder harder
she grieved   I was grown a woman   I was grown
without affinity

For the calling   her eroded hands   cupped like a chalice
she offered me the blasted world as if to say   this is our
sacrament drink   I would not   this is all there is   I
could not   I left school   I left   she faded   the
island faded   styles changed   you hid the dusty
painting in the attic   But I am still there   the one in the
middle ground   my face bruising the lines of soft white
sheets   my hand raised as if to push against the frame

Policeman Cleared in Jaywalking Case

The city policeman who arrested a juvenile girl for jaywalk-
ing March 11, has been cleared of any wrongdoing by the
Alberta law enforcement appeal board.

The police officer contended the girl had not co-operated during the first five minutes after she was stopped, had failed to produce identification with a photo of herself on it, and had failed to give the policeman her date of birth.

The case was taken to the law enforcement appeal board after the girl was arrested, strip-searched and jailed in the adult detention centre.

– *Newspaper report*

(In the black community 'to signify' indicates an act of acknowledgement of sharing, of identifying with.

The girl was fifteen. An eyewitness to the street incident described her as 'terrified'.)

Look you, child, I signify   three hundred years in swarm
around me   this thing I must   this uneasy thing
myself the other   stripped down to skin and sex   to
stand   to stand and say   to stand and say before you all
the child was black and female and therefore mine   listen
you walk the edge of this cliff with me at your peril do not
hope to step off safely to brush stray words off your face to
flick an idea off with thumb and forefinger   to have a
coffee and go home comfortably
Recognize this edge   and this air carved with her silent
invisible cries

Observe now this harsh world   full of white works   or
so you see us   and it is white   white washed male and
dangerous even to you   full of white fire white heavens
white words   and it swings in small circles around you
so you see it   and here I stand black and female   bright
black on the edge of this white world   and I will not blend
in   nor will I fade into the midget shades   peopling your
dream

Once long ago   the loud tropic air   the morning rushing
by in a whirl of wheels   I am fifteen drifting through hot
streets shifting direction by instinct   tar heel soft under
my shoes I see shade on the other side of the road   secure
in my special dream I step off the curb   the sudden cars
crash and jangle of steel   the bump   the heart stopping
fall into silence   then the distant driver crying 'Oh Gawd!
somebody's girl child she step off right in front of me, Gawd!'

Black faces anxious in a fainting world   a policeman bends
into my blank gaze   'where it hurting yuh? tell me!' his
rough hand under my neck   then seeing me whole 'stand
up let me help yuh!' shaking his head   the crowd straining
on the sidewalk   the grin of the small boy carrying my
books   then the policeman suddenly stern 'what you name
girl?'   the noisy separation of cars   'eh what you name?'
I struck dumb   dumb   'look child you ever see a car in
plaster a paris?'   dumb   'tell me what's your name?
You ever see a car in a coffin!'   the small boy calling out
my name into such shame

Now female I stand in this silence   where somebody's
black girl child jaywalking to school is stripped   spread
searched   by a woman who finds that black names are not
tattoed on the anus   pale hands soiling the black flesh
through the open door the voices of men in corridors   and
in spite of this   yea, in spite of this   black and female to
stand here and say   I am   she is   I say to stand here
knowing   this is a poem black in its most secret self

Because I fear   I fear myself and I fear your skeletal skin
the spider tracery of your veins   I fear your heavy fall of
hair like sheets of rain and the clear cold water of your eyes
and I fear myself the rage alive in me   consider the things
you make even in the mystery of earth and the things you can
an acid rain that shrivels trees   your clinging fires that
shrivel skin   This law that shrivels children   and I fear
your naked fear of all that's different   your dreams of power
your foolish innocence   but I fear myself and the smooth
curve of guns   I fear   Look, your terrible Gods do not
dance nor laugh nor punish men   do not eat or drink but
stay a far distance   watch the antic play of creation and
cannot blink or cheer   Even I fear the ease you make of
living this stolen land and all its graceful seductions   but
I fear most myself   how easy to drown in your world and
dead believe myself living   who stands 'other' and
vulnerable to your soul's disease
Look you child I signify

MERVYN MORRIS

Brief

Your dark eye is a prism
to reflect
the new world in its glass?

Shatter that rass
and roam
the darker continent
inside.

The House-slave

A drum thumps, faraway;
around the lamp my tribe of blood
are singing brothers home.

But soon that central fire will rage
too harsh for relics of the whip:
they'll burn this building,
fire these books, this art.

And these are my rooms now:
my pallid masters fled,
freeing the only home I knew.
I'll stay another night,
sounding my tutored terror of the dark.

The Early Rebels

Time and the changing passions played them tricks,
Killing the shop-soiled resolutions dead.
Gone are the early angry promises
Of rich men squeezed, of capitalists bled.

More adult honesties have straightened ties
And brushed the dinner-jackets clean,
Maturer minds have smelt out fallacies
And redefined what thinkers mean.

Hope drives a chromium symbol now
And smiles a toothpaste passion to the poor,
With colder eloquence explaining how
The young were foolish when they swore
They'd see those dunghills dank and dreary
All replaced by bright new flats:
Good sense was never youthful fury
And rash young promises by brats. . . .

'Let's drink a loyal toast to dedication:
We mean the same but youth is past;
We are the fathers of our nation,
The thinking leaders come at last.
Cheers for the faith of simple minds,
Cheers for the love of humble friends;
Love does not alter when it finds
That we have redefined its ends.'

To an Expatriate Friend

Colour meant nothing. Anyone
who wanted help, had humour or was kind
was brother to you; categories of skin
were foreign; you were colour-blind.

And then the revolution. Black
and loud the horns of anger blew
against the long oppression; sufferers
cast off the precious values of the few.

New powers re-enslaved us all:
each person manacled in skin, in race.
You could not wear your paid-up dues;
the keen discriminators typed your face.

The future darkening, you thought it time
to say good-bye. It may be you were right.
It hurt to see you go; but, more,
it hurt to see you slowly going white.

For Consciousness

Ol' plantation wither,
factory close down,
brothers of de country
raisin Cain in town.

An now dem in de city
sweatin blood dem fin'
is jus like de same system
dem mean to lef behin':

but agents of de owners dem
is harder now to sight –
plenty busha doan ride horse
an some doan t'ink dem white.

In de new plantation story
firs' t'ing dat have to know
is who an who to tackle
when de call to battle blow.

Valley Prince

Me one, way out in the crowd,
I blow the sounds, the pain,
but not a soul
would come inside my world
or tell me how it true.
I love a melancholy baby,
sweet, with fire in her belly;
and like a spite
the woman turn a whore.

Cool and smooth around the beat
she wake the note inside me
and I blow me mind.

Inside here, me one
in the crowd again,
and plenty people
want me blow it straight.
But straight is not the way; my world
don' go so; that is lie.
Oonu gimme back me trombone, man:
is time to blow me mind.

Family Pictures

In spite of love
desire to be alone
haunts him like prophecy.

Observe: the baby chuckles,
gurgles his delight
that daddy-man is handy,
to be stared at, clawed at,
spitted-up upon;
the baby's elder brother
laughs, or hugs, and nags
for popcorn or a pencil
or a trip.

And see: the frazzled wife
who jealously
protects the idol infant
from the smallest chance
of harm, and anxious
in the middle of the night
wakes up to coughs; and checks,
and loves, and screams
her nerves; but loves him
patient still: the wife
who sweets the bigger boy

and teases him through homework,
bright as play.

But you may not observe
(it is a private sanctuary)
the steady glowing power
that makes a man feel loved,
feel needed, all of time;
yet frees him, king of her
emotions, jockey of her
flesh, to cherish
his own corner
of the cage.

In spite of love
this dream:
to go alone
to where
the fishing boats are empty
on the beach
and no one knows
which man is
father, husband, victim,
king, the master of one cage.

One, Two

I
Lying in the dark together
we
in wordless dialogue
defined community.

II
You switch the light on to inspect
an alien remark.
And now your body stutters.

No more lying in the dark.

Peace-time

bomb-disposal
combed the area
and declared it clean

but love i cannot
guarantee
safe conduct

through the rubble
of my dreams –

i've read
too many people
blown to bits

by land mines
lying silent
in the dust

long after
all those bells
and all that joy

long after solemn treaties
had been signed and sealed

LEROY CLARKE

Where Hurricane

For The Mighty Chalkdust and Black Stalin

I

. . . where hurricane,
Janet the merciless jammette of winds
and flaying fibril . . .
The sea gave up serpents
to wring the neck of a whole continent
a voyeur . . .
leaving the coughs of butterflies
on the mast-tail

sink slow
          sink fast . . .
how many tribes aboard . . . !

so we came here
          soft coughing coughs
          each bauble an island . . .
spearless, armless . . .
beheaded totems
          vastness and funereal
          depth without root-proboscis . . .

II

bayonets of fire
          of spit
plunge with tourists' laughter
down the hatch.
an Actor wants to take the world,
bleeds in de bamboo:
                    ah good . . . ah good
                    God knows ah good
                    please recognize me . . . !
log of the sea tells it . . .
log of the land tells it . . .
come,

you cut-wrists, you . . . you . . . you
testify.
throw up those murdered corpses . . .
the chain of debris lengthens
like ants with news of a dying pus . . .

police gun down chile.
actuh sues actor.
now a boy-scout
                  now a general . . . a president . . . !
(can't keep up with
              the change of uniforms)
and so we see
nation rise up
            nation fall down
                  bap!

archipelago of salt and flour
— no yeast.
we parade
          souls like old fruit
muttering a rosary of flies . . .
dey hoist dey flag at midnight sharp . . .
                  Amen
dey bury coffins without de bodies . . .
                  Amen
dem an de dead who hang 'round de house . . .
                  Amen
dem skull-face, dem cow-foot, dem blood-eye . . .
                  Amen

dey cyar fool me doh
somebody go hav to pay dear
                m'dear
somebody go hav to pay
            wid dey blood . . .
                Amen
. . . to de crossroad
. . . to de crossroad
          Sandals . . . sandals . . .
mongoose an snake
dance de stick . . .

bois . . . bois
bois . . . bois
Is me de boisman, I ent fraid . . .
wid tongue in meh mouth, eyes sharp in meh head . . .
you know, I ent fraid
Is me de boisman, I cud never fraid
Rats stay in dey hole, snake tight like dey dead
tell dem shorty, I ent fraid
Aberdeen son, is me, me one
bush shaking, monkey on the run
ah tall fuh so
I ent fraid,
I cud never fraid
I is de only boisman dat ah fraid . . .

Mongoose an snake
dance de crab . . .
bois . . . bois
bois . . . bois

E. A. MARKHAM

Don't Talk to Me about Bread

she kneads
deep into the night
and the whey-coloured dough

springy and easy and yielding to her will

is revenge. Like a rival,
dough toys with her. Black-brown hands in the belly
bringing forth a sigh.

She slaps it, slaps it double with fists
with heel of hand applies the punishment
not meant for bread

and the bitch on the table sighs
and exhales a little spray of flour
a satisfied breath of white

on her hand

mocking the colour
robbing hands of their power
as they go through the motions, kneading . . .
She listens for the sigh which haunts

from the wrong side of her own door
from this wanton cheat of dough
this whey-faced bitch rising up

in spite of her fight, rising up
her nipples, her belly, rising up
two legs, dear god, in a blackwoman's rage . . .

Laughing at her, all laughing at her:
giggling bitch, abandoned house, and Man
still promising from afar what men promise . . .

Hands come to life again: knife
in the hand, the belly ripped open, and she smears
white lard and butter, she sprinkles
a little obeah of flour and curses to stop up the wound.

Then she doubles the bitch up
with cuffs, wrings her like washing
till she's the wrong shape

and the tramp lets out a damp, little sigh
a little hiss of white
enjoying it.

An Old Thought for a New Couple

She is not sure
if her failure
was important.

Death strikes
at his eyes again.
He puts on his glasses

and her smile returns.

Rewrite

Beauty screws her new
leg into place and gains
advantage. Blame the limp,
she says, on Progress: who's
for a game then?

　　　　　　I'll play,
let me play, says the Beast
sick of being upstaged again.

The hoof in the chest –
a new experience to Beast –
puzzles him: for so long
it had been *his* role to give
these beauties pleasure.

Late Return

'What an odd name, Markham, for a Montserratian!' –
Canadian tourist in Montserrat

'There is no Markham in the Directory.' – Telephone
Exchange

I

The ruin, at least, was something; the yard
with face half-rutted was the boy no girl would kiss
except in retrospect; blotches of soil erupting
like teenage lust: a tangle of green – sugarapple,
mango, sour now, outgrowing the graft of family name;
other fruit, near-fruit . . .
With no young scamp to lizard vertical for juice,
your nuts are safe: weeds cling
in parody to trunk (like boys born after you, tall,
or long-abandoned sons made good, defying dad
to wish them better) unharnessed
by Nellie's line on which the great, white
sheets of the house would flap their wings in rage.
Fringed Afro of arrogance:
their better view of the sea taunts us, close
to earth, flaunting fruit too high to get at;
some beyond-the-milk stage bunched as if in decoration.
Well before dark, my challenge from below, half-
remembered, no-more-to-be-taken-up, peters out:
mine is a garden, not of Eden, but of youth.
Suspecting things to be as honest, as accurate as they seem,
that this bit of family, untended, past its best
season, reflects something in me, I reach
for the camera I don't possess. Someone in Europe,
in America, will find this quaint. For me, a tourist-
polaroid to arrest decline.

II

I am home again, perhaps two generations late.
I think, when the jumble of accusation, of longing,
clears: I am the juvenile not yet exiled.
This rock is a springboard
into water, into sea.
Sea is safe mattress

for the pole-vaulter, beyond sand;
my ocean-liner, vast and reliable, absorbing
shock, proof of completed journeys near to risk,
knowing the way to 'abroad'. The jump
is voluntary as coming to a road which forks:
sudden pressure from behind makes you choose
without benefit of signpost. Now this:
Montserrat has caught up with the world,
impatient of late-comers, of its children, foreign-ravaged,
straggling home without humility. (High-flying
Concorde boxing people's ears, is enough.)
Others have been unpersoned
through the idiocies of politics. I, who seek no public
cut to advancement, am an Economic
not a political dissident.

Familiar picture: Man and suitcase,
contents not from this place; professional migrant
eyeing the landscape. My unpaid guide tells a story
of a potato patch, a villa-patch cleared
too soon. A riot of green is the penalty.
Less young in energy, we must try again.

III

Later, second thoughts come to the rescue
and puncture self-conceit: things affecting you
affect not only you, etc. 'Most of what matters
in your life takes place in your absence' is a verdict
with the threat drained out. (In that absence, woodlice
ate your house.) But something of you
lives here, a voice not heard in twenty years,
stubbornly locked in the present. The mind,
like a cat's paw, tries to trap stray cloud of memory,
mists of past, raindrops thrown by an unseen hand . . .
Inevitably, it locates you in the third person.

Is he a late developer?
He was sure of it, then, hot afternoons
stumped by Latin homework, bowled by the Physics
master before he took guard, before he was ready.
At home, out of the team, without Excursion
to Antigua to represent the School, he had to make do

with books; books one day, hopefully, to be swapped
for passport. Here, he watched the ants

materializing from nowhere
to attack the remains of lunch. He thinks –
Regam Reges Reget . . .: Such communication systems
    grow out of . . .
Amabam Amabas Amabat (Uncomfortable, the
    imperfect tense)
Amavero Amaveris Amaverit . . .

(What is the consequence if I do not kill these ants?)

His colleagues half-way to Antigua to play the big
    match,
he imagines he sees them, ants on the boat. He can
advise them. Ivan's late-cut is dangerous. At trials,
Ivan *twice* cut the ball in the air, and got away with it:
Five runs. Ivan will be caught in Antigua before he
    scores . . .
Capio Capere Cepi Captum . . . Were we ants, boys
from School, we would find a way
to cross sea,
get message to Ivan. These ants, he notices,
place information above life: what makes them do it?
Could it be they love one another? Too foolish
a notion for a boy early in his teens
who didn't make the team, and must settle for Latin:
Amavi Amavisti Amavit.

He thinks:
after the bombs, will the ants be here?
(Maybe he has not become a scholar
to sustain such thoughts.) He thinks of a passport
stamped, stamped in Antigua, stamped in the next island,
stamped here; luggage searched, questions asked,
and is not ashamed of the obvious:
absence of love. We haven't learnt from the ants.

      IV
Again the question: do I unpack?
(Releasing echoes of *Wanderer*, of *Seafarer*, of Salesman,
1st Generation migrant hawking knick-knacks

at the door? Do I hope to dazzle
for an hour, a week, and move on? Isn't it here
that others, with my history, have underestimated
their capacity for low goals?)

To unpack or not? The case represents
all the skill I have, success, over the years
of reducing the contents of many into one –
like absorbing disciplines into a single brain
(Nellie must have felt this way, here, after the first
cassava-bread: reaping the root, peeling, washing,
grinding at the Mill – man and boy treading pole –
the white, poisonous cassava piling up in its box,
   its coffin . . .
Over-night Press; sifting, baking on hot plate:
thin, light cassava-bread.) What of this remains
in my case?

The opened case, inevitably, won't close.
A moment of panic: could the fart of Concorde
on its way to Venezuela, have got into your things?
No, this is man-menopause, faking new consciousness.
I no longer wish to prevent bits of Montserrat
smuggling in

though night sounds of crickets and dogs weigh nothing,
bats no longer have a house to be blind in;
Scots at the Agouti, Canadians at Vue Pointe
travel lightly in my head. The biography that grows
and grows in my baggage, started life a pamphlet, an
   underlined
name, a literate slave at Riley's reading the declaration
of emancipation. Nimcom has filled the years
since 1834, and my case won't close.

And more: Under the bathtowel, samples of beaches
still free to all. Here and there, memory of kindness,
of beauty, verbs of local colour TO DANCE TO SING – TO
   LOVE?
They belong here: is it crude of me to smuggle them
into that dark place where part of me still lives?

Grandfather's Sermon and Michael Smith

Let the cow, the horse, the camel, the garden-bee — let the
mud-fish, the lobster, the mussel, eel, the sting-ray, and the
grunting pig-fi — let these, and the like of these, be put on a
perfect equality with man and woman!
— *Walt Whitman* (1819–92)

I

Echoes of the Hymns return,
the frayed little knot in a cemetery,
people standing as if in need
of practice: is this how to outlive
something dead of natural causes?
Somehow it was better inside, sagging
with the weight, bending a knee
to the strange little god of a grandfather
whose voice lacked timbre, the highish pitch
right for the man's unprepossessing
look. His favourite hymns, Nos 182 and 527
in the Methodist Hymnal
come back now with the whiff
of these unnatural deaths, these killings
of near friends, this contempt
for what it takes to live.
The killer, the new god of power
will claim to be a man like other men
babbling, from a script, the language of love.

II

The clans are fighting a mile away.
They paint their faces, wear bits of grass and bark
to tell us this is happening at an earlier time.
Do not believe it, this is wishful thinking;
they wear suits and conquer the centuries
by aircraft. In capital cities
they shake each other's hands, careless
of what smears them.
They are what old men fearing, feared to predict.

A familiar animal lives on this hill,
puts on clothes during daylight
and affects human speech: you know him.

Dangerous to women after dark, particularly
those he would own: one returns from his embrace
with a shattered jaw, ribs broken.
Why do we pretend not to recognize him?

These are your grandchildren, old man –
lay-preacher, tailor, Overseer, modestly
letting the horse outlive you –
By croaking out that ancient song, by pleading asthma
you have not prevented them inheriting your earth:
Sometimes the Light surprises
the Christian while he sings . . .
is a coy way to approach you, Michael Smith.
But what is strange to a dead man?
To march in the street to his cause is strange.
To live with his death is strange.
To play the poet, imperial in arrogance,
and colonize this *subject*, is worse, ridiculous
as reading a few lines, in a public place,
for Peace. *Vanity of Vanities, Saith the Lord:*
All is Vanity. Yet, we must do it.

You are ageless, Michael Smith, grandfatherly
when it suits, you are anybody's.
The men in suits have given you away.
Don't let their dupes turn you into a hero.

III

And will they now name a bookshop
after you, a mini-shrine
where we can come and salve conscience,
the pious and the hypocrite among us
oozing virtue and well-meaning,
and let the killers off the hook?
Some who wished you dead will buy your poems:
no one will stop them.

IV

Older, from the death of friends
we are the old men now. We preach
when we can, not knowing how to lament
those many, many dead unknown to us:

so we abuse you, Michael Smith, with excess
of sentiment.
My voice is no sweeter, my command no surer
than a grandfather who for an hour stayed
God's hand and stopped a hurricane which threatened
    genocide:
his voice is now mocked by bandits who rule this land
killing for the people's good.
If you could believe it you would return to misquote
godless lines;
to turn Whitman's 'heresy' into an island's hope
and demand with us
that some be hanged by their ties,
their well-pressed suits and fake dashikis.
But who will prevent killers in the congregation
saying *Amen* to this?

DENNIS SCOTT

Homecoming

The wind is making countries
in the air, clouds dim,
golden as Eldorado voyages.
                              Those hills
harbour a sea of dreams, they told
us; and as children we were
sad, wanting a rainbow.
                              Now
heart-sailed
from home I name them
Orient, Africa,
New York, London's white
legend; the ports have
a welcoming ring — no end
to their richness, their tumble.
The sirens sing.
                              But

again, again these
hot and coffee streets reclaim
my love. Carts rumble.
The long horn of a higgler's voice
painting the shadows midday
brown, cries about harvest,
and the wind calls back
blue air across the town; it tears
the thin topographies of dream, it blows me
as by old, familiar maps,
to this affectionate shore, green
and crumpling hills,
like paper in the Admiral's fist.
The rain comes down.

                    There is a kind of tune
we must promise our children,
a shape that the quadrant measures,

no North
to turn them
away from the dissonant cities,
the salt songs,
the hunger of journeys.

                    It is time to plant
feet in our earth. The heart's metronome
insists on this arc of islands
as home.

Grampa

Look him. As quiet as a July river-
bed, asleep, an trim' down like a tree.
Jesus! I never know the Lord could
squeeze so dry. When I was four
foot small I used to say
Grampa, how come you t'in so?
an him tell me, is so I stay
me chile, is so I stay
laughing, an fine
emptying on me –

laughing? It running from him
like a flood, that old molasses
man. Lord, how I never see?
I never know a man could sweet so, cool
as rain; same way him laugh,

I cry now. Wash him. Lay him out.

I know the earth going burn
all him limb dem
as smooth as bone,
clean as a tree under the river
skin, an gather us
beside that distant Shore
bright as a river stone.

Uncle Time

Uncle Time is a ole, ole man . . .
All year long im wash im foot in de sea,
long, lazy years on de wet san'
an shake de coconut tree dem
quiet-like wid im sea-win' laughter,
scrapin away de lan' . . .

Uncle Time is a spider-man, cunnin an cool,
im tell yu: watch de hill an yu si mi.
Huhn! Fe yu yiye no quick enough fe si
how im move like mongoose; man, yu tink im fool?

Me Uncle Time smile black as sorrow;
im voice is sof as bamboo leaf
but Laard, me Uncle cruel.
When im play in de street
wid yu woman – watch im! By tomorrow
she dry as cane-fire, bitter as cassava;
an when im teach yu son, long after
yu walk wid stranger, an yu bread is grief.
Watch how im spin web roun yu house, an creep
inside; an when im touch yu, weep . . .

Epitaph

They hanged him on a clement morning, swung
between the falling sunlight and the women's
breathing, like a black apostrophe to pain.
All morning while the children hushed
their hopscotch joy and the cane kept growing
he hung there sweet and low.
　　　　　At least that's how
they tell it. It was long ago
and what can we recall of a dead slave or two
except that when we punctuate our island tale
they swing like sighs across the brutal
sentences, and anger pauses
till they pass away.

For the Last Time, Fire

That August the birds kept away from the village, afraid:
      people were hungry.
The phoenix hid at the sun's center and stared down
      at the Banker's house,
which was plump and factual, like zero.
Every good Banker knows
there's no such bird.

She came to the house like an old cat, wanting
a different kind of labor.
But the Banker was busy, feeding his dogs, who were nervous.
Perhaps she looked dangerous.
The child threshed in her belly
when she fell. The womb cracked, slack-lipped,
leaving a slight trace of blood on the lawn. Delicately,
the phoenix placed the last straw on its nest.

Mrs So-and-so the Banker's wife beat time
in her withdrawing room. Walked her moods
among the fluted teacups, toying with crusted foods.
The house hummed Bach, arithmetic at rest.
The phoenix sang along with the record,
and sat.
But the villagers counted heads, and got up.

So, logical as that spiral worming the disc to a hole in the
      center,
one night there were visitors, carrying fire. The dogs died
      first.
Then they gutted everything.

Something shook itself out of the ash.
Wings. Perhaps.

Mouth

Shut the gallery, lock the door.
Here is a painting of the poor.
                              She's boiling
something to feed four.
And a dog's face, watching her. The shadow of
her shack slices the bright
enamel of a plate. Dust
over all. A rancid, yellow sun. Her head throws
back, longing.

             The composition circles to the pot
leading the critics' gaze. You'll notice, what
is paddling there against all reason in
the soup is not a fly, not seasoning:
                    for, half day Saturday, his day is done.
                    Savouring the water, warm around his throat,
                    a gentleman relaxes in the sun,
                    a fat suburban pooler;
                    treads water, gracefully, afloat
                    at the edge, where it's cooler.
                    He doesn't know
                    what's cooking.

             The spoon will soon come down.

             They will crunch him, and swallow
             gristle and all, and spit out the head
             like thyme, like a fly.
             Every mouth
             must be fed.
             They will leave nothing
             for the dog

                         which will
shamble down from the picture and
crawl through the gallery and
lick the canvasses clean and

Version

Beg a ten cent mista —
de lickle bwoy sick, cyaan
eat (if him stop, who going to play
who going to play
who going to drop
who?)
All roun Jamdown
youtman a move —
one beat, yu no see't?
riddim sweet

but a soun cyaan full yu, yu
chuck an yu chuck
but de pocket have hole
an de lickle bwoy sick, sick
cyaan done. A neva see a rockers sweeta
dan rent when yu have it, a neva
catch a dubside dreada
dan bread if yu cyaan mek it
da tune de irie but a dead cyaan check it,
punch a nex one mista,
version —

if de lickle bwoy dead, session done, bruk up
speaker an all, no-use
time (who going to dread
who going to dread
who going to bleed
who?) no more excuse-time; headline-news time
running in de street time,
cool an red. Sky

juice time.

Weaponsong

I wanted to praise   too
the slow quiet queens   forever fertile
burying guns   in their bellies
under the dusty lignum vitae trees
and laughing   hungry boys at traffic signals
trapped in the amber   breaking
windows with their bullet eyes   and higglers
fat as cushions   under green umbrellas
fingers crooked   like a trigger
and the smell of schoolgirls   learning
to bleed   so bright   knowing
every catch   but safety

set those songs to music
(they do not mention love   nor its cost)
play them a wild parade   the shredding flags
will tickertape   like maggots
in the air   the speakers exploding
down each black street   and time
receive back my spent city

More Poem

'No more poem!' he raged, eye red;
'A solitary voice is wrong,
Jericho shall fall, shall fall
at the People's song!'

So. Only I-tongue have the right
to reason, to that sense of dread.
Man must keep silence now, except
man without bread.

No. See the flesh? It is cave, it is
stone. Seals every I away from light.
Alone. Man must chant as Man can
gainst night.

ANTHONY McNEILL

Don

For the D

'To John Coltrane, the heaviest spirit'
– Inscription, *Black Music*, Leroi Jones/Imamu Baraka

may I learn the shape of that hurt
which captured you nightly into
dread city, discovering through
streets steep with the sufferer's beat;

Teach me to walk through jukeboxes
and shadow that broken music
whose irradiant stop is light;
guide through those mournfullest journeys

I back into harbour Spirit
in heavens remember we now
and show we a way in to praise,
all seekers to-gather, one-heart:

and let we lock conscious when wrong
and Babylon rock back again:
in the evil season sustain
o heaviest spirit of sound.

The Victors •

Hauled up from the field by obscure
radar, the birds, homing, fly past.
Distanced, they seem
like white dots tracking a screen.
These are the egrets.
Their home, earned on successful
invasion, lies south.
Essentially foreign
they fly in absolute grace to

arrive at nests fashioned in
a drained, alien country.
But despite that accurate radar
they fail to fit.
Uneasy the victors fly south in guilt.

Residue

I
The wind is crisp and carries
a tang of the sea. The flowers
burn richly against the grass.
The grass itself shines and is precious.

II
Ahead, the sky and the ocean
merge in a stain of blue. On the beach
yesterday, lolloping tourists
were posting umbrellas like crosses.

III
This morning I chose to stay home,
To watch the cats and think of
Columbus. And the grass is precious
merely because it belongs to us.

Saint Ras

Every stance seemed crooked. He had
not learned to fall in with the straight
queued, capitalistic, for work.
He was uneasy in traffic.

One step from that intersection
could, maybe, start peace. But he dread-
fully missed, could never proceed
with the rest when the white signal

flashed safe journey. Bruised, elbowed-in,
his spirit stopped at each crossing,
seeking the lights for the one sign
indicated to take him across

to the true island of Ras.
But outside his city of dreams
was no right-of-passage, it seemed.
Still-anchored by faith, he idled

inside his hurt harbour and even
his innocent queen posed red
before his poised, inchoate bed.
Now exiled more, or less,

he retracts his turgid divinity,
returns to harsh temporal streets
whose uncertain crossings reflect
his true country. Both doubt and light.

Dermis

When my flaps peel back, I am seen
As a tiger cunning and dread.
My form fleers up above your bed.
Allowed in, I become your dream.

Then claws reconnoiter your skin.
Hooked to your flesh, my fang-mouth sucks
Up your life in scarlet. The prick
Of my sex lets vampires in.

Cropped into this harsh terrible
Creature, I will ravish you innocent
Princess. Flashing down stiff,
I'm meant to smash or disable.

When the screen darkens the last African,
Go so girl! Sleep out of my eye
Hurrying up from Zambesi
To lodge in the steppes of your brain

A beast with the ache of a man.

A Wreath for the Suicide Heart

Somebody is hanging:
a logwood tree
laden with blossoms
in a deep wood;
The body stirs left
in the wind;
If the wind
could send
its miracle-breath
back to that person,
I tell you it would;
Love is Earth's mission,
despite the massed dead;
On the night of the hanging
The autumn moon bled

JUDY MILES

Suicide?

Seaweeds
sulk upon the rock;
black sand teems with stones.

Here
in this green and black holiday place
death is a white fowl, strangled,
slapping the eye.

Memory
washes like a tide
over the mind . . .
Until at last a barb of guilt
harpoons these hours to his face.

For when his heart, driven before a gale
of loneliness, sought in our
hearts a harbour and a home
no sign we gave
to anchor our compassion in his soul.

Not silence itself was our sin;
for touching hands
turn silence to a delicate,
exquisite thing, beautiful
as the slender breath of a dawn campfire
on this beach; and eloquent
as a lone seagull's flight.

Why
is tenderness usually late
or, if it does come,
frail as foam?

Seasons Greetings, Love and Revolution

Taxiing to 71 via Tijuana
the tires raised dust and dirty imps
rushing to open the door
brush the windshield ineffectually
with a rag, hoping for a nickel
or even a dime from the rich turistas.
No Aztec golden rings adorned their fingers
only eczemas set in grimy hopes
that each turista was santa claus
travelling incognito.

I was home. I recognized
poverty, filth and flies,
the shanties clutching
the knees of the hillside,
the garbage heap of homes
at the bottom of the arroyo.

Inside dark stores
in shadows cast by wings of buzzards
I cowered
as rich turistas haggled
over the price of a poncho.
And in the hotel bar
where I saw my very first Mexican fag
swallow the dregs of a drink
left by some woman he did not know
I wished that I had seen instead
the hot embrace
of the Latin lover
with the guerilla.

KEVYN ARTHUR

Gospel

If when they brought the good news
one of us Americans said 'Thank God!'
         think:
In the city, where the streets
are macadamed complications on
old Guaca's simple comings-and-goings,
where, on the hidden midden,
Mrs Ramsey's Rum Shop stands,
old Guaca would have understood
with an understanding mutilated
by the explanations of an empty tomb.

This Carib head that 'was so hard
a spanish broadsword could not cleave it
at one stroke'
would have recognized implicitly,
as he had recognized the fact
but not the implications
of the three big ships,
that Maboya had a vanquisher
apt to be appeased by prayer;
that Don Antonio and the padre
(one with sword and fire
the other with Fire and the Sword)
and he, and all his people, and Vespucci,
were subject to
some one most mighty King of all the kingdoms.

And Mrs Ramsey,
sweetening her stained cup,
would have looked up
through a virgin Mary, mediatrix,
the battalions of booze,
the salt cries of hardworked, blinded men
(shrines, wherein the Eternal Light glimmered)
to her store of Ambrosia,

when all that had been meant was
'Thanks be that we
and some things are.'
And one most minute moment of it all
was that fantastic minute when Vermejo shouted 'Land!'

I Saw Three Ships

If only those scraps from Aleppo, from Qumran
– those magical markings on frail bits of paper –
could fold me that vessel the Christians call Faith:
a strong paper clipper to sail through this puddle
and slice through the acrid surf sizzling my hull.

Old Mary Jordan had it,
who eked her tethered days out in Cheapside
huddling in her pew's hard prow
and never breaking from the anchor of her Church:
an aged Ophelia drifting to her doom,
floating in the foldings of her faith.
Her crackling voice couldn't reach the nearest nave
but yet she knew she had no need to fear;
she knew that she communed
most clearly, regularly, with her God.

So spar *me*, Somebody!
Graft me a mast to my innards,
rig fat bellies of sail to my bulwark,
hang out a light, and a Truth that could lead me,
gimme a star and pit me against
this whim and this puddle's wild raging!
O let my skill, or Mayhap, blow me to
the Holy Hill, to the Gods' dwelling!

PAMELA MORDECAI

Tell Me

So tell me what you have
to give: I have strong limbs
to make a lap of love
a brow to gaze at in
the quiet times half light and
lips for kissing: I'm well
fixed for all love's traffic

And further, I've an ear
open around the clock
you know, like those phone
numbers that you call at
anytime. And such soft eyes
that smile and ferret out
the truth. Extraordinary

eyes, and gentle – you can see
yourself. It's strong and warm
and dark, this womb I've got
and fertile: you can be
a child and play in
there: and if you fall and
hurt yourself, it's easy

to be mended: I know
it sounds a little much
but that's the way it seems
to me. So tell me, brother

what have you to give?

For Eyes to Bless You

Those times I have you when my flesh
wants nothing near it, you don't know
and even now you can't find out
that masquerade, that play.
It's old as woman, old as birth
that's joy and riddance both at once.
You will not know how much how
frequently, in that same way, I want
my body back. So do not ask
that what I said a week, a month
ago should be what I say now:
the only protest you may make
is that my eyes no longer bless
you – for the rest, the fires
that you lie so quietly against
are me: mercurial as hell
and heaven fixed in one
perpetual counterpoise:
there your intrusion may not reach.
That is a field where powers do
battle, principalities war on.
And what I say about it all
is little gauge. For eyes to bless
you then must be enough . . .

Shooting the Horses

This dawn he rose early again
and went after the horses;
he traps them manes glowing
ripe tangerine like Tintoretto
apocalypse horses-of-morning

snap-snap with his little
black box shoots the world
as it was the first day
green gold with strong legs

and a mane to be tossed
and the damp Mona plains
to be eaten like fire . . .

And what do you seek
my beloved, in the seed
of the day, when the tenderest
leaf of green light breaks
the earth of the dark?

What coin pulls you
wet from me, clutching
your little machine
obliging you capture
the crucified trees, their crosses
of shadows haunting
the rest of this Sabbath?

Is it wisdom or hope that you stalk?
Would you have me walk
with you?

Shall I sleep as you follow
the hooves of those shadows
the footprints of mountains
the musk of the mists
the tracks of the earliest earth?

I will leave you my love.
It was Eve who first
murdered the morning

ROGER McTAIR

Guerillas

Is this where idealism ends
In the fanfaronade of a streetcorner bar?

A shell of silence holds the air
Crisp between us, anxious for discourse.

Don't dig no blues, someone yowls,
Smashing our silence. We stumble
Into speech.

A patrol enters, armed
The sergeant toasts the crowd.
Everywhere, bar, beach, office, street
The charade of official camaraderie
Unfolds.
And every rank in uniform struts the role.

'We are all guerillas now,' you say,
Making sure the patrol has left, careful
Not to let the statement jump
Beyond the boundaries of discretion.

'We have our psychic exile, negative
Resistance; no insurgence, no acquiescence
Either. Just lying low,
Working out procedures for a long campaign.'

We stand outside the bar watching
The office crowd troops home.
Barroom noises disgorge on the street.
'Despair is temporary,' you say, 'like a daze
From bad rum or rhetoric.'
An armoured car goes by.
'Tempus fugit, don't dig no blues!'

Politics Kaiso

The old calypsonian sings:

And people talking –
Men widout education
Is Minister of Education,
Men widout culture
Run de Ministry of Culture;
And is a fine situation, leading
To obliteration
When de Minister of Finance
Need de finance more than we . . .

Dem who was to solve de problem
Become de problem now,
Dem who was to re-make history
Fighting history – an' how!

Dem who had
'Detached analysis and scientific perspective'
Lose dey perspective and need analysing
Now . . .

And is a fine situation, bankruptcy
The projection
When foreign carpetbaggers
Have more influence than we . . .

And de people saying –
Dey who was to save de nation
From foreign ministration
Wid ovahseas education an' BBC elocution
Send for foreign ammunition
An' automatic weapon
To show de Hooligan population
And children of de nation – just who
Is de Massa now . . .

Yes! Is a fine situation
Leading to annihilation
When de first brain in de nation (and
Third brain in universal compilation)
Send for imperialist intervention to save

De blasted nation
From foreign ministration –
An' Hooligans,
Such as
We . . .

Port of Spain, March 1970

OLIVE SENIOR

Ancestral Poem

I
My ancestors are nearer
than albums of pictures
I tread on heels thrust
into broken-down slippers

II
My mother's womb impulsed
harvests perpetually. She
deeply breathed country air
when she laboured me.

III
The pattern woven by my
father's hands lulled me
to sleep. Certain actions
moved me so: my father
planting.

When my father planted
his thoughts took flight.
He did not need to think.
The ritual was ingrained
in the blood, embedded
in the centuries of dirt
beneath his fingernails
encased in the memories
of his race.

(Yet the whiplash of my
father's wrath rever-
berated days in my
mind with the inten-
sity of tuning forks.
He did not think.
My mother stunned wept
and prayed Father

Forgive Them knowing not
what she prayed for.)

One day I did not pray.
A gloss of sunlight through
the leaves betrayed me so
abstracted me from rituals.
And discarded prayers and
disproven myths
confirmed me freedom.

IV
Now against the rhythms
of subway trains my
heartbeats still drum
worksongs. Some wheels
sing freedom, the others:
home.

Still, if I could balance
water on my head I can
juggle worlds
on my shoulders.

Epitaph

Last year the child died
we didn't mourn long
and cedar's plentiful

but that was the one
whose navel-string we buried
beneath the tree of life

lord, old superstitions
are such lies.

WAYNE BROWN

Noah

Everywhere fish wheeled and fled
Or died in scores, floating like eggs.
From his mind's ark, Noah,
Sailor for the kingdom of Truth's sake,
Watched the water close like mouths
Over the last known hills. Next day
He slept, dreaming of haystacks.

Water woke him. He stood, arms folded,
Looking out of a porthole, thinking nothing,
Numbed to a stare by horizon's drone, and the
Dry patter of rain. On the third day,
Decisive, sudden, he dragged
Down the canvas curtain and turned
Inward to tend his animals, his
Animals, waking with novelty.

Locked, driven by fatigue, the ark
Beat and beat across the same sea,
Bloated, adrift, finding
Nothing to fasten to.
Barnacles grew up the sides like sores. Inside,

Noah, claustrophobic, sat and watched
The occupants of his ark take on
New aspects, shudder into focus, one
By one. Something, he thought, must come
Of this. Such isolation! Such concentration!
Out of these instinctual, half-lit lives,
Something: some good, some Truth!
That night a dropped calf bawled to its feet,
Shaking off light like dirt.

Noah, an old man, unhappy, shook
His head. Birth was not the answer,
Nor death: his mind's ark stank
Of birth and death, would always,

Sundering, stink. Outside,
The hard insistent patter of rain
Saying 'Think, Noah, think! Break this
Patter of rain, man!' But only animals
Moved in his mind.
                        Now, unbodied by raindrops,
The patter continued, empty, shelled,
Clambering down along itself like crabs.
Driven, impotent, he neared despair.

Finally one bird, unasked, detached itself
And battered around inside his skull.
Thankfully Noah released it, fearful,
Hoping, watching it flit and bang
Against wind, returning each time
Barren. Till one day, laden with lies,
It brought back promise of fruit, of
Resolution and change.

Now animals and men crowded the gangplank,
Peering eagerly about the returning hills
For some sign of change. Noah conducted them,
Drifting among valleys with breaking smiles,
Naming, explaining, directing: Noah, released,
Turned once more outwards, giving thanks.

Relief dazed them: nobody realized
Nothing had changed. Animal and man
Settled quietly to old moulds, un-
Remembered seasons of death and birth,
Led by the bearded one, the prophet, Noah
Rejuvenated, giving thanks on a hill,
Moving among known animals and men
With a new aspect, giving thanks . . . While,
Leaking, derelict, its mission abandoned,
The ark of his mind
Wallowed empty westward
To where all rainbows
Drown among waves

Ballad of the Electric Eel

When Earth slept, like a pig in the sun
Bellying out of its warm mud in places,
Eel lay at the bottom of the ocean
Like a shambles of coils in an empty carpark
Or a magnet: one root for the sea's motion.

Dispossessed while sleeping by sunlight and wave,
Woke to a waterworld poisoned with fish
Some bigger than himself. When the whale's cave
Loomed over him, eel had to bite the dust.
That was his first and last lesson. Learned fast,

Fell into slices, sent his tail end
Landward to reconnoitre while he watched from the weeds.
When the serpent went down under Woman's heel eel
Laughed toughly, like Widmark, and grew a reef.
Now he was bedded in rock.

Fish flourished, the coral reef
Worked like a seacraft riding on oil.
Eel was its system's analyst.
His eyes screwed down to far stars in space,
His jaws fell open like compasses, he set out

To run the world strictly by impulse.
Now he is king of the mineral dark,
Earth's ticking time bomb, inset like a diamond.
When he glides from his cave the tide climbs abruptly,
Waves sever a headland, and men wage wars –

When he withdraws
Long currents drag whole streets empty,
And men in mid-sentence stand and gape
Like machines,
Their brains gone completely blank.

England, Autumn

Perhaps one should say truthfulness rather than truth in order to purge it of the high-flying or high-flown sonority which Larkin is so sceptical of.
— *Christopher Ricks*

But, doesn't heaven
prophesy still over England?
Since when was lightning ironic,
or thunder without sonority?

You ought to walk with me, critic,
you should not have to ask
your old houseboy, returning, to
translate the wind,

don't you know that, however
composed into eloquent postures,
these drystone walls, these hedgerows
are less than the rage that made them?

You should ask more of literature,
not sceptical, ask it the wind's name,
ask Prospero that, ask Satan, aye,

and ask any glad-eyed, terrified
hare whom the moor discloses
if Truth, high-flying, doesn't still

on occasion stoop from a smoking sky,
or an imperilled mortal 'I'
break from your carapaced 'one'.

You could still say 'Man' and make
the walls fall down; ask that felon lit
by horizon!

Or walk with me, mister, walk with
me, Sir, through any starched
maternity wing, with its silence of
libraries, with its doctors like dry
undertakers, and watch
as some tiny, rage-suffused

warrior, your 'first Englishman',
medalled with mucus and beribboned
in blood,
crashes into the light now, and like this
bad, unkempt, distempered poem
glares around him, bellowing

The Bind

All young men dream,
but, at thirty-five,
isn't it time you learned?

What you can lose will be lost.
What they cannot take
from you is the pain
of loss, the enduring pearl of pain –

that is yours,
till you learn to live at last,
without such punctual heartbreak.

Then they will take that too.

FAUSTIN CHARLES

Fireflies

(For Shiva Naipaul)

Like you, I preferred
The firefly's starlike little
Lamp, mining, a question . . .
– 'Lampfall', *Derek Walcott*

Every night the fireflies were our eyes
When we read the book of life backwards
Seeing the shadow of a name spelt out on wet leaves;
Our mother knew the longest, loneliest summer
As our father's face curved into grass;
Along the epitaph, the fireflies' lanterns furled into cloud,
A prophet's beard, God's smallest eye
Circling bad blood in the lineage;
A brother's annunciation in the new moon:
TIME WILL TELL,
Time will tell of the father's generation
Knotted in worlds beyond the family tree
Of the sacrifice by the mother-who-fathered-me:
The good-queen wife and the once-upon-a-time king
Carved out in ikons of the rich house
Where one day in a lonely corner
An epileptic great aunt thought she saw
Her jewel-box opened by a field-mouse,
As she stuttered her sister's name outside
The wedlock of a son-in-law;
Time will tell of the long journey
Of the desired one, floating on a fired flower
Swelling the seeds of her spouse,
In sips of her father's blood;
The betrothed enters the temple
In the subtle smile from the reclining, four-handed god
And hearts rise in the holiness of the sacred cow;
The family's divining rod
Proclaims the dowry from generation to generation.

Time will tell of marriage:
The life of trust,
Security ringed by the male lust
When the ego fails
The passion is greater than the act
And the wife's duty is nobler than love's gift,
For love lies where the gods are;
Flames of venus, the fireflies draw the honeymoon carriage
To a seaside end
Where a fisherman-friend, sooth-sayer, worshipper of the
     moon's rise
Will tell the story of the pundit's fall from paradise.

Sugar Cane

The succulent flower bleeds molasses,
as its slender, sweet stalks bend,
beheaded in the breeze.

The green fields convulse golden sugar,
tossing the rain aside,
out-growing the sun,
and carving faces
in the sun-sliced panorama.

The reapers come at noon,
riding the cutlass-whip;
their saliva sweetens everything
in the boiling season.

Each stem is a flashing arrow,
swift in the harvest.

Cane is sweet sweat slain;
cane is labour, unrecognized, lost
and unrecovered;
sugar is the sweet swollen pain of the years;
sugar is slavery's immovable stain;
cane is water lying down,
and water standing up.

Cane is a slaver;
cane is bitter,
very bitter,
in the sweet blood of life.

CYRIL DABYDEEN

Rehearsal

Language the chameleon seeks to explain the chameleon
reality. — A.I.

Old father tongue sticking out
over the fenced yard,
scampering out from the coop,
this reptilian self
breaking out without a warning —

changeable again, across the barrier
scattering feathers —
a life gone rampant
in dreams; the insane among us presenting
emblems from the scuttled sea —

all talk, old words, dropping scales
the dung of reality, moon-shape
pitching stars from the tips
of my fingers, blood oozing at the thighs
wetting the ground to form our roots

Words and Legacy

My father's life is alchemy
he tightens a fist at the wind
he plunges himself with an anger

into the night. He berates all-comers
with a dagger-kill. He listens
to the howling wind presaging his own death.

I wake up from a dream after the first cock-crow
I remember how folklore is vivid
in nightmares

how in frenzy a father's words
become the thin edge of a blade
he goes on living from day to day

making the sun blink

The Fat Men

1

The porch diminishes the fat men.
The fat men diminish the porch.
They play a game with their broad tongues.
Wind rattles the roof; a house
comes down with the thunder-clap
of wild laughter.

No one will tame them: these men
of the earth: these players
who sit still, their bellies growing huge
as houses. One is a cloud; he smiles;
sun comes between his eyes.

2

Maupassant would've found use
for these men: their spacious under-arms
as incubators. Chickens, like apples, rolling out
from under the sun of their arm-pits,
the organic heat of body,
the sweat of sun, the rattling of board bodies,
the wind and the rain.

3

The soil knows no difference.
Not only the French have their fat men.
They are the productive of the earth.

Fruit, of the Earth

I imagine myself
a mouth

you an apple
me a mother-mouth
brother-mouth
sister-mouth
munching / munching

remembering how
once upon a time
the season was
palpable escape
with the slice
white slice / red slice

eagerly munching
aunt-mouth
grandmother-mouth
before balance of
payments became crucial
in a tropical state

when suddenly
starapple / mango
papaw / sapodilla
take their place
oozing a nation's
sweet distaste.

MARLENE PHILIP

Oliver Twist

Oliver Twist can't do this
if so do so
touch your toe under we go
touch the ground and a merry go round,
and mother oh lady says to jump
mother oh grady says to cry
mother oh lady says be white
mother oh grady says be black,
       brown black
       yellow black
       black black
       black pickney stamped English
singing brown skin girl
stay home and mind baby,
growing up la di dah polite
pleasing and thank you ma'm, yet so savage
       union jacked in red
       in white
       in blue
and dyed in black to welcome Her
tiny hand moving slowly backward
slowly forward
painted smile on regal face
from the stately 'buh look how shiny'
black limousine with air conditioned crawl,
and little children faint and drop
black flies in the heat singing
Britons never never never
shall be slaves and
all that land of hope and glory
that was not,
black flies in the heat singing
of Hector and Lysander
and such great names as these,
but of all the world's great heroes

there's none that can compare
with a tow row row row row row
of the British Grenadiers and
little black children
marching past stiffly white bloused
skirted blue
overalled and goin' to one big school
feelin' we self look so proper –
a cut above our parents you know,
man we was black
an' we was proud
we had we independence
an' massa day done,
we goin' to wear dat uniform
perch dat hat
'pon we hot comb head
jus' like all dem school girls
roun' de empire
learning about odes to nightingales
forget hummingbirds,
a king that forgot
Harriet Tubman, Sojourner Truth
and burnt his cakes,
about princes shut in towers
not smelly holds of stinking ships
and pied piper to our blackest dreams
a bastard mother, from her weaned
on silent names of stranger lands.

Salmon Courage

Here at Woodlands, Moriah,
these thirty-five years later,
still I could smell her fear.
Then, the huddled hills would not have
calmed her, now as they do me.
Then, the view did not snatch
the panting breath, now, as it does

these thirty-five years later, to the day,
I relive the journey of my salmon mother.

This salmon woman of Woodlands, Moriah
took the sharp hook of death
in her mouth, broke free and beat
her way upstream, uphill; spurned
all but the challenge of gravity,
answered the silver call of the moon,
danced to the drag and pull of the
tides, fate a silver thorn in her side,
brought her back here to spawn with
the hunchbacked hills humping the horizon,
under a careless blue sky.

My salmon father now talks of how
he could walk over there, to those same hills,
and think and walk some more with his dreams,
then that he had,
now lost and replaced.
His father (was he salmon?)
weighted him with the mill stones of
a teacher's certificate, a plot of land
(believed them milestones to whcrc he hadn't been),
that dragged him downstream to the ocean.

Now, he and his salmon daughter
face those same huddled, hunchbacked hills.
She a millstoned lawyer, his milestone
to where he hadn't been.
He pulls her out, a blood rusted weapon,
to wield against his friends
'This, my daughter, the lawyer!'
She takes her pound of dreams neat,
no blood under that careless blue sky,
suggests he wear a sign around his neck,
'My Daughter is a Lawyer',
and drives the point home,
quod erat demonstrandum.

But I will be salmon.
Wasn't it for this he made the journey

downstream, my salmon father?
Why then do I insist on swimming
against the tide, upstream,
leaping, jumping, flying floating,
hurling myself at, under, over,
around all obstacles, backwards
in time to the spawning
grounds of knotted dreams?
My scales shed, I am Admiral red,
but he, my salmon father, will not
accept that I too am salmon,
whose fate it is to swim against the time,
whose loadstar is to be salmon.

This is called salmon courage my dear father,
salmon courage,
and when I am all spawned out
like the salmon, I too must die –
but this child will be born,
must be born salmon.

LORNA GOODISON

The Mulatta as Penelope

Tonight, I'll pull your limbs through
small soft garments
your head will part my breasts
and you will hear a different heartbeat.
Tonight, we said the real goodbye, he and I
But this time I will not sit and spin and spin
the door open to let the madness in.
Till the sailor finally weary of the sea
returns with tin souvenirs and a claim to me.
True I returned from the quayside
my eyes full of sand
and his salt-leaving smell
fresh on my hands
but you're my anchor awhile now
and that holds deep.
I'll sit in the sun
and dry my hair
while you sleep.

For Don Drummond

Dem say him born
with a caul,
a not-quite-opaque
white veil
through which he visioned
only he knew.

At birth dem suppose
to bury it
under some special tree.

If we had known
we could have told them
it was to be,
The Angel Trumpet Tree.

Taptadaptadaptadada . . .
Far far East
past Wareika
down by Bournemouth
by the sea,
The Angel Trumpet
bell-mouthed sighs
and notes like petals rise
covering all a we.

Not enough notes
to blow back the caul
that descend regularly
and cover this world vision
hiding him from we.

Find a woman
with hair like rivers,
a waist unhinged
and free;
emptied some of the sorrow
from the horn's cup;
into the well below her belly.
She promised to take the caul
from his eyes:
to remove the cold matter
that clouded his eyes;
and stand between him
and
the trumpet tree duppy.
The promise dead like history.
Dead like she.

When the caul come again
and covered his eyes,
this time the blade rise
like notes in a scandal
on a street corner

Far far East
past Wareika.

From a Bridge view
the crowd holds notes
One gone . . .
Don gone . . .

Lay me down for the band must rest/ Yes, Music is my
    occupation.
I tired a hold this note, you hold this memory/ For J.F.K., For
    Me.
Mek the slide kotch/ is right here so I stop.
Belleview is the view I view/ Sometime I think the whole
    world mad too.

Behold the house of his feet,
the brown booga
tongue ajar, a door that blow and open and close no more.

Fold the dark suit pressed under newspaper,
'Murder' screamed the morning paper,
Bring the felt hat
where the caul would hide
to slip down sly and cover his eyes.

And this time do the burial right fi we
Bury The Don under the Angel Trumpet Tree.

JOHN ROBERT LEE

Return

Except for the fat
and raucous
cancanesse,
you'd see no one.
At first
you'd never know that he was there,
alone
in the darkness of his memory;
guiding as the stick that tapped out curbs for him,
it led him
far beyond
the choking bags of meal

You only saw him
when you heard
his thumbs come
drumming
on the dumb
shop-counter board.
Then they,
leading him,
danced him
to the rim of memory's night,
to the hum of rushing waters,
to the numb-
                    ing crash of whirling forests;
                    with the black
                    Damballa,
he knew his soul again . . .

Sitting there,
with Africa wrinkled over him,
          his aged veins
          Limpopo's dams,
his body seem it dead,

       done dead
       as dead
       as de holes
       in his head.

Only the hyp-
notic
beat, beat, beat-
ing of the skin on bone
on blind and silent wood,
could tell you
of the darker rush of the rushing waters
of the deafening crash of the crashing barks
of the joyous fear in Legba's heart . . .
        a prodigal soul
        of a wandered son
has wandered back again.

Kite

for all revolutionary groups.

    Now hawk, wind's jockey, sitting tight;
then prancing nectar addict
humming
       to darting ash of black bird;

         turn   climb   claim again the bird-rite;
but: caught majesty:
     for all it might
fixed to cord.

     (linked liberty: as day frees night.)

now, corbeaus' scare, hanging loose, broke,
          victim of crossing lines, no line;

       all   night;   all   day;
mangy, mateless,
mute.

third world snapshots

I

out that black hole of bush
have spewed this bouldered hush
of slipping stream, this pushing
back of roots. And women washing.

II

a new clear view for today:
far from the Pentagon, this two by four,
and your copra in the blistering heat,
and below the blasted trees, your
children's bodies falling out.

or again:
the outboard of your faith, the
nets of the years' woven strengths,
the safe bay of familiar sand, all
gone to nothing. With our sky.

III

may the pride of the Old and the New not forget
that out of these rejected Nazareths
still come the Bread and the Fruit and
the Eternal Coal of the children's faith.

JOHN AGARD

Waiting for Fidel

The Cubana bird touched down
tore the blanket of heat
from around the taut faces
waiting
for a slice of history

a people starved of freedom
and hungry for heroes

Then suddenly there you stood
breath of the Sierra Maestra
proud as tall green cane

you could have been a lover
come home from a long journey

But now something disturbs our sleeping guts
something close to pain

and an untouchable sadness
turns like a key
in the door of history

Shall we walk in or turn back?

Pan Recipe

First rape a people
simmer for centuries

bring memories to boil
foil voice of drum

add pinch of pain
to rain of rage

stifle drum again
then mix strains of blood

over slow fire
watch fever grow

till energy burst
with rhythm thirst

cut bamboo and cure
whip well like hell

stir sound from dustbin
pound handful biscuit tin

cover down in shanty town
and leave mixture alone

when ready will explode

VICTOR QUESTEL

Tom

I
The wrong that are
our ancestors,
square the deal.

I have no grief
for words to
flounder upon

for the way lost
is the way
lost

and revolution
is the scandal
of poverty
sandalled to the
dust of processions.

II
Arches don't rise here
though for some
they fall with
each step.

III
To fashion consciousness
is
still to cut a figure,
yet another
pound of flesh,
have the gift
of the grab
steeled to
the mind.

It's anti-climax
my avuncular
smile said.

and here
triangular
betrayals
bay at the moon

necked to the crane of memory
yoked to the oil-
slick of our shores

waves of survival
for the slickest.

This Island Mopsy

No Slip a deep Gulley
Ah man in leg trap believe me
Ah clean bowl every woman back to the Stand
Because they couln't read the flight
Of me China Man.
— *The Mighty Bomber*

Listen to this story
'bout meh long time Mopsy
Listen to this rumour
'bout meh girlfriend Sandra

Now this was a real happening
come home late one evening
find Sandra groaning
de girl
She didn't want meh loving

Chorus: Woman come in different shapes
      different sizes
      Offering different poses
      different prizes (*Repeat*)
      I might look like Mickey Mouse
      but I always have woman inside meh house

Look at meh crosses Lord
meh Mopsy calling the Mighty Crucifix ah fraud
Look at meh crisis Lord
meh Mopsy claiming I was a fraud

Come home no food in de place
She hair undo

tears all over she face
Ah get blasted vex
pull out meh bull boy
and bus' it across she chest

She fall down on she knee
and cry as hard as she can
stay please
you is my man
you ain't fraid to mek meh bawl
in pain
from right now ah go start
loving yer again.

Boy yer see dis creature call 'oman
don't bother wid no gentle touch
rough she up don't mek no fuss

Treat she like how the Multi-national
treat dis territory
sink yer hand in she country
what yer get take it for free

Extract what yer coud before she start
to fret and boil
When she sugar done
man drill for oil
Then break all ties
ignore she consternation
and leave she wid a new
growing population.

Chorus: Woman come in different shapes
　　　　different sizes
　　　　Offering different poses
　　　　different prizes (*Repeat*)
　　　　I might look like Mickey Mouse
　　　　but I always have woman inside meh house

347

GRACE NICHOLS

Waterpot

The daily going out
and coming in
always being hurried
along
like like . . . cattle

In the evenings
returning from the fields
she tried hard to walk
like a woman

she tried very hard
pulling herself erect
with every three or four
steps
pulling herself together
holding herself like
royal cane

And the overseer
hurrying them along
in the quickening darkness

And the overseer sneering
them along in the quickening
darkness

sneered at the pathetic –
the pathetic display
of dignity

O but look
there's a waterpot growing
from her head

Without Song

The faces of the children
   are small and stricken and black
They have fallen
into exile
moving without song
or prayer

They have fallen
into mourning
moving to the shrouds
of tares

The faces of the children
   are small and stricken and black

They have fallen
into silence
uttering no cry
laying no blame

And the sun burns to copper
yet the rains, the rains gather
like diamonds
in the fleece of their hair

Old Magic

She, the mirror
you break in seven pieces

the curse you think
you leave behind

the woman make young
with old magic

the one you going
sleep with

the one you going
think is kind

KENDEL HIPPOLYTE

good morning

i woke this morning
the taste of silence
smell of banana in the room
the memory of your breast like sapodilla in my teeth

no objects in this room
no thing more real than the other
the table waited, breathing
the chair sat
quietly, saying nothing

the bowl, too
was saying nothing in particular
it only said banana, orange
and its perfect mouth
dilated slightly when it said
pineapple

sun-shaft, breaking darkness
at the one crack in the louvers
shattered silently into photons
and scattered the sun-seed
deep into the corners

the house ached with the night before
you could have walked through
walls that were walls only
out of habit
yearning for the single, the separate
soft sex of objects with the light between them

last night
has left the whole house dipped in milk
i feel the nipple of each object
if i rub the light switch one more time . . .

you burst like grapes in my memory

and everything is rounded
i find their centres without thinking
now, as yesterday and all
the other flattened surfaces
curve backwards into spheres and crescents
i swing upwards again like a bell's tongue
laughing inside you.

Jah-Son/ another way

I

who was born, not of a virgin but a real woman
whose father vanished like the holy ghost
who walked the usual crooked mile out from the high wild
   mountains of green childhood
down through the mono-crop plantations of the schools
and out into the alleys short-cuts back-streets
side-stepping from the blocks of bank and church
by-passing glass doors glaring windows, watching his
   reflection
blur into the men and manikins arranged inside
dodging the traffic of emotional commerce, the
blaring smiles honking handshakes of the
   up-and-coming-at-you 1600cc boys
who ran from three-striped foxes taxidermized love-birds and
   sunday citizens
who was jobless, had no fixed abode
who slept in fishing-boats and therefore under stars
whose mind was a tenement-yard of heresies
his head a shaggy thunder-cloud of darkening questions
his beard glistening with treasons and with ecstasies
who had burned churches blasted government buildings
and grown a garden on their waste –
all in his head
who one day abandoning the highway scramble for the
   golden fleece
went on to seek the lamb
whose name was Jason till he came to know himself
and then became Jah-Son.

II

but where you going, Jason?
look you mudda crying
you brudda an' sista trying
to get some sense into your head
but dem cyah penetrate; your dread
too thick and knot-up; too much o' tangle
mangle-up question clot-up like blood-stain drying
in you brain – Jason, you go go insane!
Jason, you go dead!

III

there has to be
another way
                    'Too dam' lazy! Ain't he is a carpenter?
                    So why he doh fin' work?'
there has to be
'Oh god Jason, not now!
You cyah just leave me now!'
           another way
                    'Come brother, will you give your heart
                    before it is too late?'
           has to be
'Comrade, the struggle needs
a thinking man like you.'
           another way.

IV

Jah sey
Jah Rastafari sey:
see I trod
through valley
see I trod

through town, through stinking alley
see I search
for you
for youth who search
for truth

see I trod
come
I make Man
into God

an' dem a-step outa de shitty
dem vank
lef de school, lef de church, lef de bank
lef de people mek o' concrete and steel
who divide and subtract but cyah feel
de yout' ban that
dem noh wan' that
dem mash it on de ground
as dem step outa de town
outa Sodom and Gomorrah fi go higher!
dem a-shake de city dust offa dem feet
an' a-flash dem natty dread inna de street
dem a-chant an' a-wail an' a-hail bongo-nyah
Jah-Jah children trod creation on a trail o' bloodfire!

who wan' go
will go
who wan' stay
will stay
whatsoever whosoever will

there is a hill called Zion
a sinking ground called Babylon
a so Jah sey

     v
a so?
a really, really so?
a two years now Jah-Mighty
an' i still doh know.

here: no cement, no steel
yet something cold
no clock, no wheel
but something
turning wrong and going back.
chaliss burning in my hand, but still
something that i doh hold
this not the way

but where to go?

     VI
out of the forest, leaving

the twisted track that snaked through bush and coiled round
    hill
and never led to Zion
turning his back
on blighted gardens, broken earthen-pots
on songs that quavered and then gradually had shrilled to
    quarrels
on praises that became as thin as smoke
he went down from the psalmist's hill
without hope, not a toke of ganja
nothing to draw on
but himself

VII

down into Mammon's kingdom: among the derelict the
    broken the insane
the ones for whom the city's alleyways are made, the
    back-road side-street shit-lane
people the shanty-minded and the minds like cul-de-sacs, the
    shingles of
dismantled person the 2×4 existences of shaking age with
    newsprint
peeling off their cracked skins letting in the cold draught of
    the cosmos,
among the dead-ends of socio-economico-political processes
    the snuffed-out
butts of a city's nervous smouldering, Jason among them

has to be

VIII

his life resembled theirs now, driftwood.
cross-currents, ill winds of circumstance
would drag him to a sand-spit of existence
another fool of time who'd lost his substance
and the way home.
he looked on at the dredged and dregged survivors
heard the future like the rumour of a storm
and the present a loud silence.

this?
another cripple at the pool?
and yet how to shout 'No!'

to the enormous opening mouth of Nothing?
no way?

      no way

      IX
he lifted up his eyes, last time –
Zion hill was green and far away.
his gaze dropped to his feet:
barren sidewalk, thin-lipped gutter, asphalt street
and saw grass
and saw how earth itself had shifted, split the sidewalk
how seeds exploding in green flame had caught small fires
all along the cracks and weaknesses of urban surfaces
grass laughing fiercely everywhere once you were looking for
   it
Zion, shining where it had always been, will always be
NOW, no other time, no other place, NOW
NOW as the grassflesh blazes into singing
splitting the sealed-slab silence of blind city sidewalks
and rustling, passing the word downwind along the
   pavements
illumining, witnessing your metamorphosis

     Jah-Son.

DIONNE BRAND

From *Epigrams to Ernesto Cardenal in Defense of Claudia*

35   Ars Poetica (III)
'on being told that being Black is being bitter'

give up the bitterness
he told my young friend/poet
give it up and you will be beautiful.
after all these years and after all these words
it is not simply a part of us anymore
it is not something that you can take away
as if we held it for safekeeping,
it is not a treasure, not a sweet,
it is something hot in the hand, a piece of red coal,
it is an electric fence, touched,
we are repulsed, embraced and destroyed,
it is not separate, different,
it is all of us, mixed up in our skins,
welded to our bones
and it cannot be thrown away
not after all these years, after all these words
we don't have a hold on it
it has a hold on us,
to give it up means that someone dies,
you, or my young poet friend
so be careful when you say give up the
bitterness.
let him stand in the light for a moment
let him say his few words, let him breathe
and thank whoever you pray to
that he isn't standing on a dark street
with a brick,
waiting for you.

From *Military Occupations*

In the 5 a.m. dusk
grains of night's black drizzle, first stones
boulders of dark
sprinkle the open face
open eyes, incense of furtive moths
badluck's cricket brown to the ceiling
I am watching two people sleep

in the morning smoke light
my chest and its arms cover my breasts,
the ground, wet, the night before,
soil scented,
the open vault of the morning,
scented as the beginning and end of everything
after a while, villainy fingers the eyes
daubs the hills disenchant
and the mouth lies in its roof
like a cold snake

coals lit
and contained in clay, glowing
a horizon like a morning coal pot,
still an old woman stooping – cold
churches coral their walls on the ridge
I could exchange this caribbean
for a good night's sleep
or a street without young men

the ghost of a thin woman
drifts against the rim of the street
I thought nothing was passing
in the grey light before the crying animals
when I saw her dress and her pointed face
I am climbing the steps to the garbage dump
a woman frightens me.

In the pale air overlooking the town
in the anxious dock
where sweat and arms are lost
already,
the ship and the cement

drop against the metal skies
a yankee paratrooper strangles in his sheet

prayers for rain,
instead again this wonderful sky

an evening of the war and those of us looking
with our mouths open,
see beauty become appalling,
sunset, breaths of grey clouds streaked red,
we are watching a house burn

all afternoon and all night
each night we watch a different
fire burn
Tuesday, Butler House
Wednesday, Radio Free Grenada
Thursday, The Police Station
A voice at the window looking
'the whole damn town should burn'
another 'no too many of us will die'

eyes full of sleep lie awake
we have difficulty eating
'what's that' to every new sound
of the war

In the 5 a.m. cold light
something is missing
some part of the body, some
area of the world, an island
a place to think about
I am walking on the rock of
a beach in Barbados
looking to where Grenada was
now, the flight of an american bomber
leaves the mark of a rapist in the room

of every waking
what must we do today
be defiant or lie in the
corridor waiting for them
fear keeps us awake
and makes us long for sleep

it is my chest,
a green-water well
it is 5 a.m. and I
have slept with my glasses on
in case we must run

the last evening,
the dock and the sky make one,
somewhere, it has disappeared,
the hard sky sends
military transports
the darkness and my shoulders
meet at the neck
no air comes up
we have breathed the last of it

In the Grand Etang
mist and damp
the road to Fedon
fern, sturdy,
hesitate
awaiting guerrillas

October 19th, 1983
this poem cannot find words
this poem repeats itself
Maurice is dead
Jackie is dead
Uni is dead
Vincent is dead
Vincent is dead
dream is dead
lesser and greater
dream is dead in these antilles
windward, leeward
Maurice is dead, Jackie is dead
Uni is dead, Vincent is dead
dream is dead
i deny this poem
there isn't a hand large enough
to gesture this tragedy
let alone these words

dead insists itself on us
a glue of blood sticks the rest together
some are dead, the others will not mourn
most wait for the death announcements
Maurice is dead, Jackie is dead
Uni is dead, Vincent is dead
dream is dead
lesser and greater
dream is dead
in these antilles
windward, leeward
reality will die
i refuse to watch faces
back once again
betrayal again, ships again,
manacles again
some of us sold each other
bracelets, undecorative and unholy
back to god
i cannot believe the sound
of your voice any longer
blind folded and manacled
stripped
Bernard, Phyllis, Owusu, H.A.!
what now!
back to jails in these antilles!
back to shackles! back to slavery!
dream is dead
lesser and greater
drowned and buried
windward, leeward
a dirge sung for ever
and in flesh
three armoured personnel carriers
how did they feel
shot, shut
across Lucas street
this fratricide, this hot day
how did they feel
murdering the revolution
skulking back along the road

the people watchful.
the white flare
the shots
the shot, the people running,
jump, flying,
the fort, fleeing
what, rumour, not true
please, rearrested not dead
Maurice is dead
at 9:30 p.m. the radio
Jackie is dead. dea . . .
9:30 p.m. the radio
dream is dead
in these antilles
how do you write tears
it is not enough, too much to say
our mouths reduced,
informed by grief
windward, leeward
it is only october 19th, 1983
and dream is dead
in these antilles.

October 26th, 1983
A fortnight like the one in May
without duplicity
sodden and overcast
we would have held them off a few more days,
god, usually so reliable on matters of hardship
could not summon up a drop of rain

October 27th, 1983
And rain does not rust bombers
instead it looks for weaknesses in farm implements

October 27th, 1983 – evening
the sky does not have the decency
to shut up

Those in the market square
they will betray you
they will eat your food
and betray you

they will lift you on their shoulders
and they will denounce you
When push comes to shove
they will have change for an american dollar
they will pocket your grief
they will sing hymns to your killers
the press will report their happiness

when we left
I took my diary, my passport
and my Brecht,
this is security too

when we left
friends watched us go
'so you're leaving
how lucky for you'
and we saw
their 'will you send for me?'

DAVID DABYDEEN

Slave Song

Tie me haan up.
Juk out me eye.
Haal me teet out
So me na go bite.
Put chain rung me neck.
Lash me foot tight.
Set yu daag fo gyaad
Maan till nite –

Bu yu caan stap me cack floodin in de goldmine
Caan stap me cack splashin in de sunshine!

Whip me till me blccd
Till me beg.
Tell me how me hanimal
African orang-utan
Tell me how me cannibal
Fit fo slata fit fo hang.
Slice waan lip out
Waan ear an waan leg –

Bu yu caan stap me cack dippin in de honeypot
Drippin at de tip an happy as a hottentot!

Look how e'ya leap from bush to bush like a black crappau
Seeking out a watahole,
Blind by de sunflare, tongue like a dussbowl –
See how e'ya sip laang an full an slow!
Till e swell an heavy, stubban, chupit, full o sleep
Like camoudie swalla calf an stretch out in de grass, content,
Full o peace . . .
Hibiscus bloom, a cool breeze blow
An from a hill a wataflow
Canary singin saaf an low . . .

Is so when yu dun dream she pink tit,
Totempole she puss,
Leff yu teetmark like a tattoo in she troat!

She gi me taat
She gi me wife
So tear out me liver
Or stake me haat
Me still gat life!

Men and Women

So me saary.
Bu when yu grow old an yu voice weak an yu mout dribble
An yu foot-battam crack,
Is too late
Foh seh saary.

Bu me still saary.

Kase me drink rum an beat yu
Young saaf wet-eye face.
Kase me gi yu big belly year after year
Nine pickni foh feed, an me run way wid sweet-hooman
Sport all me inheritance whore-house.
Kase yu wuk in de field maaning till night, bruise-
Up yu small haan an yu skin peel in de sun.
Kase when yu sit dung an roll roti, or rock baby in hammock,
Yu na sing glad-glad like odda hooman
How yu mout sour like aachar.

Me come back now, bu now yu old
An yu na know me
How yu mind weak
An yu eye dull.
Bu blood stir in me bady still when me look pun yu,
Like laang-time, when yu was me midnight bride,
Bright, fresh, hopeful, an me lay yu dung dunlopilla bed –
Downstairs dem a beat drum, dem a sing love saang, dem a
    dance in de firelight! . . .

An me saary bad!

FRAGANO LEDGISTER

On Parade

faces in a door a row of faces
becoming a line of soldiers blurring in the eye
on parade in a triangular fort saluting the standard

general in the limousine you remember that posting
when there was no enemy you watched
and nothing came from the mountains
your men stood guard with dead faces
there had been no action for centuries
no one had come to trade to question
no one had left to trade to question

general in the restaurant you remember the constant urging
ceaseless vigil ceaseless vigil you must not sleep
so you watched and grew bored and returned to the city

it begins to rain
fat clouds have come down from the mountains
be calm general nothing will happen
there will be no war the farms and city are safe
each day you command closer watch
demand constant vigil the mountains are evil

you are afraid of a world without mountains
you dream of faces in a door

The Cities Have Fallen

how is the gold become dim
  – *Lamentations* 4 vi

we have come to the end of a dream
no more pianos at seven in the evening
no more tea on cool verandahs
no more cocktails   no more brie
we have come to the end of a dream

too many stones in the field to plough
too many masters   too little pay
we have come to the end of a dream

there is no more music but music of hate
no room for vision but vision of storms
we have come to the end of a dream

FREDERICK D'AGUIAR

Letter from Mama Dot

You are a traveller to them.
A 'West Indian working in England';
Or Friday, Tonto or Punkawallah
Sponging off the state. Our languages
Remain pidgin like our dark, third,
Underdeveloped world. I mean their need
To see our children cow-eyed and pot-bellied,
Grouped or alone in photos and naked,
The light darkened between their thighs . . .
And charity's all they give: the cheque
Once in a blue moon, when guilt's
A private monsoon, posted to a remote
Part of the planet they can't pronounce.
They'd like to keep us there.
Not next door, your house propping-up
Theirs; your sunflowers craning over
The fence, towards a sun falling
On their side; begonias that belong
To them shouldering through its tight
Staves; whilst their roots mingle.
So when they skin lips to bare teeth
At you, remember it could be a grimace
In another setting: the final sleep
More and more of us meet in our prime,
(Your New Cross fire comes to mind);
Who dream nowadays of peace.
You know England, born there, you live
To die there, roots put down once
And for all; the same England brought
With them, though ageless, unseasonable.
Drop me a line soon, you know me,
Neva see come fo see . . .

On Duty

Gun-metal is somehow cool even in this heat.
They press the cherished barrels to their cheeks
From time to time. Little else is done,
Nothing said, except to blow into the neck
Of uniforms or peer down the sight of a rifle.

It sharpens a wavering landscape under the nose,
And the capillaries of a browned, dust-caked leaf,
Including a man's lean, guarded figure, stepping clear
Of trees; whose bare soles seem to skip along
The steamy, bitumen-road, with hardly a touch.

It's a fragrance he loves, recalling days
When the giant Barber-Green unrolled its linoleum
Through the heart of this country . . .
It's a sight they have waited for all morning,
Beaten by this hottening monument hoisted now

To its zenith, rehearsing the features of this man,
Sure to come hot-stepping it along to quench
His thirst at the official tap on the town's pipeline.
They have him lie face-down on the bonnet
Of a patrol car; it's a brand's warmth;

Its windscreen wipers poised on a dusty arc.
The engine's steady pulse drowns his own,
For it churrs and churrs, churning this memory
Like a broken record: how in broad daylight
They ordered three he knew to do press-ups

Till exhausted, then to run, barely able to break
Out of tottering before the guns blazed,
Giving his name as witness in the heat of it all
And now this . . . a pistol to his head, they fire
An instruction, 'Bwoy, we goin g'e yu a chance, run!'

BIOGRAPHICAL AND
EXPLANATORY NOTES

Biographies and notes are given here in the sequence in which the works to which they refer occur in the book. A full bibliography of poetry publications is given. Publishers' names are included only where they are of historical interest, or as a finding reference for recent works which should be available. Where appropriate, a discography is also given. All records are LPs unless otherwise indicated. (It seemed beyond the scope of this volume to give a discography for contributors who are primarily musicians rather than poets.)

THE ORAL TRADITION

ANONYMOUS SONGS recorded by J. B. MORETON. His book, *West India Customs and Manners*, published in London in 1793, was written as a guide for prospective emigrants. He was against slavery, saying that in Britain 'the beasts of the field are better protected by the laws than slaves in the West Indies'. He lived in Jamaica, which he obviously liked, observing that 'all ranks and denominations of people are more friendly, kindly and hospitable, than in colder countries'. He incorporates these work-songs and dancing songs in the text. (See also Introduction and his own work, page 112 (and note, page 395).)

'GUINEA CORN.' Probably a work-song, on the call-and-response pattern, with scope for improvisation (from *Columbia Magazine*, vol. II, May 1797).

ANONYMOUS SONGS recorded by ROBERT RENNY. His *History of Jamaica*, published in London in 1807, the year in which the slave trade was abolished, approves of this legal watershed as necessarily involving 'a rise in the value, and an improvement in the condition, of the Negro'.

'New-come buckra' – 'As soon as the vessel in which the author was passenger arrived near to Port Royal in Jamaica, a canoe, containing three or four black females, came to the side of the ship, for the purpose of selling oranges, and other fruits. When about to depart, they gazed at the passengers, whose number seemed to surprise them; and as soon as the canoe pushed off, one of them sung the following words, while the others joined in the chorus, clapping their hands regularly, while it lasted . . . The song, as far as we could hear, contained nothing else, and they continued singing it, in the manner just mentioned, as long as they were within hearing.' (op. cit., p. 241.)

'One, two, tree' – Renny notes that this 'was, in the year 1799, frequently sung in the streets of Kingston'. J. M. Phillippo (see page 373 below) also cites it, probably following Renny.

'MY DEERY HONEY.' Anonymous song recorded by SAMUEL AUGUS-TUS MATTHEWS. This, described as a 'sweet song with soft drum', was one of four negro songs published by Matthews in St Bartholomew's English-language newspaper, *The Report of St Bartholomew*, on 18 May 1805 (only a small proportion of the white population were Swedish-speaking). The softened consonants, *sh* for *s*, *ch* for *c*, seem to have been common in earlier dialects. The plaint of the woman looking for her absent man, and preparing the house, a meal (peas and pork) and the bed for his return, ends in her frustration being taken out on the empty bed.

'aucung' – probably 'ah cong', i.e. 'I came'.
'bine' – possibly 'bind', 'wine', or even 'boil' (cf. substitution of *n* for *l* in Jamaican folk pronunciation of 'lignum-vitae').

'FREEDOM A COME OH!' A current Trinidadian work-song which must date from the abolition of the slave trade in 1807 since it refers to King George. George III was on the throne then, while William IV was king at the time of emancipation. Not surprisingly, abolition was at first understood to mean emancipation by many of the slaves, and in the interim of twenty-seven years before emancipation, the belief was widespread that their local masters had failed to implement the king's ruling, as in the next song.

ANONYMOUS SONGS recorded by MATTHEW GREGORY 'MONK' LEWIS. The novelist 'Monk' Lewis kept a journal of his two visits to his plantations in Jamaica, 1815–16 and 1817–18, which was published in London in 1834 as *Journal of a West India Proprietor*. Although he condoned slavery as a necessary evil, he was a benevolent master who did what he could to improve conditions for his own slaves, and won their gratitude for it (see 'Negro Song at Cornwall'). He concluded his book, 'What other negroes may be, I will not pretend to guess; but I am certain that there cannot be more tractable or better disposed persons (take them for all in all) than my negroes of Cornwall. I only wish, that in my future dealings with white persons, whether *in* Jamaica or out of it, I could but meet with half so much gratitude, affection, and good-will.'

'Song of the King of the Eboes' – Lewis tells (pp. 227–8) how a copy of this song was produced in evidence at the trial of two leaders of a proposed rebellion. A gathering of 250 slaves had been observed by an overseer, ostensibly attending a funeral but in fact electing a 'King of the Eboes' and planning 'a complete massacre of all the whites on the island'. The 'King' was sentenced to be hanged, and his 'Captain' to transportation.

'Mr Wilberforce, make we free' – i.e. 'has made us free' (see note to preceding song). William Wilberforce joined the abolitionists in 1787 and became the prime mover in the Parliamentary campaign which finally persuaded the House to approve the abolition of the slave trade in 1807.

'eerie' – occurs only here. Cassidy (the Jamaican lexicographer) suggests a derivation from English 'airy' = 'gay', but it may be an African word, and the same word as has come to the fore recently in Rastafarian parlance, 'irie', a general term of approval, 'great, wonderful'.

'A Negro Song' – Lewis comments: 'The song of a wife, whose husband had been Obeahed by another woman, in consequence of his rejecting her advances.'

'Lucea' – a town in Jamaica (pronounced 'Lucy').

'A Popular Negro Song' – Lewis relates (pp. 322–4) the incident which gave rise to the song (of which he gives only the chorus). A planter in the same neighbourhood some thirty years earlier had become notorious for his cruelty in having sick slaves 'carried to a solitary vale upon his estate, called the Gulley' where they were 'thrown down and abandoned'. The bearers were told 'not to forget to bring back his frock and the board on which he had been carried'. One poor soul, who had been secretly rescued and nursed back to health, later met his master by chance in Kingston, whereupon the master seized him and claimed him as his slave, but when his story was heard, public indignation was so great that the planter, Bedward, had to flee. The story passed into the region's folklore, turning up in a Jamaican Anansi story recorded by Jekyll in 1907 (*Jamaican Song and Story*, p. 48), which has the chorus 'Carry him go 'long', and in a Guyanese folk-song with the chorus 'Dead, dead, me na dead yet', both of which suggest a direct line of transmission.

'QUACO SAM.' A Jamaican folk-song which can be dated from internal evidence to between 1812 and *c.* 1825 (the Regency gown and the use of the whip suggest lower and upper limits respectively) (see Barbara Lalla, 'Quaco Sam, a relic of archaic Jamaican speech', *Jamaica Journal*, no. 45[1981]). Versions of the song have been taken down from old people in Jamaica during this century; an incomplete early text also exists, on some earthenware. Mr Ray Fremmer has in his collection a plate and a jug, and the Institute of Jamaica has three saucers, each bearing a black, underglaze transfer print of an illustrated verse of the song. The saucers also have overglaze colour, clumsily applied. Typical of the wares which were then being cheaply mass-produced for the popular market, and which were often decorated with illustrated verses or mottos, they were manufactured *c.* 1840 (probably in Staffordshire since they were shipped from Liverpool), for a Kingston merchant, Rebecca Brandon, who was exploiting the expanded market in post-emancipation Jamaica. The text given here in the main gives precedence to the early readings, and an attempt has been made to sort out the confusion arising from similar phrases in the second halves of the two final verses. The versions taken down in this century are in fact remarkably close to the older text: eloquent testimony to the strength of the oral tradition.

Quaco Sam seems to have been a celebrated dancer or entertainer, but nothing else is known about him (the African day-name, Quaco, for a boy born on a Wednesday, obviously did not have its later pejorative associations). European influence can be seen in the song's metre and rhyme (and the tune, 'The White Cockade'), but it remains one of the most moving artistic expressions of the slave days to have survived. (Note compiled with the assistance of Barbara Lalla, Ray Fremmer and Lionel Burman. – Ed.)

'Cuba' – the African day-name for a girl born on a Wednesday.

'Mek me ax' – 'Let me ask'.

''cotch reel' – scotch reel (there had been considerable Scottish immigration to Jamaica in the late eighteenth and early nineteenth centuries).

'road da' – early text only; modern versions have 'row da' which is possibly correct, although the sense 'road' is not impossible if one imagines the woman hurrying late to the fields on Monday morning after a weekend of revelry.

'weh de people-dem da run' – the early text has 'da nigger der a wuk', which is unsatisfactory in that it breaks the otherwise rigid rhyme-scheme.

'all come behin' me' etc. – 'all who arrived for work after me got a beating'.

'centung' – obscure (presumably something used in the cultivation of cane which has become obsolete, as modern versions repeat 'Wid me hoe da me shoulder' in both of the final verses). The illustration to this verse on the earthenware shows a long spear-like tool, carried on the shoulder.

'chacolata' – breakfast, snack (of any food), here taken to the fields in a 'pan', or closely lidded metal container.

'laugh' – early text only; modern versions have 'nyam' ('eat'), presumably by association with 'chacolata'. (In the early version, this half-line is transposed with 'Me da mash putto-putto'.)

ANONYMOUS SONG recorded by J. M. PHILLIPPO. James Phillippo (1798–1879) went to Jamaica as a young missionary in 1823 and spent the rest of his life there, as pastor of the Baptist church of Spanish Town. In his book, *Jamaica: Its Past and Present State* (London, 1843, 1969; New York, 1857), he notes this song with the comment, 'These ballads had usually a ludicrous reference to the white people, and were generally suggested by some recent occurrence.'

'WAR DOWN A MONKLAND.' A Jamaican work-song, still current, alluding to the Morant Bay Rebellion in Jamaica in 1865. (Queen Victoria having dismissed a petition from Jamaicans for land to help them combat appalling poverty – from the song it appears that local opinion held that the petition was not delivered – anti-government rioting broke out in Morant Bay after troops had fired on demonstrators. Governor Eyre called in reinforcements and put down the rebellion with such severity – nearly 600 died – that a royal commission was sent from England to investigate the affair, with the result that Eyre was dismissed.)

'Monkland . . . Chiggerfoot' – places in the Morant Bay area.

'Newcastle' – a garrison town in the hills above Kingston.

'TWO MAN A ROAD.' Jekyll calls this 'a rough game': 'A line of girls stretches along each side of the road and in front of them stand the two combatants armed with sticks. One is a Coromanti (one of the African tribes) and the other a Kingston or downtown boy . . . Whoever can disable the other and snatch one of his girls across the road is the winner.' (The Koromantyn slaves had a reputation for fierce fighting.) It presumably originated either before, or shortly enough after, abolition, for those born in Africa to be distinguishable from the majority. It is interesting for its symbolic contest between the African and the urban sophisticate.

'MAS' CHARLEY.' The Panama Canal, begun in 1904 and completed in 1914, was built with largely West Indian labour. The opulence of workers returning from Colón was both envied and mocked.

'Me rarabum why' – 'a nonsense phrase' (Jekyll).

'I HAVE A NEWS.' A dancing song, interesting in that it shows that travelling professional musicians had, at least on occasion, taken over from the local musicians who were to be found on every estate in the old days.

'Mowitahl' – Mowatt Hall in Jamaica.

'August pork' – 1 August was, and is, celebrated as the anniversary of Emancipation Day. (It is now also Independence Day.)

'Not if the pork even purchase self' – 'even if the pork itself is already purchased'.

'THERE'S A BLACK BOY IN A RING.' A ring game. 'The boy inside the ring chooses his partner, whom he leaves there after the dance. She obtains release by choosing another partner, whom she leaves behind. So there is alternately a boy and a girl in the ring.' (Jekyll.) Jekyll also records an Anansi story in which Anansi sings this song to Screech-owl before killing and eating him, but with the words mockingly altered to, 'There's a blind boy in a ring'. The variant 'There's a brown girl in the ring' has become well known internationally since Boney-M's version topped the hit parade in the late sixties.

'shamador' – Jekyll glosses, 'possibly a corruption of "camerado"'.

'THEM GAR'N TOWN PEOPLE.' A dancing song about the making of the road to Newcastle in Jamaica, for which local labour was used. In the post-Emancipation period, an unwillingness to work in the fields meant there was a large pool of ready labour for other projects. Newcastle became an important garrison, and saved many soldiers' lives by its high elevation, being, at 4,000 feet (1,200 metres), free of the yellow-fever mosquito. Above Gordon Town the terrain is precipitous, the road needing many 'tunnels' or cuttings. It was finished in the mid nineteenth century.

'follow-line' – 'Strangers are called "follow-line" because, as they come down from their homes in the higher hills, they walk in strings' (Jekyll).

'A ten pound order' – a £10 contract.

'number nine tunnel' – had a particularly bad accident record.

'ITANAMI.' A Guyanese folk-song that vividly conveys the fear which such natural hazards as the Itanami rapids on the river Potaro instilled into the early prospectors, or 'pork-knockers'.

MICHAEL MCTURK. 1843–1915. Born in Liverpool from a family associated with Guyana for 150 years, McTurk became a sugar-planter in the Essequibo region and subsequently a pioneer in the interior.

Like Wilson Harris in this century, he became a surveyor and lived for several years with the Amerindians, becoming eventually a travelling magistrate in the interior. His vernacular poems were published originally in the Georgetown newspaper, *Argosy*, under the pen-name Quow, and later in a collected edition. They offer wry comment on Guyanese society of the times, through the persona of 'Quow' addressing his friend 'Jimmis'.

Poetry: *Essays and Fables in the Vernacular*, Georgetown, Guyana, 1899, 1949.

'Jonah bin nyam w'ale' – the joke is that the story is back-to-front, with Jonah eating the whale, which is imagined as a fish with scales to be scraped (verbs can cause confusion).

'ratta . . . ol' fiah-'tick . . ./fowl' – all proverbs.

'dem Ba'jan nagah' – jokes against people from other parts of the Caribbean are common in all communities.

'"cookoo an shad"' – a Barbadian dish of a baked 'bread' with fish.

'no you wan bin' – 'you are not the only one to have been'.

'Quow' – McTurk habitually signed himself 'Quow', which was originally an African day-name but became a derogatory term for an albino or light-skinned person (he was white).

EDWARD A. CORDLE. 1857–1903. Born in Barbados from a family whose name first appears in Barbadian records in the 1850s. A former classical scholar of Harrison College, he wrote a hugely popular column of vernacular verse under the title 'Overheard' in the Bridgetown *Weekly Recorder*. A collected edition was published posthumously. The poems are letters from 'Lizzie' to her friend 'Susie' about her life with 'Joe', and matters of topical importance. After Cordle's death, an admirer, Archie C. Greaves, resurrected 'Lizzie and Joe' in the *Herald* newspaper, writing new verses which went on to become as popular as the original.

Poetry: *Overheard*, Bridgetown, Barbados, 1903.

'Lizzie Discourses on the Small-pox' – 118 Barbadians died in a smallpox epidemic between February 1902 and April 1903. The island was put in quarantine, which halted trade and caused great hardship to the populace.

'Uh woud did hah to try' – 'I would have had to try'.

JAMES S. MARTINEZ. C. 1860–C. 1945. Born in Belize, Martinez received little formal education, following his father round the logging camps of the mahogany forests. He is the first of the Caribbean's popular (published) vernacular poets to come from the world he portrays in his poems. Like McTurk and Cordle he was published first in the local newspapers and subsequently in a collected edition. About half of the work collected is in standard English, with a sentimental Edwardian flavour, but his unremarkable homespun philosophy is interwoven with a conscious portrayal of a society hitherto unrecorded.

Poetry: *Caribbean Jingles*, Belize, [1920].

MARCUS MOSIAH GARVEY. 1887–1940. The Jamaican black nationalist leader, who founded the Universal Negro Improvement Association in Jamaica in 1914 and took it to America in 1916, is not usually thought of as a writer, but he understood the importance of verse, and particularly sung verse, as a means of disseminating ideas. In Harlem his weekly newspaper *Negro World* drummed up a large following, and in 1919 he launched the Black Star Line, a steamship company intended to link black communities in the USA and the Caribbean. In 1920 at a massive UNIA convention in New York he was elected provisional president of the 'African Republic'. With the commercial failure of the Black Star Line, he was convicted in 1923 of mail fraud, over the sale of Black Star stock, and in 1925 began serving a five-year sentence in Atlanta Penitentiary. In 1927 his sentence was commuted and he was deported to Jamaica, where he kept the movement going, and held a big convention in 1934. He subsequently moved his headquarters to London, where he died in 1940. His movement has, if anything, assumed greater importance since his death, having laid the foundation for all the black-liberation movements of this century, from the Black Power of the sixties to the broad-based Rastafarianism of today.

Poetry: *The Poetical Works of Marcus Garvey* (ed. Tony Martin), Dover, Massachusetts, The Majority Press, 1983.

'Keep Cool' – presumably written while Garvey was in prison, this song, set to music by Alexander Seymour, became a hit in America in 1927.

'Centenary's Day' – from a volume of UNIA Convention Hymns, all written by Garvey, published in Kingston in 1934. It commemorates the centenary of Emancipation, and presents a more tolerant view of the white races than is often associated with his movement.

'To Afric's shore' – Garvey believed that the black people of the Americas should return to the homeland, Africa, and that the separateness of the races should be maintained.

SLIM AND SAM. 'Slim' Beckford and Sam Blackwood were popular Jamaican street singers in the 1930s, performing mostly round the markets of Kingston, but also going on tours of the countryside. They jointly composed topical and humorous words to existing mento songs, which they sang to Sam's guitar accompaniment, while Slim performed as lead singer and sold copies of the words for a penny each. Large crowds formed wherever they sang, and many of their songs have passed into the folk repertoire (for instance, 'Johnny Tek Away Mi Wife'). In the forties they also made more formal theatre appearances. Both seem to have died in the mid-forties. (See Godfrey Taylor, 'Slim and Sam: Jamaican street singers', *Jamaica Journal*, vol. 16, no. 3, 1983.)

'Sandy Gully' – the wartime US Air Force base of Vernamfield.
'go get a bite' – i.e. look for a job.
'Mus-Mus' – the Jamaican word for 'mouse'.
'yu goin pupuputoo' – 'you are going to be terrified'.

'SLY MONGOOSE.' A Trinidadian song which became the first recorded calypso; Lionel Belasco recorded a version of it for the Victor Gramophone Company in 1914. Knolly La Fortune's verses are from his 'Ballad of Play Bois'.

'DIS LONG TIME, GAL.' A Jamaican folk-song on the timeless theme of mutability.

'Peel-head John Crow' – the large black turkey-vulture, which has a sinister appearance with its bald head.

'LINSTEAD MARKET.' An earlier version of this Jamaican folk-song was recorded by Jekyll; his chorus line was 'Oh not a light, not a bite'. As with many folk-songs, key, rhythm and tempo could be varied in performance, and this song is now usually performed in a fairly fast, cheerful manner.

'DOG SHARK.' A Trinidadian folk-song. The unsuccessful fisherman returns to his family with only a dog shark, unfit for human consumption. The hungry family eat it, and one by one fall ill.

'SAMMY DEAD OH.' A soulful Jamaican folk-song. Sammy's success as a grower of provisions was the cause of his death in that jealousy prompted his neighbours to use obeah against him.

'GLORY DEAD.' A snatch of folk-song (Trinidadian, she thought) quoted by Jean Rhys (see note page 402) in one of the *Letters*.

'TROUBLE OH.' A Trinidadian spiritual.

'ZION ME WAN GO HOME.' A Rastafarian chant which would be repeated over and over to a heavy, rhythmic accompaniment of drums and other instruments.

'Zion' – Rastafarians have taken the Biblical story of the exile of the Jews in Babylon as a model of their own exile from Africa, 'Zion', to which they hope to return.

'Et'iopia' – the ultimate spiritual homeland, the West African peoples coming originally from there, and the former Emperor of Ethiopia, Haile Selassie I (known as Ras Tafari), head of the Coptic Christian Church, being regarded as divine.

LOUISE BENNETT. b. 1919. Born in Jamaica, she began to write as a teenager and has performed her work professionally since 1938. She also broadcast on radio, and from 1943 wrote a regular Sunday column in the *Gleaner*. She began to collect folklore material all over Jamaica, and in 1945 won a scholarship to the Royal Academy of Dramatic Art in London. In Britain she worked for the BBC and for repertory companies, in America she performed and broadcast and, based in Jamaica again since 1955, she has continued with a distinguished career as 'Miss Lou', the persona of her poems, and as a warm champion of the folk tradition. She has toured and lectured in many countries, in the Americas, Europe and Africa, and has been given many awards for her work, including the MBE.

Poetry: Some early volumes including her poems were published in Jamaica in the forties, and there have been two substantial collections of her poems: *Jamaica Labrish*, Kingston, 1966; *Selected Poems* (ed. Mervyn Morris), Kingston, Sangster's, 1982.

Records: *Children's Jamaica Songs and Games* (USA, 1957); *Miss Lou's Views* (Kingston); *Listen to Louise* (Kingston); *Once Upon a Time* (Kingston); *Anancy Stories* (Kingston); *Carifesta Ring-Ding* (Kingston); *The Honourable Miss Lou* (Kingston, Sublime Arts Music, 1980); *Yes M'Dear* (London, Island, 1983). (NB. *Listen to Louise* and *Yes M'Dear* both include some poetry.)

'Back to Africa' – 'Bun Grung' is a place-name (Burned Ground).

'Colonization in Reverse' – throughout the 1950s and until immigration regulations were tightened in 1962, some 300,000 West Indians, a majority of them Jamaicans, came to Britain, encouraged by official blandishments. Many found work with London Transport and in the Health Service; others were unable to find work.

'I feel like me heart gwine burs' – spoken with an 'English' accent.

'Dutty Tough' – the first four lines are proverbs (cf. 'Dem Belly Full', the Bob Marley song, page 64).

'Rain a fall but dutty tough' – i.e. rain has fallen but the ground is still hard.

'Fe cut we yiye pon bread' – 'to look away from bread'.

'All dem deh weh dah fahs wid me' – 'all those who are taking liberties with me'.

'Excitement': 'blue-boot' – 'to put on blue-foot fe go climb leben steps' was a proverbial saying for 'to smarten oneself up for a court appearance' (the court house had eleven steps; 'blue' of boots seems to have meant 'black and shiny').

'one man' – the gun-toting politician was, in fact, Alexander (later Sir Alexander) Bustamante, who eventually became Prime Minister.

'Independance' – written to commemorate Jamaican Independence, 1962. (The 'a' spelling is an indication of the pronunciation here, as contrasted with the self-consciously 'posh' pronunciation in the following poem.)

'When daag marga him head big' – a proverb, 'big-headedness is a sign of weakness'.

'When puss hungry him nose clean' – proverbial, 'to survive one may have to get dirty'.

'Daag wag im tail fe suit im size' – another proverb.

'formula' – a pun on 'formula' as 'baby's milk' (at Independence Jamaica is like a new-born baby).

'nuff jackass rope' – a compactly ironic conclusion, suggesting (a) tobacco for the coming adult Jamaica ('jackass rope' is the local name for a kind of tobacco sold in a thick twist), (b) rope to tie a jackass (i.e. an obstinate fool who needs firm handling), (c) an allusion to the English and Jamaican proverb 'give a man enough rope and he will hang himself'.

'Independence Twenty-One' – a fitting sequel to the last poem, written to commemorate the twenty-first anniversary of Independence in 1983. From stanza 7 on, it is a clever collage of Jamaican proverbs, the folk wisdom pointing lessons for the young nation.

'play buggy-widouten-tup' – to have no real foundation, to be pretentious.

'Bignadoa, an cocohead no deh a barrel' – to be a bragger ('bignadoa') when you haven't even got food ('cocohead' is a starchy vegetable).

'no macca, no Crown' – 'no prickles, no Crown Imperial flower' (which grows from a cactus-like plant).

'de dumplin tun fla-fla' – the dumpling dough is so thin from a shortage of flour (a sign of poverty) that it has to be made into fritters ('fla-fla').

'Marga cow is bull muma' – 'the thin cow may be the mother of a bull'.

BRUCE ST JOHN. b. 1923. Born and educated in Barbados, where he taught from 1942 to 1945. He went to Britain on a British Council scholarship, and obtained a diploma in physical education in 1947. He returned to teach in Barbados, and took a London University external degree. He studied at the Royal Conservatory of Music in Toronto in 1956, and later won a Canadian Aid Fellowship to take an MA in

Spanish at the University of Toronto, 1962–4, where he did further research, 1967–8. Since 1964 he has taught Spanish at the Barbados campus of the University of the West Indies. He has published numerous articles on Spanish and Caribbean literature, and won the Bussa Award for Poetry in 1973. He is best known as a performer of his poems.

Poetry: *Bruce St John at Kairi House*, Port of Spain, Trinidad, 1974, 1975; *Joyce and Eros, and Varia*, Bridgetown, Barbados, 1976; *Bumba-tuk I*, Bridgetown, 1982.

Records: *The Foetus – Pains*, Barbados, 1973 (45 rpm); *The Foetus – Pleasures*, Barbados, 1973 (45 rpm).

'Follow pattern kill Cadogan' – Barbadian proverb, 'slavishly copying others may lead to disaster'.

'Wuh sweeten' etc. – Caribbean proverb.

'De higher monkey go' etc. – Caribbean proverb of African origin.

'Choke 'e collar . . . boots' – proverbial, i.e. 'newly acquired status symbols can bring ridicule'.

'Wuh in ketch yuh en pass yuh' – proverbial: 'what hasn't caught up with you hasn't overtaken you'.

'Ashe cyaan play nor Sobers needuh' – in 1973 both Arthur Ashe, the champion American tennis player, and Garfield Sobers, captain of the West Indies cricket team, were boycotted for having played in South Africa.

'Evah fool got 'e sense' – Barbadian proverb.

'LORD KITCHENER' (ALDWIN ROBERTS). b. 1922. Trinidadian calypso-nian, who was in England recording a steady stream of calypsos in the fifties. Since returning to Trinidad in 1963, he has been the chief rival to Sparrow's dominance of the calypso, becoming Road March King ten times; he is known for his catchy tunes which adapt well to the steel-band range. 'Miss Tourist' was chosen for the Road March in 1968.

'Jou'vert' – 'Jour ouvert' (pronounced 'joo-vay') is Carnival Monday morning, the start of the main two-day festivities.

'mas' – carnival (from 'masquerade').

'THE MIGHTY SPARROW' (SLINGER FRANCISCO). b. 1935. Born in Grand Roy, Grenada, Sparrow has been the acknowledged champion of calypso since the mid-fifties, winning the title of monarch seven times since 1956, and producing an unwavering stream of calypsos, most of them witty, many of them serious satire. He was the first really to exploit the recording market and now has some forty albums to his credit.

'The Yankees Back' – the American bases, such as Chaguaramas in Trinidad, which the British had allowed on the islands in wartime without consulting local governments and which had therefore been resented (although the economic benefits they brought were welcomed), had been gradually run down after the war. A decade later, Sparrow was singing of the Americans' return as a similarly mixed blessing.

'Pointe-a-Pierre' – Trinidad's major oil refinery. Bought by Texaco from the Trinidad Oil Company in 1956, it became Texaco's largest refinery outside the USA.

'Pitch Lake' – one of the great natural wonders of Trinidad.

'Ste Madeleine Cane' – a major sugar refinery in Trinidad.

'Women does make we suffer' – the injured pride of the Caribbean men who were frequently dependent on their women's earnings with the GIs was an old calypso theme.

'Get to Hell outa Here' – a satire on the late Prime Minister of Trinidad, Dr Eric Williams, to whose campaigns Sparrow had earlier lent his considerable influence. In 1965 Dr Patrick Solomon, one of the members of his Cabinet, resigned after being accused of intervening to secure the release of a relative from police custody. In the old tradition of satire by mimicry, the song allows Dr Williams's response to the affair, quoted verbatim in the chorus, to work its own mischief.

'who vex loss' – 'anyone who gets annoyed will be the loser.'

'John John' – a poor district of Port of Spain.

'P.N.M.' – the People's National Movement, the party headed by Dr Williams.

'THE MIGHTY CHALKDUST' (HOLLIS LIVERPOOL). b. 1940. Trinidadian schoolteacher who chose an appropriate sobriquet when he became a calypsonian in 1966, after some years of writing for other calypsonians. 'Brain Drain' brought him to the public's attention in 1968, since when he has been respected for sticking to serious social comment. He won the calypso crown in 1976 and 1977. He has also become an expert on the history of calypso, conducting valuable research among veteran calypsonians, and helping to gain for calypso the serious respect it deserves.

'Horace James and Errol John' – an actor and playwright active in Caribbean theatre and cultural activities in London at that time.

'Expo' – Expo 67, in Montreal.

'C. L. R. James' – Trinidadian writer and historian who lives in Britain.

'Andrew Beddoe' – folk musician particularly interested in the African tradition.

'Peter Farquhar and Sukie' – Farquhar and Lionel Seukeran were talented politicians in opposition to the ruling party.

'Saldenah' – a band leader.

'parang' – Trinidadian tradition of Afro-Spanish origin, in which bands of musicians go from house to house in the weeks before Christmas, singing religious songs in exchange for hospitality.

MARC MATTHEWS. b. 1937. Born and educated in Guyana, obtaining a diploma in design. He teamed up with Ken Corsbie to become the Dem Two performance group (subsequently, with others, All Ah We), touring throughout the Caribbean and in Canada. He received a Bussa Award for his work as actor, writer and producer, and researched and produced several documentaries for radio and multi-media presentation. He now works in London as a fabric designer, and has set up a new performance group with two women, He and She.

Poetry: *Hear Nuh* (forthcoming).

Record: *Marc-up: Marc Matthews and Friends* (with others), Barbados, 1978.

'Buxton, Fyrish' etc. – places on the east coast of Guyana.

'Pompeii, Tanta doux, Bhagwandeen . . . / Sai John' – personal names.

'trench water' – 'canal water': Guyana's low-lying coastal plains are drained by a complex canal system.

'swank' – a lime-juice drink.

'cuss-cuss an sugar' – a children's sweet, made from grated coconut after the milk has been extracted.

'jinghi seeds' – these are split open and eaten.

'back-dam mettagee' – a dish of mixed vegetables grown on the provision grounds outside town ('back-dam').

'buxton spice' – a variety of mango.

'Pass Plaisance' – 'past Plaisance' (a place).

'las' lick' – the children's chasing game, 'he' or 'tag'.

'jamoon' – a fruit.

'potagee' – Portuguese (there is a sizeable Portuguese community in Guyana).

DELANO ABDUL MALIK DE COTEAU. b. 1940. Born in Grenada, he was first taken to Trinidad at the age of two, and grew up between Grenada and Trinidad. He has lived most of his adult life in Trinidad. He became involved in the Black Power movement in the sixties (he was given the same Muslim name as Michael X, Abdul Malik, when he became a Muslim in 1968), and began to compose and perform poetry out of that experience. Since 1975 he has become well known for his one-man shows at the Little Carib Theatre, Port of Spain (such as 'Bad Poet' and 'Whirlwind'), in which he has used drum and steel-band accompaniment to some of his poems. He first performed in Britain in 1983. He is a compelling performer, who uses the rhythm and music of the voice, rather than gesture, to hold his audience.

Poetry: *Black-Up*, Port of Spain, 1972; *Revo*, ibid., 1975; *Voice of the Whirlwind*, ibid., 1980.

Record: *More Power*, Port of Spain, DAMD Productions, 1982.

'Butler riots' – Uriah Butler was a Grenadian-born union leader in the Trinidad oilfields in the thirties. He led a famous hunger march on Port of Spain in 1935, and called a strike in 1937 which led to widespread disturbances.

'Marryshow' – Grenadian politician, regarded as the father of Federation.

'Federal / Funeral' – the West Indian Federation, which had been founded in 1958 as the hope of the future, collapsed in 1962 after the withdrawal of Jamaica.

'Independence / Blood c-l-a-a-t / flags' – following on the breakdown of Federation, Jamaica and Trinidad both became independent in 1962. The flag of Trinidad and Tobago is crimson, with a white-edged, black diagonal stripe ('blood claat' – i.e. 'cloth' – is used as a term of abuse in the Caribbean).

'Carifta' – Caribbean Free Trade Association.

'Toussaint' – in the wake of the French Revolution, Toussaint L'Ouverture, greatest of the 'Black Jacobins', led the slave uprising in St Domingue which has since come to be known as the Haitian revolution. It established the first independent republic in the Caribbean, which was later suppressed by Napoleonic forces. Toussaint was captured and taken to France, where he died in prison in the Jura in 1803.

'Garvey' – see biographical note on page 376 above.

'Fanon' – Frantz Fanon was the Martiniquan psychiatrist who, through his involvement with the Algerian struggle, became the philosopher of the anti-colonial movement, with his classic studies, *Peau noire, masques blancs* (*Black Skins, White Masks*), 1952, and *Les Damnés de la terre* (*The Wretched of the Earth*), 1961. He died of leukaemia in 1961 at the age of thirty-six. His reluctance to leave his work in Algeria meant that by the time he arrived in America for treatment it was too late.

'wid force / dey take me' – Malik was arrested during the Black Power disturbances in Trinidad in 1970, and charged, along with about a dozen others, with conspiracy to riot and desecration. A subsequent charge of sedition was dropped. He was held on Nelson Island for two weeks.

'Powell' – Enoch Powell, British politician, prominent in the sixties for his controversial call for the repatriation of immigrants.

PAUL KEENS-DOUGLAS. b. 1942. Born in Trinidad and raised in Grenada. He studied sociology in Canada and at the University of the West Indies in Jamaica. Having written his first vernacular poem in

1974, he began to work in broadcasting in Trinidad and to perform his own work on radio. He took part with the performance group Is We, and from 1976 ran his own shows with the group Creola, the name borrowed from his radio programme. Since 1979, when he went professional, he has performed in the USA, Canada, Britain and all over the Caribbean. He is now interested in making dramas out of his stories, for children to perform; by treating Caribbean subjects he feels he can help to give them a Caribbean identity, otherwise, he says, 'our children will be like Americans soon'.

Poetry (with some prose): *When Moon Shine*, Port of Spain, Trinidad, 1975; *Tim Tim*, ibid., 1976; *Tell Me Again*, ibid., 1979; *Is Town Say So*, ibid., 1981; *Lal Shop*, ibid., 1984.

Records: *Savanna Ghost*, Port of Spain, Keensdee, 1977; *One to One*, ibid., 1978; *Tim Tim*, London, AP Promotions, 1979; *Fedon's Flute*, Keensdee, 1980; *Is Town Say So*, ibid., 1982; *Bobots*, ibid., 1984.

'Cari – com' – Caricom is the short name of the Caribbean Economic Community. Carifta, its predecessor, was disbanded.

'oil don't spoil' – Trinidad is the envy of the rest of the Caribbean for its oil wealth. Dr Williams's famous statement on the seventies' oil boom, 'Money is no problem', was satirized by the calypsonian, The Mighty Bomber, in the words used here.

'weed' – ganja, marijuana, the smoking of which is a religious observance of Rastafarians.

'Greenidge meantime' – GMT, but cf. the West Indies cricketer, Gordon Greenidge.

'Douen' – in folklore, the spirit of a child who died before being baptized, imagined with its feet turned backwards.

'pitch' – one of the natural phenomena of Trinidad is its pitch lake.

'Walter Raleigh' – Raleigh first put in to Trinidad in 1595 on his way to Guyana in quest of El Dorado, the mythical city of gold.

'Starsky / an hush' – an ironic allusion to the popular American TV series, 'Starsky and Hutch', about a police duo, one blond and confident (Hutch) and the other dark-haired and volatile (Starsky).

'God gave me toots' – i.e. 'teeth'. A Grenadian joke: the remark, made by Walter Levine ('Dun'), a colourful local character, now dead, became a catch-phrase in Grenada.

'Redhouse' – building in Port of Spain housing the parliament and law courts.

'Doc' – Dr Eric Williams, academic historian and prime minister of Trinidad and Tobago, 1956–81.

F. 'TOOTS' HIBBERT. b. 1942. A Jamaican reggae musician who has been playing with his group Toots and the Maytals since the early sixties. They were the first group to record a song using the word 'reggae' (which was transferred to the music from Jamaican sex-talk), with 'Do the Reggay' in 1968. They now record on the Island label. This song is from the LP *Knock Out*, 1981.

'down in the valley' – this phrase, like 'trod in creation', is much used in Rastafarian speech, with its strong Biblical sonorities (cf. Psalm 23, 'the valley of the shadow of death'; the valley of the bones in Ezekiel: 37). The antithesis between the valley (of suffering, 'Babylon') and the mountain (of spiritual joy, 'Zion') has been taken up from Revivalism and given a distinctive Rastafarian symbolism.
'Arawak Indians' – the indigenous people of Jamaica.

PETER TOSH. b. 1944. Born Peter McIntosh in Jamaica, he was a member of The Wailers reggae group from 1962 to 1973, since when he has produced a number of singles and albums on his own. At the famous Peace Concert in Jamaica in 1978, attended by leaders of the rival political parties, he made an impassioned speech on the theme of his song 'Equal Rights' (see note, page 389, to Oku Onuora, 'Reflection in Red'), to the effect that political window-dressing was meaningless if the social conditions of the poor were not improved. Later in the same year he was arrested and badly beaten by the police (artists who speak out for the urban 'sufferers' know that they risk harassment and worse). He records on the Virgin label. This song is from his *Equal Rights* album, 1977.

'Clarendon / Portland / Westmoreland' – parishes of Jamaica.
'high / low' – i.e. 'light / dark' (of skin colour).
'Brixton / Neasden / Willesden' – districts of London with a large West Indian community.

JIMMY CLIFF. b. 1944. Jamaican reggae musician. One of the early singers of ska, he toured with Byron Lee in the early sixties and was signed by Island Records. He achieved international popularity in the late sixties and in 1971 starred in Perry Henzell's film, *The Harder They Come*, composing and performing the title song. He has since recorded several albums for Warner Brothers, but has not repeated the success of *The Harder They Come*, which had a tremendous impact, particularly in Jamaica, where the youth saw their lives for the first time treated seriously on film. (The novel of the same title was written after the film.)

'a pie up in the sky' – a phrase with an interesting history in the oral tradition. It has passed into the proverbial lore of the English-speaking world from a ballad written by Joe Hill (the Swedish-born songwiter active in the American labour movement who was executed in Utah in 1915 on an unsubstantiated murder charge, despite President Wilson's intervention on his behalf). The ballad satirizes the church for offering only philosophical comfort when it should be offering practical aid. Sung to a hymn tune of what Hill calls the 'starvation army' ('In the sweet bye and bye'), and echoing several similar choruses in the American Sankey & Moody hymnal (e.g. 'We shall be satisfied by and by'), Hill's ballad has the chorus: 'You will eat, bye and bye, / In that glorious land above the sky, / Work and pray, live on hay, / You'll get pie in the sky when you die.'

BOB MARLEY. 1945–81. Revered reggae musician, he was born in St Ann, Jamaica, but lived in Trench Town, an impoverished district of Kingston, as a child and a young musician. He became a national star with 'Trenchtown Rock' in 1971, and an international star in 1975 with his *Natty Dread* album. His original group (with Peter Tosh and Bunny Wailer) was known at first as The Wailers, but after he became well known they were billed as 'Bob Marley and the Wailers'. He toured North America and Europe, bringing to a wide public a lyrical protest on behalf of the underprivileged 'sufferers'. He brought a Rastafarian consciousness to his great musical talent and professionalism, deepening popular music's self-image. He died of cancer. (Legon Cogil and Carlton Barrett played and arranged with The Wailers in the early seventies.)

'De rain a fall' etc. – cf. Louise Bennett, 'Dutty Tough'.

CHRISTOPHER LAIRD. b. 1946. Born in London of Trinidadian parents, he has lived in Trinidad since 1952. He did his first degree and teacher training in London, then taught in Port of Spain for seven years. With Victor Questel, q.v., he edited and published the literary magazine, *Kairi*, 1974–9. He ran a theatre in Port of Spain in 1974, and was a founder member of the Trinidad and Tobago Television Workshop. Now a full-time producer/director of television programmes in Trinidad, he has written, directed or edited some seventy programmes for television, including the first Caribbean 'soap' operas and a made-for-TV film written and directed by Derek Walcott. He co-scripted and edited a documentary, *Village to Best Village*, which won a special prize at the Commonwealth Festival of Film and Television in Nicosia in 1980. He is well known as a performer of his poetry.

FREDERICK WILLIAMS. b. 1947. Born in Jamaica, he came to England at the age of sixteen. He started writing in 1966, and has read his poetry on Radio Nottingham (where he was involved with a black-community arts project). He lives in London and has performed at a number of venues, including the poetry reading at the first International Book Fair of Radical, Black and Third World Books in March 1982 (available on record and tape).

Poetry: *Moving-up*, Nottingham, 1978.

'Me trow me corn, me no call no fowl' – Jamaican proverb, 'I am not responsible for what follows my action.'

BONGO JERRY. b. 1948. Born Robin Small in Jamaica, he was impressed as a child by his father's copies of Langston Hughes's and J. A. Rogers's books, and went on as a teenager to study Marcus Garvey and Haile Selassie, becoming a Rastafarian. He started creative writing in 1967 and made an immediate impact with works such as 'Mabrak', which electrified audiences in the late sixties and was published in *Savacou* in 1971.

'Mabrak' – a Rastafarian word meaning 'black lightning' (i.e. 'black revelation' as opposed to the culturally dominant associations of light with whiteness and truth, and blackness with obscurity and evil).

'Babylon' – the Rastafarians' term for their present exile in modern society, and by extension the capitalist system or its agents, e.g. the police.

'Ras' – the title for sanctity in Rastafarian parlance.

'the white world must come to blood bath' – it has long been an axiom of Garveyism and Rastafarianism that the East/West power blocs would destroy each other with their arms race (the assumption that the black races would survive needs revising, in the light of current projections of the consequences of nuclear war).

'ITYOPIA' – i.e. Ethiopia. The syllable 'I' has special significance for Rastafarians. From a mistaken reading of the Roman numeral in Haile Selassie I, it has been seen as a symbolic reversal of the vernacular use of 'me' for both standard English 'I' and 'me', which was felt to be indicative of black people's lack of self-respect. To Rastafarians the use of 'I' thus symbolizes black pride, and unique forms have been adapted from ordinary speech to reinforce this, such as 'I-and-I' for 'we', 'irie' (see note on 'eerie' in 'Song of the King of the Eboes', page 371), and a number of words in which the first syllable has been replaced by 'I', like 'Ityopia' and 'Ital' ('vital').

EDDY GRANT. b. 1948. Born in Guyana, Grant came to England as a boy, and became a musician. From the beginning, he was both singer and song-writer, having his first no. 1 hit with the group The Equals and the song 'Baby Come Back' in the late sixties. He now lives in Barbados, where he has his own studio, writing and producing his records, and playing all the tracks. He is internationally known for his hit singles 'I Don't Want to Dance' and 'Electric Avenue', and his album *Killer on the Rampage* (1982), from which this song is taken.

LILLIAN ALLEN. b. 1951. Born and raised in Jamaica, she came to Canada in 1969. Founder of the performance group, Domestic Bliss, she was the first to take the dub style to Canada, and is now well known in Toronto. She has also performed in Britain.

Poetry: *Rhythm an' Hardtimes*, Toronto, Domestic Bliss, 1982.

Record: *De Dub Poets* (with Clifton Joseph), Toronto, Voice Spondence, 1984.

'Cool breeze' – proverbial, 'good while it lasted'.

LINTON KWESI JOHNSON. b. 1952. Born in Jamaica, he came to London in 1963, where he was educated at Tulse Hill Comprehensive School and London University, graduating in sociology in 1973. He began to write in the early seventies and rapidly gained a name for himself as an impressive spokesman for a sector of British society whose experience had never before been so powerfully expressed. On stage he uses a plain, low-key delivery, which is an effective vehicle for the impassioned content of his poems, while on his records he usually speaks his poetry over a musical accompaniment. He was awarded a C. Day Lewis Fellowship in 1977, and has now won considerable acclaim in Britain, with a broad-based audience also in Europe, America and the Caribbean. He has his own record label, LKJ, and works closely with the Brixton-based organization, Race Today.

Poetry: *Voices of the Living and the Dead*, London, Race Today, 1974, 1983; *Dread Beat and Blood*, London, Bogle L'Ouverture, 1975; *Inglan is a Bitch*, London, Race Today, 1980.

Records: *Poet and the Roots*, London, Virgin, 1977 (45 rpm); *Dread Beat and Blood* and *Poet and the Roots*, ibid., 1978; *Forces of Victory*, London, Island, 1979; *Bass Culture*, ibid., 1980; *LKJ in Dub*, ibid., 1980 (music tracks from the poems without vocals); *Making History*, ibid., 1984.

'ganja planes flyin high' – illicitly grown marijuana worth millions of dollars is flown out of Jamaica in light aircraft to America.

MUTABARUKA. b. 1952. Born Allan Hope in Jamaica, he became a Rastafarian as a teenager, although he describes his artistic standpoint as one of black consciousness, rather than a specifically Rastafarian one. He was the first of the new generation of Jamaican oral poets, beginning to write in 1968 and to perform from the early seventies. As a performer of his poetry he has made tours of America, Cuba, Nigeria and Europe, as well as the Caribbean (he was briefly imprisoned in Nassau, in the Bahamas, on the grounds that he was a bad influence on young people). He uses a musical accompaniment on his records as a means of reaching a wider audience, but attaches more importance to the word. He now has his own band, High Times Players, and his own record label, High Times.

Poetry: *Outcry*, Kingston, Jamaica, 1973 (with Faybiene); *Sun and Moon*, Kingston, 1976; *First Poems, 1970–79*, Kingston, Paul Issa, 1980.

Records: *Everytime A Ear De Soun*, Kingston, High Times, 1980 (45 rpm); *Naw Give Up*, ibid., 1981 (45 rpm); *Hard Times Love*, ibid., 1982 (45 rpm); *Drug Culture*, Kingston, Poets, 1982 (45 rpm); *Ode to Johnny Drughead*, Chicago, Alligator, 1983 (12-in., 45 rpm); *Check It!*, Kingston, High Times, 1983; *Word Sound of Power*, USA, Heartbeat, 1984/5.

'bee gees' – the pop group, the Bee Gees, popular in the late sixties.
'creative art centre' – there is a prestigious Creative Arts Centre on the Jamaican campus of the University of the West Indies.

OKU ONUORA. b. 1952. Born Orlando Wong in Jamaica, he became involved as a teenager with Rastafarian community groups, helping with the distribution of the black revolutionary newspaper, *Abeng*, and the founding of a community school, Tafari. He says, 'I was educated through Rastafari, through a man I respect, Negus.' In 1970 he was imprisoned for armed robbery. He began to write seriously in prison in 1971–2, and with Mervyn Morris's help he was first given radio time; then, from January 1977, he was allowed out of prison under guard to give performances of his poetry. A public campaign for his release resulted in his being freed shortly after publication of his first book of poems. He then studied at the Jamaica School of Drama, headed by Dennis Scott, for two and a half years, and has since performed his poetry in Britain, Holland, Germany, Switzerland and Cuba. On his records he makes use of music with some poems, but says that he really prefers the words 'ital' (i.e. 'pure, natural').

Poetry: *Echo* (under the name Orlando Wong), Kingston, Jamaica, Sangster's, 1977 (reprinted under the name Oku Onuora, Amsterdam, 1982).

Records: *Reflection in Red*, Kingston, Kuya, 1981 (12-in., 45 rpm); *Wat a Situashan*, ibid., 1981 (12-in., 45 rpm); *I a Tell*, Kingston, PAM, (12-in., 45 rpm); *Dread Times* (single, no details); *We a Come* (ibid.); *Pressure Drop*, USA, Heartbeat, 1984.

'pressure drop' – title of a song by Toots and the Maytals.
'den den den den den' – the voice is used to suggest a studio reverberation.
'Rema / an Jungle' – tough districts of Kingston.
'de man Peta, Waila' – Peter Tosh, q.v., one of the original group, The

Wailers, whose song 'Equal Rights' is quoted in the following lines.

'justice -tice -tice' etc. – the inflection of the voice is repeated exactly, but with fading intensity, to a whisper.

'a sad, sad / song / a redemshan' – cf. Bob Marley's 'Redemption Song', which he performs with acoustic guitar alone, and which captures the soulful mood of the spiritual.

'free Michael Bernard' – a public campaign to free Bernard (the stress is on the second syllable) was eventually successful after the sole witness, on whose evidence he was convicted, retracted his statement which had been made under duress.

'down with isms and schisms' – 'Isms and schisms', which was used in one of Bob Marley's songs, has become one of the catch-phrases of the oral culture. In performance, Oku Onuora sometimes gives this line as 'down with capitalism', and declines to choose one as the preferred reading, saying 'that is the point with oral art: each performance is different'.

'babylon kingdom' – see note to Bongo Jerry, page 387.

BRIAN MEEKS. b. 1953. Born in Montreal of Trinidadian and Jamaican parents, he came to Jamaica in 1956, and read economics at the University of the West Indies in Trinidad. After postgraduate studies in Jamaica 1974–6, he worked as a journalist and presenter with the Jamaican Broadcasting Corporation, which he left in 1981 to work in Grenada. He now teaches government at the U.W.I. in Jamaica. He has been composing poetry since 1969, and has given many performances of his work, sometimes making use of the flute. His work is published in *Savacou* and a forthcoming edition of *Focus*.

'bammi Negrah / yam' – Staple starch foods of the mass of the people ('bammi' is a flat bread made from cassava, and 'Negro yam' a variety of yam which is coarser than the preferred 'white yam'). These foods and their class connotations (as with saltfish) are here contrasted with the white bread made from imported wheat flour.

'Jones town . . . Rema' – slum districts of Kingston.

'Gleaner' – the main Jamaican daily newspaper.

MICHAEL SMITH. 1954–83. Born and raised in Kingston, Jamaica, he began to write at thirteen, with a poem protesting about Ian Smith's Rhodesia. From a Social Development Commission Workshop in Jones Town, he was selected in 1975 for the Jamaica School of Drama, where he studied at first part-time, eventually graduating in 1980, by which time he was well known in Jamaica as a performer of his poetry. He acknowledged the influence of Walter Rodney, the Guyanese political philosopher who was active in Jamaica at that time, and of the Rastafarian movement, as well as the effect of Marcus Garvey, q.v., and black American writers such as Langston Hughes. He performed at Carifesta in Barbados in 1981, and in Britain, France, Holland and Italy in 1982, winning acclaim as one of the most talented of the young generation of oral poets, who electrified audiences wherever he performed. He resisted the notion of his poems on the page, but had reluctantly planned a book. On 17 August 1983 he was stoned to death by four men at Stony Hill, Jamaica, outside the Jamaica Labour Party headquarters. Although he belonged to no political party, he had on the previous evening heckled a minister of the JLP government at a local political meeting. The following day, on his way to visit a friend, he was challenged by the four men. A witness reported that he replied, 'I-man free to walk anywhere in this land.'

Records: *Word*, Kingston, Light of Saba, 1978 (45 rpm); *Me Cyaan Believe It* and *Roots*, London, LKJ, 1980 (45 rpm); *Me Cyaan Believe It*, London, Island, 1982.

'Sing a song a cent' etc. – an ironic adaptation of two folk-songs, the English nursery rhyme, 'Sing a song of sixpence', with its blackbirds, and the Jamaican folk-song (sometimes attributed to the Maroons): 'Docta bud a cunny bud / Hard fe dead / Yuh lick im down, im fly away / Hard bud fe dead.' (The doctor-bird, a kind of humming-bird, is the national bird of Jamaica.).

'I an I . . . / . . . trod tru creation / Babylon' – see notes to F. 'Toots' Hibbert, page 385, and Bongo Jerry, page 387.

'"It's a hard road to travel"' etc. – in performance this was sung; cf. the song of the same title by Jimmy Cliff.

'teck everyting mek a muckle' – an ironic allusion to the Jamaican proverb, 'Ebery lickle mek a muckle', which itself is derived from the Scots proverb, 'Many a mickle makes a muckle' – 'many small things can add up to something great'. (There was a great deal of Scottish immigration to Jamaica in the eighteenth century; Robert Burns himself had a passage booked, but a lawsuit kept him in Scotland.)

'Cyaan mek blood out a stone' – a proverb common to Britain and Jamaica.

'cow never know de use a im tail' etc. – cf. the Jamaican proverb, 'Whcn cow tail cut off, Godamighty brush fly.'

'mek a bruk im . . . neck' – 'let me break his neck'.

'one a de P dem' – a member of the PNP, the People's National Party, one of the two main political parties in Jamaica.

VALERIE BLOOM. b. 1956. Born in Jamaica, where she trained as a teacher, she came to England in 1979, and studied English and Caribbean literature at the University of Kent. She has made radio and television appearances in England and Jamaica and is becoming well known as a performer in the Louise Bennett tradition.

Poetry: *Touch Mi; Tell Mi*, London, Bogle L'Ouverture, 1983.

'Trench Town Shock' – see note to Bob Marley, page 386.

'Ban yuh belly' – for a woman to bind her belly is to steel herself against grief (the navel being regarded as the source of strength).

'tief from tief God laugh' – a Jamaican proverb.

'Sta Fay' – 'Sister Fay'.

'Long neck pear' – a variety of avocado pear.

'fe wi' – 'our'.

'shet pan' – i.e. 'shut pan', a lidded container.

THE LITERARY TRADITION

ANONYMOUS. 'A Pindarique Ode' etc., 8 stanzas. Kingston, Jamaica, R. Baldwin, 1718. Published at the time of Lawes's arrival, it is the earliest extant poem published in Jamaica. Only known copy in Chetham's Library, Manchester, England. Reprinted Evanston, Illinois, 1942.

FRANCIS WILLIAMS. *c.* 1700–*c.*1770. A free-born Jamaican black chosen by John, second Duke of Montagu, 1690–1749, to be the subject of an experiment to prove that a negro was as educable as a white man, and therefore sent to England for education at grammar school and Cambridge University. He returned to Jamaica and, being refused government service, set up a school in Spanish Town. All we know of him is derived from Edward Long's hostile account in his *History of Jamaica*, 1774, and an anonymous portrait in the Victoria and Albert Museum, London, *c.* 1740. He wrote English verses as well as Latin, but only this ode has survived, written *c.* 1759 when Haldane arrived. His Latin is good, of a respectable, university standard (despite Long's attempts to discredit it), and shows considerable dexterity in its word-play: for instance, in the pertinent ambiguity of case in the 'candida'/'nigra' antithesis: 'candida' having a similar ambivalence to 'fair', in that it signified both 'white' and 'beautiful, morally attractive'. 'Occidui' means 'western' but also 'falling'.

NATHANIEL WEEKES. Born Barbados, *c.* 1730. In 1752 he published an effective satire in the manner of Pope, *On the Abuse of Poetry*, in which he condemned the current extravagance in poetry, including the pastoral vogue: 'All what they say amounts to just no more / Than what ten Thousand Thousand said before: / Condemn'd, and justly, to the Grocer's Hands, / To be transported into foreign Lands.' Two years later, in 1754, he published in London his own pastoral poem, *Barbados*, with the apologia, 'Descriptive poetry is not unjustly esteem'd, when executed in a masterly manner.' It is the first long (c. 1,000 lines) poem on a West Indian subject, modelled on a European tradition but already dealing in distinctively Caribbean topics. It seems to have attracted little notice, unlike Grainger's *Sugar-Cane*, as no later writers refer to it. He anticipated Grainger's poem with a section on the cultivation of the cane, but his better judgement was uneasy, calling it a subject more fit 'for Prose than Song'. In the same year he published *The Choice of a Husband, an Epistle to a Young Lady*. In 1765 he published a satiric poem on the degeneracy of the priesthood, *The Angel and the Curate*. His last poetic work was *The Messiah; a Sacred Poem*, London, 1775. A medical dissertation in Latin was published in Edinburgh in 1799 by Nathaniel Weekes of Barbados, either the poet or possibly his son.

JAMES GRAINGER. 1724–67. Born Berwickshire, Scotland; studied medicine at Edinburgh, and settled as a physician in London in 1753, where he became part of Dr Johnson's circle. His first publication, 'Ode on Solitude', 1755, was 'extolled by Dr Johnson as "noble"'. In 1758 he translated Tibullus and Sulpicia. He gave up medical practice to become a tutor, and in 1759 accompanied his pupil to St Kitts, where he married the Governor's sister and 'practised physic with great reputation and success'. His major poetic work, *The Sugar-Cane*, published London, 1764, was written there, and shown, on a visit to England, to Dr Johnson, who ridiculed a passage which had been intended as a mock-heroic parody. It is possible that Dr Johnson, an abolitionist, was embarrassed by his former protégé's advice on the management of slaves. Grainger spent the rest of his life in St Kitts. *The Sugar-Cane*, a poem of some 2,500 lines in four books, is a practical guide to the cultivation of sugar; he calls it a 'West India georgic' (Virgil's *Georgics* having become fashionable at the beginning of the eighteenth century), and acknowledges Dyer as a model. Apart from certain descriptive passages, such as the earthquake, it is mainly pedestrian verse, adequate to its functional purpose, with advice as to soils, weather lore and the management of slaves. As a doctor he was interested in their health, and while favouring the abolition of 'heart-debasing slavery', imagined a future where 'of choice, and not compell'd; / The blacks should cultivate the cane-land isles', displaying an ambivalence characteristic of the more philanthropic members of the planter class. *The Sugar-Cane* was reprinted in Jamaica in 1802. Grainger is the only early poet of the Caribbean to have achieved a lasting reputation outside the islands: his poem has been regularly included in surveys of eighteenth-century poetry.

'solfaterre' – volcano (Author's note).

'banshaw' – 'This is a sort of rude guitar, invented by the Negroes. It produces a wild pleasing melancholy sound.' (Author's note.) It seems to have been a lower-toned instrument than the modern banjo. Robert Renny writes of 'the banja, or merriwang' as a 'kind of violoncello' with 'a simple monotony of four notes' (*A History of Jamaica*, London, 1807).

'the vast circle' – the tradition of dancing and singing in a ring, while individuals take turns to perform in the centre, is well documented.

'the drum' – the drum was banned by law at certain periods of British rule.

JOHN SINGLETON. British-born writer who spent time in the West Indies and produced a poem of nearly 2,500 lines on his experiences there (as far as is known, his only work). *A General Description of the West Indian Islands, as Far as Relates to the British, Dutch, and Danish Governments, from Barbados to Saint Croix* (Barbados, Esmand & Walker, 1767) is the first non-occasional poem known to have been published in the Caribbean. It shows the influence of the growing vogue for the sublime and picturesque, and contains several passages of compliment to his hosts on his tours, as well as betraying the racial prejudice typical of the period. It was reprinted in Dublin in 1776, and London, 1776 and 1777.

'Cerberean yell' – Singleton sees the classics come to life in the West Indies. In Greek mythology, Cerberus was the watch-dog of hell.

'sulphurous unsound' – 'This mode of expression (the using the last of two adjectives for a substantive) though bold, is not new to those who are conversant with the Greek or Roman poets. The prince of poets, the divine Milton, often uses it, and under his authority I am safe.' (Author's note.)

'doleful way' – 'The adventurous traveller must be very cautious how he treads, and let the negroe guides conduct him, lest he sink in the burning sulphur. I was credibly informed that Mr Sims, the father of a very worthy gentleman now living, walking carelessly, slipt in, and had he not been secured by jack boots, must have been scalded to death; but, notwithstanding, he was miserably burnt.' (Author's note.)

'But see what strange procession . . .' – the details of the funeral are authentic: the white robes, the women with their rattles, the unruly coffin with demands of its own, the pouring of libations on the grave, and the singing, can all be confirmed from other sources, and closely mirror West African custom, but Singleton's is an unusually complete and impressive description.

'Archimages' – 'i.e. chief magicians among the Obeah negroes. – This word is often used by Spenser' (Author's note).

'mysterious speech' – African languages are still occasionally used in ritual contexts.

'Corybantian brass' – the Corybantes were the companions of the goddess Cybele, who followed her with wild dances and music.

'sistrum' – a metallic rattle used in sacred rites by the ancient Egyptians.

'Rhea' – another name for Cybele, the centre of whose cult was at Mount Ida in Phrygia.

ANONYMOUS. The eighteen-year-old author of *Jamaica* and *A Poetical Epistle*, both written in Jamaica in 1776 and published together in London in 1777, writes in his Preface: 'Having gone to our principal settlement in the West Indies, at a very early period, I was no less captivated with the beauty of the Island, the verdure of the country, and the deliciousness of the fruits, than I was disgusted with the severity of the inhabitants, the cruelty of the planters, and the miseries of the slaves: the first I endeavour here to celebrate; the last to condemn.' For one so young, his poems (of some 400 and 80 lines respectively) show remarkable assurance. Already the Caribbean literary tradition was established enough for him to make rhetorical capital from rejecting it in his anti-slavery cause.

'th'Anana' – the pineapple.

'The marrowy pear' – the avocado pear.

'milky apple' – the custard apple.

'cooling tamarind, that fans the fire' – the tart-tasting tamarind was renowned as an aphrodisiac.

'No sighing slave there' – an allusion to Lord Mansfield's historic judgement in 1772 in the case of the slave, Somerset, that his American owner could not enforce a right of property over him in England, since slavery 'never was in use here, nor acknowledged by the law'. This occasioned Thomas Cowper's lines: 'Slaves cannot breathe in England; if their lungs / Receive our air, that moment they are free' (*The Task*, bk II). Some 14,000 slaves in England at the time were freed by the edict.

'slaves for freedom die' – 'During what the Planters term rebellion, but what a philosopher would call a brave struggle of an injured people for their lost liberties: During these, the Negroes will die amidst the most cruel torments, with the most obstinate intrepidity.' (Author's note.)

'Caesars' – 'Names given by the Planters to their slaves' (Author's note).

J. B. MORETON. See note to 'Anonymous Songs', page 369 above. Moreton continues: 'The virtue and chastity, as well as the lives and properties of the women, are at the command of the masters and overseers; they are perpetually exposed to the prostitution of them and their friends: it is pity that there is not some law to protect them from abuses so tyrannic, cruel and abominable.' Its pathos and sociological value apart, this European-style ballad is interesting as the earliest-known use of the vernacular by a white writer (Moreton calls it 'the negroe dialect').

'Altho'' – the sense of this in the context is not clear.

'the field' – in the complex hierarchy of a slave-based society, the field slave held what was regarded as the lowest position. The relative status of master and overseer is also graphically illustrated here.

'missess' – i.e. the master's wife, not the overseer's.

'buss my rassa' – kiss my arse.

JAMES MONTGOMERY. 1771–1854. Born Ayrshire, Scotland; father a Moravian minister. In 1783, while he was at the Moravian school in Yorkshire, his parents were sent out to the West Indies as missionaries, where both shortly died. He spent most of his life in Sheffield, where he became well known as a religious poet and hymn-writer. William Bowyer, the publisher, commissioned an abolitionist poem from him: *The West Indies* (a poem of some 1,000 lines in four parts) was first published in Bowyer's handsome folio volume, *Poems on the Abolition of the Slave Trade*, London, 1809, and subsequently in several cheap editions. In 1827 he voiced his opposition to the 'science' of justifying racism by cranial measurement in a paper read before the Literary and Philosophical Society of Sheffield, which was published in 1829 as *An Essay on the Phrenology of the Hindoos and Negroes*.

'Charib people' – in fact, the archipelago was inhabited by two main Amerindian peoples at the time of Columbus's arrival, the Caribs and the Arawaks, but in the early literature the term 'Caribs' tends to be used indiscriminately. It is estimated that in 1492 the Indian population of the island of Hispaniola (now Haiti and the Dominican Republic) was between 200,000 and 300,000. By 1514 it was 14,000; in 1570 two villages remained. Extermination was often locally total and horrifyingly rapid, but the chapter of ethnocide was not quite closed. Small Carib communities do still survive in St Vincent and Dominica, while a remnant of the Arawak people lives in South America.

'For guilty ages, roll'd the tide of slaves' – historians estimate that between 1505 and 1865, when the last slave trade (to Cuba) was abolished, about 10 million Africans were shipped to the Americas on the notorious Middle Passage, of whom more than 4 million went to the Caribbean. These appalling statistics mask an even greater misery: approximately 20 per cent died on the voyage, and another 30 per cent within three years of arrival.

M. J. CHAPMAN. b. Barbados, d. 1865. M.A.Cantab; M.D. Edin. *Barbadoes and Other Poems* was published in London in 1833. 'Barbadoes' is a descriptive poem of some 2,000 lines, arranged in two parts, with the narrative of a Barbadian day giving it cohesion. Chapman says his intention was to 'do justice to his country' and to 'protest against ... the current of frantic innovation, that threatens with almost instant ruin both colonies and empire': it was published in the year in which the Emancipation Bill was passed. The volume includes translations from the Greek poets, and he went on to translate into verse the Greek pastoral poets, Theocritus, Bion and Moschus, in 1836. He practised medicine with distinction for many years in London, publishing *Ling's Educational and Curative Exercises* in 1856, in favour of the therapeutic effects of physical exercise.

'Guinea's shore' – the negroes believed that at death their souls returned to Africa; funerals were thus the occasion of rejoicing; cf. John Singleton, above, page 107.

WILLIAM HOSACK. 1808–83. Born Scotland, the eldest son of John Hosack of Glengaber, Dumfriesshire. His family came to live in Jamaica, at Bull River, possibly in 1824 when William's Scottish farm was offered for let. He is buried at St Michael's Church, Dumfries. His poem, *The Isle of Streams, or, The Jamaica Hermit*, London, 1879, (some 100 stanzas), was first published anonymously in an incomplete version in Jamaica in 1833, under the title, *Jamaica, a Poem*, in the *Jamaica Monthly Review*. It is one of the best poems of the type.

'the dark Maroon' – the name given to members of several communities of escaped slaves in Jamaica (originally the Spanish-owned slaves who remained when the British took control of the island in 1655), who preserved their independence in hill towns and villages by successfully fighting off the British forces sent to subdue them. In 1739 peace was negotiated with Cudjoe, the leader of the Maroons, which granted them their own land.
'the welcome shell' – on the plantations, a conch shell was blown as a signal.
'Mummers' – the John Connu Christmas revellers: an African tradition of elaborately masked festivities adapted to the New World's Christian calendar.
'the Gumby's unabating beat' – 'The goombay is a rustic drum, being formed of the trunk of a hollow tree, one end of which is covered with a sheep's skin' (Robert Renny, *A History of Jamaica*, London, 1807). It is an African word for an African instrument.

'impromptu' – the ability to compose extempore was esteemed among the African *griots*, and a number of early commentators note the importance of the art of improvisation among the Africans in the West Indies.

ROBERT NUGENT DUNBAR. British-born poet, who spent many years in the Caribbean, which formed the subject of most of his verse. He died in Paris in 1866. His earliest publication was a poem in a very sonorous style on the death of Princess Charlotte, *The Lament of Britannia*, London, 1817. Like Hosack he uses the Spenserian stanza for his first Caribbean poem, in the descriptive genre, interspersed with lyrics: *The Cruise, or A Prospect of the West Indian Archipelago* was first published in London in 1835 (97 stanzas). His intention was to remedy the general lack of knowledge about the West Indies by 'a glance at their picturesque beauties and natural treasures', envisaging a new interest in the islands as a field for white immigration after emancipation. Much of the poetry in this volume is graceful, though sometimes saccharined. He followed the favourable reception of *The Cruise* with *The Caraguin*, in 1837, interesting as the earliest narrative poem on a West Indian subject and for its introduction of a Latin American ambience to the literature of the British Caribbean. It is a long poem in three cantos, based on fact, which relates the tragic love-affair of a British-born girl with a Venezuelan, who turns out to be a pirate and her father's murderer, and is executed. The narrative is competently presented; its tendency to be romantically vapid gives way to a ring of truth in the presentation of the obeah woman, Mimba. In 1839 he published *Indian Hours, or Passion and Poetry of the Tropics*, comprised of another long narrative poem with a South American element, and a collection of lyrics. Most of *The Cruise* and a selection from his lyrics were reissued as *Illustrations of the Beauties of Tropical Scenery*, in 1863.

'Lorraine' – Claude (1600–82), the French painter known in England as Claude Lorraine, whose landscapes on classical themes came to symbolize the ancient glories of the Old World.

'Caraguin' – 'a native of Caracas' (Author's note).

'The Sybil' – 'The practitioners of *Obeah* are generally old, and of a strikingly ugly and forbidding aspect. A harsh and ill-favoured exterior, or any personal deformity are much to their advantage, as they add to the natural dread and awe in which they are held by the Negroes.' (Author's note.) Her name, Mimba, is the African day-name for a female born on a Saturday.

'those old rods / To serpents turn'd' – in a note, Dunbar traces the origin of the word *obeah* to the Egyptian word for serpent, *ob*, and cites Moses' warning against the demon Ob, translated in the Bible as 'Charmer, or Wizard, Divinator aut Sorcilegus'. He concludes: 'We are filled with a mysterious and awful feeling, when we contemplate the fact of our actually witnessing, in our own times, a living remnant of the superstitions of one of the most ancient and wonderful nations of the earth.'

'Orissa' – 'The fountain of life, and Creator of the Universe' (Author's note). In fact Olorun is the supreme deity in Yoruba cosmology, under whom are many Orissas, among them Ogun and Shango, but Dunbar is right in that it is to these that intercession is made, Olorun being regarded as too lofty to be concerned with human affairs.

'the mighty Snake' – 'Many of the Pagan natives of Africa believe that the Supreme Being is too highly exalted to concern himself about his creatures, and leaves the government of the world to the *Fetishes*. These *Fetishes* are most frequently deified Snakes, to whom no injury or insult can be offered under pain of death.' (Author's note.)

'The Royal Veil' – 'The ceremony of invitation used in Africa by kings to the ladies they intend to honour with their bed. Covered with the Veil, the lady is from that moment sacred to the King: but to refuse it is treason and death.' (Author's note.)

HENRY GIBBS DALTON. Born Guyana, educated in England. His *Tropical Lays and Other Poems*, which was published in London in 1853, relates that most of the poems in it were written in his youth. His chief contribution lies in his perception of the indigenous Indian's predicament and of the Guyanese landscape as poetic subjects (as in 'The Carib's Complaint' and 'The Essequibo and Its Tributaries'), thus founding what has become traditional in Guyanese poetry. He also wrote *The History of British Guiana*, 1855.

HORATIO NELSON HUGGINS. 1830–95. Born St Vincent, son of Horatio N. Huggins (1787–1861), a lieutenant in the Southern Regiment in St Vincent and later a captain in the Trinidad Militia Regiment, who owned land in Trinidad from the 1830s, when the family probably moved to Trinidad. The younger Horatio Nelson Huggins was Rector of St Phillip and St Peter in Savonetta, Trinidad, 1864–7, then Rector of St Paul's, San Fernando, and also Chaplain of San Fernando Hospital. He became a canon sometime after 1891, and died in Trinidad in 1895. His only known poetic work, *Hiroona*, written 'in later life', was published by his descendants in Trinidad in 1930. It is an extraordinary work: subtitled 'an historical romance in poetic form' it could also be termed the first Caribbean epic poem. Its subject is the rebellion of the St Vincent Caribs against British rule in 1795, in the wake of the Haitian revolution, which ended in the deportation by the British of the Caribs 'as a tribal nation' to Roatán Island in the Bay of Honduras. Huggins had 'in his early years heard and committed to memory the many stories of the Caribs as handed down by tradition', and composed his poem 'to perpetuate the memory of that ancient tribe'. For all his nineteenth-century racial and Christian bias, Huggins's driving force is a perception of the unalloyed tragedy of the Caribs' fate at the hands of empire, culminating in the curse of his Carib hero, Warramou, on the British, with which he ends the poem. Although 5,080 Caribs were deported, a century later Roatán Island had a population of 2,000, mostly negroes.

Huggins's confident handling of his long poem (twelve cantos, in 348 pages), in a flowing narrative style which occasionally reaches peaks of dramatic or poetic intensity, is a considerable achievement, but he is most remarkable for the originality, at the peak of British imperial history, of his lonely anti-colonial vision.

'Hiroona' – Huggins adapted the Carib name for St Vincent, 'Hiroon', for metrical convenience.

Canto XII – Huggins skilfully lent weight to his real predictions as to the future of the white man in the Caribbean by combining them here with 'prophecies' which were fact by his own day: the 1812 eruption of Soufrière, and emancipation in 1834.

'*Bondieu*' – Warramou's father, the Carib chief Chetwaye, had received a Christian education from the French.

'remember me' – a Shakespearian echo, cf. the ghost of Hamlet's father.

EGBERT MARTIN ('LEO'). 1859–87. Born Guyana. His verses for the national anthem were written in honour of Queen Victoria's Jubilee in 1887 and were awarded first prize of £50 by an English newspaper. They are typical of a considerable body of patriotic verse written by British West Indians for the 'mother country' right up until the Second World War.

Poetry: *Poetical Works*, London, 1883 (under pseud. 'Leo'); *Leo's Local Lyrics*, Georgetown, Guyana, 1886.

'clown' – in its archaic sense of 'peasant'.

THOMAS MacDERMOT ('TOM REDCAM'). 1870–1933. Born Jamaica. Journalist, novelist and author of a poetic drama about Columbus in Jamaica, *San Gloria*, as well as a poet, and the first Jamaican Poet Laureate (appointed posthumously). He wrote under the pseudonym 'Tom Redcam' (his name reversed).

Poetry: *Orange Valley and Other Poems*, Kingston, Jamaica, Pioneer Press, 1951; *Brown's Town Ballads*, Kingston, 1958.

'Cuba' – in 1895, led by José Martí, the Cubans embarked on their
second War of Independence against Spanish rule.

'Doan liard, nor tief, nor obeah' – the practice of obeah (witchcraft)
was illegal in the British islands.

DONALD MCDONALD: Born Antigua. All that is known of McDonald
is his volume of First World War verse, from which the proceeds were
to go to the West India Contingent Fund. Verse, rather than poetry, it
is none the less competent, and typical of its period.

Poetry: *Songs of an Islander*, London, 1918.

ALFRED CRUICKSHANK. *c.* 1880–*c.*1940. Born Trinidad. A skilful
versifier with a very Trinidadian feeling for satire, he spoke out
against social evils, and espoused the Garveyist position on the
Ethiopian war.

Poetry: *Poems in All Moods*, Port of Spain, Trinidad, 1937.

'The Convict Song' – an impressive early attempt to harness the
rhythms of the oral tradition's work-song to literature.

WALTER ADOLPHE ROBERTS. 1886–1962. Born Jamaica, the son of an
Anglican clergyman who supported the Cubans in their War of
Independence. He became a journalist in 1902, working in America
from 1904. He went to France in 1913 as a war correspondent,
returning to the USA in 1917. He founded the Jamaica Progressive
League in 1936, and returned to Jamaica in 1949. He wrote nine
novels, several books on history, biography, travel and politics, and
three books of poetry, the first two of which are in the European
classical tradition, while the third shows a greater interest in specifi-
cally West Indian themes.

Poetry: *Pierrot Wounded*, New York, 1919; *Pan and Peacocks*,
Boston, 1928; *Medallions*, Kingston, Jamaica, 1950.

'On a Monument to Martí' – see note to Thomas MacDermot, 'Cuba'.
Martí was killed on the first day of the fighting. (This poem and 'The
Maroon Girl' are from *Medallions*.)

CLAUDE MCKAY. 1889–1948. Born Jamaica. Having been born and
raised in the Jamaican countryside and come to Kingston as a young
policeman, McKay was encouraged to write by the English-born
folklorist, Walter Jekyll, who recognized his talent, and the need for an
indigenous literature. After publishing two volumes of verse in the
Jamaican vernacular (he became known as 'Jamaica's Bobbie Burns'),
he left for America in 1912, where he became part of what has come to
be known as the Harlem Renaissance, with a volume of verse pub-
lished in 1922. In 1928 he published his first novel, *Home to Harlem*,

which created a literary sensation. *Banana Bottom*, his only novel with a West Indian setting, was published in 1933. He visited England and Russia in the twenties, and later lived in Morocco for a while, but returned to America, not Jamaica as he had promised himself. He became an American citizen in 1940 and a Roman Catholic in 1944. A gentle man, outraged by the world's brutality, he died in America in disillusion and poverty. Since his death, recognition of his stature as a visionary poet of the Jamaican and black experience has grown steadily.

Poetry: *Songs of Jamaica*, Kingston, Jamaica, 1912; *Constab Ballads*, London, 1912; *Spring in New Hampshire*, London and New York, 1920; *Harlem Shadows*, New York, 1922; *Selected Poems*, New York, 1953 (the selection, made by McKay himself, includes no vernacular poems); *The Passion of Claude McKay: Selected Prose and Poetry 1912–1948* (ed. Wayne F. Cooper), New York, 1973.

Critical study: James R. Giles, *Claude McKay*, Boston, 1976.

'Nuff rock'tone in de sea . . . sun' – a Jamaican proverb. 'Only those who have experienced it can know about hardship.'

'gou'd' – natural containers such as gourds were used, as well as modern ones like the 'karasene pan', to fetch water from the standpipe. It was (and is) traditionally the children's job, morning and evening.

'sud' – 'get a beating, lathering.'

'The White House' – this has the triple resonance of (1) the white people's house; (2) the white-finished architecture typical of prosperous America; and (3) the U.S. President's residence.

'If We Must Die' – written as an anti-lynching poem, this, McKay's most famous poem, was first published in 1919. During the Second World War Winston Churchill quoted it in the House of Commons, and a copy was found on a dead soldier on the battlefield.

JEAN RHYS. 1890–1979. Born Ella Gwendoline Rees Williams in Dominica, she came to England in 1907. Her unhappy early years in London and Paris are chronicled in her last work, *Smile Please*, and provide the inspiration for her early fiction. She used the pen-name Jean Rhys from 1924. Despite the early support of Ford Madox Ford, at this stage her writing was little known, and she dropped into obscurity until her sensational reappearance in 1966 with *Wide Sargasso Sea*, which draws on her youthful experience of Dominica to reconstruct the tragic story of the first Mrs Rochester in *Jane Eyre*. This novel won two awards, the Royal Society of Literature Award and the W. H. Smith Award, and secured her reputation, but her comment on its success – 'It has come too late' – reflects her tragic perception of her own life and the human condition generally. She wrote what she termed 'mediocre "poetry"' all her life; in a letter she wrote, 'I began writing [my poems] aged 12, having discovered that they are a cure for sadness and easily done – not like prose which can be a *terrible* worry to me.'

'Our Gardener' – the last creative work published in her lifetime, in the *New Review*, 1977.

'Obeah Night' – written in the spring of 1964 when she was finding difficulty in finishing Part II of *Wide Sargasso Sea*. At a friend's suggestion she turned to something different to break the deadlock, and wrote this poem which enabled her, as she put it, to 'see' the book. 'Only when I wrote this poem – then it clicked – and all was there and always had been.' By substituting for the materialist Mr Rochester of the first draft a man consumed by very real passion for Antoinette, a passion which is plausibly channelled to the 'angry love' of the poem, she was able to make the book true to her first impulse to write, 'vexed', as she said, by Charlotte Brontë's 'portrait of the "paper tiger" lunatic, the all wrong creole scenes, and above all by the real cruelty of Mr Rochester'.

'that sea' – the poem explains the book's title, which had first been mooted in 1961.

'Béké' – i.e. Buckra, white people (Dominican creole).

'Locked Hearts' etc. – cf. the popular song 'I'm going to lock my heart and throw away the key' which Jean Rhys mentions in another of her books.

'*Edward Rochester or Raworth*' – she wrote, 'I think there were several Antoinettes and Mr Rochesters ... Mine is *not* Miss Brontë's ... Mr R's name ought to be changed. Raworth? A Yorkshire name isn't it? The sound is right.'

(All quotations from *Jean Rhys: Letters 1931–1966*, ed. Francis Wyndham and Diana Melly, London, Deutsch, 1984.)

FRANK A. COLLYMORE. 1893–1980. Barbadian poet, teacher, actor, editor and broadcaster, one of the fathers of West Indian literature. He had lifelong associations with Combermere School, where he taught from 1910 to 1963, and with *Bim*, the literary periodical, which he edited from its third issue in 1942 until 1975. He was awarded the OBE in 1958, and an honorary degree from the University of the West Indies in 1968. His glossary of *Barbadian Dialect* was first published in 1954, and the 1973 edition of the literary journal *Savacou* was dedicated to him.

Poetry: *Thirty Poems*, Bridgetown, Barbados, 1944; *Beneath the Casuarinas*, ibid., 1945; *Flotsam*, ibid., 1948; *Collected Poems*, ibid., 1959; *Selected Poems*, ibid., 1971. Light verse: *Rhymed Ruminations on the Fauna of Barbados*, ibid., 1968.

J. E. CLARE MCFARLANE. 1894–1962. Born Jamaica. Late Financial Secretary, Jamaica. He had an important influence on Jamaican poetry from the twenties onwards, founding the Jamaica Poetry League and editing the region's first poetry anthology, *Voices from Summerland* (London, 1929), which he followed with *A Treasury of Jamaican Poetry* (London, 1949). He also published the first critical survey of Jamaican poetry, *A Literature in the Making* (Kingston, Jamaica, Pioneer Press, 1956).

Poetry: *Beatrice*, Kingston, Jamaica, 1918; *Poems*, Kingston, 1924; *Daphne*, London, 1931; *Selected Poems*, Kingston, Pioneer Press, *c.* 1953; *The Magdalen*, Kingston, 1958.

'On National Vanity' – first published *c.* 1948.

PHILIP MANDERSON SHERLOCK. b. 1902. Born Jamaica and educated there, obtaining first-class honours in the University of London external BA degree in 1927. One of the fathers of West Indian letters, with a tireless and scholarly interest in all things West Indian, and the folk traditions in particular. He has spent a lifetime as an educator, first in Jamaican schools, and then, from its inception in 1948, at the University of the West Indies, which he headed as President (Vice-Chancellor) from 1963 to 1969. Since then he has been Secretary to the Association of Caribbean Universities and Research Institutes Foundation, based in Miami. After a distinguished record of public service, he was knighted in 1967. He has published sixteen books, mainly educational works on folklore and Caribbean history. His most recent work is a biography of Norman Manley (London, 1980). His poetic output has been small but impressive, making a significant contribution to the literary renaissance which accompanied the nationalist movements of the forties and fifties.

Poetry: *Ten Poems*, Georgetown, Guyana, Miniature Poets Series, 1953.

'Pocomania' – a cult mixing revivalism with ancestral-spirit possession; the leader is called a Shepherd.
'Long Mountain' – a long, low mountain just outside Kingston, Jamaica.
'Daventry' – the site of the BBC transmitter.
'A beauty too of twisted trees' – cf. Louis Simpson, 'Jamaica'.
'Ezekiel too saw the dry bones live' – Ezekiel 37 has particular significance in the black culture of the Americas, where legendary sermons evoking the raising of the bones have crossed into the oral culture and surfaced in popular song.
'cactus-land . . . / Hollow men stuffed with straw' – cf. T. S. Eliot's 'The Hollow Men', 1925.

UNA MARSON. 1905—65. Jamaican feminist, journalist, playwright and poet, important as the first Caribbean woman poet of note, and as an early innovator of the vernacular in poetry: her blues poems were the first to adapt musical rhythms to verse in the Caribbean (in America, Langston Hughes had shown what could be done). In London in the thirties, she became Secretary of the League of Coloured People in London, edited their journal, and became Haile Selassie's private secretary. She was also active with the Women's International League for Peace and Freedom, and the International Alliance of Women. After returning to Jamaica in 1936, she founded the Readers and Writers Club, and the Jamaica Save the Children Fund. She went back to London in 1938 to work for the BBC World Service. Back in Jamaica in 1945, she worked on the Pioneer Press, which published low-cost editions on subjects of local interest. After an unhappy private life, in about 1960 she married an American widower, but the marriage failed. As well as poetry, she wrote three plays.

Poetry: *Tropic Reveries*, Kingston, Jamaica, 1930; *Heights and Depths*, ibid., 1932; *The Moth and the Star*, ibid., 1937; *Towards the Stars*, London, 1945 (mostly reprinted from the earlier work).

'you colour is high' – a 'high', or light, skin-colour was the passport to social advancement in colonial days.

'Politeness' – cf. William Blake, 'The Little Black Boy': 'And I am black, but O, my soul is white.'

VIVIAN VIRTUE. b. 1911. Born in Jamaica, he was hailed as one of the bright stars by the Jamaica Poetry League in the 1930s. He was co-founder of the New Dawn Press and on the advisory board of the Pioneer Press, and has been Vice-President of the International PEN (Jamaica Centre). He has translated the work of Spanish- and French-Caribbean poets, among them eighty sonnets from the French of José María de Heredia. He retired as a civil servant in 1961 and now lives in London.

Poetry: *Wings of the Morning*, Jamaica, 1938.

'Wild Ishmaels' – Ishmael was the son of Abraham, of whom it was prophesied, 'And he shall be as a wild-ass among men; his hand shall be against every man, and every man's hand against him' (Genesis 16:12).

'The Hour' – commemorates Jamaican Independence, 1962.

ARTHUR J. SEYMOUR. b. 1914. Born and educated in Guyana. One of the fathers of West Indian literature. He founded the literary journal *Kyk-over-al* in Guyana in 1945, and maintained it with a high standard of literary and critical contributions until 1961. He recognized early on the importance of the language and traditions of the folk culture in building a national literature, carrying articles on these subjects in *Kyk-over-al*, and made important experiments in incorporating folk rhythms and local subjects into his own poetry. He is a prolific poet who has published a long series of small books of his poetry. The larger collections are *The Guiana Book*, Georgetown, Guyana, 1948; *Selected Poems*, ibid., 1965, 1983; *Images of Majority*, ibid., 1978. *AJS at 70* (ed. Ian McDonald) commemorated his seventieth birthday in 1984.

'yellow metal / . . . sweet crystal' – the quest for El Dorado, the city of gold, had motivated the early European colonists, particularly in Guyana. Sugar production did not become a major commercial enterprise until the mid seventeenth century, requiring the huge labour force which the slave trade maintained throughout the eighteenth century. In the nineteenth century, owing to the joint effect of world conditions and the loss of the labour force (after Emancipation in the British territories in 1834, most former slaves were unwilling to work on the plantations), sugar production in the West Indies declined.

'other races came' – between 1838 and 1924 indentured labourers were brought in to work the cane plantations, chiefly from India, with some from China, Java and other countries. About half a million Indians came to the Caribbean during this period.

'FIRST OF AUGUST' – Emancipation Day.

'Straighten its knees and stand erect' – cf. the climactic image of Césaire's *Cahier d'un retour au pays natal*, written in 1939, of the black races rising to their feet.

'Ibu' – the Ibos are one of the peoples of present-day Nigeria.

'I was a boy' – the season of kite-flying in the dry, windy weather around Easter is one of the indelible memories of a Caribbean childhood.

PHYLLIS ALLFREY. b. 1915. Born Dominica, where her father was Crown Attorney. Founder of the Dominica Labour Party, she was elected a federal MP and made a minister of the Federal Government. Since the failure of Federation, she has remained active in Dominica politics and as a journalist; she is editor of the *Dominica Star*. Her novel, *The Orchid House*, in some senses a forerunner of Jean Rhys's *Wide Sargasso Sea*, was published in 1953.

Poetry: *In Circles: Poems*, England, 1940; *Palm and Oak: Poems*, London, 1950; *Contrasts*, Barbados, 1955; *Palm and Oak II*, Star Printery, 1973.

ERIC MORTON ROACH. 1915–74. Born Tobago, where he became a schoolteacher after leaving school, until he joined the army in Trinidad in 1939. After the war he returned to Tobago as a civil servant, married, and in 1954 left his job to devote his time to writing. In 1960 he returned to teaching, and moved to Trinidad in 1961, where he worked chiefly as a journalist until in 1973 he again resigned in order to give more time to his writing. He committed suicide by swimming out to sea in April 1974. As well as contributing poetry to local journals and the BBC *Caribbean Voices* programme, he was the author of an unpublished novel and a radio serial, and a playwright, with three of his plays published by the University of the West Indies Extra-Mural Department: *Belle Fanto* (1967); *Letter from Leonora* (1968); *A Calabash of Blood* (1971). A collection of his poems (ed. Danielle Gianetti) is in preparation. 'Love Overgrows a Rock' is an early poem, from 1957; the others are from the early seventies.

'Piarco' – Trinidad's international airport.
'poggoes' – the Tobago name of the yellowtail bird.
'At Guaracara Park' – Guaracara Park is a large sports centre in south Trinidad, the site of the annual Southern Games, which are trials for international athletics events. Written in 1970, the poem was inspired by the coming visit of the famous Kenyan sprinter, Keino, to the Southern Games in 1971.

GEORGE CAMPBELL. b. 1916. Born in Panama of Jamaican parents, he was brought to Jamaica as a small child, and educated in Kingston and New York. Earning his living as a journalist, he was one of the poets prominent in Edna Manley's *Focus* group in Jamaica in the 1940s. Derek Walcott describes the impact of his *First Poems* on him in *Another Life*.

Poetry: *First Poems*, Kingston, Jamaica, 1945, New York and London, Garland Publishing (vol. 10 in the Yale series, Critical Studies on Black Life and Culture), 1981; *Earth Testament* (with drawings by Edna Manley), Kingston, Jamaica, 1983.

BARBARA FERLAND. b. 1919. Born and educated in Jamaica. In England she worked for the music department of the British Council. Her output of verse has been small but impressive; she contributed to the BBC *Caribbean Voices* programme, and her poetry has appeared in a number of journals and anthologies.

JOHN J. M. FIGUEROA. b. 1920. Born Jamaica. He first taught at London University, was Professor of Education at the University of the West Indies 1957–73, and Professor of Humanities at the Centro Caribeño,

Puerto Rico, 1973–6. Since then he has held posts at the University of Jos, Nigeria, at Bradford College, Yorkshire, England, at the Open University, Milton Keynes, and with Manchester Education Committee. He has written widely on educational and literary topics, editing the first substantial anthology of Caribbean poetry, *Caribbean Voices* (vol. 1, London, 1966, 1982; vol. 2, London, 1970, Washington DC, 1973; combined edn, London, 1971). He has long championed the eclectic approach to art, asserting, with Terence, that 'nothing human is alien to me'.

Poetry: *Blue Mountain Peak*, Kingston, Jamaica, 1943; *Love Leaps Here*, Liverpool, 1962; *Ignoring Hurts*, Washington DC, 1976.

'*Dixerat*' – 'she had spoken' (Latin).
'*lachrymae rerum*' – an evocative phrase, roughly, 'the sadness of things'.

WILSON HARRIS. b. 1921. Born and educated in Guyana, he became a government surveyor, spending a good deal of time in the interior with the Amerindians, whose myths he has used in his work. He became well known as a poet, with much of his early work published in *Kyk-over-al*. He came to England in 1958 and immediately began work on his first novel, *The Palace of the Peacock*, which was published in 1960. Since then he has become one of the great novelists of the Caribbean, the pioneer of the poetic voice in prose (he no longer writes poetry, as such). He is now based in England, while lecturing and teaching all over the world. He has published two collections of critical essays, *Tradition, the Writer, and Society* (London, New Beacon, 1967) and *Explorations* (Aarhus, Denmark, Dangaroo Press, 1981).

Poetry: *Fetish*, Georgetown, Guyana, Miniature Poets Series, 1951; *The Well and the Land*, Georgetown, 1952; *Eternity to Season*, Georgetown, 1954, Kraus Reprint, 1970, rev. edn, London, New Beacon, 1978. (The early editions of his poetry were published under the pseudonym, 'Kona Waruk'.)

'Laocoön' – in book II of Virgil's *Aeneid*, a priest who failed to save his people because they would not heed his warning about the Trojan horse, and was then powerless to save himself or his sons from the twin serpents which the goddess Minerva sent to destroy him.

MICHAEL ARTHUR LEMIÈRE HENDRIKS. b. 1922. Born in Jamaica and educated there and in England. He has been general manager of the Jamaica Broadcasting Corporation, international director of Thomson Television International, chairman of the Arts Council of Jamaica and president of International PEN (Jamaica Centre). He co-edited the *Independence Anthology of Jamaican Literature* (1962), and has published many short stories, essays and articles on literary criticism, business and politics. He now lives in England.

Poetry: *On This Mountain*, London, 1964; *These Green Islands*, Kingston, Jamaica, 1971; *Muet*, Walton-on-Thames, Surrey, 1971; *Madonna of the Unknown Nation*, London, 1974; *The Islanders*, Kingston, Savacou, 1983; *The Naked Ghost*, Walton-on-Thames, Surrey, Outposts Publications, 1984.

'D'où venons nous?' etc. – the title of a painting by Gauguin.

BASIL MCFARLANE. b. 1922. Born in Jamaica and educated at the University of the West Indies. As well as a poet, he is a journalist and art critic, the author of *An Introduction to Jamaican Art*.

Poetry: *Jacob and the Angel, and Other Poems*, Georgetown, Guyana, Miniature Poets Series, 1952, Kraus reprint, 1970.

'Coyaba' – the Arawak heaven, where the good go at death (Author's note).

'cassava milk' – the starchy cassava root, native to central America, is ground to a white flour and then boiled, before being made into bread.

GLORIA ESCOFFERY. b. 1923. Jamaican painter, journalist and teacher, as well as poet. She studied at McGill University, Montreal, and the Slade School of Fine Arts, England, and lived long in England before returning to Jamaica. She now teaches English at a rural community college in Jamaica, paints, and exhibits her work from time to time, and writes as an art critic, contributing regularly to *Jamaica Journal*. In 1976 the Jamaican government awarded her the Order of Distinction for her services to the arts. Her output as a poet has been small but of high quality.

Poetry: *Landscape in the Making*, Kingston, Jamaica, 1976.

'Wai oh! Aic! Ehcu!' – the local cries of lament are balanced with the Latin equivalent, 'Eheu!'

LOUIS ASTON MARANTZ SIMPSON. b. 1923. Born Jamaica. He went to New York in 1940, and served with the US Army in Europe 1943–5. After the war he studied at Columbia University. After five years as an editor in New York, he turned to academic teaching in America, in which he has had a distinguished career. He has been Professor of English and Comparative Literature at the State University of New York, Stony Brook, since 1967. He has won numerous literary awards, including the Prix de Rome, the Hudson Review Fellowship, the Columbia University Medal for Excellence, two Guggenheim Fellowships, and the 1964 Pulitzer Prize for poetry. He is the author of numerous books, including the autobiographical *North of Jamaica* (1972; published in Britain as *Air with Armed Men*), a novel, *Riverside Drive* (1962), a critical study of James Hogg (1962), several critical works and anthologies, and ten volumes of poetry. He is a US citizen and is often thought of as an American poet, but he has continued to draw on his Jamaican experience in his work, and brings the critical eye of an outsider to the American scene. Denis Donoghue has said of him: 'His conscience works, by remembering what America has forgotten.'

Poetry: *The Arrivistes*, New York, 1949; *Good News of Death* in *Poets of Today II*, ibid., 1955; *A Dream of Governors*, Middletown, Connecticut, 1959; *At the End of the Open Road*, ibid., 1963; *Selected Poems*, New York, 1965, London, 1966; *Adventures of the Letter I*, New York and London, 1971; *Searching for the Ox*, ibid., 1976; *Armidale*, Brockport, NY, 1979; *Out of Season*, Deerfield, Massachusetts, 1979; *Caviare at the Funeral*, New York, 1980, London, 1981; *People Live Here: Selected Poems 1949–83*, Brockport, NY, 1983; *The Best Hour of the Night*, New York, 1983.

'Jamaica': '. . . a cathedral' – the city of Port Royal, Jamaica, a haven for pirates, sank under the sea in the earthquake of 1692.
'The Battle' – the Battle of Bastogne, December 1944, in which the advance of the Allied forces across Europe following on the Normandy landings was checked by an unexpectedly fierce German counter-attack in the Ardennes.
'A Fine Day for Straw Hats': 'the Palisades' – the name of the long arm of land which encloses Kingston harbour, at the tip of which Port Royal stands.
'Working Late': 'Russia' – Louis Simpson's mother came from Russia; cf. his poem 'Why Do You Write about Russia?' in *Caviare at the Funeral*.

JAMES BERRY. b. 1924. Born in Jamaica. Came to England in 1948 and has since been continuously involved in both social and cultural activities with Britain's black community. He is a popular performer, reading his poetry throughout the country and appearing on radio and television. He has held a C. Day Lewis Fellowship and a Minority Rights Group arts award, and has served on the Community Arts Committee of the Arts Council and the Literature Panel of the Greater London Arts Council. He won first prize in the National Poetry Competition for 1981 with 'Fantasy of an African boy'.

Poetry: *Lucy's Letter*, 1975, enlarged and republished as *Lucy's Letters and Loving*, London, New Beacon, 1982; *Fractured Circles*, ibid., 1979; *Chain of Days*, London, OUP, 1985.

Edited: *Bluefoot Traveller* (anthology of UK Caribbean poets),

London, 1976, rev. Harrap, 1981; *Plan Poets* (Progressive League anthology), London, 1983; *Dance to a Different Drum* (Brixton Festival anthology), London, 1983; *News for Babylon* (anthology of UK Caribbean poets), London, Chatto & Windus, 1984.

'Length of time gets rope buried' – James Berry ends all of his 'Lucy' poems with a Jamaican proverb. Lucy lives in London.

'Cleopatra's Needle' – one of the sights of the Thames Embankment in London.

JAN RYNVELD CAREW. b. 1925. Born and educated in Guyana, and at universities in America, Czechoslovakia and France. He is best known as the author of six novels, including *Black Midas*, but has written poetry throughout his career, as well as numerous stage, radio and TV plays which have been performed in Europe, Canada and the USA. He now lives in Chicago and is Professor of African and American Studies at Northwestern University.

Poetry: *Streets of Eternity*, Georgetown, Guyana, 1952; *Sea Drums in My Blood*, Port of Spain, Trinidad, New Voices, 1980.

'Our Home': 'Fanonesque' – see note on page 383 above.

'half a millennium' – when Castro ousted the American-backed Batista regime in Cuba in 1959 virtually 500 years had elapsed since Columbus's 'discovery' of the Americas.

'The Cliffs at Manzanilla' – like the Morne des Sauteurs in Grenada (used by Derek Walcott in *Another Life*), the cliffs at Manzanilla in eastern Trinidad are where a group of Caribs leapt to their deaths rather than be taken and enslaved by Europeans.

'Savacou and Hurricane' – the bird-god and wind-god of the Caribs.

'Faces and Skulls': 'Benin' – artefacts from the royal city of Benin, now in southern Nigeria, which from the thirteenth to the eighteenth century was one of the most highly organized states of West Africa, are world famous.

MARTIN WYLDE CARTER. b. 1927. Born and educated in Guyana. A politician and historian as well as a poet, he was active in the early nationalist movement and was imprisoned for some months in 1953 when direct rule was imposed from Britain. His voice of quiet commitment came to symbolize the idealism of the period. He later became Minister of Public Information and Broadcasting, and represented Guyana at the United Nations.

Poetry: *The Hill of Fire Glows Red*, Georgetown, Guyana, Miniature Poets Series, 1951; *To a Dead Slave*, Georgetown, 1951; *The Hidden Man*, ibid., 1952; *The Kind Eagle*, ibid., 1952; *Returning*, ibid., 1953; *Poems of Resistance*, London, 1954, Georgetown, 1964; *Poems of Shape and Motion*, Georgetown, 1955; *Conversations*, ibid., 1961;

Jail Me Quickly, ibid., 1963; *Poems of Succession*, London, New Beacon, 1977 (about half reprinted from earlier work); *Poems of Affinity 1978–80*, Georgetown, 1980.

(Of the poems here, the first three are from *Poems of Resistance*, the next three from new work in *Poems of Succession* and the last three from *Poems of Affinity*.)

'For a Man Who Walked Sideways': 'The bruised heel' – cf. the heel of Adam unparadised, bruised by the serpent.

'Laocoön' – see note to Wilson Harris, 'Laocoön', page 408 above.

EVAN JONES. b. 1927. Born in Jamaica, and educated there, in the USA and at Oxford University. In the fifties he did a variety of jobs, including refugee relief in the Gaza Strip, furnace man in a bubble-gum factory and teacher of English at an American university. Two of his plays were performed in Jamaica in the fifties: *Inherit This Land*, and *A Figure of Speech*. He has been in England writing full-time since 1956, primarily for films and television. His TV work includes the BBC series *The Fight against Slavery*, and among others he wrote scripts for *King and Country*, *Funeral in Berlin*, *Outback*, *Escape to Victory* and *Champions*. He now lives near Bath. Most of the poems here were written in the fifties. 'The Song of the Banana Man', an important early use of the vernacular, much anthologized and much loved, was written in 1952 as a conscious experiment to find a distinctively Caribbean voice; 'The Lament' was written about ten years later. *Tales from the Caribbean*, a book of stories for children, was published in 1985.

'November, 1956' – the time of the Hungarian uprising, the Suez crisis and General Eisenhower's re-election for a second term as President.

'The Song of the Banana Man' – Golden Grove, in eastern Jamaica, is a small town in the middle of low-lying, fertile, plantation country, which used to be on tourist itineraries; the parish of Portland, a few miles to the north, is mostly mountain land (the John Crow Mountains), the typical small farmer's terrain. Banana-growers would bring their crop down from the hills to a number of small ports where the banana boats would call in. Nowadays, more road transport and fewer ports are used.

'janga' – a crayfish.

'Gros Michel . . . Lacatan' – varieties of banana.

'The Lament of the Banana Man' – see note to Louise Bennett, 'Colonization in Reverse', page 378.

ELLSWORTH MCGRANAHAM 'SHAKE' KEANE. b. 1927. Born St Vincent and educated there and at London University. He became a teacher and broadcaster with the BBC, 1952–65, working on the *Caribbean Voices* programme. He had been playing as a jazz musician in London from 1962, and from 1965 made it his living in Europe. In 1973 he returned to St Vincent as Director of Culture. He now lives in New York.

Poetry: *L'Oubli*, [Barbados, 1950], *Ixion*, Georgetown, Guyana, Miniature Poets Series, 1952; *Volcano Suite*, St Vincent, 1979; *One a Week with Water*, Havana, Cuba, 1979 (winner of the 1979 Casa de las Américas Prize for poetry).

'Shaker Funeral' – published in 1950; an early attempt to catch the rhythm of an intensely West Indian scene. The Shakers are a Pentecostal sect so named because they express the coming of the holy spirit in paroxysms of movement.
'Volcano Suite' – St Vincent's volcano, Soufrière, erupted on Good Friday, 13 April 1979.

DANIEL WILLIAMS. 1927–72. Born New York, raised St Vincent. He read law at London University and became a barrister. His poetry has been broadcast on the BBC and published in Caribbean literary magazines and anthologies. He was killed in a road accident.

'We are the Cenotaphs' – published in 1951; an early yet mature approach to the problem of coming to terms with history.

ANDREW SALKEY. b. 1928. Born in Panama of Jamaican parents and educated in Jamaica and at London University. After living and working in London from 1952 to 1976 as broadcaster, editor, teacher and reviewer, as well as creative writer, he moved to Amherst, Massachusetts, where he is Associate Professor of Writing at Hampshire College. He has edited and written more than thirty books, and received many awards, among them a Guggenheim Fellowship, the Deutscher Kinderbuchpreis, the Sri Chimnoy Poetry Prize and the Casa de las Américas Poetry Prize (for *In the Hills where Her Dreams Live*).

Poetry: *Jamaica*, London, 1973; *In the Hills where Her Dreams Live*, Havana, Cuba, 1979; *Away*, London, Allison & Busby, 1980.

'Remember Haiti, Cuba, Vietnam' – all had historic revolutions in which an imperial, or quasi-imperial, power was ousted by relatively puny forces: Haiti (as St Domingue) in 1789, Cuba in 1959, Vietnam in 1975.
'Soufrière': 'bauxite' – the ore from which aluminium is smelted, an important mineral resource of the Caribbean, frequently US-controlled.
'Clearsightedness' – Claudia Jones (1915–64) was a Trinidadian poli-

tical activist, and editor of the first West Indian newspaper in London.

'Postcard from Mexico, 16.x.1973': 'Olmec head' – The Olmec people, whose artefacts are the most ancient in the Americas, carved stone heads up to nine feet tall. They were found at La Venta on the Gulf of Mexico and removed to a more accessible site at Villahermosa. The flat noses and thick lips of the carvings are more usually taken to suggest mongoloid features.

HENRY BEISSEL. b. 1929. Born in Cologne and educated at London University, he went to Canada in 1951. He became a Canadian citizen in 1956, and has been president of the League of Canadian Poets. He is also well known as an academic, a translator and a dramatist: his best-known play is *Inook and the Sun*. He lived and taught in Trinidad in the mid-sixties, and wrote a number of poems on Caribbean subjects.

DEREK WALCOTT. b. 1930. Born and educated in St Lucia, he studied at the University of the West Indies, Jamaica, and in New York on a Rockefeller Fellowship. In 1959 he founded the Trinidad Theatre Workshop which he directed until 1977. His plays have been staged there, as well as all over the Caribbean, in North America and Britain. His best-known play, *Dream on Monkey Mountain*, was filmed by NBC television in 1970 and in its production by the Negro Ensemble of New York won the prestigious Obie Award in 1971. His poetry has been published in Britain by Cape from 1962 and Faber since 1982, and in New York by Farrar Straus & Giroux since 1964. Robert Graves said of his 1962 collection, 'Walcott handles English with a closer understanding of its inner magic than most (if not any) of his English-born contemporaries.' He has won many awards for his poetry, including the Guinness Award, the Royal Society of Literature Award, the Cholmondeley Award, the Jock Campbell/New Statesman Award, the Welsh Arts Council Award and the Heinemann Award. For many years he contributed critical articles and reviews to the *Trinidad Guardian*, but his most important critical works are the essays, 'What the Twilight Says' (which formed the preface to *Dream on Monkey Mountain and Other Plays*), and 'The Muse of History' (in *Is Massa Day Dead?*, ed. Orde Coombs, New York, 1974; an excerpt is published in *Critics on Caribbean Literature*, ed. Edward Baugh, London, 1978). In recent years he has spent part of each year teaching at various American universities, including Harvard, but he is still based in the Caribbean and continues to produce his plays there. He has the range and power of a great poet.

Poetry: *25 Poems*, Port of Spain, Trinidad, 1948, Bridgetown, Barbados, 1949; *Epitaph for the Young*, Bridgetown, 1949; *Poems*, Kingston, Jamaica, c. 1952; *In a Green Night*, London, 1962; *Selected Poems*,

New York, 1964; *The Castaway*, London, 1965; *The Gulf and Other Poems*, London, 1969; *The Gulf*, New York, 1970 (including 13 poems from *The Castaway*); *Another Life*, London and New York, 1973; *Sea Grapes*, London and New York, 1976 (texts not identical); *The Star-Apple Kingdom*, London and New York, 1980; *Selected Poetry* (ed. Wayne Brown), London, Heinemann, 1981; *The Fortunate Traveller*, London, Faber & Faber, and New York, Farrar, Strauss & Giroux, 1982; *Midsummer*, ibid., 1984.

Plays: *Henri Christophe*, Bridgetown, Barbados, 1951; *Dream on Monkey Mountain and Other Plays*, New York, 1970, London, 1972; *The Joker of Seville and O Babylon*, New York, 1978; *Remembrance and Pantomime*, New York, 1980.

Critical Studies: Edward Baugh, *Derek Walcott: Memory as Vision: 'Another Life'*, London, Longman, 1978; Robert D. Hamner, *Derek Walcott*, Boston, Twayne, 1981.

'A Far Cry from Africa' – an allusion to the uprising of the Mau Mau, an organization of Kikuyu militants, against British rule in Kenya in 1952. By 1956, 100 Europeans, 2,000 African loyalists and 11,000 rebels had been killed.

'the blood of both' – Walcott has both African and English ancestry.

'*Another Life*, Chapter 20' – the passage relating the death of Harold Simmons. Walcott's superb autobiographical poem tells the story of the growth of an artist's consciousness, paying particular tribute to his friend, the painter, Dunstan St Omer (whose work is on the cover of this book), his first love, Andreuille, and his friend and mentor, the painter, lepidopterist, botanist, folklorist and antiquarian, Harold Simmons. When Walcott had worked on the poem for a year and was casting about for a structure for it, news came (7 May 1966) that Harry had killed himself, at the age of fifty-two. After an uncongenial life in the Civil Service he had withdrawn to his preferred life as an artist among the people in the hill village of Babonneau, St Lucia, where mental breakdown finally got the better of him. His death, which crystallized the dimension of loss and failure, enabled Walcott to get his poem into perspective; he wrote, 'When I began this work, you were alive, / and with one stroke, you have completed it!' The creative act was, as always, in precarious balance with the self-destructive one.

'to dip rain-water over his parched boards' – the pouring of a libation on the ground for the dead is an African tradition which has survived in the Caribbean.

'*pour* Msieu Harry Simmons' – the first language for some 70 per cent of St Lucians is a French creole.

'Forest of Europe': 'Joseph Brodsky' – the Russian-born poet in exile in the USA, who writes now in English.

'Mandelstam' – the Russian poet persecuted under the Stalin regime, who died in custody in Siberia in 1938.

' "The rustling of ruble notes by the lemon Neva" ' – see no. 222 in the *Complete Poetry*, New York, 1973.

'Gulag Archipelago' – it was western publication of Alexander Solzhenitsyn's novel, *The Gulag Archipelago*, in 1974 which prompted the Soviet authorities to deport him.

'The Spoiler's Return' – one of the great vernacular poems of the Caribbean, a peak of satire, with its twin ancestors of the Trinidad calypso tradition with its 'picong' and the European tradition of satiric poetry. The most recent of Walcott's poetry here, first published 1982, although he has long made creative use of the vernacular in his poetry.

'Spoiler' – 'The Mighty Spoiler' (real name Theophilus Phillip) was a famous calypsonian in Trinidad from the late 1940s to his death in 1959. Termed the 'genius of the absurd' by Gordon Rohlehr, he asserted in his best-known song, 'Bed Bug', quoted in the poem ('I going to bite them young ladies, partner' etc.) that he wished to be re-incarnated as a bed bug in order to get at the women. It is particularly appropriate that Walcott should use his persona as he used to sing about the absurd confusions which resulted from having a twin brother (Walcott has a twin brother, Roderick, also a playwright).

'Laventille' – a hillside shanty-town district of Port of Spain.

'Desperadoes' – a famous steel-band.

'Lord Rochester' – the first four lines of the quotation form the opening of Rochester's 'Satyr (against Reason and Mankind)', first published 1675. His poem continues: 'I'd be a *Dog*, a *Monkey*, or a *Bear*. / Or any thing but that vain *Animal*, / Who is so proud of being rational.' Walcott adapts the Rochester to end with another quotation from Spoiler. He also uses Rochester's metre.

'V. S. Nightfall' – V. S. Naipaul in fact used the phrase 'An area of darkness' as the title of a book about his first visit to his grandfather's homeland, India, which had been 'an area of darkness' to him as a child growing up in Trinidad, but Walcott wittily adapts the phrase to suggest here the critical pronouncements on Caribbean society for which Naipaul is famous.

'and black still poor, though black is beautiful' – an allusion to the Black Power campaign of the 1960s, in which one of the most effective slogans was 'Black is Beautiful'.

'Bedbug the First' – Spoiler's song went, 'And I calling myself King Bedbug the First.'

'Rodney' – Walter Rodney, the Guyanese philosopher and Marxist historian, who was assassinated in 1980.

'what sweet in goat-mouth sour in his behind' – proverbial.

'Attila . . . Commander' – calypsonians.

'Uganda' – an allusion to the Amin regime in Uganda, notorious for its use of violent political repression.

'the Savannah' – the Queen's Park Savannah is a large park and meeting-place in Port of Spain, where people go to stroll, gossip and buy snacks (e.g. green coconut, opened with a headsman's chop of the cutlass).

'a twelve-thirty show' – midday cinema show patronized particularly by the young unemployed, who feed their fantasies there.

'Rastamen . . . locks' – Rastafarian men wear their hair in long, uncombed, 'natty' (i.e. 'knotty') locks, 'dreadlocks'.

'Frederick Street' – the main street in Port of Spain.

'I want to fall' – Spoiler's catch-phrase.

'Arnold's Phoenician trader' – the 'grave Tyrian trader' of Matthew Arnold's 'The Scholar-Gipsy' who sails on 'To where the Atlantic raves', to trade with 'the dark Iberians'. There is a prosperous Levantine community in the Caribbean.

'the children of Tagore' – i.e. the people of Indian descent in Trinidad, roughly half of the population (Tagore was a Bengali poet).

'funeral shroud' – in India, white clothes are worn for funerals.

'curry favor and chicken' – curried chicken is an Indian dish sold from roadside stalls and popular with all Trinidadians.

'you bald, black justices' – the corbeaux on the municipal rubbish-dump are large, black vultures with naked heads.

'ibises' – the scarlet ibis, of a spectacular brilliance, is the national bird of Trinidad and Tobago.

'Caroni Plain' – an area of Trinidad largely populated by East Indians.

'tabla' – an Indian drum.

'bleached flags' – the Hindu prayer flags.

'a green sea' – the endless fields of blue-green sugar-cane, which in Trinidad is cultivated by a mainly Indian labour-force, typically the most disadvantaged social group. Walcott's is one of the few poetic voices heard to protest on their behalf.

'Catch us in Satan tent, next carnival' – the 'tents' (they are now mostly permanent structures) were originally the rehearsal venues for the calypsonians, but the nightly performances there in the season are now as important as the two days of carnival itself. Each tent is associated with a particular performer; Walcott uses 'Satan' as if it were a calypsonian's name, which it well could be.

'Quevedo' – Raymond Quevedo, the calypsonian 'Atilla (sic) the Hun' who became a politician in 1946.

'Maestro . . . / . . . The Duke of Iron' – calypsonians.

'the monarchy' – at each year's carnival a calypso monarch is chosen.

'the old re-minor key' – in the early days most songs were in one of four minor keys.

'those who gave . . . / fatigue' – i.e. those who heckled.

EDWARD KAMAU BRATHWAITE. b. 1930. Born Lawson Edward Brathwaite in Barbados, he won the Barbados scholarship for 1949 to study history at Cambridge University. After producing a study of the development of creole society in Jamaica, 1770–1820, for the PhD degree at Sussex University (published by OUP in 1971), he taught at a university in Ghana for seven years, and then returned to the Caribbean, where he now teaches history at the University of the West Indies, Jamaica. Since he began to be well known as a poet, in the sixties, he has received many awards for his poetry, among them an Arts Council of Great Britain Poetry Bursary, the Cholmondeley Award, a Guggenheim Foundation Fellowship, a Bussa Award, a Casa de las Américas Prize and a Silver Musgrave Medal (Jamaica). He has done more than perhaps any other single person to foster a serious concern for a living Caribbean poetic tradition, and has pioneered a constructive and scholarly interest in both the literary beginnings of Caribbean literature and its folk base. From his work with the Caribbean Artists Movement, founded in London in 1966, and now publishing important literary collections under the Savacou imprint in Jamaica, to his own continuing poetic odyssey, he has confirmed the vision of the early pioneers and made a unique contribution to Caribbean letters. Bridging the divide between the oral and scribal traditions, he has produced recordings of his work, and regularly gives readings of his poetry, and lectures, in both Britain and North America as well as the Caribbean. He has produced checklists of Barbadian and Jamaican poetry as the first stage of a Caribbean poetry bibliography, has written plays for schools, and has recently published a critical essay, *History of the Voice* (London, New Beacon, 1984).

Poetry: *The Arrivants* (a trilogy): *Rights of Passage*, London, 1967, *Masks*, London, 1968, *Islands*, London, 1969, reissued in one volume, London, 1973; Penguin Modern Poets no. 15 (with Alan Bold and Edwin Morgan), London, 1969; *Other Exiles*, London, 1975; *Black + Blues*, Havana, Cuba, 1976 (winner of the Casa de las Américas Prize); *Mother Poem*, London, 1977; *Sun Poem*, London, OUP, 1982. There have also been pamphlet-sized editions of individual poems.

Critical study: Gordon Rohlehr, *Pathfinder: Black Awakening in 'The Arrivants' of E. K. Brathwaite*, Trinidad, 1981.

Recordings: *Rights of Passage*, London, Argo, 1969 (4 sides, 33 rpm); *Masks*, London, Argo, 1972 (2 sides, 33 rpm); *Islands*, London, Argo, 1973 (4 sides, 33 rpm); *Mother Poem* (discussion and reading), London, ATCAL c/o Africa Centre, 1980 (2 cassettes).

'Horse Weebles' – a sequence from *Mother Poem* incorporating dialogue from Brathwaite's early vernacular poem,' 'The Dust', first published in *Rights of Passage* and performed by Walcott's company in Trinidad in 1969.

'meroë' – ancient centre of African culture (Author's note).

'Starvation' – a poem in the Jamaican vernacular, where 'Horse Weebles' is in Barbadian. Its ethos is Rastafarian, and its setting, Jamaica.

'don drummon' – see note to Lorna Goodison, 'For Don Drummond', page 427.

'nyah bingeh' – Rastafarian warriors. (The term is from East Africa, the name of a religio-political cult which was anti-colonial and involved spirit-possession, in the early years of this century. In Jamaica it is also the term for a ceremonial gathering of Rastafarians.)

'dem dream a abyssinia' – the Rastafarians' Zion, the homeland to which they hope to return.

'trenton' – 'pig; unclean (non-ital) food, and by extension, non-Rasta (Babylonian) men' (Author's note).

'barbican . . . red hills / . . . skyline drive' – prosperous suburbs of Kingston.

'babylon' – by analogy with the Jews in the Bible, the Rastafarians' term for their present exile, be it Jamaica as here, Britain, or wherever.

'skull / . . . white cock o' deat'' – the magic emblems of obeah.

'dese bogle blues' – Paul Bogle, the Baptist deacon, was executed for his part in the Morant Bay rebellion in Jamaica in 1865 (see note to 'War Down a Monkland', page 373). He is now one of the Jamaican national heroes and a famous statue to him by Edna Manley stands outside the Morant Bay Courthouse.

EDWARD LUCIE-SMITH. b. 1933. Born Jamaica; in 1946 came to England where he was educated at King's School, Canterbury, and Oxford University. In the sixties he was one of the poets known as The Group. He has since become well known as an anthologist and an art critic, with more than thirty books to his credit. He has also published a historical novel on Gilles de Rais, and an autobiography, *The Burnt Child*, London, 1975. In 1961 he won the John Llewellyn Rhys Memorial Prize, and was given an Arts Council Award. He is a Fellow of the Royal Society of Literature.

Poetry: *The Fantasy Poets, no. 25*, Eynsham, Oxford, 1954; contributions to *A Group Anthology* (which he co-edited), London, 1963; *Confessions and Histories*, London, 1964; *Towards Silence*, London, 1968; *The Well-Wishers*, London, 1974.

ABDUR-RAHMAN SLADE HOPKINSON. b. 1934. Born Guyana, educated there, in Barbados and at the University of the West Indies, Jamaica, where he was active in theatre as actor and director. After teaching in Jamaica and Trinidad, where he acted with Derek Walcott's Trinidad Theatre Workshop, he studied at Yale University Drama School on a

Rockefeller Foundation Scholarship, 1965–6. After teaching at the University of Guyana for two years, he returned to Trinidad and Walcott's company. In 1970 he founded the Caribbean Theatre Guild, but had to give up the stage in the early seventies, when he became increasingly ill with renal failure. He moved to Canada in 1977 and is now a Canadian citizen. He became a Muslim in 1964, taking the name Muhammad Abdur-Rahman (he was born Clement Alan Slade Hopkinson). He has written several plays which have been staged in the Caribbean.

Poetry: *The Four, and Other Poems*, Bridgetown, Barbados, 1955; *The Madwoman of Papine*, Georgetown, Guyana, 1976; *The Friend*, ibid., 1976.

'*oriens et occidente lux*' – the motto of the University of the West Indies, 'And a light rising in the west'.

'Rass Rass Rass' – in the Caribbean vernacular, 'rass' is a swear-word (a contraction of 'your ass'); in Rastafarian parlance 'Ras' is the appellation of holiness.

'euphorbia' – a tropical variety of the large *Euphorbia* genus has a mass of white flowers.

IVAN VAN SERTIMA. b. 1935. Guyanese poet who contributed work to local literary journals and anthologies in the sixties. 'Volcano' is an early poem, first published in 1958.

Poetry: *The River and the Wall*, Georgetown, Guyana, Miniature Poets Series, 1958.

EDWARD ALSTON CECIL BAUGH. b. 1936. Born Jamaica and educated at the University there, at Queen's University, Ontario, Canada, and the University of Manchester, England. He is now Professor of English at the University of the West Indies, and has recently been Visiting Professor of English at the University of California, Los Angeles (1980), and at Dalhousie University, Canada (1983). His most substantial critical work is a study of Derek Walcott's autobiographical poem *Another Life: Derek Walcott, Memory as Vision* (London, Longman, 1978). His poetry has been published in journals and anthologies, and he contributed to *Seven Jamaican Poets* (ed. Mervyn Morris), Jamaica, 1971.

'Memphis' – the city where Martin Luther King was assassinated in 1968.

'Cinna the poet' – cf. Shakespeare's *Julius Caesar*, III. 3.

'The Carpenter's Complaint' – in the Caribbean the making of a coffin is traditionally not just a commercial service but a tribute to the dead, regarded as an honour by the maker and attended with much ceremony.

'waters' – rum.

'*schottische*' – a dance introduced into England from Europe in 1848 and thence to the Caribbean, where, with the quadrille, it has remained popular in country districts.

HOWARD FERGUS. b. 1937. Born Montserrat. Educated locally, and at the University of the West Indies, and the Universities of Bristol and Manchester. From 1970 to 1974 he was chief education officer of Montserrat, and became, in 1975, the first Speaker of Montserrat's Legislative Council. He is now resident tutor for the UWI in Montserrat, where he runs a creative-writing workshop. He has published a number of booklets on Montserrat's history and society.

Poetry: *Green Innocence*, Montserrat, 1978.

'Look for rain tonight' – cf. Shakespeare's *Macbeth*, where Banquo's last words before his murderers strike are, 'It will be rain tonight,' to which a murderer rejoins, 'Let it come down.'

'Ethnocide' – the two main indigenous races of the Caribbean, the Arawaks and Caribs, had very distinct cultures, the Arawaks being peaceful, the Caribs warlike. The Arawaks were hospitable to the Spanish and were quickly exterminated. The Caribs fought, and survived.

'Lament for Maurice Bishop' – see note to Dionne Brand: from 'Military Occupations', page 429.

'Fort Rupert' – Bishop renamed Fort George after his father.

CLAIRE HARRIS. b. 1937. Born Trinidad. She has read English, education and communications at universities in Ireland, Jamaica and Lagos. Her first poems were published in Nigeria in 1975. She has been based in Canada since 1966.

Poetry: *Translations into Fiction*, New Brunswick, Canada, Fiddlehead, 1984; *From the Women's Quarters*, Toronto, Williams-Wallace, 1984.

MERVYN MORRIS. b. 1937. Born Jamaica, and educated there and at Oxford University on a Rhodes Scholarship. He won a tennis blue at Oxford and has captained the Jamaica team. He now teaches at the University of the West Indies in Jamaica, in the English Department, and has been instrumental in encouraging the younger Jamaican poets, particularly those in the oral tradition. As a critic he has written widely on Caribbean literature, and has edited two anthologies, *Seven Jamaican Poets* (Jamaica, 1971), and (with Pamela Mordecai) *Jamaica Woman* (London, Heinemann, 1980).

Poetry: *The Pond*, London, New Beacon, 1973; *On Holy Week*, Kingston, Jamaica, 1976; *Shadowboxing*, London, New Beacon, 1979.

'dunghills' – Kingston's notorious 'Dungle' was a shanty-town built over the municipal rubbish dump.

'For Consciousness' – i.e. progressive consciousness. (Author's note.)

'Valley Prince' – a tribute to Don Drummond (see note to Lorna Goodison, 'For Don Drummond', page 427). One of his pieces was titled 'Valley Princess'.

LEROY CLARKE. b. 1938. Born Trinidad. Both painter and poet, he has been based in New York since 1967, and has exhibited widely all over North America, in the Caribbean and in Brazil. He has published two portfolios of drawings, the second, *Douens*, being a visual exploration of similar themes to those in the poetic sequence of the same title. He now lives in Trinidad again and is working to establish an arts centre in Aripo.

Poetry: *Woman, Woman*, 1971; *Tonight My Black Woman*, 1971; *Taste of Endless Fruit*, 1974; *Douens*, New York, 1981.

'The Mighty Chalkdust and Black Stalin' – calypsonians.

'Janet' – hurricane Janet struck the southern Caribbean in 1955 with particularly severe results.

'dem skull-face, dem cow-foot, dem blood-eye' – signs of the malignant supernatural.

'crossroad' – the place associated with Legba, the limping West African/Caribbean god, the intermediary between man and the other gods, and the first to be invoked. 'Legba, old man at the crossroads . . . mirror at the gate . . . poet-keeper of the word . . . blender of the fates . . . all that and more he rises here in the Poet exhilaration to initiate a New Day.' (Author's note.)

'bois . . . bois' – the cry of the bands of stick-fighters (a survival from the old French vernacular of Trinidad).

E. ARCHIE MARKHAM. b. 1939. Born Montserrat. He is a graduate in English and philosophy, has taught in England, built houses in France and directed the Caribbean Theatre Workshop in the West Indies. He has also lived in Germany and Sweden, and during 1983–5 was in Papua New Guinea as a media coordinator, but he has long been based in England where, in the seventies, he held a creative-writing fellowship at Hull College of Higher Education and a C. Day Lewis Fellowship in Brent. He is assistant editor of *Ambit* magazine.

Poetry: *Cross-fire*, Walton-on-Thames, Surrey, 1972; *A Black Eye*, Bettiscombe Press, n.d.; *Mad*, Solihull, War., 1973; *Love Poems*, Cambridge, 1978; *Games and Penalties*, Middlesex, 1980; *Love, Politics and Food*, Cambridge, Massachusetts, 1982. His selected poems, *Human Rites*, was published by Anvil Press, London, 1984.

'Late Return': '*Regam Reges Reget*' – the schoolboy is reciting the conjugation of Latin verbs. (The future tense of 'to rule' is followed by the imperfect, future perfect and, later, perfect tenses of 'to love'. '*Capio*' etc. – the parts of the verb 'to catch': 'I catch, to catch, I have caught, caught.')

'of *Wanderer*, of *Seafarer*' – two of the earliest surviving poems in the English language, recorded in the Exeter Book in the tenth century, with a powerful elegiac sense of exile from the pleasures of life.

'poisonous cassava' – the root of the bitter cassava contains hydrocyanic acid until cooked. The cassava mill and press are reminders of an old way of life.

'Agouti . . . Vue Pointe' – 'venues of island night-life: the Agouti rough-and-ready; the Vue Pointe, sophisticated hotel entertainment' (Author's note).

'Nimcom' – 'the name of the literate slave on Riley's estate, mentioned above, who on 1 August 1834 was invited to read aloud to the assembled company the Declaration of Emancipation and did so with ease' (Author's note).

'Grandfather's Sermon and Michael Smith' – Michael Smith (q.v.) was a young Jamaican poet who was stoned to death in a sectarian murder in August 1983.

'The clans' – in 1983 E. A. Markham was working in a remote part of Papua New Guinea.

'will they now name a bookshop / after you' – a topical London allusion, a bookshop formerly named after two Caribbean heroes from the old colonial days, (Paul) Bogle (Toussaint) L'Ouverture, having been renamed after the Guyanese political philosopher, Walter Rodney, assassinated in 1980.

DENNIS SCOTT. b. 1939. Born Jamaica and educated there. Poet and man of the theatre, he is a director, playwright, actor and dancer. He has been a member of the Jamaica National Dance Theatre Company, and editor of *Caribbean Quarterly*. As Principal of the Jamaica School of Drama he has played an important role in developing the talents of some of the young oral poets. Recently he has been Associate Professor of Directing at Yale University.

Poetry: *Journeys and Ceremonies*, Jamaica, 1969; *Uncle Time*, Pittsburgh, 1973 (winner of International Poetry Forum Award and Commonwealth Poetry Prize); *Dreadwalk*, London, New Beacon, 1982.

'Homecoming': 'like paper in the Admiral's fist' – to convey the landscape of the West Indian islands, Columbus is said to have crumpled a sheet of paper.

'Uncle Time': 'a spider-man' – Anansi, the West African/Caribbean trickster folk-hero who can change from spider to man.

'Version' – i.e. the dubside of a record, the instrumental version of a song with the vocal track dubbed out.

'yu no see't?' – one of the oral culture's catch-phrases.

'sky juice' – the name of a brilliant red syrup which is sold with shaved ice from street barrows.

'Weaponsong': 'boys at traffic signals' – boys who clean windscreens for a few cents while the lights are red.

ANTHONY MCNEILL. b. 1941. Born Jamaica. He has studied at Johns Hopkins University and the University of Massachusetts at Amherst. He was joint editor (with Neville Dawes) of the anthology, *The Caribbean Poem*, 1976. In 1985 he was awarded a U.S.I.S. fellowship to the International Writers Program, University of Iowa.

Poetry: *Hello Ungod*, Baltimore, 1971; *Reel from 'The Life-Movie'*, Kingston, Jamaica, Savacou, 1975 (an imperfect edition of 1972 was withdrawn); *Credences at The Altar of Cloud*, Kingston, Institute of Jamaica, 1979.

'Don' – see note to Lorna Goodison, 'For Don Drummond', page 427.

'Babylon' – see note to E. K. Brathwaite, 'Starvation', page 419.

'The Victors' – The cattle egret (*Ardeola ibis*) was unknown in the Caribbean before 1950. Common in tropical Africa and Asia, it crossed the Atlantic to colonize northern South America, from where it has spread throughout the Caribbean basin. Large, white birds, they are conspicuous for their regular flights between roosts and feeding grounds at dawn and dusk.

'Saint Ras' – 'Ras' is the Rastafarian term for 'holiness'.

'queen' – the Rastafarian term for 'wife'.

JUDY MILES. b. *c*. 1942. Born Trinidad. Educated at the University of the West Indies and the University of British Columbia, Vancouver. She began to publish her poetry in Caribbean journals in the mid-sixties. She has been based in Canada for many years.

KEVYN ARTHUR. b. 1942. Born Barbados. Educated there and at Ohio and Yale universities. Now runs an oriental-rug restoration business and is a part-time teacher of English and philosophy at the University of Bridgeport, Connecticut. His poems and other writings have been published in various journals, including the 1983 American Poetry Association anthology. He is working on a life of Jesus.

'was so hard . . . etc.' – a quotation from Bryan Edwards's *The History . . . of the British Colonies in the West Indies*, 1793 (Author's note).

'Maboya' – the Devil in the Caribs' cosmology (Author's note).

'Vermejo' – Rodriguez Vermejo, a sailor from Seville, the look-out on the *Pinta* who first saw land in the Americas (Author's note).

'Cheapside' – a street in Bridgetown, Barbados, near St Mary's Church
(Author's note).
'I Saw Three Ships' (ll. 19–23) – cf. Psalm 43:3 (Author's note).

PAMELA MORDECAI. b. 1942. Born Jamaica. Educated there, in the
USA and at the University of the West Indies. She has taught English
in schools and at Mico Teachers' College, and has worked extensively
in the media, especially television. She has written on Caribbean
literature and developed curriculum materials in language arts for the
Caribbean. She is publications officer for the Faculty of Education at
the University of the West Indies in Jamaica, and edits the *Caribbean
Journal of Education*.

   Poetry: (co-editor of and contributor to) *Jamaica Woman*, London,
Heinemann, 1980; *Shooting the Horses* (forthcoming).

ROGER MCTAIR. b. 1943. Born Trinidad. He began to write in his early
teens, and was first published in Clifford Sealey's *Voices*. He is a
veteran of many poetry readings, but is now reluctant to read in
public. He lives in Toronto as a freelance writer and film-maker.

'Politics Kaiso' – 'In March, 1970, students demonstrating against the
   government were denounced as hooligans by the Prime Minister,
   Dr Eric Williams (who was Oxford-educated and touted as the
   "Third Biggest Brain in the World", 1955–57). The nation erupted in
   a wave of protest that denounced colour prejudice, ministerial and
   party corruption, administrative ineptitude and the general stupid-
   ity and insensitivity of the ruling circles. A State of Emergency was
   declared, during which an American task force waited off-shore.'
   (Author's note.)

OLIVE SENIOR. b. 1943. Born Jamaica. Educated there and in Canada.
She has worked as a journalist, in public relations, as a freelance writer
and researcher, and in publishing. She is managing director of the
Institute of Jamaica Publishing Company Ltd and editor of *Jamaica
Journal*. Her poems and short stories have been published in journals
and anthologies. Her book, *A–Z of Jamaican Heritage*, was published
in 1983.

'cedar' – the wood traditionally used for coffins.
'navel-string' – the burial of a child's navel-string under a tree of good
   omen is an African custom surviving in the Caribbean, and here
   linked with the Christian myth of the tree of life.

WAYNE BROWN. b. 1944. Born Trinidad. Educated there and at the
University of the West Indies, Jamaica. He was Gregory Fellow in
Poetry at the University of Leeds, England, has been Information

Officer at the US Embassy, Port of Spain, writer-in-residence at UWI, Jamaica, and is now a journalist, writing a daily column for the Trinidad *Guardian*. In 1966 he founded and edited *Impact*, a weekly news magazine at the UWI, in 1975 he co-edited an anthology, *21 Years of 'Poetry and Audience'*, and in 1980 became co-founder of the Eric Roach Trust for Literature and the Arts. He has published a biography of Edna Manley (London, 1975), and has edited a selection of Derek Walcott's poetry, q.v.

Poetry: *On the Coast*, London, 1972 (winner of the Commonwealth Prize for Poetry, and Recommendation of the British Poetry Book Society).

FAUSTIN CHARLES. b. 1944. Born Trinidad. Educated there and at the Universities of Kent and London. He has lived in England since 1962, and is at present a part-time teacher for the Inner London Education Authority. His first novel, *Signposts of the Jumbie*, was published in 1981.

Poetry: *The Expatriate*, London, 1969; *Crab Track*, London, 1973.

'Fireflies' – Shiva Naipaul, the younger brother of V. S. Naipaul, has written a novel titled *Fireflies* in which, as in V. S. Naipaul's novel *A House for Mr Biswas*, the gradual West Indianization of a Trinidad Brahmin family from India is charted. The title image of the fireflies alludes to the head of the family's anecdote about a boy whose family was so poor that he had to trap fireflies in a bottle in order to have light to study by.

'our father's face curved into grass' – Derek Walcott and Shiva Naipaul (like Faustin Charles) lost their fathers at an early age and were raised by their mothers.

'the mother-who-fathered-me' – a Trinidadian expression (used by George Lamming and Edith Clarke).

'water lying down, / and water standing up' – a traditional Caribbean riddle to which the answer is 'sugar-cane'.

CYRIL DABYDEEN. b. 1945. Born Guyana. Having moved to Canada in 1970, he is now a Canadian citizen, and the only West Indian member of the League of Canadian Poets. For 1984–6 he is Poet Laureate of the city of Ottawa. He has won three prizes for his poetry, and has also published a volume of short stories, *Still Close to the Island*, Ottawa, 1980.

Poetry: *Poems in Recession*, Georgetown, Guyana, 1972; *Distances*, Vancouver, Fiddlehead, 1977; *Goatsong*, Ottawa, Mosaic, 1977; *Heart's Frame* (forthcoming).

'The Fat Men': 'Maupassant' – cf. his famous story 'Boule de Suif'.

MARLENE PHILIP. b. 1947. Born in Tobago, and raised both there and in Trinidad, studying at the University of the West Indies before moving to Canada in 1968 to study law. After practising law for seven years, she has now given it up in order to write full-time.

Poetry: *Thorns*, Toronto, Williams-Wallace, 1983; *Salmon Courage*, ibid., 1983.

'Harriet Tubman' – the American abolitionist who helped hundreds of fellow-slaves to freedom in the North before the American Civil War.

LORNA GOODISON. b. 1947. Born Jamaica. Educated there, and in New York. She is also an artist who has exhibited in Jamaica and Guyana, and has illustrated her own *Tamarind Season* and Mervyn Morris's *On Holy Week*, among the books mentioned here. In 1983 she took part in an International Writers' Program at the University of Iowa.

Poetry: *Tamarind Season*, Kingston, Jamaica, 1980.

'For Don Drummond' – Don Drummond was a brilliant Jamaican trombonist who in the late sixties suffered from an increasing mental illness. In 1969 he stabbed and killed his girl-friend, gave himself up to the police, and later committed suicide.
'a caul' – in Jamaican folklore, those who are born with a caul can see duppies (ghosts).
'Wareika' – a hillside Rastafarian settlement at the eastern extremity of the city of Kingston.
'Belleview' – Kingston's main mental hospital.

JOHN ROBERT LEE. b. 1948. Born St Lucia. A graduate of the University of the West Indies in Jamaica and now a librarian in St Lucia, he worked for several years in the theatre, and for radio and television. Since 1979 he has been active in the Christian ministry, teaching, preaching and contributing a weekly Christian column to the main local newspaper.

Poetry: *Vocation*, St Lucia, 1975; *Dread Season*, St Lucia, 1978; *The Prodigal*, St Lucia, 1983; *Possessions*, St Lucia, 1984.

'*cancanesse*' – a loud, rowdy woman (the shopkeeper) – a St Lucian creole term (Author's note).
'*Damballa*' – a god of the highway (Author's note).
'Legba' – the Dahomean/Haitian god of the gateway, the crucial link between man and the other gods (Author's note).

JOHN AGARD. b. 1949. Born Guyana. Having been acting and writing since he was a teenager, he toured the Caribbean with the All Ah We performance group (with Ken Corsbie, Marc Matthews, q.v., and Henry Muttoo), giving 160 performances. He coined the term 'poet-sonian' for his work. He came to England in 1977, and now works for the Commonwealth Institute giving talks to schools. He has written several books for children using the Guyanese vernacular, including *I Didn Do Nuttin* and *Two Hole Tim.*

Poetry: *Shoot Me with Flowers*, Georgetown, Guyana, 1973; *Quetzy de Saviour* (a story in verse), Georgetown, 1976; *Man to Pan*, Havana, Cuba, 1982 (winner of the Casa de las Américas Prize); *Limbo Dancer in Dark Glasses*, London, Greenheart, 1983.

'Waiting for Fidel' – written when Castro visited Guyana in 1973.

'Sierra Maestra' – mountains where the guerrillas trained, but cf. Castro's 'Declaration of the Sierra Maestra', 12 July 1957.

'Pan Recipe' – the pan is the instrument of the steel-band (see Glossary).

VICTOR DAVID QUESTEL. 1949–82. Born Trinidad. Educated at the University of the West Indies there, completing a PhD in 1981. He made an unpublished study of Derek Walcott's work, and contributed numerous articles on literature to Caribbean journals.

Poetry: *Score* (with Anson Gonzalez), Port of Spain, Trinidad, 1972; *Near Mourning Ground*, Diego Martin, Trinidad, 1979; *Hard Stares*, Diego Martin, The New Voices, 1982.

'This Island Mopsy' – The Mighty Bomber is a calypsonian. The calypsonians' attitude to women, as satirized here, has long been notorious.

'meh bull boy' – a bull's penis, used as a whip.

GRACE NICHOLS. b. 1950. Born in Guyana, she came to Britain in 1977. She has had poems published in several journals, and has given readings of her poetry, some for the Poetry Society, over the last few years. She has written three books for children and is just finishing her first adult novel, set in Guyana.

Poetry: *I is a Long-Memoried Woman*, London, Karnak House, 1983 (winner of the 1983 Commonwealth Poetry Prize); *The Fat Black Woman's Poems*, London, Virago, 1984.

KENDEL HIPPOLYTE. b. 1952. Born St Lucia, and educated there, becoming involved in dance and drama in his late teens and taking part in a creative-writing workshop. He taught for two years before studying at the University of the West Indies, Jamaica, where he ran a theatre group for which he wrote plays. He returned to St Lucia to teach literature at a secondary school, and work for the Department of Culture. He is still active in the theatre and has written four plays.

Poetry: *Island in the Sun, Side 2*, The Morne, St Lucia, 1980.

'Jah-Son' – symbolic name for a Rastafarian, Jah (from the Biblical 'Jahweh') being the term for god.

'I trod / through valley' – see note to F. 'Toots' Hibbert, 'Never Get Weary', page 385.

'I make Man / into God' – the root of Rastafarian self-respect is the perception that man is holy. Like the Quakers, they construct no church between themselves and their god.

'shitty' – ironic term for 'city', popularized by Peter Tosh, q.v.

DIONNE BRAND. b. 1953. Born Trinidad. Educated there and at the University of Toronto. She has been active in black-community work in Toronto and has become well known as a black, socialist and feminist poet in Canada. She worked for a year as an information/communications coordinator in Grenada until the American invasion in October 1983, when she returned to Canada.

Poetry: *Fore Day Morning*, Toronto, 1978; *Earth Magic*, Toronto, 1980; *Primitive Offensive*, Toronto, Williams-Wallace, 1982; *Winter Epigrams and Epigrams to Ernesto Cardenal in Defense of Claudia*, ibid., 1983; *Chronicles of the Hostile Sun*, ibid., 1984.

'from *Military Occupations*' – about the events in Grenada in October 1983. (Maurice Bishop, who had led Grenada since the overthrow in March 1979 of the corrupt Gairy regime in a bloodless revolution, was placed under house arrest on 12 October 1983 by an extreme leftist faction, led by Bernard Coard. After a week of crisis, with many ministers resigning, a mass protest culminated in a crowd of several thousands freeing Bishop from house arrest. Supposedly under Coard's direction, the military fired into the crowd, and isolated and then shot Bishop and several senior ministers. This gave the USA and governments of other Caribbean states hostile to the socialist regime of Bishop the looked-for excuse to invade Grenada and re-establish a right-wing regime there. They took over the island on 25 October, creating an international furore. Many Grenadians apparently welcomed the invaders as liberators.)

'Jackie' – Jacqueline Creft, Education Minister.

'Uni' – Unison Whiteman, Foreign Minister.

'Vincent' – Vincent Noel, trade-union leader.

'Bernard, Phyllis' – Bernard and Phyllis Coard.

'Owusu' – Liam James, head of the security forces.

'H.A.' – General Hudson Austin, head of the People's Revolutionary Army.

DAVID DABYDEEN. b. 1955. Born in Guyana, he moved to England in 1969. He read English at the universities of Cambridge and London, completing his doctorate in 1982. He is now on a research fellowship at Wolfson College, Oxford University, and is a lecturer at Warwick University. He won the Quiller-Couch Prize for Poetry at Cambridge University in 1978.

Poetry: *Slave Song*, Mundelstrup, Denmark, Dangaroo Press, 1984. (Winner of the Commonwealth Poetry Prize.)

'Slave Song' – David Dabydeen says that his poems are 'an exploration of the erotic energies of the colonial experience': 'The slave addresses his Master (mentally of course). He asserts his manhood, his dignity and his instinct for survival through his surreptitious lust for the white woman, his Mistress. He will not be beaten down or reduced to utter impotence . . . His dream of her allows him to survive his condition of squalor.'

FRAGANO LEDGISTER. b. 1956. Born in London, and educated in Jamaica at the University of the West Indies. He has worked as researcher, actor, journalist, herdsman and general factotum. He has lived in New York since 1982. His poetry was represented in the 1983 edition of *Focus*.

FREDERICK D'AGUIAR (pronounced *Dee-ag-ur*). b. 1960. Born in London of Guyanese parentage, he grew up in Guyana and returned to London in 1972. He writes: 'Like most children of that period I was "posted home for a proper upbringing". The experience of living there is the basis for my understanding and imagination about life here in Britain. "Mama Dot" in a forthcoming collection of poems provides a focus as a grandmother-figure for tackling the diaspora of black people worldwide. The death of the last of my grandmothers, while I was still at school, sparked off my first poem.' His poems have appeared in journals, among them the *Poetry Review*.

'Friday, Tonto or Punkawallah' – Third World figures attendant on white men (Crusoe, the Lone Ranger and the Indian raj).

'New Cross fire' – the fire at a house in London in January 1981 in which thirteen young black people died. The black community felt at the time that the fire was the result of racialist arson.

'Neva see come fo see' – like James Berry in his Lucy poems, Frederick D'Aguiar ends with a proverb (many of the Mama Dot poems are in the vernacular).

'Barber-Green' – 'a machine used to pave roads with bitumen, so-called because of its green colour and ability to convert rough track into smooth road' (Author's note).

GLOSSARY

a – of; is
aachar – tamarind
ackee – in Jamaica, part of the fruit of a tree, which, when cooked, resembles scrambled eggs
ascorden – according
au – I
awe – I, us
ax – ask

baas – boss
Babylon – Rastafarians' term for their present exile (see note, page 387)
baby mother – mother
backra – white person, people
backwud – retort, answering back
bagabone – thin child ('bag of bones')
bagasse – cane-stalks, the refuse of the sugar process, ground, dried and used as fuel
bahl – bawl, yell, cry
Ba'jan Barbadian
bammi – a flat bread made from cassava
bans – lots
barn, bawn – born
bawn grung – birthplace
beebah – beaver hat
bickle – victuals, food
bignadoa – bragger, boaster
big-smady – grown-up, adult person
biout – without, unless
bite – small amount of money; a paid job
bittle – victuals, food
bitty – money
boasify – boastful
bohbohl – bribery, 'fiddle'
bongo-nyah – the way of Rastafari; a Rastafarian
boogooyagga – lack of sophistication

bo'-'tick – stick-fighting stick ('bois-stick')
bredda – brother
brigah – boasting
bruck – break; broken
buckra – white person, people
bud – bird
bumby – bye-and-bye, later on
bump-an-bore – pushing and jostling
bun – burn; fire (of a gun)
bung – bound
busha – overseer (cf. earlier form, 'obissha')
buss – kiss (standard eighteenth-century usage)
bwile – boil
bwoy – boy

cack – cock, penis
caff – cough
cah-cah-dah – a pittance
caiso – calypso (this is thought to be the original African form of the word, and is the traditional cry of audience approval)
calaloo – leaf vegetable, like spinach
camoudie – a kind of snake
cane-piece – field of sugar-cane
caution – warn
cella – the space under a house, used for storage (in the Caribbean, houses are built on masonry pillars to deter termites)
chan – can't
chap – chop; exchange (words), answer back
check – be aware of, appreciate
chiggoes – insects whose grubs hatch under the skin and cause irritation
chink – holes in the roof
cho – an exclamation (about equivalent to 'heck!')
chuck – move rhythmically to music
claat – cloth
cloaz – clothes
cocohead – a root vegetable, a staple starch food
cole – cold
collobree – humming-bird (French 'colibri')
coocoomacca – a wood noted for its hardness
corbeau – turkey-vulture (its Eastern Caribbean name, cf. John Crow)
corn – Indian corn, maize
cotta – ring-shaped head-pad for carrying loads
crabin – craving
crappau – toad

craps – scrap
crosses – tribulation
cudjo – cudgel
cunny – cunning, clever (cf. Scots 'canny')
cuss-cuss – curses, abuse
cutacoo – a basket woven from palm leaves, particularly an obeah-man's bag
cyaan – can't
cyaan done – endlessly
cyah, cyar – can't

daag – dog
dahta – woman, women
dasheen – a vegetable
dashiki – African-style, loose, collarless shirt
dead – corpse
deh – they; there; their
deh so – right there
Demeradah – Demerara
do' – door
doah – although
done – finished
dread – awesome (Rastafarian usage); a Rastafarian; hair worn in the long, knotty Rastafarian style
drei – dry
driber – slave-driver
dub – see page xli
dung – down
dungle – dunghill, rubbish heap (the name of a Kingston shanty-town, now demolished)
dung-tung – down-town
duppy – ghost, spirit
dutty – earth, ground; dirty

eben – even
Ebo – a West African people, now more usually spelled Ibo or Igbo; their territory
ebry – every
een – in
eerie – joyful (cf. modern 'irie', q.v.)
eh – eh; ain't
en – ain't; end
ert – earth
ess – if
exvise – advise (a malapropism)

e'ya – he

fa – for
fabour – prefer
facety – proud, impudent
fahs – bold, uppity
fatigue – heckling
fe – for, to
fedda – feather
fete – party
fe yu – your
fi – for, to
fiah – fire
fiah-tick – fire-stick, firewood
fi-him – his
fi-me – my
fine – find
fingah-tacking – gloves
fla-fla – fritters
foofah – whose
fum – beat, whip
fum-fum – a whipping, beating
fus – first

gah – go
gahn – gone
galang – go along; 'so long' (valedictory)
ganja – marijuana, the smoking of which is a religious observance among Rastafarians (a Hindi word)
gi – give
gin'am – gingham
grudgeful – envious
guaba – guava
Gubbena – Governor
gubbye – goodbye
gungu – a small, green bean, 'peas' in Jamaica
gwaan, *gwan* – go on
gyaad – guard

hact – act
haffe, *haffi* – have to
hag – hog, pig
hare – hear
hat – hot, painful; to hurt
hawbah – harbour

haxin – asking
heaby, hebby – heavy
hebben – heaven
herb – ganja, q.v.
higgler – street vendor (cf. 'to haggle')
Hinglan – England
Hinglis – English
hipsaw – to dance with a sinuous hip movement
hisin – rising
hoat' – oath
hooman – woman
hyah – higher

I-and-I – I, we, me, us (Rastafarian usage)
ile – oil
inna – in
irie – great, lovely, wonderful (a general term of approval in Rastafarian usage, in widespread use since 1974; cf. 'eerie')

Jah, Jah-Jah – God (Rastafarian usage, from the Biblical 'Jah-weh')
Jamdown – Jamaica
jammette – bawdy woman
John Crow – turkey-vulture (Jamaican name)
jook, juk – jab, pierce
jook up – hitch up
jump, jump up – dance
junk – chunk
junka – chunky

kaiso – calypso (see 'caiso')
kase – because
ketch – reach, catch
kin – skin
kin-teet – smile, smiles (lit., 'skin-teeth')
koo – look
kotch – hold, stay
kub – coop

Laard, Lard – Lord
lagniappe – makeweight
lambie – conch
lebben – leaven
lebin – eleven
leka – let
liard – liar

lib – live
libbin – living
lick – hit, beat
lick dung – knock down
lickle – little
lilly – little
limers – people passing time on the street with friends
linga – weaken, be ill

macajuel – boa constrictor
macca – prickles
mackey massa – originally the polite greeting of a slave to his master (Twi 'makye' = good morning), the phrase developed, satirically, another meaning in another context: by punning on 'macca' – 'prick, prickle', a very common word – it came to mean in sexual contexts 'virile partner', and is still current today
madda – mother
man – friendly term of address, used irrespective of age or sex
mannis' – impertinent
mareno – vest
marga – thin (French 'maigre')
Maroon – see note under William Hosack (page 397 above)
mas – master; carnival (from 'masquerade')
mash – crush
massa – master
matty – friend, confidante, or more generally 'people'
mek – make, let
mento – a traditional Jamaican song-and-dance form, characterized by lyrics expressing social comment and an off-beat banjo or guitar strum

nah – no; not
nana – term of respect for an older woman
nare – near
naseberry – sapodilla
natty – knotty
natty dread – long, uncombed Rastafarian locks; a Rastafarian
nebah – never
needuh – neither
Negrah yam – a coarse variety of yam, a staple starch food
nuss – nurse
nyam – eat

oba – over
obeah – witchcraft

obissha – overseer (later 'busha')

oder – other

oonoo, oonu – you, pl. (Jamaican usage)

ouk – out

pahn – grab

palam-pam – noise, confusion

pan – on, upon; steel-band instrument, invented in Trinidad in the forties, and made by tempering the head of an oil-drum to give a number of different notes

pap lack – burgle (lit., 'pop lock')

pat – pot

pat'ole – pothole

paze – peas

peely – bald-headed

peeny-wally – fireflies

peetle – people

pickney, picny – child, children (from Spanish/Portuguese for 'small child')

picong – biting, satiric comment ('piquant')

po – poor

poinsettia – shrub the upper leaves of which turn scarlet around Christmas

poke – pork

pon – on, upon

pop – break; crack (a whip)

putto-putto – mud

pyah-pyah – insignificant

quatty – obsolete coin worth a penny halfpenny ('quarter' of a sixpence)

quinge up – huddled, cowering

rack – rock

rahtid – irate, fearsome (lit., 'wrath-ed')

rap – to declaim in a rhythmic, oratorical style

Ras – holiness (Rastafarian usage)

rass, rassa – contraction of 'your ass'; an obscenity; a term of contempt

rasta – Rastafarian

ratta – rat, rats

Regen – Regency

riddim – rhythm

rig-jig – a lively, crowded dance

roach – cockroach

roti – unleavened Indian bread, cooked on a griddle

rung – round

saaf – soft

salfish – saltfish (usually cod from the north Atlantic; a traditional protein food in the Caribbean, traded for rum)

sangaree – Spanish *sangria*, wine diluted with citrus juice

sapodilla – a fruit

sarradee – Saturday

satta – sit

scrunter – scrounger, sponger

sef – self

seh – say, says, said

seine – fishing net   .

sense – since

shac-shac – shaker, rattle, used in music-making

shay-shay – a dance (French 'chassé')

shet pan – pan with a lid ('shut')

shirt-jac – the short-sleeved shirt-cum-jacket adopted in the tropics as an alternative to the formal northern suit

shu't – shirt

si – see

sinting – things (lit., 'something')

ska – Jamaica's first amplified popular music, which developed during the early 1960s as a fusion of American urban blues and Jamaican rural folk music (see 'mento'). It is characterized by off-beat rhythms, with riffs and raucous instrumentation

skellion – spring onion, shallot, scallion

slata – slaughter

smaddy – somebody; person, people

soja – soldier

swalla-henkychi – neckerchief

swips – takes deftly

taat – thought

tajo – meaning uncertain; possibly the name 'Tajo, Tacho', a Latin American diminutive for 'Anastasio'

tan – stand

tanky-massa – gift from master (lit., 'thankyou, master')

tap – top; stop

tatta – father; grandfather

tawn – thorn

teata – theatre

tek – take

tep – step

tief – steal, thieve; thief

ting – thing
tink – think
toke – St Lucian word for the butt of a marijuana cigarette
tory – story
trash – to separate the edible part of a crop from the remainder; to cut
    out dead or redundant growth
trimble – to cause to tremble, to shake
tripe – guts
tru – through
tun – turn
tup – stooped

uh – I
usy – use, treat

vank – reject, spurn
'vice – advice
vosh – wash

wa'k good – go well, farewell
wan – a, one; want
warra – what
wase – waste
we – we, us, our
weeble – weevil
weed – ganja, q.v.
weh, whey – what; who; which
whai – a cry of alarm or lament
who an' who – who
who-fa, whofah – whose
wi – will
wid – with
wine – to dance with a sinuous hip motion; a movement of that sort
    (originally 'to wind your waist')
wood-anch – wood-ant
wud – word, words
wuh – what
wut – worth

yah – here; truly, you know (lit., 'you hear')
yam – a root vegetable, a staple starch food
yanga – a dance step with bent knees
yaw sah – you hear (pronounced 'yah sah')
yerry – hear

Glossary

yerry seh – hear say, hear tell
yiye – eye, eyes
yiye-water – tears
yo – you, your

INDEX OF POETS

John Agard, 343–4
Lillian Allen, 73–4
Phyllis Allfrey, 171–2
Kevyn Arthur, 312–13
Carlton Barrett, 64
Edward Baugh, 273–5
Henry Beissel, 241–2
Louise Bennett, 31–8
James Berry, 205–10
Valerie Bloom, 94–6
Dionne Brand, 356–62
Edward Kamau Brathwaite, 255–63
Wayne Brown, 322–6
George Campbell, 177–9
Jan Carew, 211–13
Martin Carter, 214–19
'The Mighty Chalkdust', 46–7
M. J. Chapman, 115–16
Faustin Charles, 327–9
LeRoy Clarke, 287–9
Jimmy Cliff, 63
Legon Cogil, 64
Frank Collymore, 151–2
Edward Cordle, 16–18
Alfred Cruickshank, 137–9
Cyril Dabydeen, 330–32
David Dabydeen, 363–4
Frederick D'Aguiar, 367–8
Henry Dalton, 124–5
Robert Dunbar, 121–3
Gloria Escoffery, 195–7
Howard Fergus, 276–7
Barbara Ferland, 180–81
John Figueroa, 182–4

Slinger Francisco, see 'The Mighty Sparrow'
Marcus Garvey, 22–3
Lorna Goodison, 337–9
James Grainger, 104–5
Eddy Grant, 72
Claire Harris, 278–80
Wilson Harris, 185–6
A. L. Hendriks, 187–92
F. 'Toots' Hibbert, 61
Kendel Hippolyte, 350–55
Allan Hope, see Mutabaruka
Abdur-Rahman Slade Hopkinson, 268–71
William Hosack, 117–20
Horatio Nelson Huggins, 126–9
Bongo Jerry, 69–71
Linton Kwesi Johnson, 75–8
Evan Jones, 220–25
Shake Keane, 226–31
Paul Keens-Douglas, 56–60
'Lord Kitchener', 41–2
Knolly La Fortune, 25
Christopher Laird, 66–7
Fragano Ledgister, 365–6
John Robert Lee, 340–42
'Leo', see Egbert Martin
Hollis Liverpool, see 'The Mighty Chalkdust'
Edward Lucie-Smith, 264–7
Thomas MacDermot, 132–3
Donald McDonald, 134–6
Basil McFarlane, 193–4
J. E. Clare McFarlane, 153
Claude McKay, 142–5
Anthony McNeill, 306–9

Roger McTair, 317–19
Michael McTurk, 13–15
Delano Abdul Malik De Coteau,
    49–55
E. A. Markham, 290–98
Bob Marley, 65
Una Marson, 158–62
Egbert Martin, 130–31
James Martinez, 19–21
Marc Matthews, 48
Brian Meeks, 87–9
Judy Miles, 310–11
James Montgomery, 113–14
Pamela Mordecai, 314–16
J. B. Moreton, 112
Mervyn Morris, 281–6
Mutabaruka, 79–82
Grace Nichols, 348–9
Oku Onuora, 83–6
Marlene Philip, 333–6
Victor Questel, 345–7
'Tom Redcam', *see* Thomas
    MacDermot
Jean Rhys, 146–50
Eric Roach, 173–6

Aldwin Roberts, *see* 'Lord
    Kitchener'
W. Adolphe Roberts, 140–41
Bruce St John, 39–40
Andrew Salkey, 235–40
Dennis Scott, 299–305
Olive Senior, 320–21
A. J. Seymour, 165–70
Philip Sherlock, 154–7
Louis Simpson, 198–204
John Singleton, 106–9
Slim and Sam, 24
Robin Small, *see* Bongo Jerry
Michael Smith, 90–93
'The Mighty Sparrow', 43–5
Peter Tosh, 62
Ivan Van Sertima, 272
Vivian Virtue, 163–4
Derek Walcott, 243–54
'Kona Waruk', *see* Wilson Harris
Nathaniel Weekes, 102–3
Daniel Williams, 232–4
Francis Williams, 101
Frederick Williams, 68
Orlando Wong, *see* Oku Onuora

ACKNOWLEDGEMENTS

For permission to publish or reproduce the poems in this anthology
grateful acknowledgement is made to the following:

JOHN AGARD: for 'Waiting for Fidel' from *Shoot Me with Flowers*
(Georgetown, Guyana, 1973), to the author, and for 'Pan Recipe' from
Man to Pan (Havana, Cuba, 1982), to the author and Casa de las
Américas, Havana. LILLIAN ALLEN: for 'Belly Woman's Lament' and 'I
Fight Back' from *Rhythm an' Hardtimes* (Toronto, Domestic Bliss,
1982), to the author. PHYLLIS ALLFREY: for 'The Child's Return' and
'Love for an Island' from *Palm and Oak* to Curtis Brown Ltd on behalf
of Phyllis Shand Allfrey. KEVYN ARTHUR: for 'Gospel' and 'I Saw
Three Ships' to the author. CARLTON BARRETT and LEGON COGIL: for
'Dem Belly Full' to Rondor Music (London) Ltd. EDWARD BAUGH:
'Colour-scheme' from *Seven Jamaican Poets* (ed. Mervyn Morris,
Kingston, Jamaica, 1971), 'Truth and Consequences' from *The Sunday
Gleaner Magazine* (9 April 1978), 'Country Dance' from *One People's
Grief: New Writing from the Caribbean* (ed. Robert Bensen) (vol. 8, no.
3 of *Pacific Quarterly* (Moana)), and 'The Carpenter's Complaint', to
the author. HENRY BEISSEL: for 'Pans at Carnival' from *Voices* (vol. 1,
no. 6, 1966, Port of Spain, Trinidad), to the author. LOUISE BENNETT:
for 'Back to Africa', 'Colonization in Reverse', 'Dutty Tough' and
'Independance' from *Jamaica Labrish*, for 'Excitement' from *Selected
Poems* (ed. Mervyn Morris, Kingston, Jamaica, 1982), and for 'Inde-
pendence Twenty-One' from *Inside Jamaica* (vol. 2, no. 3, 1983), to
the author. JAMES BERRY: for 'My Father' from *Melanthika* (ed. N.
Toczek *et al.*), 'Ingrown' from *Lucy's Letter* (1975), 'Back to Home-
town Kingston' from *Bluefoot Traveller* (London, 1976), 'From Lucy:
Holiday Reflections' from *Lucy's Letters and Loving* (London, New
Beacon, 1982), 'Fantasy of an African Boy' from *Poetry Review* (vol. 71,
no. 4), and 'Distance of a City', to the author (some texts revised).
VALERIE BLOOM: for 'Trench Town Shock (A Soh Dem Say)' and 'Wat
a Rain' from *Touch Mi; Tell Mi* (London, 1983), to Bogle L'Ouverture
Publications Ltd. DIONNE BRAND: for the excerpt from 'Epigrams to
Ernesto Cardenal in Defense of Claudia' from *Winter Epigrams*
(Toronto, Williams-Wallace, 1983), and for the excerpt from 'Military
Occupations' from *Chronicles of the Hostile Sun* (ibid., 1984), to the

author. EDWARD KAMAU BRATHWAITE: for 'Schooner' from *Other Exiles* (London, 1975), and for 'Horse Weebles' from *Mother Poem* (London, 1977), to the author and Oxford University Press; for 'Harbour' and 'Starvation *and* Blues' from *Black + Blues* (Havana, Cuba, 1976), to the author and Casa de las Américas, Havana, and to the Longman Group for 'Starvation', reprinted as 'Springblade' in *Third World Poems* (ed. E. K. Brathwaite). WAYNE BROWN: for 'Noah' and 'Ballad of the Electric Eel' from *On the Coast* (London, 1973), to the author and André Deutsch Ltd, and for 'England, Autumn' and 'The Bind' from *Trinidad and Tobago Review* (vol. 6, nos. 1/2, 1982), to the author. GEORGE CAMPBELL: for 'History Makers', 'In the Slums' and 'Holy' from *First Poems* (Kingston, Jamaica, 1945; New York and London, Garland Publishing, 1981), to the author. JAN CAREW: for 'Our Home', 'The Cliffs at Manzanilla' and 'Faces and Skulls' from *Sea Drums in my Blood* (Port of Spain, Trinidad, New Voices, 1980), to the author. MARTIN CARTER: for 'University of Hunger', the excerpt from 'I Come from the Nigger Yard' and 'Till I Collect' from *Poems of Resistance*, and for 'There is No Riot', 'For a Man Who Walked Sideways' and 'The Great Dark' from *Poems of Succession* (London, 1977), to the author and New Beacon Books Ltd, and for 'As New and as Old', 'Bent' and 'Our Number' from *Poems of Affinity*, to the author. 'THE MIGHTY CHALKDUST' (Hollis Liverpool): for 'Brain Drain', to the author. FAUSTIN CHARLES: for 'Fireflies' from *Crab Track* (London, 1973), and for 'Sugar Cane' from *The Expatriate* (London, 1969), to the author. LEROY CLARKE: for 'Where Hurricane' from *Douens* (New York, 1981), to the author. JIMMY CLIFF: for 'The Harder They Come', to Island Music Ltd. FRANK COLLYMORE: for 'Ballad of an Old Woman', 'Monkeys' and 'Triptych', by kind permission of Mrs Ellice Collymore. CYRIL DABYDEEN: for 'The Fat Men' and 'Fruit, of the Earth' from *Distances* (Vancouver, Fiddlehead, 1977), 'Rehearsal', first published in *Canadian Literature* (University of British Columbia, 1982), and 'Words and Legacy', first published in *Fiddlehead* (University of New Brunswick, 1980), to the author. DAVID DABYDEEN: for 'Slave Song' and 'Men and Women' from *Slave Song* (Mundelstrup, Denmark, 1984), to the author and Dangaroo Press. FREDERICK D'AGUIAR: for 'Letter from Mama Dot' and 'On Duty', to the author. GLORIA ESCOFFERY: for 'No Man's Land' from *Landscape in the Making* (Kingston, Jamaica, 1976, reprinted in *Caribbean Poetry Now*, London, 1984, ed. Stewart Brown), to the author and Hodder & Stoughton Ltd; for 'After the Fall' from *Bim* (41, 1965), and for 'Farewell to a Jovial Friend' from *Bim* (46, 1968), to the author; for 'Twins' to the author and the Gleanor Co. Ltd, Kingston, Jamaica. HOWARD FERGUS: for 'Ethnocide' and 'Forecast' from *Green Innocence* (Montserrat, 1978), and for 'Lament for Maurice Bishop', to the author. JOHN FIGUEROA: for 'Birth is . . .' and 'At Home the Green

Remains' from *Love Leaps Here* (Liverpool, 1962), and 'Portrait of a Woman (and a Man)' from *Ignoring Hurts* (Washington DC, 1976), to the author. LORNA GOODISON: for 'The Mulatta as Penelope' from *Focus* (Kingston, Jamaica, 1983), and for 'For Don Drummond' from *Tamarind Season* (Kingston, Jamaica, 1980), to the author. EDDY GRANT: for 'War Party' to Greenheart Music Ltd, Antigua, represented in the UK by Intersong Music Ltd. CLAIRE HARRIS: for 'Framed' and 'Policeman Cleared in Jaywalking Case' from *Fables from the Women's Quarters* (Toronto, Williams-Wallace, 1984), to the author. WILSON HARRIS: for 'Charcoal' and 'Laocoön' from *Eternity to Season* (London, New Beacon, 1978, © Wilson Harris), to the author and New Beacon Books. A. L. HENDRIKS: for 'Hot Summer Sunday', 'Boundary', 'The Migrant' and 'Will the Real Me Please Stand Up?' from *Madonna of the Unknown Nation* (London, Workshop Press, 1974), and for 'D'où venons nous? etc.' from *The Islanders* (Kingston, Savacou, 1983), to the author. F. 'TOOTS' HIBBERT: for 'Never Get Weary' to Island Music Ltd. KENDEL HIPPOLYTE: for 'good morning' and 'Jahson/another way' from *Island in the Sun, Side 2* (The Morne, St Lucia, 1980), to the author. ABDUR-RAHMAN SLADE HOPKINSON: for 'The Madwoman of Papine' from the book of that title (Georgetown, Guyana, 1976), for 'Tycoon, Poet, Saint' from *Caribanthology 1* (ed. Bruce St John), and for 'December 1974: a Lament' from *The Friend* (Georgetown, 1976), to the author. BONGO JERRY: for 'Mabrak', to the author. LINTON KWESI JOHNSON: for 'Bass Culture' from *Dread Beat and Blood* (London, Bogle L'Ouverture, 1975), to the author and Bogle L'Ouverture Publications Ltd, and for 'Reggae fe Dada', first published in *Artrage* (London)(no. 6, 1984), to the author. EVAN JONES: for 'Genesis', 'Walking with R.B.', 'November, 1956', 'The Song of the Banana Man' and 'The Lament of the Banana Man', to the author. SHAKE KEANE: for 'Shaker Funeral' from *L'Oubli* (Barbados, 1950), 'Coming Back' from *Bim* (51, 1970), and 'Soufrière (79) 1' from *Volcano Suite* (St Vincent, 1979), to the author. PAUL KEENS-DOUGLAS: for 'Tell Me Again' from the book of that title (Port of Spain, Trinidad, Keensdee Productions Ltd, 1979), and for 'Wukhand' from *Tim Tim* (ibid., 1976), to Keensdee Productions Ltd and Good Vibes Records and Music Ltd. 'LORD KITCHENER' (Aldwin Roberts): for 'Miss Tourist' to the author. KNOLLY LA FORTUNE: for verses to 'Sly Mongoose', to the author. CHRISTOPHER LAIRD: for 'The Sea at Evening', to the author. FRAGANO LEDGISTER: for 'On Parade' and 'The Cities Have Fallen', first published in *Focus* (1983), to the author. JOHN ROBERT LEE: for 'Return' and 'Kite' from *Vocation* (St Lucia, 1975), and for 'third world snapshots' from *Possessions* (St Lucia, 1984), to the author. EDWARD LUCIE-smith: for 'The Wise Child' (© 1964), and 'Imperialists in Retirement' (© 1964) from *Confessions and Histories*; 'Your Own Place' (© 1968), from *Towards Silence*; and

Acknowledgements

'The Hymn Tunes' (© 1964), from *A Tropical Childhood*, to the author; used by permission. BASIL MCFARLANE: for 'Arawak Prologue' from *Seven Jamaican Poets* (ed. Mervyn Morris, Kingston, Jamaica, 1971), to the author. J. E. C. MCFARLANE: for 'On National Vanity' from *The Independence Anthology of Jamaican Literature* (ed. A. L. Hendriks and C. Lindo, Kingston, 1962), to the estate of J. E. C. McFarlane. CLAUDE MCKAY: for 'Fetchin Water' from *Songs of Jamaica* (Kingston, Jamaica, 1912), and for 'Subway Wind', 'The White House', 'If We Must Die' and 'Baptism' from *Selected Poems* (New York, 1953), by kind permission of Hope McKay Virtue. ANTHONY MCNEILL: for 'The Victors', 'Residue', 'Saint Ras' and 'Dermis' from *Hello Ungod* (Baltimore, Peaceweed Press, 1971), reprinted in *Reel from 'The Life-Movie'* (Kingston, Jamaica, Savacou, 1975), for 'Don' from *Reel* etc., and for 'A Wreath for the Suicide Heart', first published in *Focus* (1983), to the author. ROGER MCTAIR: for 'Guerillas' and 'Politics Kaiso', to the author. E. A. MARKHAM: for 'Don't Talk to Me about Bread', first published in *Love, Politics and Food*, 'An Old Thought for a New Couple', first published in *Bluefoot Traveller* (ed. James Berry, London, 1976), 'Rewrite' from *Games and Penalties*, all reprinted in *Human Rites* (London, Anvil Press, 1984), and for 'Late Return' from *Human Rites*, to the author and Anvil Press Poetry Ltd; for 'Grandfather's Sermon and Michael Smith' to the author and South Head Press Poetry, Australia. BOB MARLEY: for 'Trenchtown Rock' to Cayman Music Inc., administered in the UK by Leosong Copyright Service Ltd. DELANO ABDUL MALIK DE COTEAU: for 'Oui Papa' from *Revo* and 'Motto Vision 1971' from *Black Up*, to the author. MARC MATTHEWS: for 'Guyana not Ghana', first published in *Savacou* (Kingston, Jamaica) (3/4, 1970/71), to the author. BRIAN MEEKS: for 'Las' Rights', and for 'The Coup-clock Clicks' first published in *Savacou* (14/15, 1979), to the author. PAMELA MORDECAI: for 'Tell Me', first published in *Bim* (63, 1978), for 'For Eyes to Bless You', first published in *Savacou* (14/15, 1979), and for 'Shooting the Horses', to the author. MERVYN MORRIS: for 'Family Pictures', 'The Early Rebels', 'The House-slave', 'To an Expatriate Friend' and 'Valley Prince' from *The Pond* (London, New Beacon, 1973), and for 'Brief', 'For Consciousness' and 'One, Two' from *Shadowboxing* (ibid., 1979), to the author and New Beacon Books; for 'Peace-Time', first published in *Focus* (1983), to the author. MUTABARUKA: for 'Revolutionary Poets' and 'The Change' from *The First Poems*, and for 'Free Up de Lan, White Man' and 'You Ask Me', to the author. GRACE NICHOLS: for 'Epilogue', 'Waterpot', 'Without Song' and 'Old Magic' from *I is a Long-memoried Woman* (London, Karnak House, 1983), to the author. OKU ONUORA: for 'Last Night' and 'Pressure Drop' from *Echo*, and for 'Reflection in Red', first published in *Savacou* (14/15, 1979), to the author. MARLENE PHILIP: for 'Oliver Twist' from *Thorns* (Toronto, Williams-Wallace, 1983), and 'Salmon Courage' from *Salmon Courage* (ibid., 1983), to the author and Williams-Wallace Inc. VICTOR QUESTEL: for 'Tom' from *Score* (published jointly with Anson Gonzalez (Port of Spain, Trinidad, 1972), and 'This Island Mopsy' from *Near Mourning Ground* (Diego Martin, Trinidad, The New Voices, 1979, © Marian Questel), by mind permission of Mrs Marian Questel. JEAN RHYS: for 'Our Gardener', first published in *New Review* (4/41, 1977), and for 'Obeah Night' from *Jean Rhys: Letters 1931–1966* (first published 1984 by André Deutsch Ltd, © 1984 The Estate of Jean Rhys, © 1984 Selection: Francis Wyndham and Diana Melly), to the literary executors of Jean Rhys. ERIC ROACH: for 'Love Overgrows a Rock', first published in *Bim* (vol. 7, no. 25, 1957), 'Piarco' from *New Writing in the Caribbean* (ed. A. J. Seymour, Georgetown, Guyana, 1972), and 'At Guaracara Park', first published in *Students Arts Group* (San Fernando, Trinidad) (vol. 1, no. 3, 1970), by kind permission of Mrs Iris E. Roach. BRUCE ST JOHN: for 'Bajan Litany' (also published in *North American Mentor Magazine*, 1975), 'Subtlety' and 'Wisdom', all published in *Revista de Letras* (1972), and in *Bumbatuk 1* (Bridgetown, Barbados, 1982), to the author. ANDREW SALKEY: for 'Remember Haiti, Cuba, Vietnam', 'Soufrière', 'Postcard from Mexico' and 'Dry River Bed' from *Away* (London, Allison & Busby, 1980), to the author and Allison & Busby; for 'Clearsightedness', first published in *Ambit* (London), (91, 1982) and 'A Song for England' from *Caribbean Voices 2* (ed. John Figueroa, London, Evans, 1970), to the author. DENNIS SCOTT: for 'Homecoming', 'Grampa', 'Uncle Time', 'Epitaph' and 'For the Last Time, Fire' from *Uncle Time* (Pittsburgh, University of Pittsburgh Press, 1973), and for 'Version' and 'Weaponsong' to the author; for 'Mouth' and 'More Poem' from *Dreadwalk* (London, New Beacon, 1982), to the author and New Beacon Books. OLIVE SENIOR: for 'Ancestral Poem' and 'Epitaph' from *Jamaica Woman, An Anthology of Poems* (ed. Pamela Mordecai and Mervyn Morris, published by Heinemann Educational Books (Caribbean and London) Ltd, 1980), to the author and publisher. A. J. SEYMOUR: for 'For Christopher Columbus' and other excerpts from *The Guiana Book* (Georgetown, 1948), for 'The Well', first published in *Kyk-over-al* (vol. 5, no. 16, 1953), and for 'I Was a Boy', first published in *Patterns* (Georgetown, 1970), to the author. PHILLIP SHERLOCK: for 'Jamaican Fisherman', 'Pocomania', 'Dinner Party 1940' and 'A Beauty Too of Twisted Trees', to the author. LOUIS SIMPSON: for 'Jamaica' and 'Arm in Arm' from *The Arrivistes* (New York, Fine Editions Press, 1949), for 'The Battle' from *Good News of Death and Other Poems* (New York, Scribner's, 1955), for 'The Inner Part' from *At the End of the Open Road* (Middletown, Connecticut, Wesleyan University Press, 1963), for 'Back in the States' and 'Working Late' from *Caviare at the Funeral*, (New York, Franklin Watts,

447

Acknowledgements

1980, London, Oxford University Press, 1981), and for 'A Fine Day for Straw Hats', first published in *The Listener*, (5 August 1982), to the author. MICHAEL SMITH: for 'Black Bud' and 'I an I Alone, *or* Goliath', by kind permission of Mrs Nerissa Smith. 'THE MIGHTY SPARROW': for 'The Yankees Back' and 'Get to Hell outa Here', to the author. PETER TOSH: for 'African' (Words and Music: Peter Tosh), reprinted by kind permission of Virgin Music (Publishers) Ltd. DEREK WALCOTT: for 'A Far Cry from Africa' from *In a Green Night*, for 'Chapter 20: ii, iii, iv' from *Another Life*, and for 'Forest of Europe' from *The Star-Apple Kingdom*, reprinted by permission of Farrar, Straus & Giroux Inc. and Jonathan Cape Ltd; for 'The Spoiler's Return' from *The Fortunate Traveller*, reprinted by permission of Farrar, Straus & Giroux Inc. and Faber & Faber Ltd. FREDERICK WILLIAMS: for 'De Eighties', to the author.

Every effort has been made to trace the copyright holders of poems included in this anthology, but in some cases this has not proved possible. The publishers therefore wish to thank the authors or copyright holders of those poems which are included without acknowledgement above.

MORE ABOUT PENGUINS, PELICANS, PEREGRINES AND PUFFINS

For further information about books available from Penguins please write to Dept EP, Penguin Books Ltd, Harmondsworth, Middlesex UB7 0DA.

In the U.S.A.: For a complete list of books available from Penguins in the United States write to Dept DG, Penguin Books, 299 Murray Hill Parkway, East Rutherford, New Jersey 07073.

In Canada: For a complete list of books available from Penguins in Canada write to Penguin Books Canada Ltd, 2801 John Street, Markham, Ontario L3R 1B4.

In Australia: For a complete list of books available from Penguins in Australia write to the Marketing Department, Penguin Books Australia Ltd, P.O. Box 257, Ringwood, Victoria 3134.

In New Zealand: For a complete list of books available from Penguins in New Zealand write to the Marketing Department, Penguin Books (N.Z.) Ltd, Private Bag, Takapuna, Auckland 9.

In India: For a complete list of books available from Penguins in India write to Penguin Overseas Ltd, 706 Eros Apartments, 56 Nehru Place, New Delhi 110019.

PENGUIN REFERENCE BOOKS

☐ **The Penguin Map of the World**   £2.50

Clear, colourful, crammed with information and fully up-to-date, this is a useful map to stick on your wall at home, at school or in the office.

☐ **The Penguin Map of Europe**   £2.95

Covers all land eastwards to the Urals, southwards to North Africa and up to Syria, Iraq and Iran * Scale = 1:5,500,000 * 4-colour artwork * Features main roads, railways, oil and gas pipelines, plus extra information including national flags, currencies and populations.

☐ **The Penguin Map of the British Isles**   £1.95

Including the Orkneys, the Shetlands, the Channel Islands and much of Normandy, this excellent map is ideal for planning routes and touring holidays, or as a study aid.

☐ **The Penguin Dictionary of Quotations**   £3.95

A treasure-trove of over 12,000 new gems and old favourites, from Aesop and Matthew Arnold to Xenophon and Zola.

☐ **The Penguin Dictionary of Art and Artists**   £3.95

Fifth Edition. 'A vast amount of information intelligently presented, carefully detailed, abreast of current thought and scholarship and easy to read' – *The Times Literary Supplement*

☐ **The Penguin Pocket Thesaurus**   £1.95

A pocket-sized version of Roget's classic, and an essential companion for all commuters, crossword addicts, students, journalists and the stuck-for-words.

THE PENGUIN ENGLISH DICTIONARY

The Penguin English Dictionary has been created specially for today's needs. It features:

* More entries than any other popularly priced dictionary
* Exceptionally clear and precise definitions
* For the first time in an equivalent dictionary, the internationally recognised IPA pronunciation system
* Emphasis on contemporary usage
* Extended coverage of both the spoken and the written word
* Scientific tables
* Technical words
* Informal and colloquial expressions
* Vocabulary most widely used *wherever* English is spoken
* Most commonly used abbreviations

It is twenty years since the publication of the last English dictionary by Penguin and the compilation of this entirely new *Penguin English Dictionary* is the result of a special collaboration between Longman, one of the world's leading dictionary publishers, and Penguin Books. The material is based entirely on the database of the acclaimed *Longman Dictionary of the English Language*.

1008 pages   051.139 3   £2.50 ☐

A CHOICE OF PENGUINS

☐ *The Complete Penguin Stereo Record and Cassette Guide*
Greenfield, Layton and March £7.95

A new edition, now including information on compact discs. 'One of the few indispensables on the record collector's bookshelf' – *Gramophone*

☐ *Selected Letters of Malcolm Lowry*
Edited by Harvey Breit and Margerie Bonner Lowry £5.95

'Lowry emerges from these letters not only as an extremely interesting man, but also a lovable one' – Philip Toynbee

☐ *The First Day on the Somme*
Martin Middlebrook £3.95

1 July 1916 was the blackest day of slaughter in the history of the British Army. 'The soldiers receive the best service a historian can provide: their story told in their own words' – *Guardian*

☐ *A Better Class of Person* **John Osborne** £1.95

The playwright's autobiography, 1929–56. 'Splendidly enjoyable' – John Mortimer. 'One of the best, richest and most bitterly truthful autobiographies that I have ever read' – Melvyn Bragg

☐ *The Winning Streak* **Goldsmith and Clutterbuck** £2.95

Marks & Spencer, Saatchi & Saatchi, United Biscuits, GEC . . . The UK's top companies reveal their formulas for success, in an important and stimulating book that no British manager can afford to ignore.

☐ *The First World War* **A. J. P. Taylor** £3.95

'He manages in some 200 illustrated pages to say almost everything that is important . . . A special text . . . a remarkable collection of photographs' – *Observer*

A CHOICE OF PENGUINS

☐ **Man and the Natural World** **Keith Thomas** £4.95

Changing attitudes in England, 1500–1800. 'An encyclopedic study of man's relationship to animals and plants . . . a book to read again and again' – Paul Theroux, *Sunday Times* Books of the Year

☐ **Jean Rhys: Letters 1931–66**
Edited by Francis Wyndham and Diana Melly £3.95

'Eloquent and invaluable . . . her life emerges, and with it a portrait of an unexpectedly indomitable figure' – Marina Warner in the *Sunday Times*

☐ **The French Revolution** **Christopher Hibbert** £4.50

'One of the best accounts of the Revolution that I know . . . Mr Hibbert is outstanding' – J. H. Plumb in the *Sunday Telegraph*

☐ **Isak Dinesen** **Judith Thurman** £4.95

The acclaimed life of Karen Blixen, 'beautiful bride, disappointed wife, radiant lover, bereft and widowed woman, writer, sibyl, Scheherazade, child of Lucifer, Baroness; always a unique human being . . . an assiduously researched and finely narrated biography' – *Books & Bookmen*

☐ **The Amateur Naturalist**
Gerald Durrell with Lee Durrell £4.95

'Delight . . . on every page . . . packed with authoritative writing, learning without pomposity . . . it represents a real bargain' – *The Times Educational Supplement*. 'What treats are in store for the average British household' – *Daily Express*

☐ **When the Wind Blows** **Raymond Briggs** £2.95

'A visual parable against nuclear war: all the more chilling for being in the form of a strip cartoon' – *Sunday Times*. 'The most eloquent anti-Bomb statement you are likely to read' – *Daily Mail*

PENGUIN TRAVEL BOOKS

☐ *Arabian Sands* **Wilfred Thesiger** £3.50

'In the tradition of Burton, Doughty, Lawrence, Philby and Thomas, it is, very likely, the book about Arabia to end all books about Arabia' – *Daily Telegraph*

☐ *The Flight of Ikaros* **Kevin Andrews** £3.50

'He also is in love with the country . . . but he sees the other side of that dazzling medal or moon . . . If you want some truth about Greece, here it is' – Louis MacNeice in the *Observer*

☐ *D. H. Lawrence and Italy* £4.95

In *Twilight in Italy, Sea and Sardinia* and *Etruscan Places,* Lawrence recorded his impressions while living, writing and travelling in 'one of the most beautiful countries in the world'.

☐ *Maiden Voyage* **Denton Welch** £3.50

Opening during his last term at public school, from which the author absconded, *Maiden Voyage* turns into a brilliantly idiosyncratic account of China in the 1930s.

☐ *The Grand Irish Tour* **Peter Somerville-Large** £4.95

The account of a year's journey round Ireland. 'Marvellous . . . describes to me afresh a landscape I thought I knew' – Edna O'Brien in the *Observer*

☐ *Slow Boats to China* **Gavin Young** £3.95

On an ancient steamer, a cargo dhow, a Filipino kumpit and twenty more agreeably cranky boats, Gavin Young sailed from Piraeus to Canton in seven crowded and colourful months. 'A pleasure to read' – Paul Theroux

PENGUIN TRAVEL BOOKS

☐ *The Kingdom by the Sea* **Paul Theroux** £2.50

1982, the year of the Falklands War and the Royal Baby, was the ideal time, Theroux found, to travel round the coast of Britain and surprise the British into talking about themselves. 'He describes it all brilliantly and honestly' – Anthony Burgess

☐ *One's Company* **Peter Fleming** £2.95

His journey to China as special correspondent to *The Times* in 1933. 'One reads him for literary delight . . . But, he is also an observer of penetrating intellect' – Vita Sackville West

☐ *The Traveller's Tree* **Patrick Leigh Fermor** £3.95

'A picture of the Indies more penetrating and original than any that has been presented before' – *Observer*

☐ *The Path to Rome* **Hilaire Belloc** £3.95

'The only book I ever wrote for love,' is how Belloc described the wonderful blend of anecdote, humour and reflection that makes up the story of his pilgrimage to Rome.

☐ *The Light Garden of the Angel King* **Peter Levi** £2.95

Afghanistan has been a wild rocky highway for nomads and merchants, Alexander the Great, Buddhist monks, great Moghul conquerors and the armies of the Raj. Here, quite brilliantly, Levi writes about their journeys and his own.

☐ *Among the Russians* **Colin Thubron** £2.95

'The Thubron approach to travelling has an integrity that belongs to another age' – Dervla Murphy in the *Irish Times*. 'A magnificent achievement' – Nikolai Tolstoy

KING PENGUIN

☐ *Selected Poems* **Tony Harrison** £3.95

Poetry Book Society Recommendation. 'One of the few modern poets who actually has the gift of composing poetry' – James Fenton in the *Sunday Times*

☐ *The Book of Laughter and Forgetting*
Milan Kundera £3.95

'A whirling dance of a book . . . a masterpiece full of angels, terror, ostriches and love . . . No question about it. The most important novel published in Britain this year' – Salman Rushdie in the *Sunday Times*

☐ *The Sea of Fertility* **Yukio Mishima** £9.95

Containing *Spring Snow, Runaway Horses, The Temple of Dawn* and *The Decay of the Angel*: 'These four remarkable novels are the most complete vision we have of Japan in the twentieth century' – Paul Theroux

☐ *The Hawthorne Goddess* **Glyn Hughes** £2.95

Set in eighteenth century Yorkshire where 'the heroine, Anne Wylde, represents the doom of nature and the land . . . Hughes has an arresting style, both rich and abrupt' – *The Times*

☐ *A Confederacy of Dunces* **John Kennedy Toole** £3.95

In this Pulitzer Prize-winning novel, in the bulky figure of Ignatius J. Reilly an immortal comic character is born. 'I succumbed, stunned and seduced . . . it is a masterwork of comedy' – *The New York Times*

☐ *The Last of the Just* **André Schwartz-Bart** £3.50

The story of Ernie Levy, the last of the just, who was killed at Auschwitz in 1943: 'An outstanding achievement, of an altogether different order from even the best of earlier novels which have attempted this theme' – John Gross in the *Sunday Telegraph*

KING PENGUIN

☐ **The White Hotel** D. M. Thomas   £3.50

'A major artist has once more appeared', declared the *Spectator* on the publication of this acclaimed, now famous novel which recreates the imagined case history of one of Freud's woman patients.

☐ **Dangerous Play: Poems 1974–1984**
Andrew Motion   £2.50

Winner of the John Llewelyn Rhys Memorial Prize. Poems and an autobiographical prose piece, *Skating*, by the poet acclaimed in the *TLS* as 'a natural heir to the tradition of Edward Thomas and Ivor Gurney'.

☐ **A Time to Dance** Bernard Mac Laverty   £2.50

Ten stories, including 'My Dear Palestrina' and 'Phonefun Limited', by the author of *Cal*: 'A writer who has a real affinity with the short story form' – *The Times Literary Supplement*

☐ **Keepers of the House** Lisa St Aubin de Terán   £2.50

Seventeen-year-old Lydia Sinclair marries Don Diego Beltrán and goes to live on his family's vast, decaying Andean farm. This exotic and flamboyant first novel won the Somerset Maugham Award.

☐ **The Deptford Trilogy** Robertson Davies   £5.95

'Who killed Boy Staunton?' – around this central mystery is woven an exhilarating and cunningly contrived trilogy of novels: *Fifth Business*, *The Manticore* and *World of Wonders*.

☐ **The Stories of William Trevor**   £5.95

'Trevor packs into each separate five or six thousand words more richness, more laughter, more ache, more multifarious human-ness than many good writers manage to get into a whole novel' – *Punch*. 'Classics of the genre' – Auberon Waugh

ENGLISH AND AMERICAN
LITERATURE IN PENGUINS

☐ *Emma* **Jane Austen**   £1.10

'I am going to take a heroine whom no one but myself will much like,'
declared Jane Austen of Emma, her most spirited and controversial
heroine in a comedy of self-deceit and self-discovery.

☐ *Tender is the Night* **F. Scott Fitzgerald**   £2.95

Fitzgerald worked on seventeen different versions of this novel, and
its obsessions – idealism, beauty, dissipation, alcohol and insanity –
were those that consumed his own marriage and his life.

☐ *The Life of Johnson* **James Boswell**   £2.25

Full of gusto, imagination, conversation and wit, Boswell's immortal
portrait of Johnson is as near a novel as a true biography can be, and
still regarded by many as the finest 'life' ever written. This shortened
version is based on the 1799 edition.

☐ *A House and its Head* **Ivy Compton-Burnett**   £3.95

In a novel 'as trim and tidy as a hand-grenade' (as Pamela Hansford
Johnson put it), Ivy Compton-Burnett penetrates the facade of a
conventional, upper-class Victorian family to uncover a chasm of
violent emotions – jealousy, pain, frustration and sexual passion.

☐ *The Trumpet Major* **Thomas Hardy**   £1.25

Although a vein of unhappy unrequited love runs through this novel,
Hardy also draws on his warmest sense of humour to portray
Wessex village life at the time of the Napoleonic wars.

☐ *The Complete Poems of Hugh MacDiarmid*
☐ Volume One   £8.95
☐ Volume Two   £8.95
The definitive edition of work by the greatest Scottish poet since
Robert Burns, edited by his son Michael Grieve, and W. R. Aitken.

ENGLISH AND AMERICAN
LITERATURE IN PENGUINS

☐ **Main Street** **Sinclair Lewis** £3.95

The novel that added an immortal chapter to the literature of America's Mid-West, *Main Street* contains the comic essence of Main Streets everywhere.

☐ **The Compleat Angler** **Izaak Walton** £2.50

A celebration of the countryside, and the superiority of those in 1653, as now, who love *quietnesse, vertue* and, above all, *Angling*. 'No fish, however coarse, could wish for a doughtier champion than Izaak Walton' – Lord Home

☐ **The Portrait of a Lady** **Henry James** £2.50

'One of the two most brilliant novels in the language', according to F. R. Leavis, James's masterpiece tells the story of a young American heiress, prey to fortune-hunters but not without a will of her own.

☐ **Hangover Square** **Patrick Hamilton** £3.50

Part love story, part thriller, and set in the publands of London's Earls Court, this novel caught the conversational tone of a whole generation in the uneasy months before the Second World War.

☐ **The Rainbow** **D. H. Lawrence** £2.50

Written between *Sons and Lovers* and *Women in Love*, *The Rainbow* covers three generations of Brangwens, a yeoman family living on the borders of Nottinghamshire.

☐ **Vindication of the Rights of Woman**
   Mary Wollstonecraft £2.95

Although Walpole once called her 'a hyena in petticoats', Mary Wollstonecraft's vision was such that modern feminists continue to go back and debate the arguments so powerfully set down here.

PLAYS IN PENGUINS

☐ **Edward Albee** *Who's Afraid of Virginia Woolf?*   £1.60
☐ **Alan Ayckbourn** *The Norman Conquests*   £2.95
☐ **Bertolt Brecht** *Parables for the Theatre (The Good
   Woman of Setzuan/The Caucasian Chalk Circle)*   £1.95
☐ **Anton Chekhov** *Plays (The Cherry Orchard/The Three
   Sisters/Ivanov/The Seagull/Uncle Vania)*   £2.25
☐ **Henrik Ibsen** *Hedda Gabler/Pillars of Society/The
   Wild Duck*   £2.50
☐ **Eugène Ionesco** *Absurd Drama (The Rhinoceros/The
   Chair/The Lesson)*   £2.95
☐ **Ben Jonson** *Three Comedies (Volpone/The Alchemist/
   Bartholomew Fair)*   £2.50
☐ **D. H. Lawrence** *Three Plays (The Collier's Friday
   Night/The Daughter-in-Law/The Widowing of
   Mrs Holroyd)*   £1.75
☐ **Arthur Miller** *Death of a Salesman*   £1.50
☐ **John Mortimer** *A Voyage Round My Father/What Shall
   We Tell Caroline?/The Dock Brief*   £2.95
☐ **J. B. Priestley** *Time and the Conways/I Have Been
   Here Before/The Inspector Calls/The Linden Tree*   £2.50
☐ **Peter Shaffer** *Amadeus*   £1.95
☐ **Bernard Shaw** *Plays Pleasant (Arms and the Man/
   Candida/The Man of Destiny/You Never Can Tell)*   £1.95
☐ **Sophocles** *Three Theban Plays (Oedipus the King/
   Antigone/Oedipus at Colonus)*   £1.95
☐ **Arnold Wesker** *The Wesker Trilogy (Chicken Soup with
   Barley/Roots/I'm Talking about Jerusalem)*   £2.50
☐ **Oscar Wilde** *Plays (Lady Windermere's Fan/A Woman
   of No Importance/An Ideal Husband/The Importance
   of Being Earnest/Salomé)*   £1.95
☐ **Thornton Wilder** *Our Town/The Skin of Our Teeth/
   The Matchmaker*   £1.95
☐ **Tennessee Williams** *Sweet Bird of Youth/A Streetcar
   Named Desire/The Glass Menagerie*   £1.95

PENGUIN BOOKS OF POETRY

☐	*American Verse*	£5.95
☐	*Ballads*	£2.95
☐	*British Poetry Since 1945*	£3.95
☐	*A Choice of Comic and Curious Verse*	£4.50
☐	*Contemporary American Poetry*	£2.95
☐	*Contemporary British Poetry*	£2.50
☐	*Eighteenth-Century Verse*	£3.95
☐	*Elizabethan Verse*	£2.95
☐	*English Poetry 1918–60*	£2.95
☐	*English Romantic Verse*	£2.95
☐	*English Verse*	£2.50
☐	*First World War Poetry*	£2.25
☐	*Georgian Poetry*	£2.50
☐	*Irish Verse*	£2.95
☐	*Light Verse*	£5.95
☐	*London in Verse*	£2.95
☐	*Love Poetry*	£3.50
☐	*The Metaphysical Poets*	£2.95
☐	*Modern African Poetry*	£3.95
☐	*New Poetry*	£2.95
☐	*Poems of Science*	£4.95
☐	*Poetry of the Thirties*	£2.95
☐	*Post-War Russian Poetry*	£2.50
☐	*Spanish Civil War Verse*	£4.50
☐	*Unrespectable Verse*	£3.50
☐	*Victorian Verse*	£3.50
☐	*Women Poets*	£3.95

THE PENGUIN POETRY LIBRARY